The Say So

Also by Julia Franks

Over the Plain Houses

The Say So

A NOVEL

Julia Franks

HUB CITY PRESS
SPARTANBURG, SC

Cover Design: Meg Reid
Cover Illustration: Hollie Chastain
Interior Book design: Kate McMullen
Author photograph © Andrew Davis
Proofreaders: Megan Demoss, Corinne Segal

Library of Congress Cataloging-in-Publication Data

Names: Franks, Julia, 1964- author.
Title: The say so / Julia Franks.
Description: Spartanburg, SC : Hub City Press, [2023]
Identifiers: LCCN 2022038938 (print)
LCCN 2022038939 (ebook)
ISBN 9798885740074 (hardcover)
ISBN 9798885740081 (epub)
Subjects: LCGFT: Novels.
Classification:
LCC PS3606.R422575 S29 2023 (print)
LCC PS3606.R422575 (ebook)
DDC 813/.6--dc23/eng/20220818
LC record available at https://lccn.loc.gov/2022038938
LC ebook record available at https://lccn.loc.gov/2022038939

Hub City Press gratefully acknowledges support from the National Endowment for the Arts, the Amazon Literary Partnership, South Arts, and the South Carolina Arts Commission.

HUB CITY PRESS
200 Ezell Street
Spartanburg, SC 29306
864.577.9349 | www.hubcity.org

For my parents and my three brothers. And for C.

A Note from the Author

During the period between 1940 and 1964, the rates of so-called "illegitimate" pregnancy doubled and tripled in America, from 89,500 in 1940 to 275,700 in 1964. These unwed mothers came from every level of society, but middle-class Americans kept their pregnancies secret. Schools expelled unwed mothers, and companies fired them. Thousands became invisible. Those with the most financial resources were admitted to private maternity homes, where some eighty percent relinquished their children to adoption. Such homes had conflicting missions: were they supposed to be safe havens for exiled mothers, or were they adoption agencies recruiting prospective donors? The answer seems to have depended upon who was running the place. But the homes' other clients, white childless couples desperate for infants, became a powerful financial incentive: find white women to sign away their newborn babes.

Other unwed mothers didn't go to the homes, either because they couldn't afford them or because they weren't seen as desirable candidates. Race and ethnicity were enormous factors. There are few records of these women, but seventy percent of their pregnancies likely ended in adoption too, often brokered by relatives, lawyers, ministers, doctors, and freelance entrepreneurs. Most kept no records.

In all social classes and all demographics, women remember being coerced, pressured, or duped into giving up their rights, sometimes by social workers or medical professionals, sometimes by their own parents. Many recall an inability to escape an outcome that felt inevitable. But public opinion was virtually unanimous. Americans did not question the one single assumption: that in the case of unplanned pregnancy, adoption was the best solution.

Part I

The Bargain

1959

1

LUCE

I only went there once, to that Home, but I can answer some of your questions. Or try. The house had columns for one thing, like one of those antebellum mansions in some rundown romance novel, and actual wrought iron gates. The bus stop was right out front, so when you stepped onto the curb the first thing you saw was a bunch of rude messages spray-painted on the retaining wall. WATERMELON HILL, that sort of thing. (In 1959 the delinquents in our city weren't what you'd call creative.) The walkway took you down the center of this great big old lawn, and it was hard not to feel self-conscious—all those windows in the sunlight, glinting and staring down at you. I guess it was April then because the hydrangeas next to the portico were already leafing out, the bushes littered with some kind of white confetti, and it took me a beat to realize that all those little pieces of paper were playing cards, shredded into tiny pieces, a king of diamonds and a ten of clubs, but most too small to read. Whoever'd done it had spent hours at the task. Whoever'd done it might be there right now, behind that shining glass, intent and watching.

I had no idea how to behave, despite the promise I'd made to Edie's mother. Was I supposed to ring the bell and ask for Edie? Or was it like a business, where you walked right in? I rang, studied the shredded cards, the patterns in black and white and red. There. A club. It made no sense. They'd come from one of the upper windows, that was clear. But whatever fierce purpose they'd once had was now lost in that sure surrender to earth.

Inside, the sound of rattling: the clatter of a chain, sliding metal, and then the door opening and a lady with white-striped hair removing a pair of spectacles and beaming out at me. "You are our visitor! We are so happy to see you!" She had a foreign accent I couldn't place. "I am Mrs. Wentzloff." So: Russian. "Come." She ushered me into a large foyer and seated me next to a grand staircase.

I already hated the place, the damask, the sagging furniture, the faded cabbage roses climbing the wallpaper. And yes, my eyes inventoried the room out of habit: no knick-knacks, no sweaters thrown over chairs, no cups and saucers on end tables, no shoes cluttering the entryway. Just a pair of silver candlesticks on a marble tabletop. But nobody ever noticed when that sort of thing went missing.

Mrs. Wentzloff took off her glasses and peered at me. "You can wait here? Yes? You can wait here. Sit, please." She set the spectacles next to the candlesticks before turning away, the heavy paneled door swinging into place behind her, then stilling. The marble tabletop was two paces from the sofa, the eyeglasses silver, the kind old people used for reading.

I perched at the edge of the cushion, my weight on the bones of my pelvis. Elsewhere, female voices rose and fell. I strained to pick out Edie's but could not. Only Mrs. Wentzloff's. The old lady was nice enough. Friendly. And yet. There were those playing cards. The spray paint at the bus stop. *Who needs a bus? You arrdy got your ride.*

Yes. *Arrdy.* This is what I'm trying to tell you.

Without really thinking about it I rose, strode two long steps to the marble-topped table, bent forward, and palmed the glasses into my hand, then into my sleeve, then into the pocket of my coat. Done. Then I was back on the sofa, pelvic bones square on the cushion.

The pendulum in the grandfather clock hung motionless. No ticking, no nothing. My fingers explored the contents of my pocket, the lenses small and oval, the cool metal warming to my hand, the metal arms flimsy, a mitigation. From *mitis*: soft. Cognate: remediation. Or maybe it was *mederi*, like medic: heal.

Well. You'll have to decide for yourself how you feel about all this.

There was creaking above and then here she came, easing down that long staircase in a maternity smock wide as a mushroom. Everything about her seemed smudged—her swollen face and dark hair, the blousey dress, the heaviness in her walk. Her hand gripped the bannister, her feet feeling for each step, shoulders and violin neck tilting forward, face toward the floor. I tried not to gawp. She'd gone straight from being a girl to being an old woman, and I didn't know what to do about it. Stand or sit? Be cheerful or somber? Commiserate or congratulate? I could think of nothing. Just told myself I had better find a way to smile.

Then she was folding her arms around me but not too hard, not too hard at all, her shoulders bonier than I remembered, more fragile. I stepped back, my hands on her upper arms. I willed my voice to excitement. "You're going to be a mama!"

Edie flinched, then darted a look toward the swing door. "They don't use that word around here."

"Oh." It hadn't been but a minute and I'd already said the wrong thing. "Sorry." My hand snuck to my pocket, the lenses there smooth, pockless, machine-made perfect.

Edie lowered herself onto the sofa, bracing her hand against the armrest as she eased her hips to the cushion. The sigh was part of the motion. "Oh, Luce."

What did it mean? That she knew why I'd come? I sat and took her hand, heard myself chirping inanities—how the school newspaper had come out, how the chemistry teacher had been fired after a tiny little fire. Edie smiled politely into the space between us but seemed to be listening to some other message she alone could hear. I prattled on, all my stories asinine, including my reports on the protests—especially my reports on the protests. I wasn't used to seeing her like that. I wasn't used to having to struggle to keep her attention.

I remember thinking it was my turn to give back. Stand up straight.

Stay positive. "So," I said. "I do have some news. Good, I think. Remember that boy Wayne I was telling you about, from the glee club?"

That seemed to do it. Edie tilted her head, her gaze at last landing on me, examining dim memories from our past. Her eyes opened wider. In a good way. "The one who did the solo?"

"Yeah…"

"Who used to go with Kathy St. John?"

I faltered. Why in God's name would Wayne have gone with Kathy St. John? And how did Edie know something about him that I didn't? My hand cocooned in my pocket, and my thumb pressed the gentle glass depression. I nodded, tried to remember the things I'd been wanting to tell her about Wayne—that he was an Eagle Scout who liked fossils and canned asparagus and nature shows. Seven o'clock Tuesday nights if we could swing it.

But those facts seemed fragile now, like details that needed protecting. In any case they weren't important enough to bother Edie with right now. She leaned in. "Has he asked you to go with him?"

"Well, no."

"But you think he will."

I wasn't so sure. I wished I'd known about Kathy St. John. "Maybe."

Edie eased back into the wing chair, let out a satisfied sigh. "He will. He's not a fool."

I felt like I was standing at the edge of an abyss, and I'd already leaned too far. I held up my hand. "Fingers crossed." Besides. I was supposed to be the one doing the comforting. "You know your mother asked me to come. It was the only way I could get the pass."

"I'm glad you did." But her eyes went distant.

"The thing is, Edie, I agree with her in some ways." Now she jerked her chin toward me, eyes too. I paused. I had no idea how to proceed. I didn't have the heart to tell her about City Hall or what I'd learned about the sorts of things that happened there. Yes, my father practiced family law, yes he could take her case for free, but that courtroom— good Lord. "You could go back to school, graduate with the juniors, go back to working at Ivey's. They'd want you back." I wondered if that were true. "And there's loads of other stores. But that's not even the point. There's college."

Edie looked woeful.

If I'd stopped there, probably it would have been okay. But I didn't. "The thing is, Edie, you only get so many chances. Your parents...they love you." It wasn't even what I was trying to say.

Edie's attention rested on something in the wallpaper.

"I know they're not perfect and they're pretty frosted with you right now, but believe me they're in*vested*—especially your dad—and the fact that they *sent* you here—"

Edie straightened and studied me, in the old way. "My daddy hasn't called me, not once."

"But Edie. You know he thinks the world of you." It was time to stop. Just stop. But for some reason I couldn't. I dashed toward my next contention, my stupid pièce de résistance. "What if they don't take you back? What if they stop liking you? Stop *loving* you?" She was listening, her mouth partway open, her full attention targeted on me. Panic twitched through me, and I fumbled for some kind of defense. "I mean, I'm not sure you can imagine what it's like to be...left. Out there. On your own."

Edie took a long long breath, then covered her eyes with the heels of her hands and pressed. Then all that air she'd stuffed up in her lungs squeezed itself out in stifled little blasts. It took a long time, and at the end of it she whispered something strange. Something I didn't quite hear. "That's what they meant by getting us ready, isn't it?"

My stomach lowered, settled into a miasma of dread. I remember thinking that maybe I was exactly like Edie's parents. That maybe I secretly wanted exactly what they did: to make the baby go away. To lie again across Edie's double bed and sort through forty-fives and movie magazines. To sit again at the edge of Edie's world and be invited in, to know in my bones I could have that kind of order if I chose it. Yes, I *might* take the automatic-washer-electric-dryer, the kind where you don't have to hang the underwear out on the line for the clothespins to bite, and the clothes come out soft and warm in just thirty minutes' time. I *might* want that. I *might* want to have a life where there was regularity and predictability, and people said things like *darling, I've missed you so.*

Well. That wasn't the world we were going to live in, was it?

Edie had begun to cry without a sound, the way that only grandmothers did.

Inside my pocket, the wire arms of the spectacles were delicate and slim. I gripped those glasses tight, the beveled lenses pressed to the flesh of my palms, digging deep.

EDIE

I watched her clonk her way down the front walk, never mind our ten thousand talks on posture and gait, never mind my little trick about walking on glass, never mind any of it, because here it was again, *clomp, clomp, clomp*, only this time I *wanted* to hear it and only this time I could not. She was too far away. I watched, and I spread my fingers against the pane to touch that stomping rhythm, to feel it, to feel *her*. But the glass did not vibrate, and I willed her to stop, and turn herself around, and right when she got to the open gate lo and behold that's exactly what she did, she stopped and fished into her pocket and set something on the gate post, something that glittered in the light like glass, and while I was trying to figure out what that thing was, Luce Waddell passed through the iron gate and down the stairs and into the street and the flow of people and was gone. Lost.

The pedestrians absorbed her, all those people, all of them with some important place to go, every one of them, the white men in their flannel suits holding their hats against the breeze, the colored men in white shirts and dark pleated pants with their eyes that didn't land on any one thing, their women carrying paper sacks with string handles, their faces guarded too. But what showed through every one of them, white and Negro alike was something I've since seen every day of my life: a pale amber fear, every single one of them afraid of doing something improper, every one of them wanting so bad to be good it seemed to burn straight through their skin. And I remember thinking maybe it was those people, all of them, who'd be the ones to call my child a bastard, who'd already decided that I, Edie Carrigan, was supposed to give my child away. Even Luce.

But how?

2

EDIE

I'd met her two years earlier, in the lunchroom at Central High. People your age have never seen those school shirts, but in the late fifties anyone who'd ever lived anywhere near the state of North Carolina had seen them plenty. At first I thought they were a joke, with their squared white letters announcing the name of the city, but I can tell you for a fact they were not. The problem was that whoever'd made those crazy sweatshirts hadn't taken boobs into account, so the bustier a girl was, the more the name got cut off at the sides, and half the time what they ended up saying wasn't CHARLOTTE but HARLOTT. Just imagine, dozens of us in that high school wearing those shirts like it was the most normal thing in the world. When I first moved there, I kept waiting for a reaction from the students who'd grown up there, you know, a wink or a sly look, but I never did see one, and anyway in those days there was no such thing as ironical dressing so in the end I decided it was the kind of thing you were supposed to pretend you didn't see at all. And sure enough, standing in that lunch line that first day, I stopped noticing too. What I saw instead was the fact of the one student body, all that blue and white like one single organism, pulsing and moving without going anywhere at all, a big tuneless din. That and the smell of pine disinfectant, fried chicken. Starch.

I gripped my tray with both hands and dawdled at the cashier's hoping to see someone I recognized and I ended up catching the eye of a girl in my history class—Debbie—that was her name. She said hey and I decided to take that as an opening. "Where are you sitting?"

But Debbie tucked her head to one side. "*Really* sorry," she said, already moving away. She sounded like she even meant it. "We don't have extra spots."

Someone behind us jostled us both, a little girl with barrettes in her hair who seemed like she was pushing right up against us, all hurrying and no sorry-to-bother-you, nothing but a fast sidestep into the crowd, and just as she did I saw a flash of yellow, an object that could only have been a pencil hanging against her palm as if it had never heard of gravity and then disappearing up her sleeve.

I couldn't help but follow. "I saw that." The little girl in the barrettes didn't turn, but she heard me all right. You could tell by the fake purpose in her walk. "I saw you," I said. "That pencil." The girl turned around so quickly I almost ran into her, lunch tray and all. She had a face like an elf's, hair lank and dark, eyes lagoon brown, full of some dare. There was fear in that dare, yes, but something else too, a kind of dread. Or pride.

I blinked. I didn't know what to say. It wasn't even my pencil. If anything, it was Debbie's. "It's not you," the little girl said. It wasn't exactly a confession.

"What's not?" I said.

"The seats. It's not you." No mention of the pencil. It had never even happened.

"Oh." And anyway, who would steal a pencil?

"It's the groups. You know." The girl's eyes darted here and there, her head and skinny neck perched over small-boned shoulders, the rest of her body invisible in the folds of one of those sweatshirts. And those barrettes, terrible. But she wasn't actually a child, just small, and the first person in the school who'd given me any information at all about its mad little rules.

"The groups don't change."

The little girl who was not a little girl shot her eyes to the side and then back—something like an eye roll but more self-conscious, more desperate, as if there were some other reality located right next door and she was considering going there any minute. Then she bobbed her head at me, turned around, and walked to a nearby table. It wasn't really an invitation, but I followed anyway.

The table held five empty chairs. Two other girls looked startled when I approached, then, when they saw I was going to sit down, gave little tilts of their palms that could have been waves or could have been stop signs, it was hard to say. They both seemed to have trouble keeping their skin clear. I set my tray on the table.

The barrettes girl said, "I'm Lucille." The other two exchanged a glance between themselves, then introduced themselves as Alice and Libby. I sat on the edge of a chair, ready to flee if it came to it. Libby was a little bit wall-eyed, her gaze bulging at my lunch, my hands, my face. Lucille set her pile of books on the table, then flopped into a chair like a boy, no smoothing the back of her skirt, no nothing. It ballooned all around her. "Debbie sits at the married table."

I wasn't sure I'd heard that right. "The married table?"

Alice and Libby exchanged another coded look.

Lucille unrolled a paper sack and drew out a sandwich wrapped in battered-looking waxed paper. "They always sit together." She spoke with authority, never mind her size, but I heard the undertow all the same. Loads of people had one, a kind of current that dragged the meaning right out from under their words and left it in some other place. Lucille's undertow slipped along a deep oceanic floor, a swirl of ink, blue and deep as the sea.

"But we're in *high* school. They're not *married* married."

"Oh but they are. We get going early here." And there it was again, the slide of her eyes, some maimed retreat under the words. *They* get going early here.

Alice giggled. "*Life* magazine ran a feature on us. Four pages. Youngest marriage age in the country."

"We're famous all right." Lucille removed the wax paper from the sandwich, wiped a smudge of yellow from it, folded it into a little square, and returned it to her sack. "Yes sir."

Silence followed, and I tried to fill it. "Most of the parents I know in Atlanta would have a heart attack if their kids got married in high school."

"Maybe people in Georgia have some sense," Lucille offered. "But I doubt it." She could have been pretty, sort of, if she smiled and did something else with her hair, but there was a more curious quality in her, like a fish beneath the surface that had been watching you all along. The thing that attracted your eye was the movement, the sudden quick energy that was so different in purpose from your own.

"Those married students—where do they live?" I was still rearranging the idea in my mind. It was just—it was too—good Lord, I couldn't imagine it, deciding now, for once and for all, that this was the person you'd spend your life with forever and forever.

Lucille smiled the not-smile again. "With their parents, one set or the other, I guess."

By that point there should have been loads of stuff to talk about, the obvious thing, for one. "Do they sleep in the same bed?"

Alice giggled and whispered something to Libby. Lucille raised her eyebrows and tilted her head. Meanwhile a thousand other questions crowded right in. Did they cook their own dinners? Have babies? I glanced at the other two girls before lowering my voice. "Would *you* do it?"

"What?"

"Get married before you graduated?"

This time Lucille blushed, really and truly, as if she were too old to be having the conversation and at the same time too young. "Are you kidding?"

I fumbled. "Sorry."

But now she leaned in, as if she'd just thought of something really clever to say. "I wouldn't mind being *asked*."

And then I did a rude thing. I let out a little bark of a laugh, not because it was so unlikely, even though it was, but because here was this odd little person who seemed like she wanted to hide away but was at the same time so pleased with her smart little self. I slapped my hand over my mouth, but too late. Alice and Libby stopped their talk.

I hurried to put myself on the same level. "It's never happened to me either." And Mama sure as shinola wouldn't stand for it. She didn't even like the idea of young people going steady and exactly for that reason: it was halfway to being married.

Lucille tucked her chin. "Well." Something in her changed then, the sash of a window sliding open. "I'm sure the occasion is imminent. For both of us."

The occasion is imminent? Who in the world talked like that? This time my laugh came all the way out and I let it. Then I pointed at the stack of library books. "Are every one of those yours?"

Lucille glanced at the stack. "Yeah, I'm trying to revise a debate speech."

There'd been a debate club in my old school too, though why a speech required a person to carry a whole stack of books to lunch I did not know. I tented my milk carton open. "What do you do, exactly, in debate?" It was as good a thing to talk about as anything else.

"Well, it's like an argument, but with rules. And there's a judge who decides who wins."

"Huh," I said. It sounded dreadful. "I'd like to see that someday."

Lucille tilted her head, regarded me. "I'm practicing after school." She placed the sentence on the table between us, like a piece of cake she'd divided in half. But instead of waiting to see if I'd take it, she cut me off. "That's pretty short notice."

I felt annoyed, and now I wanted to get the offer back, to be whatever it was this girl had thought I was. "Today?"

Lucille waved her hand. "Besides, it's mostly politics."

What did that mean? She didn't think I liked politics? I didn't know if I liked politics or not. I wasn't even sure what-all the word included. "I'll ask my mother," I said.

The speech was dead boring, all about Russia and nuclear bombs and brinkmanship and loads of skimble-skamble about all sorts of things that might or might not happen. Lucille recited it perfectly, as if there wasn't any room for argument, as if she had iron opinions about issues I'd never even thought about, and then afterwards, before I could figure out how I felt about any of it, she turned right around and read another speech that argued the exact opposite. Only then did I see that the whole thing was an exercise and that being right wasn't the point, and anyway, arguing about events happening halfway around the world wasn't the real flesh of the thing. What made it breathe was the *way* you did it, and from then on, I just stopped listening. The words flowed or gushed or eddied around me, and instead I paid attention to the undertow. And there I saw a bare naked striving that I'd long associated with boys, a desire to accomplish, and then to accomplish something else, an ambition that gaped so large it felt as if it opened something inside me too. In Atlanta, the rules had been clear. Girls imitated the debutantes and tried to get invited to their parties. It had been about belonging. Mama had spent a lot of time figuring out where to belong and who to be friends with, and she was not one bit pleased when we moved to Charlotte and she had to start over.

But this girl Lucille was trying to do something completely different. I found myself amazed, as if someone had just come along and said, "Look here, Edie Carrigan. Look at all these *doors*."

She looked at me. "That example about Cuba, I probably need to change that."

I hadn't been paying attention to the example about Cuba. "Look, Luce." The shortened name just popped right out. Her mouth kind of opened in surprise, but you could see she didn't mind it. "Why don't you stand up straight and stop putting all your weight on one leg?"

Now her surprise changed to hurt, her hand dipping into her pocket to touch some object there. I tried to soften the criticism. "It's just that I had to take a class once on posture, and that was one of the things they told us."

She managed a nod. But then she did it, stood up straight and stopped putting all her weight on one leg, and you could see it, something in her shifting, as if the act of standing taller made her taller too.

"And maybe—" This time she shot me an openly hostile look, but I was already committed. "Maybe you shouldn't look at the ceiling? It's like you're not even talking to me."

For one moment she did look to the ceiling, as if she didn't really believe she'd ever looked there before. Then she focused her gaze on my face and kept it there. Mostly.

But that night I was the one who sat on the edge of the bathroom sink, practicing how to slide my eyes in just the right way. I never did know if I had it right because I couldn't see myself when I was doing it, and finally my sister Deirdre banged on the door and asked was I ever coming out or what?

It wasn't but a week later I got the warning. I was in the girls' room, drying my hands on the loop of damp cotton. Behind me, someone was watching, I could feel it. "I've seen you." I turned to see a pretty brunette in a yellow sweater set. Right away she started fishing through her handbag and pulled out a lipstick. "You're the new girl. You're friends with Lucille Waddell." Her voice didn't match up with the words she spoke.

"Yes," I said.

She turned toward the mirror with the lipstick and leaned forward. "It's too bad for her, in a way." She made a careful pass across her lower lip. "Because she's so very clever."

I kept my voice neutral. "What's too bad?"

"About her parents, you know, the divorce and such." You have to remember that in those days "such" meant *broken home*, and the word *broken* meant broken, which meant failed, which meant not like us. It was a big deal, not like now. The sweater girl paused, pouted her lips, watched her face as she ticked it to the left, then the right. "Lucille's a swell kid, really." The sweater girl replaced the lipstick in her pocketbook and met my eye, and that was the first time I remember seeing color that way, that underneath her high-flown importance was a pale kind of fear, a pall that actually came across to me as yellow as her sweater. She kept talking, yellow lips on yellow skin. "Two years ago, before the story came out, Lucille was a member of our club."

"Oh," I said. I wasn't an idiot. I knew I was being manipulated. "The Adelphians?"

"The Girls Good Sports." And yes, that was the real name, and don't you dare laugh at it. Like I said, it was 1957 in North Carolina and there was no such thing as irony. "You can imagine," the sweater girl said. "Everyone was horrified, wanting to help, you know. Poor thing." And I knew that was the message, the thing she wanted to tell me, to warn me about, that Luce Waddell was a "poor thing."

After she left, the yellow pall lingered. I figured the story of the divorce was true. In the weeks I'd known her, Luce had never once invited me to her house, coming instead to pick me up in the subdivision where I lived. Her parents had never once shown up in the red velvet auditorium where the debate events were held, and I'd found myself wondering who they were, how they looked. Now I leaned toward the milky-streaky mirror and puckered my lips the way the sweater girl had. I wasn't her. And I'd already chosen Luce, already promised her I'd go with her to the finals. If I'd been quicker or braver with the sweater girl I might have said something to stick up for Luce, something fierce.

I stood up straight and cocked my head to the side. *If you don't like it, you can lump it.*

But of course I hadn't said any such thing. I hadn't even thought of it. In the mirror, my blue eyes stared back at me, flecked with yellow.

LUCE

There are so many people out there who're good at making you smaller than you are, but not too many of the other kind, the kind who make you bigger. Edie was that kind, as if she had charm and grace to spare and didn't mind some of it rubbing off on someone like me. But the friendship had come too easy. I remember waiting for her to slip up, to reveal some inner meanness, some ugly insecurity hidden beneath that eggshell skin of hers. But the cost of her affection turned out to be altogether different. Edie saw you, and not just the parts you presented for her to see. That first day, she'd seen me take Debbie MacIntyre's pencil—she'd *seen* it, caught me red-handed, and all I could do was pretend it hadn't happened. But I knew. And she knew. I was transparent as a guppy around her, all my organs and bones outlined in the light. That was Edie's real tyranny. It burned, that gaze, and you always went back for more.

Take the business with the advice books. I (even I) had pilfered many looks at my sister's *Joyce Jackson's Guide to Dating*, or the beauty section in *Seventeen*. But those had been solitary exercises, sessions I hid even from myself—mainly because the gap between "is" and "should be" was too immense to leap without falling into the abyss. But Edie had every guide to dating ever published, displayed right there on a shelf at the foot of her bed, the titles all loaded with words like "beauty" and "dating" and "charm." You have to remember it was a time when such words lived unambiguous lives. Even I did not question the reign of such words, such books, such advice.

But I didn't quite share Edie's enthusiasm. Whenever the newest guide came out, she toured through the pages right there, as if this were the very volume that would reveal the secret of everlasting love, as if whatever secrets those books provided would and should be available to her. As if they were her *right*. She read her favorite parts aloud, the two of us sitting there in her bedroom on a carpet that was sleep-worthy. The whole endeavor was silly, of course, but I didn't not like it. "Hey, listen to this," she'd say. The vein in her temple traced a blue arc, and my eye went there, to that imperfection. Edie read the advice with great relish. *Do not behave like Diana on the hunt! You may have to take the lead, but you will have to use tact!*

Well. At the time I didn't understand why the books made me so uncomfortable, why they felt so...crass. Nor could I imagine myself walking around school with a strategy for capturing boys—much less telling people about it. On that day I dipped my chin at Edie and tried to soften my skepticism. "You're supposed to *trick* them?"

She paused. You could see that word "trick" traveling through her mind, the fact of it and then its implications, like a pinball lighting up levers as it banked through the machine. When her mind arrived at the place it wanted to go, she lowered the book. "It's not about *tricking* them, Luce, it's about *reading* them." She wagged a pencil at me, the gesture so exaggerated it became a parody of itself, as if she were only pretending to scold. "And stop making that face. You might learn something."

I stopped. Making that face. "What happens when they find out they've been tricked?"

She dipped her chin and lifted her eyebrows and ignored my question. "Listen to this. *Always remember that brains do not handicap a girl if she keeps them well hidden.*" This time she didn't meet my eye.

I searched her voice for some trace of sanctimony, searched her face for some indication she considered the passage especially significant, that she was reading it on purpose. But she kept her eyes right on that book. For Pete's sake. She did. She was. Reading it on purpose. I folded my arms and tried to decide if I was angry. She must have known she'd overstepped, because now she pretended to read in silence. I stewed. On the bureau, a Kodachrome of a younger Edie stared back at me with her two sisters. From another, a begowned Edie regarded me on the arm of some boy she'd gone with in Atlanta: Aster, fair-haired and big-eared. Her mother had been hoping they'd stay together forever. I wasn't all that interested in Aster, or in any other boy per se, but the photo confused me, that boy's arm draped around her shoulders in a way that made me wonder what it felt like, all that human flesh, the weight of it there, and how easy a thing it was to want that arm there, and, if you did want it, whether the fact of that want had to be to be inversely proportional to all the other things you wanted.

Now Edie lowered the book. "C'mon. Don't you want a steady?"

I sighed. It seemed a very personal question. But there was something in the marrow of it, a kind of investment—that made me want to answer it honestly. I lifted my chin and looked into those uptilted eyes. "Sure I do."

Edie cocked her head. "But?"

"But I'm not you. And I don't want to be some kind of...*project*." Because in those days the girl-as-project was a staple of life. When people talked about a girl's "potential" they usually meant the way she styled her hair. My hair had always been straight as nails, but Edie had a way of wrapping it in tiny little spirals and misting them with water. At the time they seemed important, those pin curls, mostly because she'd taken the time to show me how to do it. I hadn't got a bead on it yet, the girl-as-project business, but I already knew it was too late to have a say. My bureau was already strewn with a collection of scarves and headbands Edie had advised me to wear with specific outfits. Wear that. Yes that one. The black velvet one.

Well. I wasn't so cerebral that I didn't care about boys and popularity—I did—but in those days the project of beauty was abstract, like one of those thought experiments in physics with the ball in the elevator, a theoretical exercise, not something that could change me or my status in the world per se. I endured it and wanted to be good at it—but mostly to keep Edie's attention—anything to stave off the day when Edie Carrigan avoided my eye and carried her tray past our table to sit with the Service Club or the Pep Club or the Adelphians or God forbid the Girls Good Sports. But someday she'd come to the same decision Connie had. (Connie had said it wasn't my fault. It's just that they were obligated to ask me to leave the group because the Girls Good Sports believed in family. That's why their constitution had made the rules in the first place, and anyway, they couldn't get in the habit of bending the rules for some people but not others. That would just be a perfect nightmare. Connie was sure I'd understand. And the whole time Connie was explaining, she was patting the hair at the back of her neck to see if the curl there was holding. It was.)

3

If I had to guess I'd say that first crack must have started in the shoe department at Ivey's, where the sales clerk sat wide-kneed in front of me and spread open a size eight and a half Capezio. I slid my toes in, but my heel just did not want to go.

"I thought so," the clerk said and reached for a box on the floor next to him.

Mama frowned. "I don't know. I'd hate to see her in a nine."

And we were all of us sitting there at that moment, weighing the terribleness of the nine, when a man's thin voice interrupted from above. "I beg your pardon." The voice was accustomed to being in charge, you could tell, and belonged to a sandy-haired man in a suit so wildly plaid that you just knew it had to be the next big thing in fashion. He made a little bow and then did some motion with his hand that caused the sales clerk to nod and turn away, then introduced himself as some sort of director of some sort of department. Mr. Crowder. His features were small and handsome, his hair thick, his neck all Adam's apple and pointy chin.

Mama gave him her all-purpose smile. "We were just admiring the new shoes."

"Marvelous," Mr. Crowder said without any interest in the shoes at all, then right away changed the subject. "We've got oodles of shorts and pedal pushers coming out this summer in Misses."

"Oh," Mama said vaguely. "We haven't been over there yet."

"They're not out yet, Mrs. Carrigan. We're looking for a couple of youngsters to help show them."

Mama tilted her head.

"Your daughter has just the Ivey's look." He smiled at my mother. "And I think we know who she can thank for *that*." His appreciation was so enthusiastic that it didn't sound like real appreciation at all.

For the first time my mother sounded unsure. "We're very proud of her." She glanced at me as if trying to decide if that was true.

Mr. Crowder gave Mama another little half bow. "Good breeding always shows." Then he turned to me. "Edith, how do you feel about trying out for the summer line?"

I blinked. He was talking about a job. I right away found myself thinking of Luce, who'd just been named co-editor of the newspaper, as a sophomore, and a girl, and was practicing now for *Speak Out* on the radio and gunning for state champion in debate. Doors and more doors.

"Yes," I said. And right away I had the thought, that who would've ever predicted I'd be the one to get a job before Luce? At the time it felt like it could only be good news.

The next afternoon Mr. Crowder showed Mama and Daddy into a glass and marble office on the fourth floor, and I waited in an anteroom on an aqua-colored geometric chair. A secretary brought me a Co-Cola and set it on a white cocktail napkin on a glass coffee table. In the next room, Mr. Crowder leafed through an open file drawer and presented papers on a round table while Mama and Daddy leaned over the papers in the low glassed thrum, closed up in a world soundless as an aquarium.

There wasn't a single thing for me to do so I just watched everyone doing their tasks in the other glass compartments, every one of them busy doing something different, speaking without speaking or returning typewriter carriages or dialing telephones or putting on spectacles— tropical fish, all of them in their silent separate worlds—except—*there*, someone *was* seeing me, someone right there watching me watch, a sloe-eyed man in a bowtie and—

He looked away. He was wearing a white apron and holding some kind of metal contraption, there above his knees, the apron stained with something black. His hipbones were lean and strong and outlined like parentheses against the cotton fabric. A slow heat rose up my neck. He'd probably seen me spying on everyone there, seen me slurping down my Coke like it was going out of style. I knew some things about how to operate in the world of boys, and in those years it seemed to me that I had some say-so in it because I knew, or thought I knew, that if you managed their interest it made your life easier in all manner of ways. They paid attention to what you had to say, drove you to school, befriended the people you wanted befriended.

But this wasn't a boy. This was a man. Who *worked* here. I let my eyes slide back to his glass aquarium.

And there he was. Looking away again. Guilty.

For the first time it occurred to me that *I* was the one in the aquarium, sitting cross-ankled on that square aqua chair and poking through the remains of my ice with my straw, and that he probably thought I was older, that he'd see as soon as my parents came out that I was still a kid, but that in the meantime if I turned to look I'd find him there again, just so, and it seemed impossible to me that I, at sixteen, could have a thing in the world on a grown man. But I saw that I did, that I'd unearthed some secret totem, a clean hard stone that rolled smooth and bright in the palm of my hand, shining its peculiar cryptic power. What a thing. What a thing to grab in the grip of your palm, to honor and adore, or to hold in your pocket like a guilty coin to save for some future far-off day.

Mr. Crowder came out and handed me a clipboard and fussed over several sentences that were written there, and I tried to listen to what he was saying, but his favorite word seemed to be *youngsters*, and I found myself listening for the word, counting. I signed my name, and he tucked the pen back into his breast pocket, folded the clipboard under his arm, and returned to my parents in the office. The man with the tight white apron and the pretty hip bones was busy refolding his tripod. The strange part was that I'd seen his secret emotion without even trying, a desire painted right there on his face, in color, purple. Anyone who cared to look would see it, but the crazy thing was that nobody ever did because they were all too busy talking on the telephone and smoking cigarettes and rifling through desk drawers and sharpening pencils and looking in compact mirrors and wearing their own desires on their own faces for any old soul to see. There in the doorway: a man and a lady pointing at something on a piece of paper. The man was talking, but the lady was orange with anger, her jaw hard and her lips pressed thin, but he didn't even notice the way her eyes avoided his, the color of her emotion right *there*. Worse, he was laboring to prop himself up in the most obvious way, struggling to enlarge himself with bigger speech and magenta-colored gestures and all his effort just making the lady angrier than before.

And there, in the other office, my own parents like the others, Daddy so big and bulky holding his hand on a piece of paper while my mother ran a finger over the glass tabletop, both of them stealing glances at the pages and then at one another. I saw it for the first time, my daddy gold and striving, my mama sunk in a yellow insecurity that now seemed a permanent part of her, but also, how they suited one another, my parents, how they relied upon each other to move about in the world, how they wanted the same kind of safety for themselves and for me. People weren't happy, not really, even my parents, who had everything normal there was to want, and more. But maybe there was more to want beyond the edge of the wide flat world, something more precious and glittering. Maybe.

Then Mr. Crowder walked toward me, winked, and closed the Venetian blinds.

That was how I came to spend my afternoons downtown. I learned I didn't have the bosom for the job, but that bosoms could be professionally faked. I learned that most girls only lasted a single season. But I signed up for it anyway, not because of the money or the brush of new clothes or the warmth of lights and attention, or at least not *only* because of those things. What surprised me was the usefulness I felt, the importance of it, even if it was based on wearing pretty clothes. And of course the one who'd taught me to want that kind of usefulness was Luce.

And then there was Simon, the college student with the hipbones in the white apron who helped with the shoots, Simon of the long straight nose and the architectural face, Simon wiping dust from the backdrops, Simon setting up another pair of lights, Simon bending to raise or lower a tripod, a sci-fi paperback curled into his back pocket, Simon who liked photography and movies and called both of them *film*. Every time I posed with a beach ball or a hula-hoop, I imagined the way the photograph looked to Simon.

It wasn't too long before he was offering to take me to lunch. This wasn't as easy as it sounds because he was working, you see, and there was always something that needed to be done, some kind of equipment to be fixed, something adjusted, something moved. You can't imagine his hands, so long-boned and elegant, fingers lean as scallions, the most elegant hands you've ever seen, no matter the nails black-rimmed with all those chemicals. But that was exactly the problem, his hands, especially his right hand, mind you his *right* hand, where there was a well-worn gold ring that looked to me an awful lot like a wedding band. I remember watching him unscrew the legs of that tripod, the ring tapping against the metal. But I couldn't bring myself to ask the question straight out. "Your ring, is that an antique?"

His left hand immediately went there and turned it, those long fingers pressing and stroking that little piece of metal. He didn't even realize he was doing it. His eyes sparkled at me. "I don't know about an *antique*. But it's maybe 50 years old. A wedding ring."

"Oh." Something in me waned and faltered, a certain excitement I hadn't known I'd been feeling until it was gone. Simon hefted the tripod in his left hand, like a scepter.

"My grandfather's. He died in the war. The first one."

"Oh." And then against my will came this huge smile, all teeth I could tell without even seeing it and right after he'd said that dreadful thing about his grandfather dying in the war. I adjusted my face. "I'm sorry about the, about your grandfather."

"Battle of Verdun. He was a soldier in the German fifth."

"He was shot, then."

"Maybe. Died in combat. That was the report. Fighting for his country."

"Oh. That's awful."

But in this particular moment Simon didn't seem to mind terribly. As a matter of fact he perked right up, his eyes bright with some growing mischief. "You thought it was *my* wedding ring?"

"I did wonder."

"I'm not married. I'm only twenty-one." And here came my crazy grin again, all teeth. But he didn't seem to mind. In fact, he seemed to find that last bit of information particularly intriguing. "And what else have you been wondering?" He was grinning now too.

At that point I felt like I'd already been way too pushy and figured it best to stick to history. "What was he like, your grandfather?"

"I never met him. I mean, obviously. Isaac was his name. In 1938 my grandmother brought her kids here. She always told me the same thing. 'That man?' Simon's accent was now German, and terribly fake. 'Your grandfather? That man was very good husband. Very good father. But that man have very bad jokes.'" The corner of his mouth dimpled into a smile.

"What was her name?"

"Golda."

"Like gold?"

"Exactly. Like gold."

SIMON

Simon knew plenty of pretty girls, and people were always reminding him of that fact. His friends: "That photography gig you have is a *kick*." His father: "It's just as easy to fall in love with a Gentile as it is to fall in love with a Jew. But it's also just as easy to fall in love with a Jew." But Simon knew what he knew. Pretty girls expected to be watched. That's why they all wanted to be models. They were *watchees*.

And then Edie showed up, banging down a Co-Cola in two drags and gandering around the office like some kind of Arkady Darell hunting for Asimov's Second Foundation. Edie surprised you. Take the thing at the Dairy Queen. (Simon was all benches and booths. You could scooch right up to a girl that way. The Dairy Queen had those curved cement numbers and was so damn crowded in warm weather you practically had to sit on top of each other anyway.) Simon barely knew her and she still grilled him about the pre-med stuff. They'd just come from *Day the World Ended*, and the film'd had one of those plotlines that shook up your perspective and spilled it out—bam!—and the shape of the world looked different. You'd been reshaped. It wasn't a new message to him: the world was ending. There were giant forces at play—*giant*—and his parents couldn't see them because all their thinking was going into the one thing: the survival of their own. Half the members of Temple Beth El had thrown themselves into the fight for Negro civil rights, but his parents had gone whole hog the other direction. But their view—Zionism itself—was a step toward the particular. There were bigger forces at play. Call it what you wanted, Foundation, Empire, Galactica, it was all the same. The world—the rest of it—was moving toward connection.

That night Edie seemed to feel it too, that reshape, because she right away started asking questions about the future. She was wearing a purple sleeveless number and spooning ice cream into her mouth. Strawberry. "Did you always know you were going to medical school?" Those lifting laughing eyes. Innocent as pie.

"Yep." What a question.

She tilted her head, and her dark hair bunched all to one side and rested on her shoulder. Touching, but just barely. Or maybe not touching, he couldn't be sure. She didn't say anything. She was waiting for—yeah, the medical school question.

"It's not strictly a requirement," he said. His parents had been saving for his education since before he was born. "It's more like a path, pre-paved, that I can walk down when I'm ready. I don't have to do it. But I probably will."

Edie blinked. "Is that what you *want* to do?"

"I mean, *yeah*, I'd like to be Richard Avedon or somebody like that, but that's not what would happen." Edie scraped the spoon around the side of the cardboard dish. Did she know who Richard Avedon was? Everybody knew who Richard Avedon was. "I wouldn't *be* him," he continued. "I'd just be some hack with a camera who thought he could imitate the guy."

She licked the spoon and regarded him. "No, you wouldn't. You'd be you. And people would be mad for your pictures."

He loved that. Didn't believe it, but he loved that she said it. Even though she called them *pictures*. "You'd be mad for my pictures."

Spoon back to lips, arrested. "So would your parents. They'd be proud of you."

He gave a little laugh. "Maybe." Out in the parking lot, two cars circled, waiting for an open spot. "I'm sure I'll do it. Med school, that is. You know, you make this bargain with yourself. Study anatomy for four hours so you can go to the photo lab for one." The spoon rested lightly on her lips. He said, "It's okay. I mean, it works out."

"A bargain?" She did the head tilt again. "How does that work once you're a doctor all day?" Not a *trace* of sarcasm. Not one. She really wanted to know. "I know you'll be successful, but how does the bargain part work?"

Simon shifted his ass on the cement. "It's not just that. It's not just the success part." Jesus, that bench was hard. He took another bite of his cone in case she was wanting to jump in, but she wasn't. "It's the pride of it too. They want to be able to go back to their families and say, 'My son Simon the doctor.' It's corny. I know. But they want me to be able to have all the things they worked for and never got."

Edie was nodding slowly. No more ice cream. No more lips. She still didn't jump in.

"And if I said no, I don't like it so hot, it would be like saying they've gone and done all this work for nothing." Ha. More than that.

"So it's a question of owing?" Edie said. "To your parents, and your grandparents before that?"

"Yeah, I guess." (His mother: "Have you seen your cousin's hands? Engine grease! Embedded!") But looking in people's throats and noses and ears was mechanic work too. Just that the machine you were looking at was a human one, and instead of scrubbing off engine grease you were scrubbing off mucous and blood.

Edie folded her arms on the cement table. "How long will you owe them?"

He stopped chewing.

Edie looked embarrassed. "I'm being nosy, aren't I?"

"Nope." Yep, but he loved her anyway.

She rested her elbows on the table. "What I mean is, how long do you need to wait before you get to do the things you want?"

"I *am* doing the things I want. Right now. I'm doing them right now. This." He waved his arm at the dinky umbrellas, at the pick-up window, at the cars in the lot. "This. This is what knocks me out. This *is* doing exactly what I want. Now is when I get to do what I want." It was true.

Edie leaned in, close enough that he could smell the strawberry on her breath. Her eyes were swimming-pool blue. "I'm sorry to be so nosy, Simon Bloom."

And that right there, that "Simon Bloom." Like she saw you, straight through. The girls Simon knew would never go and do that. And they sure as hell didn't let you see through *them.* "It's okay." He was grinning like a fool. "I like it."

Edie let out a bright laugh, like some kind of fish that flips to the surface and slaps its tail at the sun.

"You're the prettiest girl I know."

Another laugh, this one smaller, more of a slow float to the surface. "Really?" Not one iota of surprise. "Thank you, Simon Bloom. And thank you for the movie. I just love Lori Nelson. She has the most amazing eyes." Simon kissed her then, right there on the bench. He didn't give a rat's ass about Lori Nelson's eyes.

LUCE

It wasn't Simon that bothered me per se. I'd been expecting him, or someone like him. What really bothered me was the job. I'd thought I'd be first, that's all. Besides. Edie didn't need a career. By the time her mother filled up that hope chest, she'd be engaged.

Outside the bus, umbrellas and fedoras and briefcases joggled along. September had come in rainy. I swiped my palm across the number seven's fogged window, wrapped my jealousy in a little package and tucked it away. Presbyterian Hospital lurched past, then Elizabeth Avenue with its homuncular bungalows, then Central High School where I was supposed to be, then the hulky block of Mr. Belk's store. The courthouse columns rose up in the front window, clarified again and again by the swish of the wipers. Out of habit, my eyes swept the building's wide stairs. I'd seen him there once, talking to a colleague, grooved gray hair combed across his head. But I was too late for that. They would have started by now. Well.

I pulled the bell cord.

The interior of the courthouse was oaken, the sound of the bailiff's voice booming right through the double doors. No one paid me any attention, even though they'd have recognized me if they took a real look. I always thought one day the old man who ran the elevator would give me some secret sign. Or one of the other Negro attendants. But that never did happen. The colored people didn't see me either.

I eased through the doors and slipped into the gallery, to my usual place, the view the same as ever: the backs of men's heads. But I knew him anyway, the round physique, the folds of skin bunched at the back of his neck, the pink scalp showing more than ever. My dad.

The cases were always about broken families. Today there was a Mrs. Gagney trying to get money from a Mr. Gagney. Dad carried a yellow pad and referred to it often. Did you, Mr. Gagney, send a check on the day of January 14, 1957? He stood close to the man and his voice rang against the lacquered wood. Sometimes it would happen when he turned back—his eyes landing on mine. You'd see the surprise in them, the happy recognition—at least for a moment, before he put on his father-face and popped his eyes at me. *I told you this wasn't the place.*

I know what you're thinking. You're thinking you feel sorry for the younger me, the me skipping school just for a glance from my dad. But it wasn't just that. I wanted to know what he did out there in the world. Wanted to know what attorneys did. Debate team was an exercise. Lawyering was a life.

The counsel for the defense was a fellow named Mr. Sweeney I'd seen before. There weren't but so many people practicing family law. And yes, they were always men, and the stenographers were always women. But Dad had already said it didn't have to be that way. *Law school's not illegal, Toots. Just expensive.*

At about 3:00 Dad stepped up to speak to the judge, and I thought it would happen right then, on his way back. But he never did look past the table, and in the end the judge ruled against Mr. Gagney, and Mr. Sweeney and Dad shook hands, and Mr. Gagney glared at the judge from over his glasses, and Dad slid his papers into his briefcase and bent over to fasten it. But still he did not look up.

Well.

I waited outside with the others. Soon enough Dad and Mrs. Gagney emerged together, the woman's hand on the inside of his upper arm, as if for protection, a pocket book on the shoulder of the other. The bag swung in range as she passed, a black leather number, the aperture a toothy brass zipper, new and shiny as a smile.

And then my father was turning around. Surely he'd see me. Surely he'd stop in the middle of that human swarm, smile broadly, take my face in both hands. *My favorite girl.*

Mrs. Gagney would let go his arm. She'd have to. *Post hoc, ergo prompter hoc.*

But already he was turning toward Mrs. Gagney, her hand on his arm cuffed in pale blue cotton, the nails pink-lacquered. The aperture in the purse was big enough for one finger, or, if you had small hands, two.

I closed my eyes tight. Held myself in.

Then they were both ambling down the hall, Mrs. Gagney and my dad. I waited a moment or two, then pressed up behind them, as if to catch them, and instead felt for the jagged teeth of that zipper—and touched *something.* Fabric maybe, or vinyl. I tweezed two fingers together—and the woman stepped away while something blue bright and light as air tailed out of her purse like a comet, gave a little catch on the teeth, and then, just as she leaned into my father, came away in my hand. I took it into my fist and followed, as if I were trying to get their attention.

You can't believe how easy that stuff was. Nobody shouted. Nobody coughed. Nobody said, "Excuse me, miss." City employees were too busy nodding at my father in deference. I fingered the fabric, something thin and polyester. A headscarf maybe, the kind you tied under your chin to keep the wind from ruining your hairdo. The scarf smelled burnt as hairspray.

You have every right to judge me. I'm not sure I can explain it, even now. It wasn't about the money, though God knows we could have used it. It was something else eating at me from the inside, something more grotesque.

Well.

The pale blue dress and my father's wide gray suit continued down the hallway, ever smaller. Again I wondered: how would it be to follow him, to touch his coat, to inhabit it, to inhabit *him*? How would it be to *be* him?

Girls like me weren't supposed to want to work, especially girls in the middle class, which was where my family was, or least where they'd started out. Career girls were liable to wind up as old maids and neurotics. Look at my mother. She'd been a secretary, but once she'd gotten married, the firm had told her it was too much. They'd sent her home, and she'd gone off the rail. And then one day she'd locked Martin out of the house, emptied his closet and cut each item of clothing in half with a pair of scissors. That same winter she'd boarded up the bay window so the neighbors couldn't see inside. It was exactly like the experts warned. I'd gotten the message. I wasn't deaf. If you didn't surrender to the female principle, you ended up a loon.

By the time I reached home, the air had grown moist and thick, like ointment. The fans whapped and the Venetian blinds tap-tapped against the window frames, their striped shadows wobbling across the floorboards. Juries of dust bunnies marshaled in the corners, and the whole place smelled of dead cigarettes.

Imagine what Edie would think. The thought made me cringe. The shape of the thing could show itself at any time. Someone like Edie'd be able to see its outline without even looking.

I knew my mother was home—she was always home—but it was a question of where. The house didn't give any clues. Guy Lombardo on the record player would've been a good sign. Rearranged furniture meant she was liable to be upbeat. Likewise the sorting of clothes or the alphabetizing of books. A bathrobe, slippers, or the television were generally bad. You never knew until you knew. Best be ready to defend yourself.

I opened the refrigerator: a bottle of milk on the top shelf with a red rubber band around the neck. The milk would be Miss Diamond's, our colored tenant's. A bowl of macaroni and cheese, two bottles of Co-Cola, a box of oranges, all with red rubber bands. Everything seemed to belong to Miss Diamond. But the milk looked fresh, and she'd told me more than once go ahead and drink all the milk you want, Miss Lucille, but you leave my oranges be, for they are my special weakness. I poured myself a glass of milk and set it on the counter. Then I counted the oranges. There were five, fat and bright and thin-skinned. I held one to my nose, took a long citrusy breath, and returned it to the bowl.

I smelled her before I heard her. Either bourbon or rum. I couldn't always tell.

I steeled myself. But all she said was, "Is that some kind of a look you're cultivating?" Which was ironic, since she was wearing that yellow duster and a hairnet. Thank the good Lord Edie would never have to see that get-up. "You know how to polish those shoes." I looked down at my saddle shoes. Nobody cared about my shoes, ipso facto. Her eyes traveled up my body. "You're exactly like your father."

"I know. Sorry." If only my father thought that. "I'll do the shoes."

But she lingered. "The school called. They said you weren't feeling well."

I froze. I'd never actually been caught. My mother hated getting phone calls from the school. Usually they were about my brother Martin.

Now she sounded defensive. "What was I supposed to say? I told them you were sick."

"I appreciate it."

And now her tone changed to something like surprise. "Are you?" She squinted at me. "Sick?" It was the voice of someone who'd found a lost object she'd long since forgotten. There, right there, behind the sofa, was the ashtray from Myrtle Beach that you hadn't seen now for some three years. Strange, because you hadn't even noticed it was missing.

I searched out the least offensive answer. "Maybe. I don't feel great."

Then, to my amazement, she produced a thermometer from the front pocket of her duster. I hadn't known she owned one. She shook the instrument and squinted at it, wrinkling her brow in concentration. She spoke to it. "When you were a baby you used to get ear infections." Even though she wasn't looking at me I loved that sentence. It seemed to me the sort of thing mothers were supposed to say. I let it rest there in the silence between us. Now her tone lifted with encouragement. "Open." She sounded like a mother, so I tried to act like a daughter. I opened my mouth. And then she actually touched me, her hand cool and tender against my hairline, her eyes searching my face, the seconds slipping too quickly into the past. I willed the mercury up, up, up. "Open."

She squinted at the instrument for what seemed a long time. "You're okay." Now her intonation was flat. "No more phone calls from the school, you hear? How do you think that makes me feel?"

"Yes ma'am."

Then she turned and her gaze fell upon the glass of milk. She held it to the window and studied it, her shoulder blades like fence slats underneath that bathrobe. "Did I buy this?" As if she were talking to herself. "When would I have bought this?"

"Miss Diamond said it was all right," I said carefully.

Suspicion in her voice. "She bought it? Miss Diamond?"

I made my tone flat. Divested. "She said I could have some every now and then."

But Mother seemed to be sorting out some puzzle in her mind. "What day is it?"

"Thursday."

"I don't think I've bought milk since, well..." She frowned into space, her lips counting.

I didn't say it. Last winter.

She bent toward the milk and smelled it. "I most certainly did not buy this."

"Miss Diamond said I could have some. Every now and then."

Mother peered at me with some kind of dawning realization on her face. "You know we can't take food from Miss Diamond. That's not the way it works." She held the milk away, as if it were sour, looked around the room for a place to set it. Then the problem of the milk just seemed to overwhelm her, and she let herself give into that private meanness that sometimes clawed up from the inside. She tipped the glass and the milk streamed to the floor and splashed up my shin, still cool. It soaked through my bobby socks, still cool. What I thought of in that moment was Edie. How glad I was she wasn't there to see me. How I would want to die.

Mother set the glass on the counter with a thwack. "We cannot take food from Miss Diamond." Then she turned and walked away, the bones of her spine jutting out like the teeth of a saw.

I listened to her shuffle down the corridor and into the living room. The milk pooled and thinned on the forest colored linoleum, a cloudy green, like Necco wafers, or a dusted chalkboard. Some part of my brain started issuing commands. Take off your shoes and socks. Store them on the porch and get the mop. Flush out the mop and wring. Rinse the shoes with the hose and set them back on the porch. They will dry some amount before school.

I poured a glass of water from the tap. What she'd said about not taking from Miss Diamond wasn't exactly correct. Mother *preferred* renting to colored women. There weren't but so many places for them to go. Which meant you could charge them more.

There was also that other fact: Most colored women were working. Miss Diamond taught science at the Second Ward School, and it hadn't seemed to damage *her* mind. She seemed perfectly normal, maybe more than normal. One summer day when I was fourteen or so and cutting through the Second Ward to get to a used bookstore on South Tryon, I'd walked past the open door of a laundromat and heard a gaggle of women talking so loudly I'd stolen a look into the darkened space to get a look at whatever the party was. There was Miss Diamond stepping toward another Negro lady with the corners of a sheet in each hand, both of them laughing the kind of laugh that was nothing like the way Edie laughed but was also exactly the way Edie laughed, loose and free. The way people only ever laughed when they were around someone they loved.

Come Monday morning those ladies had jobs, and in their pocket-books money they'd earned for themselves. Come Monday night they returned to single rented rooms. They didn't seem to be having nervous breakdowns.

I wasn't crazy about the term *old maid*. *Spinster* I could live with. Spinsters walking the corners of those sheets toward one another, hands to hands.

Sometimes on a Sunday Miss Diamond wore lavender high heels, leather pumps that one time prompted my mother to raise the rent five dollars because she said anybody who could afford shoes like that was liable to have enough money and then some. Miss Diamond also had a yellow dress dotted with lavender flowers she wore with those shoes, but not to school, never to school. School days she walked to the bus stop in plain brown flats and flannel skirt, a brown satchel in one hand and a paper bag lunch in the other. In a different time period, or a different part of the world, I might have come right out and asked her what it meant to earn her own money. Whether being on your own meant being on your own for good. But you have to remember that in those days it was hard to imagine such a conversation. Maybe for her too. And it was years before I realized it was Miss Diamond's rent that kept the roof over our heads.

I knew what I knew: that I couldn't stay in my mother's house, couldn't run the risk of becoming her carbon copy. That I didn't want to be like my sister, Martha, who'd graduated from high school and found a job at a druggist's counting out Miltown and Thorazine. That I didn't want to be a stenographer or a telephone operator or a typist. Nor was I pretty enough to be a stewardess or a sales girl. That spring I'd seen a photograph in *Life* magazine, a full-page portrait of a colored girl holding a cardboard sign. The caption said the girl was one of ten thousand Negroes who'd traveled to Washington to march for voting rights. The girl was wearing a white blouse with a black string tie at the neck. She looked purposeful, as if she'd decided to worry only about meaningful things, changing the country maybe, and freedom, not try-ing to get into the Girls Good Sports or making her hair do something it wouldn't. Or at least, that's what I'd supposed at the time. Which was what it was all about, supposing, that and figuring out what it was you were allowed to want. I'd wanted what that girl had, to worry about important things, to be able to see the difference between my enemies and my friends. There was a war brewing in Little Rock and another one brewing against nuclear proliferation. In school we had air raid drills, and Mr. Armstrong showed a map of the world with a red stain seeping across the continents. Scientists like Linus Pauling were calling for an international ban on nuclear testing, and I wished I were a boy so I could join the National Committee for a Sane Nuclear Policy. Or any of the other things that were so much bigger than me.

Well. It would take a college degree. Miss Diamond had one. So what if other women didn't finish theirs. Some of them did. The ones who really wanted to, the ones who didn't quit to get married. The old maids.

The intellectual type of man usually is interested in a woman who flatters his ego rather than displays equal or superior intellectual ability to his own.

And maybe that was true. The more my mother stayed home, the more she drove my dad away. One thing was certain. He'd been proud of my grades, proud of every spelling bee and every recital and every essay, proud enough to call me his smartest girl.

Just not proud enough to stay.

4

"It's so *obvious*." Luce had her theories and didn't mind saying them out loud.

I shook my chocolate milk for an overlong time, and then shook it some more. We could talk about most anything, Luce and I, but not about that. Luce didn't know about boys, how the right one could turn your body electric as live wire. And telling her would be halfway to admitting everything else. "What do you mean?"

"You know. So they can do *that*." She slid her eyes sideways as if *that* were happening just over her shoulder. Two tables away, Fred and Nancy Tate leaned shoulder to shoulder, blissfully wedded in some glittering twin of a cafeteria worlds away from this one. I was just glad Luce wasn't looking at me. I know what I was afraid of seeing: shock, maybe, disappointment definitely, and worst of all, disgust.

I never did lie outright, to Luce or to my folks, like some part of me knew even then I'd end up defending my case in front of Luce, or my parents, or maybe St. Peter himself, how I'd say I hadn't really and truly lied, I just hadn't told my parents about the darkroom to begin with. It was the only place at the Blooms with a lock on the door and to enter it was to step into one of Simon's movies after the nuclear bombs had hit: all red mystery and pans of glassy fluids and the smell of underground chemicals, photographs hanging on a string; the tail fin of a Firesweep, a fry cook in a white rectangular hat, a hand with long lacquered nails tilted outward like an offering, peculiar objects and people all broken apart and splashed together in splendid secret combination.

And all the while that high-volt fire fizzing and zinging through your skin, the charge of it, the risk.

Simon called the photographs *films*, and that's how the whole place was, a film, a motion picture, and we were the stars in it, and what happened in that darkroom happened in another person's story that was not mine, to another girl named Edie Carrigan, Simon's sinewy arms and white chest floating in the red gloom, the girl on the quilt on the cement floor a film version of me because the real me would have been embarrassed by the physicality of it all, the nakedness of it, the sudden focus on the parts of the body I was supposed to keep hidden. The two figures on the floor were James Dean and Natalie Wood, or Montgomery Clift and Elizabeth Taylor because I, Edie Carrigan, didn't have it in me to break my parents' heart.

The film version of us floated palely in that gloom, our bodies like buoys, our future a miracle blowing from the horizon.

It was the one unspoken rule I knew my parents held most dear, and I was breaking it.

I was breaking it. Some days I let Simon convince me and other days I did not. Or at least that was the way I made it out, putting him off at times of the month I thought were unsafe, because it just wasn't right, and on other days, especially if he'd been able to get some rubbers, letting myself give in. I never did ask where in the world they'd come from, and if I thought of those foil-wrapped packages at all, say, during class, I told myself I wouldn't need them again and that I really meant it this time— unless—well, there was always Unless. I kept Unless there, in a tiny closet in my mind, wrapped up in a box in case I needed it. I couldn't *plan* to go to the darkroom with Simon. Planning would mean I was responsible for what happened there. Planning would mean I was guilty.

I also believed what they said about rinsing. That pregnancy came from the union of two germ cells, the female and the male, which was probably why my mother kept a bottle of Zonite in the back of the bathroom closet, behind the deodorant and the Kotex pads, probably too why the label on the bottle promised two things: to combat an odor more grave than bad breath and to kill all germs. All meant all. Right?

It worked for a long time, almost a year, and maybe would have worked forever if our plans hadn't gone sideways that first week of senior year when everything happened all at once. That morning I woke to the sound of the ringing phone and my mother's carpet-cushion steps. I rolled onto my side and pulled the bedcovers to my chin. The windows were still half dark, the floor littered with dirty clothes and textbooks and a felt lion with tortoise-shell eyes and a note from a girl named Marian Smythe who'd invited me and Luce to join the homecoming committee. I'd told her yes, and Luce had told her yes too, because it was everything we'd planned together, but then right away she'd gone mad for something else, some ten thousand Negro and Caucasian students who'd held a giant march in Washington, and it was all about integrating schools, and it turned out all this time a Negro dentist named Hawkins had been sitting at white lunch counters at Douglas Airport for so many days in a row that the federal government hadn't had any choice but to declare those restaurants mixed. Listening to Luce talk, I could feel it—not the possibility of integration or what it meant—but what it meant to her, to Luce, this thing out there changing her, like a steam engine pulling her toward whatever her life was going to be, and I wished I had that too.

It got to be such a big deal the debate team took on the topic too, and then the reverend at Luce's Unitarian church started organizing all manner of special events, and Luce signed right up, all the while working on about a thousand speeches for debate and telling me, Edie, don't you forget, the finals are the weekend of the tenth, and you're coming, right?

I did mean it when I said yes. I did mean it when I said I wouldn't miss it for the world.

Outside my door, Mama stepped and halted, hesitated. Then a

knock, the door squeaking open, her sitting on the edge of the bed. The news didn't make sense: a boy I'd gone with in Georgia, an automobile accident, rain on the new interstate highway, the car wedged under a truck, the top half of the vehicle ripped off, Aster's older brother dead.

Mama said I should consider all funerals *de rigueur*, and besides, the poor boy needed all the support he could get and if she had her way we'd all be back in Atlanta in a year or two anyway and I didn't want Aster to forget all about me, did I? She said I was old enough to take the bus to Atlanta by myself and Ethel Darden could meet me at the station, that I should wear her navy Peck & Peck and the felt hat with it. She slid open the closet door and pulled out a pair of cellophane-wrapped gloves and laid them on the bed.

The whole thing seemed hundreds of miles away. Mama hadn't liked Aster when I was going with him. The whole thing *was* hundreds of miles away.

Mama stopped. "Shoes." She touched a finger to her lips and stared at the bed, as if the gloves were liable to answer her question, and it might be that it did because she turned back to the closet. "Thank goodness Aster is a Methodist." In Atlanta, we'd been Catholic, but now we attended Kilgore Methodist. So as to blend, Mama said. The Methodists poured loads of sunlight into the church itself but didn't believe in confession for a person's actual soul. Mama pulled a dress from the closet, examined it top to bottom, all without turning around. "Thank goodness it's not Simon's family. We wouldn't even know how the, how his people do it."

"What's that supposed to mean?" I said. There was only one Jewish student at Central, but in Atlanta, there'd been dozens. In Atlanta, people hadn't paid all that much attention.

Mama returned the dress to the closet, slid several loaded hangers to the other end. "The world is full of other boys, Edith."

The question just spilled from me. "Are you criticizing Simon for being Jewish?" I right away regretted asking. It sounded too invested.

In place of answering, Mama hooked a coat hanger on the closet door, bent to pinch the hem of a skirt between thumbs and index fingers, and gave a series of little yanks. "You can take my gray crepe just in case."

That's when I knew the funeral was what she'd been waiting for all along, a reunion of Methodist and Baptist boys, all my old friends, a reunion of my old self and Aster, a world of young people with no Simon in sight. Arguing would only make her suspect the truth.

But the funeral was real, there my old girlfriends done up in hats and gloves, there the football squad in ill-fitting suits, there my friends from elementary school and junior high and the principal Mr. Hatch and a half dozen teachers, the girls and boys from my old gang exclaiming and kissing my cheek, the air stuffed with a giddy woe that somehow bubbled over to excitement.

At the gravesite Aster took up my hand, his fingers grasping so tight they hurt. When I made to pull away, he turned to me with such blue-eyed panic that I couldn't do it. The minister spoke, and the walnut coffin lowered into the hole they'd ripped into the grass. It sank unevenly, the head dipping and then the foot and then the whole thing sinking below the dirt horizon. Nash was in the box, and I thought about him lying there, forever. I knew all about angels and saints and heavenly hosts, but the box had nothing to do with them, and the place where Nash was going was the dirt, and that place was no place at all but a hole in the ground and no matter how fancy you made it—with the gleaming walnut and the brass handles, with the velvet tones of the minister's voice and all the people from school in their best church clothes and their shoes all polished—no matter how you dressed it up, there was still this pile of dirt, red and sandy with little rocks mixed in, red clay dust, the kind my mother hated, and it was why you had to wipe your feet when coming through the back door and into the kitchen. Twice. You had to wipe your feet twice.

Aster's hand crushed my own, never mind that we were there, the two of us together, Aster and I hand in hand in front of all his family and friends, and never mind that it was the way everyone remembered us, Aster and Edie, just like we'd always been. I didn't see any point in correcting them, so I stayed right there and let my hand be crushed while the sun yellowed the side of the minister's face and highlighted the granite headstones and the pieces of quartz in the red pile of dirt and the lifeless certain light. He never even said the thing about the holy angel watching over the grave, and I couldn't remember the prayer on my own. In the end, there were no angels, no saints, and no Virgin Mary.

After the service, people edged up to shake Aster's hand or to hug him. They said it was a miracle he was alive or that it was a miracle the entire car hadn't slid under the truck, or they said thank God his life had been spared, if only by inches, or that it just went to show that God had a purpose in mind for him. Aster stared or muttered, and I ended up making excuses for him. An English teacher grasped his hand and wagged her head back and forth and Aster said nothing and I was the one who mouthed, "Thank you."

When the lady turned away, Aster said, "People don't pay any kind of attention."

The anger of that statement jarred me, a well of it there, crimson and deeper than I'd ever expected, and I was afraid to look at it all the way to the bottom. "She's just being nice."

At that he swung around to face me and grabbed my arms, his face much too close, his eyes pinning mine, as if he meant to shake me in front of all those people. His skin was patchy and red, freckled with broken confetti, light blond stubble catching the sunlight like grains of sand. And all that ruddy anger. "It wasn't *him*, Edie. It was me."

A thread of panic curled and coiled inside me, ready to spring. "What do you mean?"

His hands clenched my very bones, and I knew people must be look- ing at us. His words hissed out in a hard whisper. "It wasn't him *driving*. I was the one driving. He was *letting* me drive. I *asked* him." His eyes were pale and liquid, his breath vinegar.

"But…"

He looked around like a man in a spy film. The people who'd been watching—it wasn't so many as I'd supposed—looked away. He bent toward me. "You can't tell a *soul*." But beneath those words charged an electric countercurrent that said the opposite, that said he was in truth leaving everything up to me, that telling or forgiving or condemning or ignoring was all in my hands. And then, as if relieved, he let go my arms and said in a matter-of-fact voice loud enough for anyone to hear, "My parents don't want anyone to know."

"But...why?"

All his furtiveness was gone now, and he jabbed his head at me as if it were obvious. He sounded amused and hopeless and reckless. "They don't want any of their friends to know the truth." A primitive dread stirred underneath me, some ugly goliath just now waking to recognize my presence on its close-cropped grass. I stared at him too long, then folded my arms around him and felt his arms encircle my shoulders, then my waist. Then his hands slid lower. I tried to make space between us, but he didn't let go, and I wasn't about to make a scene, right there and right then. A few yards away, his black-clad mother pointed her veiled face exactly in our direction, and if she thought her son's behavior was inappropriate, she didn't show it one bit. If she thought her son posed any kind of hazard to himself or to me, she didn't show that either. Certainly I couldn't blame her for anything that happened later.

Years later I wondered why I hadn't been smarter. Maybe I could have learned something from that weekend and that funeral service, with everyone going around pretending and Aster talking too loudly and behaving too rudely and daring me to say otherwise. At the time I didn't know the not-telling could become its own secret sin.

I never did tell about Aster's confession, even back in Charlotte. Instead I stayed in bed and dreamt of piles of dirt, of peering up from a hole, the path of escape floating above me out of reach, and it was impossible to get back onto the surface where the rest of the world lived, impossible to get out of the dirt. Then I dreamed of Aster, naked and dead and bleeding, his male parts distorted and enlarged, and of a dreadful looming shame.

I packed the funeral away, buried in the furthest reaches of my brain, but the next time the phone rang before breakfast, I knew. I could hear the murmur and blur of Mama's voice in the front hall, the tones and cadences disconnected from any single event that had come before. "Oh Margaret...Oh no...Oh the poor boy," and it was all perfectly clear that there was another poison Thing making its way into our kitchen, and that the whole family'd better wait in that swollen silence to find out what it was, and then my mother cradled my shoulder, and

I knew that the poison was meant for me. Aster had had an *accident*, something about the garage and a running car engine, but whatever it was hadn't killed him, and all the adults were surprised and relieved, and anyway the fuss wasn't about him being hurt or not hurt but rather about his parents and my parents. They'd seen something that terrified them. Mr. Eriksen checked his son into a hospital in Atlanta where letters and visits were forbidden, and I imagined white hallways and rooms with bars on the doors, doctors with hair that stood straight up on end, and lecherous grinning inmates. The world, it seemed, was full of danger, not the playground kind I'd known as a child, when there'd been certain rules about when to cross a street or how fast to push the merry-go-round. Back then we'd thrilled to the ride's windy speed and the rush of air that made our eyes water, the heavy grip of the handles, the terror of letting go. This new danger was bigger, people making decisions that forced them spiraling out of the orbits of their lives. It was impossible to see at which point they would fly off, or where if ever in the wide world they would land.

And then I was unwrapping pin curls and clamping the bobby pins between my lips when the smell of metal and old hair spray settled on my stomach and lingered so long that my insides flopped and my throat constricted and I gagged. At breakfast the food leered, rivers of golden egg yolk pooling around mountains of grits, squares of butter melting in the center. My stomach lurched again, and I nibbled at a piece of bacon, not for its taste, but because it was the only thing on my plate that didn't run yellow. The crunch and the salt of it steadied me. By the time I left for school, I'd forgotten I'd been sick to my stomach. I'd forgotten it so well that I was surprised when it happened again the next day. I ate more bacon and then after breakfast opened a sleeve of Ritz and ate one of those too. The rest I stowed in my pocketbook.

I swished my mouth with Listerine. It couldn't be that. It just couldn't. In the mirror, my face was white and goggle-eyed. There were loads of things that made girls sick. The funeral in Atlanta, Aster Eriksen's broken face, my mother's bias against Simon. Hormones.

My sister Deirdre rapped on the bathroom door and squeezed her voice right through the crack. "Guess who's *heeeere*." Behind the roller shade I saw Simon's Fairlane parked in the driveway. Surprise.

Five minutes later I pulled open the Ford's door. As if by agreement, neither of us said a word until we'd cleared the subdivision. Then Simon glanced at me. "Well?" His eyes watched the road, but all I heard was the fear in his voice. "What's going on?"

None of the explanations I could muster made sense, not the funeral or the dirt, not the leering inmates nor my mother's secret plans to get me away from Simon, and then before I knew it I was crying, covering my face with my hands and choking out the only explanation that made any kind of sense. "I've been sick." That, at least, was true.

Simon swerved the sedan into a filling station, the faded red hose dinging beneath the tires. He turned a long stare at me. "What do you mean?"

Now I was wishing I'd given a different reason. "You know. Tired," I said.

"Not throwing up?" You could see the undertow beneath his features, grabbing.

I couldn't look at him square. "A little, some, in the morning."

"How long?"

I glanced at him, then away, the hood of the Fairlane stretching before us.

"I don't know…a few days, maybe more. It's hard to—"

And right then the undertow caught up and swallowed him whole. He groaned, slumped over the steering wheel, and pressed his forehead into the enamel. All I could see was the back of his head, his gray and blue seersucker jacket walling around his shoulders, obscuring all but the edge of his hairline. There in the curve of that neck and the slump of those shoulders and even in the weave of that fabric was everything that was important to me, there where his dark hair bristled down in a v, right into the hollow at his spine, where the last filaments traced delicate feathers before disappearing into his clothes.

Aster's hair was coarse and colorless, like the negative of a photograph, the sky and day around him lightless glass, a place I could not would not see.

Simon's breath moved in and out, and it occurred to me I'd remember the sound for a long time, that I wanted to retreat into that seersucker with him, to get right under that coat. I looked down at my hands, now folded in my lap. How had I been so stupid?

Simon lifted his head, sighed, and said he would see what he could find out. Then he took my head between his palms and studied my face, his thumb stroking my cheekbone. "In the meantime, don't do anything. In the meantime sit tight."

5

LUCE

I remember foisting a certain edition of *Parade* on Edie. At the time I thought it might bring her out of her sourpuss mood. We were lying crossways on her bed, the voices of her parents buoying up from the kitchen. "Look." Marilyn Monroe giggled up from the page of the magazine, right next to Arthur Miller. "*He's* Jewish."

It worked, but not the way I'd hoped. Not even close. Edie lay her hand on mine and looked at me as if befuddled. "Luce, I think I'm going to have a baby. I'm scared frozen." I right away closed my eyes. But Arthur Miller still smiled there in the dark, guarded, as if he were evaluating the camera lens, not the other way round. My mind was stuck there, on that careful smile. It wasn't even the right idiom. Scared *stiff* was the way you were supposed to— "Oh Luce, please don't tell me I'm a terrible person. I already know that. I know. I just—I *know*."

But I wasn't thinking that per se. I wasn't thinking anything, except that if I met Edie's eyes it would be real, and I'd be in it too. Participating.

Which was in all cases better than not participating. No, what I was thinking was something much worse, something that scurried out from some nasty part of my soul, and sat up, and sniffed, intrigued that anything so awful could happen to someone as charmed and pretty as Edie. It was a tiny feeling of *glee*.

What a small person I was—minuscule. That Edie couldn't see that was amazing. That she'd chosen me, kept choosing, kept waiting at my locker to hear how the other editors liked my story ideas, kept sending me pep notes, the script looped fat as valentines. Well.

When I opened my eyes she was pressing her knuckles against her eyes, like a little kid, her shoulders quivering. I knew there was supposed to be a correct response, something I was supposed to do, but I didn't know what it was. If the roles had been reversed, she would have known. I imagined her there, comforting me. And then I knew what to do. I scrambled forward to the edge of the bed and patted her shoulder, pat, pat, pat, then decided perhaps stroking was better. So I stroked.

Edie pulled me into her arms and cried.

I knew what my job had to be. What we needed first was someone who knew something about bodies and the way they worked, and I was de facto not qualified. We'd all read about girls who went away. We'd all read magazine articles about the homes. And one summer I'd sat in the old Carnegie Library and read a book by a fellow named Alfred Kinsey that said two-thirds of men and half of women were having sex outside marriage and that heavy petting was so common as to make virginity a technicality. If Mr. Kinsey was right, then the girls at Central—the whole *country* really—was pretending. I couldn't quite believe that.

But now Edie was asking for my help, and I wanted to be able to save her. The thing to do was go back to the library. It seemed square, even to me, but it was information. It was a start.

Edie carried the encyclopedia by its spine and covered the "A" with her hand. There wasn't really any other thing that started with the letter "A," she said. At first I thought she was putting me on, but she wasn't. I took the book from her and flipped through the pages. The listing said abortion was *the expulsion of a human fetus before viability*. And,

See miscarriage. But neither Edie nor I had any idea exactly how such a process occurred. I read aloud from the *History* section. *Abortion has been practiced in many cultures throughout human history.* Blah, blah, blah… Edie broke in. "Skip to the part about now."

I turned the page and put my finger on the word MODERN. *Hospitals are now making efforts to reduce the number of therapeutic abortions performed. Most institutions allow a woman to plead her case in front of a committee of hospital administrators but typically reject those requests unless her life is in danger.* I stopped.

"What?" Edie said.

I let my eyes race through the paragraphs. "Nothing important." In my pocket, I traced the edge of the Honor Society pin I'd found at the sink in Home Ec.

"What? Your mouth is going all twitchy."

The pin was heavy and hard. It had slipped into my pocket easy as pie.

Edie leaned toward the open book. "I can tell when you're fibbing, you know."

This was true. I took a breath and tried a dismissive tone. *In some cases, but not all, hospitals might grant a therapeutic abortion if the patient agrees to sterilization…*

When the word registered, Edie's features shrank and dropped.

I finished the sentence, tried to keep the shock from my voice. *Mostly in cases of Negroes and indigents.*

A long pause. Silence echoed against the marble floors. "What are indigents?"

My eyes scanned the text ahead. My heartbeat tapped in my throat. I felt myself balanced over a great abyss and did not dare peer down. Instead I curled my fingers around the NHS pin, its front beveled with artwork, its backside cold, hard, and liquid smooth. Before my membership had been revoked, I'd once had one exactly like it. "Like hobos," I think I said. *Indu*, within. *Egere*, need. "It doesn't mean you." But I wasn't a hundred percent sure.

Edie let out a breath. The weight of that phrase *Negroes and indigents* had not landed on her, on us. And I'm ashamed to tell you this: We were *relieved*, both of us. We saw it as a grievous imbalance, but it wasn't happening to us. We were *relieved.*

But that sentence never did go away. I already knew there were people out there whose bodies and dreams did not matter to the wide white world and whose bodies and dreams were ipso facto not supposed to matter to us. What got my attention was the book's tone, its matter-of-factness. For many years that smug sentence stayed entrenched there in my mind, dug in deep.

I set the books and the journals back on the shelf, my hand finding again the gold pin in my pocket. It belonged to Natalie Lindstrom, who'd screamed when she'd noticed it missing. And I mean that literally. Right in the middle of Home Ec class. She screamed. In a day or two I'd have to set it back on the edge of the sink where I'd found it.

Edie said, "I'll ask Simon." That burned me up a bit, since he was the one who'd got her in this fix to begin with. But I didn't argue. People out there were getting illegal abortions. Somehow. It was just that getting information about such a thing was a mystery. We'd all read magazine columns about emergency rooms being full on Monday mornings, women bleeding to death on the weekends. They were getting abortions somewhere.

It wasn't until years later that I learned that most of the women who were bleeding to death on the weekends were the ones who were performing the procedure upon themselves.

EDIE

Simon told me the boy's name was Herbert Womack, and that he was supposed to know everything about anything. Simon didn't know what-all that might include and he didn't want to find out, just that people said if you were in a jam, go to Womack—as long as you were willing to shell out some dough.

The fellow wanted $500. The money was supposed to be in increments of twenties, and it was supposed to be unmarked, and Simon was supposed to have it ready in a brown paper sack, and I was supposed to carry it that way in my pocketbook. I was to pack a small suitcase and leave it in the trunk of the car. I'd drive to the Howard Johnson's on Liberty Boulevard, and at 8:30 I'd park on the front side of the lot and roll down the driver's side window. I had to be alone. If I acted jumpy or erratic or did anything at all unexpected, or if there were another person in the car, the man would not stop, but if I followed instructions, he would approach me and ask if I knew where he could buy a pack of cigarettes, and I was supposed to say this: "The lobby sells only unfiltered." The man would tip his hat, walk over to his car, and get in. After two or three minutes, I was supposed to look at my watch and start my car and follow him. He would drive slowly so as not to lose me, then park in the lot of another motor hotel and wait, and I was supposed to park far away from his car, take my suitcase and check into a room, telling the clerk I wouldn't be staying but the one night. Fifteen minutes later I should expect a knock on the door.

I sat on the edge of the motel bed. The table lamp spilled a pool of light into the gloom, and after a few minutes I heard the scratch of shoes on concrete. The shoes stopped. There was a light knock, polite. I crossed the room and the shadows moved beneath my feet.

At the door was the same heavyset man I'd spoken to earlier, this time with a brown case in his hand, his hat pulled low enough I couldn't see his eyes. He said "Evening, miss," and touched his hat. I hesitated. Had he said "miss" with a sneer or had I imagined it? I couldn't see beneath his expression, which was too layered and too masked. Acne scars spread across his cheeks and chin. I moved to let him in, and he shut the door behind him and set his hat on the little desk. He held out his hand. "I have to ask you for the payment first, miss. You understand." Stubbles of hair sprouted from the acne scars. I gave him the paper sack with Simon's tuition money, and he sat at the little desk and counted it into neat stacks of twenties. His body spilled over the sides of the chair, and there was something odd about his feet, and I saw that his shoes were loafers, and the heels were uneven, tilted, worn more on the inside than the out, and the leather was brown, even though the suit was black.

"Right." He turned the stack of bills on its side, tapped and squared it, then returned it to the sack. He stood. Even in the glow of the lamp I could not see the clues that should have been in his face. He opened the case on the bed and removed what looked like a shower curtain, spread it out over the mattress. "I like to make this as simple as possible for girls in your position, you understand. If you do everything I say, it will turn out fine, and you can go right home." He looked at me expectantly. I stared. "You're gonna have to take off your underthings, miss. It's the only way."

I excused myself and closed the bathroom door behind me, hesitated one moment, then turned the latch as slow as I could to prevent the bolt making a sound. Then I sat on the edge of the bathtub and peeled down my stockings, then my garter belt, then my panties. My slip and pleated skirt I left on, and rolled up the panties and the garter belt in the stockings and left the whole tidy package on the back of the commode. But then I changed my mind and put the little bundle behind the shower curtain on the edge of the tub, out of sight. I slid the lock open. My legs were trembling.

He was sitting in the chair holding a jar of clear liquid in one hand and a syringe in the other. He inserted the syringe into the jar and began to draw the liquid into it. "For the pain," he said.

"What is that?"

"Sodium pentothal."

"What does it do?"

"Makes you groggy."

"Like beer?"

"Yeah." For the first time he showed interest. "Why, you like beer?"

"No." I sat carefully on the bed, the shower curtain cool and a crackly against my legs.

He set the jar on the table and his elbow on the table and aimed the syringe toward the ceiling. "Then it's not like that. It just makes you sleepy, hear? Relaxed. You'll just be relaxed, miss, then you'll maybe fall asleep and when you wake up it'll all be over."

Fear swelled through me. "Wake up?"

"That's how we do it."

"But can't I just stay awake? I could pretend I was at the dentist."

"No, you can't. This here pain is a different kind of pain." He inserted the thumb of his other hand into his mouth and gnawed on the nail, then glanced at it. "And anyway, you need it on account of the noise, you hear? Because what you don't want is for the people next door to call the cops." His jaw worked in a tiny chewing motion. "You don't want that, do you? Everyone knowing you're here." His elbow still rested on the table, the syringe pointing straight up. "You're gonna have to roll up that sleeve."

I looked down at my folded hands and shook my head. I didn't look up. I couldn't tell him the truth. It felt too presumptuous, too rude. That I was afraid of being asleep in his presence. As if a person in my position had the right to make such judgments.

"You don't get it, miss. This is what we call a requirement for this operation."

I shook my head again and kept my eyes on my hands in my lap because you can't just come out and say a thing like that. And anyway I knew if I had to say it I'd cry, so instead I looked at my hands and shook my head as hard as I could, and it might be that was the thing that brought me back to my body and my own mind. I didn't want it. I wasn't having it. "I don't like shots." The way it came out sounded thin and whiny, like a little girl's voice.

Right then I saw the crimson undertow beneath the man's mask, a movement of annoyance—or disdain. He nibbled on his thumbnail, the muscles jumping in his jaw.

"I'd like to have the money back."

He didn't say anything for a long moment, and the color of anger washed his face, but he hid it right away. Then he looked at his watch, as if he were deciding something. "Right-O. Suit yourself," and he reached into the brown case and pulled out the brown paper sack and set it on the dresser. Then he folded up the shower curtain and pushed it into the case. He rolled down his sleeves, put his coat on, then picked up his hat from the table and put it on his head. "Right-O."

I slid the bolt and listened to the scratch of his shoes on the pavement, then the ignition of a car's engine. Beneath my pleated skirt, I was naked. The wool shirred against my thighs, and my skin was metal-cold.

There was only one real doctor, Womack said, and he might or not might be able to help, he didn't know, only that the fellow was bona fide medical, and he, Womack, would have to be the one to set it up. The instructions were just as complicated as before. Simon would have to take me to an address on Front Street. There was a garage there, and the doctor said he'd park there, and his car was a maroon Bel Air sedan. Simon was to pull up next to it, and I was supposed to get out of the car with calm and poise, as if I were meeting someone I knew. Do not act nervous or sneaky. Just get right out and walk right over. The doctor would take me to the place where the abortion would be done. In two days, at seven o'clock in the evening, he would deliver me back to the same garage. He would wait with me there until Simon arrived to pick me up.

Two days. I was supposed to be on the bus to Raleigh for the debates. I'd promised Luce I'd go. Wouldn't miss it, not for all the world.

The doctor drove me down a street of crowded houses, the front yards littered with tires and rusted metal. He asked me to close my eyes and lean against the headrest as if I were sleeping, for my own safety, he said. I did it. The permission slip my parents had signed was zipped inside my pocketbook. And here I was, missing the debates.

Next to me, the doctor began talking. He explained we were going to park in front of a two-story house and that he was going to go in, and that in five minutes I was to get out of the car purposefully, as if I lived there, and then walk right up the path, open the door and go in, as if I'd been there a hundred times before.

Even on the doorstep I could hear the televisions playing different shows, two or three of them. One was an episode of *Hopalong Cassidy*, the one with the singing bandit.

A woman in her sixties with a soft jowly face met me at the door and said her name was Mrs. Ennis. She motioned me to sit at a chipped Formica table, then fished two Dixie cups from a package and filled them with ice and lemonade. The lemonade was cold, and I was glad to hold the cup in my hand. It gave me something to do when the woman sat down across from me. My other hand clamped on the sack of money in my lap.

Mrs. Ennis said it was the other Mrs. Ennis who did the abortions, the younger one. She said the younger Mrs. Ennis would not be putting me to sleep. She'd be using a catheter and a solution, and I'd stay in the bedroom with two other girls for a couple of days after that. Mrs. Ennis said there would be cramping and then blood.

How much blood?

That depended on the individual and how far along she was.

Howdy, Pardner! Hopalong Cassidy said, and beyond that, under-neath it, there was a sound like moaning, something like a ghost drain-ing away, and I remembered the casket swaying into the ground, the pile of red dirt, and the mourners. For the first time it occurred to me that dying and death weren't really and truly the same thing. One was a process that was scary and painful, but the other was something worse, a *result*, something arid and lonely and permanent. One was the terror of feeling your car slide into a truck, and the other was a pile of sand and red clay, little pieces of quartz glinting in the sunlight.

Mrs. Ennis was watching me. "You know," she said, and for one moment the two words sat there by themselves in the space between us, like deserted islands. "I can see that you're worried." She paused, gauging my reaction. "I can also see that you're a good girl. In point of fact it's the good girls that get in trouble, because y'all are the ones that don't know how to take care of y'all's selves."

What did that mean?

"But y'all ought not get rid of that baby. Children are precious, a precious gift. God gives a gift and we got to cherish it and hold it in our hearts. Keep it safe for Him." She paused again, her eyes on my face.

I opened my mouth but immediately shut it again.

Mrs. Ennis poured me more lemonade, as if we were having a little luncheon and talking about what I'd learned in school that day. "Me, I love children," Mrs. Ennis said. "I love every child. Y'all ought to have that little one and give it to me."

I took a long pull of the lemonade so that I wouldn't have to say anything, and then I scraped the edges of the cup with my teeth. Curls of wax fell upon my tongue, and the wax and the sweet lemonade and the sound of *Hopalong Cassidy* made my stomach watery.

Mrs. Ennis filled the silence. "I can give you a place to stay. It's a lit-tle house out in back." She motioned toward the window and a peeling carriage house leaning against a tree. I moved to the window, if only for an excuse to get away from the elder Mrs. Ennis. There was a little door on the side of the carriage house with four panes of glass that had been covered from the inside by a towel. A small, high window in the front of the building was also covered. I wondered if the someone who was in there now had covered the windows or whether the elder Mrs. Ennis had gone and done that.

"I'd say you got a good bit of time yet," Mrs. Ennis said. "Young girl like you." Her eyes flicked down to my belly. "You probably wouldn't have to be there but three months, especially if you get yourself one of them girdles that cinches up."

Then she said, "You wouldn't have to pay a slap nickel." There was a sly upward lilt in her voice. "Room and board for free." Then she said, "All I'm saying is that if you don't want that baby, then I do. That's all I'm saying."

I don't remember the rest of the conversation, only that the floor moved and tilted away so that my feet had to stretch downward to find it, but then the floor rotated and went all slidey like a merry-go-round gaining speed, and then Mrs. Ennis was holding my arm and saying something about dizziness, and I couldn't explain that it was not dizziness but something else altogether and that it had to do with the strangeness of it, the news, that the woman, Mrs. Ennis, knew something I didn't, that she held some knowledge that gave her the power to see the into the future: that I, Edie Carrigan, held a possibility inside me, the possibility for a child, a real child, and try as I might, I could not—*could* not—go to the moaning room because I knew I would never ever come out. The thing about funerals, about that one funeral, wasn't that Nash was dead, because that was bad enough. The real and true tragedy of it was that he had to spend the rest of eternity in a box. Alone.

My bones were cold, brittle as metal. Someone or something was lightly slapping my cheek. "Miss. Missy." The woman leaned over me, her jowls loosing toward me, her face lined with concern. "Don't go out on me, Miss."

Go out?

"Don't go out." The woman's face was inches from mine, all gold in the light. She smelled like lemons. And soap. And sugar.

I focused on the blue of her irises. "Please let me go home."

I felt my head being eased onto the floor with a tenderness I'd somehow known to expect. "Darlin', you can do whatever it is you need to do." And somewhere in there I heard Mrs. Ennis talking on a telephone, and was the doctor there and hello, he'd made a mistake this time and if he knew what was good for him he'd better come pick up this young lady and it had better be right now.

6

I braced my hands against the back of the commode, and my stomach yanked into my throat, jerked into my mouth, then bolted out my lips. A fierce splash, and then, before I could get a breath, it happened again. *Jerk, jump, dump, splash.* Turned inside out. A brown oily slick floated on the surface of the toilet. My face was hot and moist. I leaned the heels of my hands against my thighs, then wiped the toilet seat with paper, cleaned the rim of the bowl with the brush my mother kept behind the commode, and washed my hands.

When I opened the bathroom door, she was standing right there, her head tipped forward, her eyes landing widely and terribly on my face, irises bright, spots of red leaping in her cheeks, charged and vivid, like a wild creature. Which was exactly how I felt. For half a second the two of us looked at each other there, mirror images, panicked as antelope. Then she said, "You're not going to do this to me, young lady."

There was nowhere to go. "Do what, Mama?"

"You are not going to do this. Do you hear me?" Her nostrils gave a little pulse and her irises danced green and blue, her face awash in pale green terror. "You've been sneaking around with him, haven't you?"

Sneaking? Simon and I had been seeing each other over a year, and my parents had never forbidden me to see him. I tried to make my spine go straight.

Mama leaned in so close I could see the grains of powder on her nose. "*Haven't* you?"

Then the film played out in front of both of us: the red glow of the darkroom and the photos clothes-pinned to the twine and the pans of developing fluid and the quilts all spread on the floor and the undershirt and the Dickies and crinolines and sweaters and brassiere. And me and Simon. Doing that. It was unbearable. "No, Mama. Just—"

Downstairs my sisters clamored for lunch money. My mother turned away. "You get dressed for school, but don't you dare get on that bus. I'll take you myself."

She poured a cup of coffee and set it on the table, which I actually thought might be for me because Mama never sat at the breakfast table, but then she untied her apron and did just that. She picked up the saucer with the cup and held them both in front of her collarbone with both hands and stared into the cup but didn't drink, her face full with some color I'd never seen before. Fear I'd seen, yes, and anger, but here was something else, something indigo and swollen. When I realized what it was I looked at my plate. Woe.

Mama's voice was fragile and tight. "When you were born, Edith, we had ration cards. We had a vegetable garden. Your grandmother and I darned socks."

I raised my eyes but only for a second. My mother had closed hers.

"You don't know this, Edith, because I've never told you. But I… dropped out of school. To work in a factory, to tie…paper, and strings, around…pig meat." Shame in her voice. "The smell. You cannot imagine." Her words wobbled with tears. "And I gave the money to my parents. I worked there for three years." Now her voice dropped to a stiff whisper. "And I didn't go past eighth grade."

I sat perfectly still, heard my mother sip from the coffee cup. I didn't want to hear any more, but I didn't want to not hear it either.

"I followed the rules. I did what my parents expected of me. I found your father. I didn't set my sights on any old boy just *because*. It's not fair to anybody. And we were careful. We scrimped and saved, and we waited, and we followed the rules. Do you understand that? We followed the rules, Edith. We did everything we were supposed to do."

I heard her set down the cup. On my plate, black flecks of pepper, the hardened egg yolk. I made myself look up.

Mama tipped up her chin, controlled the waver in her voice. "And then we came here, on account of the money Duke Power was offering for electric work, and for the…cost of living. Do you think I wanted to come here? But I came anyway. All because we wanted to make a life. This life." She swept out her hand and swallowed. "And because of you girls. We followed the rules, Edith."

I crossed my fork over my knife, too loudly.

And now Mama's voice seemed to have found something solid to stand on. "And now you want to throw all that away? Do you think that's fair?" And beneath it that roiling undertow: *Are you saying the rules mean nothing? Are you saying we followed the rules for nothing?*

I wasn't saying that. I didn't say that. Shame swelled my sinuses and threatened to spill out. The floor was red and white squares, and it was linoleum, and it had cost some amount of money but I didn't know how much.

"Your father could lose his job."

Was that true? I heard in her voice that it was.

"You and your sisters would be ostracized."

I felt her watching.

"We would have to move. Again."

I picked up my knife, scraped at the yellow on my plate. Now was as good a time as any to try out my new sentence. I mustered as much confidence as I could. "We're going to get married, Mama."

She set down her cup, stood, retied her apron, and carried my plate to the sink. She didn't answer.

After a while I said it again, "We're going to get married, Mama." Then I added the sentence Simon had repeated to me. "People do it all the time."

She stood at the edge of the sink, head bent over that plate as if getting it clean were the most important thing she could think of. But there was real anguish in her voice. "That would just be making it worse." She slid the frying pan into the sink and ran the faucet. "Get ready for school and we'll discuss it when your father comes home."

But we didn't discuss it when my father came home. I didn't discuss it with Daddy for thirty-two years.

SIMON

Use his words. That was Simon's plan. Show the old man how much he'd embraced his values. Take responsibility, follow through. That was what they'd taught him, right? But damn if his father hadn't parked himself in the La-Z-Boy and glued his eyeballs to the television set for good. Destruction in Quemoy, vast swathes of the place bombed out. And yeah, that was the thing—China—that got his father's attention. When the broadcast broke for a commercial, the old man rattled the paper right up to his face.

Simon stepped up, hands jammed in his pockets. "Pop…"

"Don't tell me 'Pop', Simon."

"Dad—" he said.

Paper down. Eyes sweeping over his frame.

Simon removed his hands from his pockets. Now. Tell him now. "I asked Edie to marry me. It's the right thing to do."

His father blinked, inhaled for about a week, then let go. "*Now* you want to be a hero, Simon? Now?"

"I don't want to be a hero. I want to be a respon—"

His father leaned forward in his chair, as if ready to spring right out. "This is not the way a hero behaves, Simon. A hero does not throw away his life and the life of the person he says he loves for the sake of his own ego." And now came the finger jab. "Not to mention throwing away everything his parents have worked to give him." Jab, jab, jab. "There is nothing heroic here, Simon." One more jab. "Nothing."

Goddamn his browbeating arrogance. Simon willed himself to unfold his arms, but there was nothing to do with them. Nothing. "Who said anything about throwing away my life? Or Edie's?"

"Hel*lo*!" his father almost shouted. "You did. Every time you open your mouth you say you want to throw away your life."

God*damn*. Simon knew this bit upside down and sideways. "Dad. I'm talking about *making* a life. With Edie." He needed their support. Otherwise his life became a jump into free fall. No parachute, no nothing.

"There. You said it again. I want to throw away my life please, and I'd like you to help me do it. I'd like to marry a brainless girl—"

Brainless?

"…Who hasn't even finished high school so the two of us can set up housekeeping and start a family. Please Pop. I know that we don't have any money, but that doesn't matter because we are in love." Now he threw both hands into the air. "We shall feed our children with, well, who knows, I can't be bothered to think of that. I can't be bothered to think of my future or the future of the girl I'm supposed to be in love with. Why does it matter that I don't have a college degree and my future wife doesn't have a high school diploma? Why should that matter?" He leaned back and glowered.

Jesus. He didn't know shit about Edie. Correction: He knew one thing. He knew she was a threat, an alternative to the life he'd written for his son. And that's what it was, wasn't it? His father was *jealous*. "She's not brainless." The words hung in the air, backdropped by the clipped cadences of the television.

"Maybe she is and maybe she's not, Simon. It doesn't matter, right? Because the only thing that's important is that you have love. *Love!*" He said the last word as if it were the most preposterous thing he could think of. "The reason I'm here, Simon, do you know what that is? My purpose in life, Simon, is to make sure that you do the right thing. And what you are suggesting to me is not the right thing. So. This conversation is over, Simon Levenger Bloom." He snapped up the newspaper and rattled it open. "Besides, it's too late."

"No, it is not too late."

Newspaper down. "Your mother and I have already talked to her people."

What people?

"Nice enough folks," he said. Newspaper up.

Jesus. He meant Edie's parents. Simon stepped toward him. "Where?"

He made a sweeping motion with his hand. "Over there, in that place, that...subdivision."

Simon couldn't think. His father was so thin, and so bent, and his mom—nothing like Edie's mother, God help her. Compared to Mrs. Carrigan, his mother was an old lady. "What happened?"

"What happened?" Pop's hand brushed through the air. "Nothing happened. Everyone agreed."

"Was Edie there?"

His father looked up from under his eyebrows. "Only the adults were there, Simon."

Nice. Simon didn't take the bait. "What do you mean everyone agreed?"

"Everyone agreed that both of you should marry someone from your own backgrounds, what else," he said. "Besides, you have years of school ahead of you."

But that—school—was a whole different thing. Edie was real. School was not. School was just staying in his parents' good graces. When he was finished with school and the internship and the residency, he'd still have to find something real.

His father was holding forth. "I told him: Look, we're very fond of Edie. But we also think like you do. Young people should listen to their parents. They should slow down. They should carry on family traditions. And that man, that Boyd Carrigan." Pop wagged his head in mock sadness. "I'm sorry to tell you, Simon, but he does not like you."

Now. He didn't like him *now.*

"But then, look what you did. I'll tell you who it's costing, Simon." He jabbed his index finger into his own sternum. "It's costing *me*. Four dollars a day."

"Four dollars a day?"

"For the Home."

"What Home?"

"They have *places*, Simon. They're not free. They go, they have the baby, and they're done." He snapped the La-Z-Boy upright, hoisted himself from the chair, turned up the television, and picked up his newspaper.

Simon took a deep breath. He was twenty-two years old. He crossed the carpet and cut the volume. Dropped onto the couch. "People get married, Dad. It happens all the time. It's not the end of the world. It's what the social order is built on."

This time Pop slammed the newspaper down, his face red with fury. "The 'social *order*'? The 'social *order*'? What the hell is the 'social *order*'? The social order is that if you marry Edie you will always be a second-class citizen in her family. Always. Even if you *do* finish medical school, which is unlikely. Even if you become the most brilliant physician to walk the earth since William goddamn Harvey, you will be a second-class citizen. The social order wants to *destroy* us, Simon. Maybe you would like to help in that process? Maybe you would like to build the bombs yourself. Or maybe you've forgotten about Temple Beth-El? Give them this child, give them *all* your children. Because they will be goyische, Simon. Nobodies. Here, take my child, no, take *all* my children, I want them to be nobodies so that they can join the Christian social order! Don't tell me social order, boy!"

Simon's veins had turned to metal. His father had said it twice: that his children would be nobodies, that their child was a nobody. The word sucked up the rest of the conversation and inhaled it whole. Extraordinary. Extraordinary the way he flipped such pronouncements into the air. Why? Because the old man was worried that his son would not be making more Jews. Would be a biological dead end. And why? Because that would make him a dead end too. Simon's voice came out quiet, spiteful, incredulous. "You are so afraid you won't matter, aren't you?"

The newscaster was saying something dry and smug about Khrushchev. His father trained his eyes on the television. But he'd heard him all right. You could see it in his lips. They'd compressed into a line, his chin raised two degrees too high, his eyes so focused on that television screen his son wondered for the first time if he'd be lost without it. Maybe that's why Simon slapped his palm on the wooden console, too hard. A fuzz of static buried the newscaster's clipped syllables. His father turned his face to him with such animosity Simon had to look away. The picture, which had gone jagged and sideways, resolved into the newscaster's face, unruffled once again. "Good night, and good luck."

7

EDIE

The Home sat on a little rise, a large brick building with four white columns and a long walkway straight through old-fashioned iron gates. It might have looked pretty if it weren't for the pawn shop and the laundromat on either side, or the bus stop with its battered wooden bench, the words WATERMELON HILL spray-painted across the slats. Something about those words felt worse than anything yet, because there they were, right there for Mama and Daddy to see, and I felt like whoever'd written them was talking about me.

Daddy was downright uncomfortable, you could tell, and it only got worse once we were inside. The director showed us down a freshly painted hallway, all white plaster walls, the floorboards scuffed to honey brown. He asked right away about the graffiti outside. "I assume, Mrs. Bruns, you know about that?"

She ignored the question and gestured to the oaken armchairs. She was a middle-aged lady, slim and straight, the shoulders of her suit all padded out in one of those jackets from the forties. "Thank you-all for waiting, Mr. and Mrs. Carrigan. Edith. We're always so busy these days." She closed the office door. "So many girls interviewing for so few positions. The world, as you know, has changed."

Daddy didn't give up. "It's pretty lewd."

Mrs. Bruns barely looked at him. "Sit down, Mr. Carrigan. Please." Her desk was neat, save for three stacks of paper and another of unopened mail. A pair of rubber boots stood aligned underneath the window.

Mama and Daddy lowered themselves into the chairs, and I did too.

Mrs. Bruns settled herself, elbows on her desk, hands clasped under her chin. She lifted her eyes in my father's direction. "I'm aware, Mr. Carrigan, of the graffiti. I'm also aware that times are changing." She unclasped her hands and spread them on the desk. "You must be too. There are juvenile delinquents about." She wore her hair in old-fashioned rolls on the sides of her head, which made her temples look square, like an owl. "I'm afraid our facility has become a destination for...cruising. Carloads of ogling boys. Yes, it is despicable, yes, it is lewd." She looked frankly at my father. "I hate to tell you the things they say, Mr. Carrigan." She paused, as if waiting for him to ask. "That's the reason there are no passes after five o'clock. I'm not running a freak show here."

Daddy's face went stiff. "Of course not."

"Now," she said, "I'd prefer to start at the beginning." She peered at each of us, the only person in the room who didn't seem deeply embarrassed. "Our facility is not a holding pen, Mr. and Mrs. Carrigan. Our aim is to teach. Much of the responsibility here falls upon our patients. It's their task to recognize how they've created this problem in the first place. We've found that's the only way to keep it from happening again." She went on. How if I was accepted I'd have to attend classes in hostessing and decorating and charm and makeup and cooking and, yes, that some of the girls had to take reducing and diet, because structure was the only way the girls could learn what was expected of them. Through it all, Mama and Daddy sat straight as pins. "Behavior modification has to start immediately and be enforced consistently. Our goal is simple. Make each patient eligible to reenter the world she's rejected. To provide her a second chance at marriage and happiness. Transform her."

I think it was that word *transform* that did it. Something in the atmosphere of the room shifted and loosened, and Mama let out a long breath, her features softening with relief and some other quality that opened up just for Mrs. Bruns, something like adoration. "That's exactly what we're looking for too."

The director leaned back in her chair. "Of course…not everyone is a good candidate. We limit ourselves to cases that offer the most chance of success. And the law is quite clear. The girls have to decide. Our aim is to get them ready to do that. In the best cases, girls are ready to rejoin society by the time they leave our gates. To find husbands and start afresh."

Mama and Daddy nodded.

Mrs. Bruns looked down at my application, narrowing her eyes at something she saw there. "You-all live awfully close, Mr. and Mrs. Carrigan." She studied them. "Normally Charlotte girls go to Charleston or Norfolk. But I'm sorry to tell you that at present we already have Charlotte girls at both those facilities."

Daddy looked dumbstruck. It hadn't occurred to him that I might be rejected, much less rejected from all the Homes in three states.

Mrs. Bruns gauged us. "I could make a call to Atlanta."

Right away Mama shook her head.

Mrs. Bruns watched my parents, one to the other. "If she were accepted here she'd have to be discreet."

Mama and Daddy looked at one another tentatively. But there was some purple appetite hidden in their eyes and lips, a greedy need to get one of those slots.

Mrs. Bruns didn't seem concerned. "It *has* been done…Our girls have their checkups right here in house. We have our own salon. Some of them get passes for the cinema over in Dilworth, but that's an immigrant neighborhood, mostly old people."

Mama clasped one hand in the other. "What about the…delivery?"

"At Memorial, naturally. But nowadays, Mrs. Carrigan, there are separate wards." My mother looked confused. "For the unweds." It was the first time I heard myself described with that word.

Mama was nodding, like it was the kind of language she heard every day.

Mrs. Bruns frowned, let her eye go to the window. "What she wouldn't be able to do is get on a bus. They're every one of them routed through the Square, right next to that hangout, that drugstore."

"Liggett's," I said, too quickly.

Mama and Daddy didn't seem to notice.

"Liggett's," Mrs. Bruns echoed. How peculiar that someone with a hairdo like hers should know about Liggett's. What else did she know? "She'd have to isolate herself." Mrs. Bruns leaned in again, knocked her interlaced fists on the desk and turned to look at me. "If we accept you, Edith, you'll have to make a few decisions." I could feel my parents holding their breath.

"You'll have to have a name, for one thing."

My face went hot. I hadn't been thinking about baby names.

Mrs. Bruns didn't seem to notice. "We can't have people asking was there a dark-haired Edith here from such and such a time."

Oh. She meant for me. And temporary.

Mrs. Bruns picked up a pen. "Well?"

Right now? I blinked. "Susannah."

"Very well." Mrs. Bruns made a note on the application.

Mama leaned in more, stroking the nail of her thumb with her middle finger. "What about...letters?"

"I do open the mail." Mrs. Bruns pointed at the stack of letters. An opener with a mother-of-pearl handle and a dog leg blade lay across the envelopes. "Letters from boys go directly into the trash bin." She held up a black laundry marker. "And this takes care of secondhand messages or upsetting trivia. I should also tell you that most families reroute their mail, usually through trusted relatives. You-all won't want to be explaining to anyone about letters with a Charlotte postmark. And that is worth setting up now."

Mama and Daddy exchanged glances. Maybe that meant I was accepted, or at least, almost. If I was supposed to feel something, I didn't have any idea what it was supposed to be.

LUCE

If I'd been smarter I would have stayed away from Edie's parents altogether. But it wasn't always easy. On that day I pressed the bell next to the front door, then jammed my hands into the pockets of my coat. This was a bad habit. The coat was a hand-me-down from my sister—she was nuts for houndstooth—and it was warm enough. But the seams of the pockets were already beginning to split.

Inside, Mosley was barking his head off, even though he was the one in the warm house and I was the one out here in the cold. I rang the bell again. It was Saturday. It might be Edie wasn't even home.

But then Mr. Carrigan's voice shushed the dog, and the door opened. I'd met Edie's father several times, but I wasn't sure he remembered me. "Good morning, sir."

Instead of answering, he opened the screen door and stepped out onto the porch. He was a fleshy man, hair crewcut and bristling across his forehead in the shape of an M. Despite the extra chin and extra pounds, he still had the walk of a boy entering the athletic field at the beginning of a match: restless, puffed, unsprung.

I fixed my eye somewhere near the doorbell and braced.

But his voice didn't pounce. Instead it slid up to me, sharing a secret. "I know that you know." Which part, he didn't say. I knew about the Home and the Miss Haversham lady running the place. Everybody knew about such places. We were forever reading about them in magazines. You went there and had the baby and some nice couple took it home and you went on with your life. But it was always other people who went there, not anyone we actually knew.

Personally I would have risked the abortion. But ever since that funeral in Atlanta Edie'd been a perfect mess, and I was sure it had to do with death. The fear of it. I kept my eyes right on that doorbell and thought about not replying, but couldn't imagine how that would go. The silence seemed to go a long time.

"You know what I'm talking about." I recognized Mr. Carrigan's tone. It was the one adults used when they were planning an ambush. I nodded. Inside my coat pockets, my hands balled into fists and drove down. "She's been a good friend to you." I nodded again. "And you owe her."

Owe? I supposed that was true. I tried to take up as little space as possible.

"I know how girls *talk*."

And then it dawned on me what he wanted. My fists in my pockets

loosened. I'd been keeping secrets my whole life. "Sir, you don't have
to worry about—"

"I see how you girls talk."

"I'd never—"

"It might seem harmless to you. But it's not. It wouldn't be harmless
to her, or to you, or to anyone. So it better not happen, hear?" He held
up the palms of his hands and tilted them away from each another. He
smiled without showing emotion or teeth.

"Mr. Carrigan, there's—"

"I'd have to assume it was you who did the talking, now wouldn't I?"
His voice was big and round as ever, but for all that, edged in malice. I
looked down at the doorsill. "Hear?"

The mat said WELCOME. Absurd. Absurd*ist*. What was the difference
again?

"You think it's funny?" His voice drew back, crouched now, poised
to spring. "I can tell you one thing for certain. This is on *you*." I glued
my eyes to that mat. Then his thick fingers were touching my chin,
shocking as a slap, tilting my face up toward his. "Understand?" It was
an old old message, one I already knew well: Edie is mine. This is my
family and you are not part of it. Edie is protected, and you are not.
Edie is precious, and you are not.

I closed my eyes, held my breath. Edie is beloved. You are not. My
voice came out a whisper. "Yessir."

He took his hand back. "Edith is on her way." He left the door ajar.
Well.

I had my own father and he was a good deal smarter and more accomplished than Mr. Carrigan. He had tried to fortify me. He would have
done even more if he could, would have saved me from the hallways
and the eyes that slid away from mine. Would have scoffed at the Girls
Good Sports Club and the Honor Society and every other group that
had revoked my membership on the grounds of the broken home.
Maybe he'd even have winked at the first thing I'd pocketed: a lipstick
straight out of Connie Flagler's open purse. Her favorite color: siren
red.

And make no mistake. Edie disappearing would be worse than the divorce, the whispering, the underground current of rumor that swept the Girls Good Sports and the Adelphians and the Marian Smythes right out of our lives. But I'd spent loads of time without the likes of Marian Smythe. I could do it again. I didn't owe her diddly.

Still. Sometimes I wished I'd been born in a place where people came right out and told you what was what, in a place where the causes were more definite. Or that I lived at the bottom of the ocean or at the end of the desert or in the middle of a colored neighborhood in a secret house with a secret colored family who'd envelop me in their arms and make me one of their own.

8

EDIE

In January Mrs. Bruns called to say they had a bed for me, and on that night Daddy took my suitcase out to the Roadmaster and loaded it into the trunk, and on Monday morning we rolled right past the splayed ranch houses and the close-clipped lawns and the house-wives cleaning up breakfast dishes behind sliding glass doors.

I guess I was expecting a certain kind of clientele in the Home, girls in black eyeliner maybe, who went with ducktailed leather-jacketed boys they called "cats," girls who slipped noiselessly from unloving homes, whose fathers wore sleeveless undershirts at the dinner table and smoked cigars on crumbling back stoops, whose mothers wore rollers to the market. But the first person I saw was a redhead in a pale smock the shape and color of a pink grapefruit. She showed me to my room, her belly taut and aggressive and crowned with a horrible nipply protrusion that had to be her belly button. I tried not to stare, tried not to think about the elastic of my own girdle against my own waist. The girl's name was Dotty, and she was a twenty-six-year-old telephone operator.

Four days later Dotty went over in the middle of the night and had a baby boy that weighed seven pounds and four ounces. A week after that she came to collect her things, no baby in sight, her belly gone, her eyes on something I couldn't see, her fingers fussing and fretting at the leather strap of her pocketbook, wringing and twisting.

I unpacked my suitcase and hung my extra shirtwaist in the big black wardrobe between the two beds. The Home provided smocks, but Mama had insisted I bring my linen suit with the pumps and the gloves. For afterwards, she said, which was a point in time I couldn't think about. Everything else fit in two bureau drawers: the white nightgown, the whirlpool brassieres, the two pairs of flats and two cans of hairspray, the latest Mademoiselles and house slippers, and, in the bottom drawer under the yellow skeins and the knitting needles I hadn't touched in a year, two letters from Simon and the framed Kodachrome of us on a pirate ship in the middle of a frozen sea, our faces beaming.

I'd told him everything: about the black laundry marker, about the cinema passes on Saturdays. We'd already agreed which days to meet, already marked them on the calendar, and he'd already mapped a route past Dilworth Road and into the mill town, a place that would have given my mother the hives, Thelma's lunch counter across from Mister Tire, to be exact. There was a public telephone there. I had taxi fare, I had a decent coat, and I had dimes, dimes, dimes.

The sounds of the Home drifted through a little window above the door: female voices, television, and now the drag of some heavy object being pulled across the wooden floorboards, an object that stopped in front of my door. I opened it. There stood a girl with harlequin glasses and an enormous suitcase. "Hey," I said.

"Hey." The tortoiseshell frames slanted like the brows of a jack-o-lantern, behind them freckles and wary hazel eyes. "Is this twenty-one?"

"It is." I helped her pull the suitcase over the threshold. "I'm... Susannah."

"Trudy." She said it right off and it sounded natural. Her eyes landed on my suitcase. "Did you just get here too?"

"About two hours ago," I said.

Trudy investigated the room first with her eyes, and then with her hands, opening drawers and wardrobe doors, testing the furniture and the beds, even the one with my suitcase on it.

"I think they're pretty much the same," I said.

Trudy closed a bureau drawer with a wooden squeak. Then she turned to me. "Do you have a steady?" It wasn't an invitation. It was a challenge.

For some reason I didn't want to tell her about the map Simon had drawn, or about Thelmas's lunch counter, or even the portrait of me and him framed in that cardboard ocean, the water curlicued into standing blue waves. "My parents made us break up." It wasn't a lie. I could always tell her more later. "Do you have a steady?"

Trudy sat on the edge of the bed with her palms down on either side of her hips. She seemed strangely at home. "Nope. Never did."

I blinked and sat on the other bed. "What about…the father?"

"What father?"

"Aren't you…?" I couldn't bring myself to finish the sentence.

"Preggo?" Trudy laughed a hard laugh. "They say I am."

They? "Are you?"

"Nope." The conviction in her face was featureless and blank. She stood and held out her arms, palms up. "Skinny as a rail." And there, right there, was the undertow, a plea deep and malevolent with rage that flashed and flushed and slid away. "Look," she said. "I am not like you or anybody else here. I haven't done it. Haven't even been *kissed* yet. I'm not trying to be rude, but now I'm kind of glad." The rhinestones in her spectacles glittered with light.

"Oh," I said. "You're smart then." And that word smart hung in the air between us, gilded and hard as a slap.

In the days that followed most of the girls stopped talking to Trudy. It wasn't meanness really, or it wasn't all meanness, it was more that we were all of us suspended in time, living in this one moment, where any kind of thinking about the past or the future did not compute. It didn't help that Mrs. Bruns treated Trudy like spun glass, the most fragile creature in the world, that both she and Mrs. Wentzloff shot dark looks at anyone who muttered a word against her. Nobody wanted to sit next to her at dinner. Sometimes I'd do it, but it felt like an assignment, a chore

I'd given myself, and on the days I didn't do it, I felt the red blast of her fury, and I'm ashamed to say I just stopped, ashamed to say I stayed away from our dorm room, ashamed to say that her despair and ire felt contagious, liable to spread by touch or even the very breath between us. In those days none of us had a clue. All we knew was that her baby didn't have a father, that maybe her baby didn't exist. We didn't have the imagination to guess at Trudy's life. For me it was decades before I learned about the sorts of things that happened to girls out there in the rest of the wide hard world.

Mrs. Bruns tracked our weight, and if you were too fat or too thin, you lost your Saturday pass. No films, no shopping, no hunching over the receivers of public pay phones. When I'd entered the Home I'd weighed one hundred and twenty-five pounds—I remembered exactly—but when I stepped on the scale that third week, the bar clacked down on the left, and Mrs. Bruns moved the steel indicator further to the right, and then further still until at long last the bar balanced. One hundred and thirty-six pounds. Which couldn't be right. It just couldn't.

Mrs. Bruns wrote the number on a clipboard. "I had a feeling."

A slow panic welled in my throat. No Thelma's lunch counter, no Simon. "Maybe it's…well, don't you think it's temporary?" Why in the world had I eaten the banana cream pie the night before? Or the biscuits?

Mrs. Bruns regarded me over her glasses. "Mark my words, Susannah. You won't be alone in the diet kitchen this week." She motioned the next girl up.

There was no way to get Simon a message. "What if—would it help if I—could I get my pass back if I'm back on weight Saturday morning?" I'd stop eating, that's all.

Mrs. Bruns looked up from the scale. "Susannah. It's not going to hurt you to miss a film or two." She examined my face—too much.

I froze. Stop talking, just stop talking. "No ma'am. It's not."

"A week. We'll weigh you again in a week. I'm not in the business of making deals, Susannah. You know that."

Instead of meeting Simon on Saturday I loaded up the dishes in the industrial Hotpoint, which all of us were in love with. None of us had ever used such a thing and at the time it seemed like pure magic. All you had to do was scrape off the food and then rinse and set the plates on end, the big ones and the small ones separate, and the machine took right over.

But it was no substitute for the warmth of Simon's breath, the feel of his long fingers interlaced with my own, his smell of pencil shavings and soap and his own throaty musk. At noon, he'd be arriving and sitting at the usual spot, in a booth away from the windows, and he'd be ordering a cup of coffee and reaching for one of the textbooks from his satchel.

At 12:35 the red light on the Hotpoint stopped glowing. Simon would be worried now, maybe wondering if I'd fainted or been accosted on the street. I opened the dishwasher door. Great clouds of sterile steam billowed up, the dishes too hot to touch.

Was he gathering his books and leaving? I fanned the steam away and pulled out the cutlery basket. Was he looking up and down the street? Thinking I'd been hurt? Searching?

That night at dinner, I didn't eat a single bite.

In bed I lay with my eyes wide open, the light spilling through the little windows that they called transoms, sound shifting up and down the hall, floorboards creaking, a scurrying in the walls, someone crying. It seemed to me that I had no choice but to leave my body there, doing their diets and obeying their rules, but it didn't mean my mind had to stay. It seemed to me that if I concentrated well enough I could let my mind float free, that anyway *Susannah* was a name that didn't suit me, with its lullaby s-sounds and wide-open vowels. Susannah was someone who was beautiful and wise, in control of her life, someone who knew how to behave in the Home for Unwed Mothers. The house was full of them, Susannahs and Graces and Annettes and Elizabeths—the selves we were all of us supposed to be. Our real personalities were hidden in our old names, the Pennys and Betsys and Barbaras and Judys, our other sad selves, the selves that were hiding, floating in the ether, the selves we were supposed to banish before we were allowed to get our bodies out of the Home.

That was the first night I felt her moving, and I placed my hand on my tummy, and I knew it wasn't just the growl of my stomach. It was a thrill to feel that, you know, and I decided right there that she would be a little girl. Part of it was lonesomeness, I think, this knock-down need to have someone on my side, fetus or no. To me, in that moment, she was a full-blown person, a tiny ally feeling every feeling I felt, the only person in the whole place who knew the real me was still alive, who believed in me and didn't yet know that the rest of the world considered me a failure. And right then I knew her name too—Lindy—simple and honest. Lindy, who isn't mad at me. So what if everyone else in the world wishes me different. Lindy doesn't, and Simon doesn't. But you're the one who's here with me and you're mine, and this place, these secret hallways, they're all just for now because Simon will wait for us, and Simon will come to get us because he isn't the type to run away and he isn't the type to change his mind. I promise.

We weren't supposed to talk about keeping. You'd be amazed how little time we spent talking about our futures, our plans, like we were frozen in amber. But there was one French girl who said and did things different, and when the moderator of *Queen for a Day* asked the on-air contestant what she'd do with her prize money and the contestant answered that she needed it for baby furniture, Therese waved her cigarette at the television and said, "Families don't need to buy furnitures. They can borrow furnitures."

"Oh sure. Good idea," Annette shot back.

"This is true," Therese countered. The talk about the future sent a panic into my bones, even though I'd gotten good at ignoring the very idea of it, now reciting my knitting stitches loud in my head. Knit three, pearl two.

Annette was sarcastic as ever. "Your parents spend hundreds of dollars to send you over here, but they're not going to mind if you come home begging baby cribs from the neighbors?"

Seven faces turned from the television to Therese.

"No. This is thing we do."

Annette held up a limp-wristed hand, pinky extended. "Zis is ting we do." Then she leaned in, the challenge in her voice burning on a current of need. "Who said you were *allowed*?" There was a collective drawing in: seven girls inhaling from seven cigarettes. My knitting sequence evaporated. Mrs. Bruns had said it, for one, that the law was quite clear, that the girls had to decide, that the purpose of the Home was to get us ready. We had four months to get ourselves ready.

Therese straightened. "I tell them. I take the baby with me. We are one big family. I tell the people she is my sister."

Juliette said, "That's impossible."

I heard someone say something about Therese being French, or maybe the word was *rich*, or maybe it was *bitch*, but the thought, the thing she'd said, floated there upon the air, alight and fleeting, a dangerous kiss, a threat and a promise both. No wonder they hated her. If Therese could do it, it would mean it could be done, and that would mean it was possible for us to do it too, but only if we chose to live outside of everyday life, outside of family, of school friends, of the neighbors down the street, of jobs. And in that moment I heard it—*saw* it—as if it were an actual memory, or a brand-new photograph: me and Lindy and Simon, the three of us together without the cardboard waves ready to crash upon us. The words just came out by themselves. "Maybe it's not—impossible. Maybe doing what they want is worse. I'm keeping too." And right then I knew it was true.

The faces around me closed up, the silence awkward and wide and unpopulated. In a single instant, I'd become Therese number two. Even Sally, old as my mother, wouldn't meet my gaze. Katherine stopped chewing her hair, and only Lee watched me, lips slightly parted, her hands pulling at one another. *Are you saying the rules don't mean anything? Are you saying we followed the rules for nothing?*

But my thoughts were busy rearranging themselves, like puzzle pieces clicking into some new configuration, relieved and right, even though I had no more of an idea than the man in the moon how I'd make any of it come true.

Nights I floated through corridors, drifting whitely in that yoked nightgown, yards of fabric swirling around my ankles, upstairs, downstairs, basement, it didn't matter, as long as I didn't have to face Trudy's ghastly optimism. Windowed doors stared at me blankly: the exercise gym, the clinic, the old lactation room, now shuttered of course. We'd all asked Mrs. Wentzloff about that one, and she'd obliged by telling us about the missing history, story after story spinning out in her vintage castled accent. In the old days, the girls were ruined, bless their hearts. There were not people to want the babies of the ruined girls. The families did not want back the ruined girls. In the old days the Home was to teach them jobs, to sew or to clean or to cook. They had to make the money. In the old days, the Home was to keep the girls for years, was to teach them to feed with the breasts and to take off the diapers and to put the clean ones on.

Now the diaper laundry was a beauty salon. And that night I heard it snuffle. I stopped. The door was ajar. Another snuffle. Whoever it was had heard me, maybe expected me to keep going, but in place of doing that, I pushed the door open and stepped into a darkness sulfured with Toni home permanent, the globes of hair dryers leaning together like gossips. A figure underneath cried and blew her nose in the darkness. It was Sally.

"Sorry," I stuttered. Sally was a college professor. Somewhere. "I just wondered who, I didn't know, I mean I wasn't trying to be nosy." I began to back away.

"Is that Susannah?" the older lady asked, her voice tired and lonesome. "Come here, child." The furniture in the room began to take shape. Sally waved her hand at an upholstered chair.

I sat, careful not to bang my head on the hairdryer. "This is a swell place, Sally. It's hard to find anywhere to be alone." And here I came anyway. "I should go." But even as I said it, I knew it wasn't what she wanted.

"Child..." A white flag floated up, and there was the sound of nose-blowing. Sally's face materialized, now clouded with mascara and ashy sorrow. She looked straight at me and brought her hand up to her collarbone. "I'm forty-five years old. I'll bet you didn't know that."

I wondered if I should act surprised at that number but decided it wasn't the point.

"This is going to be the last chance for me, Susannah. Even before this happened I was beginning to...to skip months." Her hand clutched at her throat. Remember I was a teenager, so I had only a vague idea what she was telling me. "So…I thought, when I skipped three months in a row, well, this is it for me." She closed her hand into a fist and pressed it into her flesh. "I want…I don't know if I can do this again."

"Do what again?"

"Say goodbye. What you said in the dayroom was true, Susannah. It *is* worse."

"It is?"

Under the grief, I saw, was anger, utilitarian and unlovely and unbending as a railroad track. "The irony is that you're supposed to give your child away out of love, but then, after the giving's done, you're not supposed to feel anything. The love just stops, just like that." She snapped her fingers weakly. "You're supposed to forget." Her voice was bitter, sarcastic, unfeminine. "Poof. But it doesn't happen that way, Susannah. " I felt my mind tumbling—and I knew one hundred percent that this was why we all avoided talking about the past and the future.

Sally was silent for a long time. "I had another one. A little girl. With curly brown hair and the reddest little face." Her voice darkened. "Her father had curly hair too. My PhD advisor at William and Mary."

"I'm sorry," I said. I couldn't think what to say, and the silence felt rude and ungainly.

"She…would have been a talented young lady. *Is* a talented young lady. Somewhere."

I tried to breathe as quietly as possible. Sally turned her face to me.

"But I worry. There's such a thing as a girl being too smart. Like having a big birthmark, or a hunched back, or any such thing people are supposed to pretend they don't see. I can't help wondering if she's unhappy."

For the first time, I knew what to say. "I have a friend like that. She's smarter than the boys, and I don't think it makes her too unhappy, being smart. I think she likes doing things like a boy, and having…" I searched for the right word "…accomplishments. And she decides things for herself." How hard it was, putting your finger on a personality. "I'm not like that, but I try to be." Luce's letters came through the mail every week, black-striped with the laundry pen. And maybe I should have told her to send them through Simon, or to bring them to Thelma's, but I didn't want to share him, share our time together.

Sally was quiet for one moment and then sighed largely. "Thank you." She dabbed at her nose. "I sound like a foolish hen. You're probably thinking, how could I have made the same mistake twice, I know. How could I have lost myself twice over two different men. I don't see how either, Susannah. Sometimes I blame it on literature." She laughed self-consciously, as if the idea were silly even to her. "The classics make you…aware. You're surrounded by such passion, all these characters you know and love who are living out rich and dangerous and meaningful lives. And you think, no, you're not going to dive into all that tumult, because it's all so messy, but it might be nice just to put your toe in for once…. And then a dashing instructor visits in the drama department and asks you to help him with the production of *King Lear*, and if you're a Shakespearean, you're thinking it's either *King Lear* or back to evenings drinking cream sherry with your mother. Well, you say yes, naturally."

"Naturally," I echoed. It wasn't a really a word I used, but somehow it fit with the moment and the strange sweet collaboration of our talk. Sally was old, and her life should have been her own, and there was nothing I could tell her she hadn't already thought.

"We produced a fine play. Opening night was…well, it was a fine production. Just grand…. The truest and loveliest Cordelia you could imagine. He did the blocking and I did the coaching. But then…then by the spring season it turned out I wasn't the only one. There was a girl, maybe a student, I never found out. And because of that I made sure he never found out about me."

I moved my head from left to right and back again.

"The funny thing is, if he'd stayed, I could have lived with it, the philandering, even if it was with students. I know it's shameful, but I'd have pretended not to know." Her voice dropped to a whisper. "I just wanted the baby. I just want this baby."

"So keep it." The words jumped out of my mouth, that loneliness rearing up again, and for the first time in a long time, I felt like Edie, and not like Susannah. Sally could be my—what? Teammate? We could show one another, show *them*.

But Sally's face dropped toward her chest, shoulders drawing in, fingers dragging at her collarbone. She didn't look up. "I'm not as brave as you. They would let me go. There'd be no bargaining with the college.

There'd be no referrals. No pension. No place for me to go." Wonder bloomed in her voice, "I'm supposed to be a role model."

I looked at my own hands, the whites of my nails bitten away. My throat squeezed up, and I swallowed. Everywhere I turned I found the same thing, the same raw nerve pulsing under the skin of everyday life, cringe-red and shuddering.

Early the next day Mrs. Bruns called me into her office. I hadn't been there since my interview, but it looked the same as ever, plain and neat with all her to-do tasks lined up in piles.

"Susannah. Sit." Even here, even now, she called me that. "I want to make something clear to you." Her face was stern, her make-up somehow mismatched against her skin. "The law stipulates that you can make any choice you'd like about your pregnancy and your future." She interlaced her fingers on her desk and regarded me closely. "Naturally we prefer that you follow our recommendations, based as they are upon scientific research and upon your health and that of the child. But we cannot force you." She leaned forward across the desk. "That said, I know what you've been saying in the dayroom."

I'm keeping too. Which of them had told her?

"And I would appreciate if you kept your particular whimsies, your...*dreams* to yourself."

How did she know?

"It infects the other girls. And it's not fair." And there was that word, popping up again. My mother had said it too. That I wasn't being fair, to her, or my father, and most definitely not to my sisters. *We followed the rules.*

"We can and will ask you to leave. Make room for some other young lady who cares about her privacy and her future. So. No more of this, you hear?"

I nodded. I wondered if Therese had been warned too.

"Now. I believe this is for you." Mrs. Bruns handed me a letter. I glanced at the return address. *Lucille Waddell, 92 Dixie Road.*

Dear Edie,

    I so miss hearing your voice and seeing your face. I talked to my father, whom you have never met. Suffice it to say he's one of the very smartest people I know (present company excepted of course). He also has a very good position at the ███ ██████████████████ ███ ███████ ██ *and he knows more than anyone about this kind of thing. He assured me that there are resources. The problem is that the state doesn't make it easy to get.* ███████ ██ ███ ██ ██ ███████ ████ ████ ████ █ ████ ██ ████ █ ██████ ██ ████ ██ *Don't worry at all, Edie. We are here for you, and we're going to help you out of this bind.*

██████ *And anyway, when you get back, you'll be starting fresh.*

    In other news everyone here at school is in a panic over the prom, especially Marian and the GGS and you know who. So predictable. If I'm honest, it does make me a little wistful, not being part of all that hoopla, but mostly I just miss YOU.

    And anyway, I'm spending more time at the Unitarian Church. You would not believe how quickly everything has changed. Reverend Cahill has moved on, and the new reverend is Sid Freeman—a professor! 30 years old!—and holy moly, is he ever ready to continue Cahill's integrationist work, even though he's not a Yankee per se. The difference is that everyone likes him, and I believe he's ready to change the church and the whole city. Reverend Freeman teaches at Johnson C. Smith (there are only two Caucasian professors.) You remember I told you about Dr. Reginald Hawkins, that Negro dentist who sat in the restaurants at the airport. Well. Some of the faculty and students want to copy his idea, to expand on it—and they invited Dr. Freeman to come. He says it's the power of being present. It's all very exciting. Young people are joining the movement and the church like mad. (We're up to 150!)

    Edie, I know you're a Catholic, but that doesn't matter. All are welcome in the church and the movement. I can't wait until you're back to your old self and can join us.

Don't worry one bit about Marian Smythe or anything else that gang thinks. When you return we'll be looking at a whole new world.

Love, Luce

9

EDIE

We watched television shows back to back, seven soap operas straight through to the evening news and *The Donna Reed Show*. Sometimes we'd try to sneak *American Bandstand*, but Mrs. Bruns seemed to be able to hear the opening music four rooms away. On that morning the set was watching us, its single eye a judgment, reluctant to go. Then the eye squeezed itself into a slit, then into a pinpoint of energy, then blinked once, electrically, and went out.

Mrs. Wentzloff had circled up the chairs, and we were most of us smoking and knitting our little caps, booties, and blankets. She was supposed to be the housemother, but she was more like a grandmother, except with a foreign accent and hair as striped as a cat's, and today she was especially cheery because of the hypothetical men who were supposed to become part of our hypothetical futures. Of course I had Simon, so none of it really applied to me, and me and Lindy just held onto that, the secret of him there.

Mrs. W. perched on the edge of her armchair and started up in her fairy-tale accent. "Girls. I know this is the question that is bother you always. Some of you are asking me already." She peered at us over her glasses. "Now. Not to worry. Here we are. Finally." She raised her index finger and waggled it. "It will be, eh, breath of relief. We are talking about information for future. What does the husband need to know?"

I waited along with everyone else, pretending at interest. It was obvious Mrs. W. was pausing for effect. She looked at each of us. "You girls will have the control." She touched both index fingers together and pointed them at Katherine. "Is the husband going to ask you did you have baby?"

Katherine shook her head.

"No." Mrs. W. pointed her little steeple at Lee. "Is the husband going to ask you did you go to bed with other man?"

Lee shook her head.

"No. He will not, because of that you will act so innocent. As if he is first man you like." Her pointer dipped toward Annette. "That means no petting." She turned back to Lee. "If he tries to pet you before wedding, you say, 'Oh!'" Mrs. W. covered her mouth with one hand. "You are so shocked. 'Oh!'" Everyone laughed, including Mrs. W. "Shocked. You see?" More giggles.

She leaned forward, as if the next bit were especially good. "Because no other man has been trying to pet you before." She waggled one finger at me. "Now. He will try to convince you. Of course. He will say, 'I love you more.' And what does that mean?"

"I respect you less!" some of the girls answered.

"Of course he will be saying every thing." Point, point, point. She paused to make eye contact with each of us. "But remember, young friends. In his heart, he will be so happy. He will believe he is first man because he will want to believe he is first man. Bless his heart. He will think he is so persuasive and so charming. I am not doubting it." All we had to do was walk the straight and narrow path and the man's own pride would steer his judgments. It was simple.

Lee raised her hand. "Are you telling us we should lie?"

"Lie?" Mrs. Wentzloff's chin retracted into her neck. "No. Of course not." She shook her head. She threw her hands wide and smiled. "You will not talk about past. This will not be the topic for talking. Not even little topic."

I'd heard this presentation before, and I'd seen how the new girls paid attention, how they wanted to believe in starting over. But beneath that hope was the undertow, the unspoken understanding that they'd be lucky if a single soul ever showed serious interest in them again, that they'd stumbled from the club of normalcy and were desperate to get back in, that marriage was the ticket to reentry. It was why they were there, why we were there. And maybe it was because I knew I had the luxury of Simon that I raised my hand and was surprised to hear Luce's what-if voice come right out. "You're supposed to *trick* them?"

Mrs. Wentzloff hesitated.

"What happens when they find out they've been tricked?"

"Ah, Susannah, bless your heart," Mrs. Wentzloff said. "You are so…honest, and I am so glad. It is trick, as you say, only if you think it is trick. If you will try to lie then it is problem you and your true love will have for later. Better to think information is something you skipped, something erased and now is not part of your life. Is not there. He will think how he likes to think." She waggled her head. "These things are okay." Her voice was a cushion, a marshmallow. "He believes in you. You both want the belief."

At the end of the hour everyone hugged Mrs. Wentzloff close, hugged her promises closer, especially the one about reinventing ourselves. For a few moments, we believed.

LUCE

Edie's letters had gotten odd. She hadn't said—she couldn't— that she was keeping the baby. But I knew her well enough to worry. And one thing was certain: that boy Simon had fallen on his face. Should do this, could do that. But as far as I could tell it was all talk, talk, talk. And anyway, Edie didn't need him. She already had a career.

My dad knew all about the ways of getting help from the state. He was a bona fide expert at helping women. That's what he did. Every day. I kept my eye on the court docket and waited. Then one day there it was: Waddell, prosecutor, affiliation hearing. I figured I'd learn at least part of what I needed to know. Affiliation, from *affiliare. Filius. Filia. Filial.*

I skipped gym class, but it didn't make much difference. By the time I arrived at the courthouse the bailiff was swearing in a girl not much older than me, her dress bright as a robin's egg in all that sea of gray. When the bailiff spoke, her hand rose white like a flag, the fingers stretched in exaggerated attention the way a kid does the first time he says the Pledge of Allegiance. A matching blue sailor hat was bobby-pinned to the back of her head, and it didn't want to stay in place. Every few minutes she repositioned it, pursing the spare clip between her lips while fretting the other through her hair and over the bright blue wool.

I'd worn my best jumper, but Dad didn't see me. He was asking the girl gentle questions. The girl—her name was Miss Ledbetter—was the complainant, and he was doing his job. Her front teeth protruded quite a bit, and she kept smiling the way a person does who thinks she's supposed to be apologizing. Worse, she had a habit of laughing while she talked, a kind of whinny, and when she opened her mouth those two front teeth showed extra white against her lipstick. Orange-red. The color put me in mind of sockhops.

It came out that Miss Ledbetter was a cashier at the Piggly Wiggly, where she'd met the defendant, Ward Thackston. Right there he was, sitting at the other table, his hair standing at flat-topped attention, the shoulders of his suit geometric, immobile. The man next to him had to be his father. They had the same broad, squared face, the same close ears, the same intent stare toward the judge, though they didn't once look or speak to one another. As I watched, the boy—Ward—swiped his palms down the front crease of his trousers.

Miss Ledbetter's parents had already paid a visit to the Thackstons, to see if Ward could be convinced to marry their daughter. He had declined. His parents weren't having it. Well. That's when the girl's parents brought the affiliation suit.

I'd seen the defense lawyer before, the silver-haired counsel Mr. Hallowell, his face going ruddy when he got excited. Now Mr. Hallowell strode to the witness stand, his two-toned shoes covering the space in four paces. "During the conception period between May 12 and August 12, 1957, did you and the defendant have sexual intercourse?" I remember stiffening with surprise. Even the way he pronounced the phrase embarrassed me. It was more like "*se*xual *in*tercourse," as if those first two syllables appalled him.

Miss Ledbetter almost whispered. "Yes." A sibilant consonant hushing across surfaces. I couldn't see much of Miss Ledbetter's waist, but if the math was right she'd be up to six months pregnant.

Mr. Hallowell's voice was unnaturally loud. "What's that you said? Can you speak up?"

"Yes, *sir*." Still barely audible. Her eyes didn't meet his, but when he turned away from her, they lifted to follow the dark fabric of his suit. Then he turned back.

"And how many times would you say you had…*se*xual *in*tercourse with Mr. Thackston?"

"I don't know."

"What would your estimate—your *guess*—be?"

"I don't know. I reckon it was two or three times a week."

"Two or three times a week. You *reck*on." Loud. "And where?"

"In the car mostly. I mean his car."

"In his car." Pause. "Is that the only place?"

"I reck—I think so."

Mr. Hallowell was still standing there, waiting, as if the answer were unacceptable. I felt my toes curl up and grip the soles of my saddle shoes. But Miss Ledbetter seemed to have some idea what Mr. Hallowell expected, because she added, "Maybe in the back of the store once."

An audible exhalation of air from the members of the jury.

"The back of the store?" Mr. Hallowell never did smile, but there was something about him—the casual way he rested his foot on the rung of a chair, the way he jingled his hands in his pockets—that told you he was enjoying himself. "What is that area exactly? Could you describe what that area is like?"

"The back of the store. You know. There's a lounge for the girls, and lockers, and then there's a place for mops and such and…"

"A couch?" For Pete's sake. He really did want that picture.

She blinked. "Yes."

"I see." He paused, too long. "Were there any witnesses who can verify that you and Mr. Thackston had sexual intercourse in the back of the store?"

She looked shocked. "Nooo…"

"You say that you had sexual intercourse in the very place where you were employed, but there were no witnesses?"

"It wasn't like that. Ward was, we were crazy for each other."

"Crazy for each other?"

"All the time." The defense attorney jingled the change in his pockets again. He didn't say anything for a moment but let the last words float above the lacquered wooden benches of the courtroom like an impulse. "Aside from the car and the back of the store, in what other locations did you have *sexual intercourse* with the defendant?" As if the location were of critical importance. Dad didn't object, so maybe it was.

Miss Ledbetter seemed to jerk her head back involuntarily. At the same time she made a kind of wheezing laugh.

"Were there any other locations, Miss Ledbetter?"

Miss Ledbetter's eyes skipped from Ward Thackston to the jury box and then to my father. Miss Ledbetter said, "I'm not sure. I mean I can't exactly remember." Dad still didn't object. Maybe he was writing the notes that would put Miss Ledbetter's tormenter in his place. I couldn't wait to see him do it, couldn't wait to see the glow of a martini reflected in his face and hear the way he'd later explain his strategy.

Mr. Hallowell sounded skeptical. "You can't exactly remember. Please note, Miss Ledbetter, that you are under oath."

Miss Ledbetter jerked her eyes from one location in the room to another: the jury, my father, Ward Thackston. Mr. Hallowell stood in front of her, jingling and jingling. Why wasn't Dad objecting? Miss Ledbetter's eyes flickered in animal agitation. Then she said in a rush, "There was once, in the bathroom in a filling station. He was always in a big hurry."

"I see." Mr. Hallowell nodded slowly. "Thank you, Miss Ledbetter. Now. Did you have *sexual intercourse* with any other men during this time period?"

"Why *no*, sir."

"Are you absolutely certain that you're remembering exactly? Were there any other…*filling* station episodes?"

There was the sound of an escaped laugh. But it was impossible to tell from where among the wooden benches and tables and flannel suits it had come. Dad said nothing. Nor was he writing anything on the yellow pad in front of him. Maybe that was a good sign. Mr. Hallowell waited for the titters to fade before he spoke again. "Miss Ledbetter?"

"No, sir."

The attorney contemplated her before making some unseen decision in his mind. "Miss Ledbetter. Did Mr. Thackston pay you to have sexual intercourse with him?"

Miss Ledbetter sat up straighter. "*No. No sir.*"

"He never *paid* you?" The way the statement swooped up into a question made it sound as if Miss Ledbetter had been foolish not to send Ward Thackston a bill. Then, as if Mr. Hallowell were trying to sort out some reasonable explanation, he said, "Did he ever give you gifts or money?"

"No."

"Did he *promise* you gifts or money?"

"No. Yes. He said he was going to buy me a dress for when I met his family."

"And did he?"

Miss Ledbetter didn't say a thing. She looked to the side and blinked rapidly then bent her head toward her lap and turned it once to the left and once to the right. Mr. Hallowell waited, and I felt a surge of gratitude. Then in a tone that was conversational and curious, he said, "Did you ever meet Mr. Thackston's family?"

Miss Ledbetter shook her head without looking up.

The attorney waited. I felt my jaw tighten with understanding. He didn't want the jury to feel sorry for the girl. When he spoke again his voice was sympathetic. "Miss Ledbetter, did you imagine that you were going to marry the defendant?"

Her face relaxed some. "Of course. We talked about it."

"And this was something you wanted to happen?"

"Of course. I mean, he talked about it as if—"

"When did you realize that Mr. Thackston wasn't going to marry you?"

She took a long breath. "When he said he was engaged to, he was engaged to, to somebody else…"

"I see." Again Mr. Hallowell left the sentence alone for several seconds. "And how long ago was that?"

"The weekend after Labor Day."

"How many months after that did you…*discover* you were pregnant?"

Miss Ledbetter blinked. "Two months, sir."

"And in those two months, how many other men did you have sexual intercourse with?"

"*None*, sir."

Mr. Hallowell said he had no further questions, and before I knew it Ward Thackston was at the witness stand. He touched his necktie, then acted as if he would loosen the tie, then seemed to think better of it. He set his hands on his thighs instead, elbows bent outward and shoulders shrugged up to his neck, so that his head appeared to rest on the block of his body.

Dad stood. I felt a thrill of pride. He had the yellow pad with him, but he didn't seem to need it. He said, "Did you have sexual intercourse with Miss Ledbetter during the conception period of May 12 to August 12?"

"Yes."

"How many times, would you say?"

"It was a few times. I don't know. Sometimes on a Saturday afternoon. Sometimes on a weekday after classes."

Dad asked if Ward Thackston had given Miss Ledbetter the impression that he might want to marry her. Ward Thackston said no. I felt a ping of triumph. *Sic semper tyrannis.* Then Dad asked if he'd used condoms. Ward Thackston said he wouldn't even know where to procure such a thing. For some reason he sounded proud about that. Then Dad said that would be all.

That was it? It didn't seem right. There was writing—he'd written something on that yellow notepad. There had to be more.

Then Mr. Hallowell was standing up and jingling his pockets again. "Mr. Thackston. Would you describe the circumstances of your relationship with Miss Ledbetter?"

"Circumstances?"

"How you met her, to start with."

"Some fellows in the fraternity told me about her. You know, that she was, that she had… That she would give it away."

"Give it away? What do you mean by that exactly, Mr. Thackston?"

"You know. Have sex relations. They said that she would have them, that she would do that with fellows who took her out."

"Who were those fellows of whom you speak, Mr. Thackston?"

"Well, in particular, there was this one guy on the baseball team that told me about her. He had been…having relations—sex relations— with her last summer but then he stopped."

"I see. And he was the one who told you about Miss Ledbetter."

"Yes."

"So you had heard of Miss Ledbetter's reputation before you met her?"

"Yeah—yes."

"Would you say that her reputation was in fact the reason you met her?"

"Yeah…Yes. I'd say that was in fact the reason I met her." Ward Thackston was making a steadfast effort to rivet his eyes on the attorney. I looked at the profile of Miss Ledbetter, who had turned her head to watch Ward with open mouth. The muscles of her face were perfectly still.

"Was there anyone else you knew who said they'd had relations with Miss Ledbetter?"

"Yeah. They talked about her. A fellow would go out with her and then the next day say that he had done it with her." Ward Thackston's eyes never strayed from Mr. Hallowell's.

"Which fellow?"

"You know." He made a gesture with his arm that suggested the other speaker might be sitting right next to him. "A guy on the team. A considerable number of guys."

"Thank you, Mr. Thackston."

Then a boy in a houndstooth jacket and a bowtie came forward as witness for the defense, and his steps were quick and leathered and nervous on the wooden floor. My father sat with his head in both hands. I willed him to put his hands on the table, but he never did move.

Mr. Hallowell went straight to the point. "Mr. Kemp. Have you ever had sexual intercourse with Miss Ledbetter?" It wasn't until then that I understood. Suddenly the courtroom with its lines of dark wood and gray flannelled bodies seemed to me the most alien of places. The state wasn't going to get a single red cent out of Ward Thackston, and my dad knew it.

I heard the sound of Mr. Kemp's voice saying yes. Such a simple word. Well. I closed my eyes and breathed. There had to be hundreds of Miss Ledbetters out there. Thousands. I fumbled in my school satchel until I found my history notebook. I wasn't ever going to be one of them. For the first time in my life, I felt as if I had a modicum of say-so. I found an empty page and began to write.

"Did you have a relationship with Miss Ledbetter two years ago?" Mr. Kemp said yes to that too.

"Did you also have sexual intercourse with Miss Ledbetter during the conception period of May twelfth to August twelfth?" The boy said yes to that too.

Then there was the spontaneous clatter of varnished wood slamming against floorboards. It was a sound that didn't belong in such a premeditated place. Nor did the raw word that came next. "Liar!" The man who'd been sitting next to Miss Ledbetter had stood up so suddenly that his chair had fallen against the wooden rail behind him. His face and neck were flushed a violent shade of pink, and a semicircle of brown hair ran from ear to ear around the bottom of his shining skull. He wore neither coat nor tie, and in the sliver of silence that followed the sound of the chair, he said, "I can tell you for a fact." In the twang of that sentence were the sound of mountains and mules. Miss Ledbetter's father. My own father stared at him with bleak surprise.

The judge slammed his gavel on the desk and told the man to sit down.

"I can tell you for a fact," the man said again, but this time he seemed less sure of himself. He folded his arms across his chest but sat down anyway.

"Proceed, Mr. Hallowell."

"Can you describe the circumstances of your relations with Miss Ledbetter?"

"We still kept in touch. You know. For old time's sake. I called her up and asked if she wanted to get a burger. Afterwards we parked. *You* know." You know.

Eventually Mr. Kemp sat down, and then the defense called a third boy. He was younger than the other two and sat grinning like a fiend the whole time, as if he and everybody else in the courtroom were all a part of some thrilling naughty joke. When Mr. Hallowell asked him to describe the circumstances of his intimacy with Miss Ledbetter, he said, "Esso. I think it was an Esso."

General laughter.

Please.

The judge banged his gavel and said, "That will be enough, Mr. Kilpatrick!"

But that wasn't the worst. For some reason Miss Ledbetter began giggling. She slicked her eyes from the judge to her parents to the other people in the room, looking for something in each face and then nervously sliding to the next. At one point her eyes landed on mine, and I was somehow dirtied by it, as guilty as the rest. And maybe I was. Miss Ledbetter's gaze skipped away, and the giggling became a frightened hee-haw laugh that went on for many anguished seconds before her father put his hands on her shoulders and brought his face close to hers. Then he shook her once, hard, and then again. Her teeth made an ivory clack, and then she stopped. For a moment she sat absolutely still, looking at her father. Then she began to cry with exactly the same force with which she'd been giggling the moment before.

In the end the jury didn't even convene. The judge dismissed the case. Ward Thackston was innocent of fathering Miss Ledbetter's baby. Miss Ledbetter would not be getting any money from him. I wrote down as much as I could.

And vowed it wouldn't happen to Edie that way. Simon wasn't *that* low, surely. My mouth tasted like ash. My father didn't move. For the last twenty minutes he'd sat with his fingers splayed on either side of his temples. I willed him to move, do *something*, say *something*. There had to be something he could do to cancel out that taste of complicity. Instead the curve of his spine bowed through his jacket, and it was that image, that hunch of defeat, that I took home with me. If I'd been Miss Ledbetter's lawyer, I'd at least have sat up straight. If I'd been in his place, I'd at least have made Mr. Hallowell work harder.

I spent the next two afternoons in the library. I learned that an unwed mother had to file an affiliation suit before she was eligible for state assistance. She had to show she'd done all she could to get the putative father to pay. In those days it was all on her. But no court in the country would permit an adjudication of paternity when the identity of the father was in question. *Exceptio plurium concubentium.* Seven years later when I took the North Carolina bar exam it was still there.

I thought about that courtroom many times in the years after that, how easy it was to ruin a reputation, how easy it was to change a life, how women have known as much for centuries, have been taught to expect it, how women had to learn to forestall impropriety, even its very appearance. It was many decades later when the #MeToo movement finally grew up thick and strong and the tables turned. This time men were the ones being accused, including men who'd never had to think about the power of allegation or how it might be wielded against them, powerful men who'd never been taught to fear sexual libel. They couldn't believe the way an accusation could change a life, ex post facto. Couldn't believe the way one charge led to the next. All they could do was stand amazed. They hadn't been raised to expect such things, and their outrage rang in the air like a gong.

10

EDIE

Dr. Maben peered at me over his glasses, chin low, the flesh of his neck bulging around it, then closed the manila folder and set it atop a cardboard container that looked to be a box of Lincoln Logs. "Every day, Susannah, there are more girls in your position." Papers stacked his desk, also dirty coffee cups and pipe cleaners and all manner of toys. It was a relief to see an office so messy, and it made my own flaws seem less pointy. Now the psychiatrist took his glasses off and set them on the folder. "We used to think that girls like you-all got pregnant because of...well, immorality." He seemed embarrassed by the explanation. "Bad apples, so to speak." He raised his eyebrows and dipped his head to the side. "Now we take a more...*scientific* view. Now we know it's more like an illness, a kind of social malaise, much like neurosis or delinquency or homosexuality. A girl like you, Susannah, can be cured." He looked at me expectantly, then ran his fingers behind his ear as if tucking away a strand of hair, then opened his palm to reveal a penny. He beamed and handed it to me.

"Thank you, sir."

He patted my knee. "We have work to do, Susannah."

I wasn't sure how to respond. He lit his pipe, the long wooden match flaring sulfurously against the waxen folds of his face. He smoothed his bald head, opened his hand again, and seemed delighted to find another penny there.

This time I smiled and held the penny against my belly. "See that, Lindy? It's a penny from the nice doctor." She didn't move though.

"Yes…" Dr. Maben said uncertainly. "Let's talk about your school. What grade were you in this year, Susannah?"

"Twelfth."

"Let's talk about that," he said. But he didn't ask about classes. He asked about my friends and then about Mama and Daddy. At first I answered honestly because that was what you were supposed to do, but the stories about my sisters and Mama and Daddy seemed boring, even to me, and Dr. Maben was growing restless.

That was when that first sentence rose like a bubble from some place inside me deep as fathoms. "You know, they never come to watch me, my parents." And, while I was still marveling at that first statement, more floated up. "They don't come to school events. Like debate." And it just went on from there, me telling him how the other kids' parents came to watch the debates, but mine did not.

Dr. Maben raised his eyebrows. Then he wrote something down. "Debate? Were you the only girl on the team?"

I nodded. It's not like it was the worst lie in the world.

"Um-hmmm. That says a good deal, Susannah." He crossed the one knee over the other and balanced his shiny pipe and stared into space. His lips puffed drily on the wood.

I couldn't remember the last time someone had told me I was saying a good deal. I wanted to say more things he'd like, but all my guesses were blind as pin-the-tail-on-the-donkey.

So I told a story about my parents, how my real father had divorced my mother when I was a child, which Dr. Maben ate right up, how my real father was a lawyer who never came to visit, and that sometimes I spied on him anyway. The doctor gulped it down. "And sometimes I steal things. Little things. Not money."

His brows shot up with interest. "Ah yes." His sentences quickened. "Of course, yes. Do you ever feel as if you need to prove yourself?"

"Oh *yes*. Almost all the time." Dr. Maben was writing busily now, his large body turned toward his desk. He scribbled and scribbled, all of it about me. I was finally able to relax.

The next week he gave me the questionnaire. *Number one: why do you think you became pregnant?* A list of ten or more choices sprawled their way down the page: *I am angry at my mother... I feel more powerful... I want to have a child to love... I want to be loved by a man... I don't believe in following the rules...* None of the statements were one hundred percent true but none of them one hundred percent false either. It just depended where you were at the moment. I *did* want to love my child, I *did* want Simon to love me, and he did, I was sure, but the forms didn't say any of that. So in the end, I penciled a slow X in each of the little boxes.

Dr. Maben read it, sighed, and returned the page to me like a failed algebra test. Then, out of the blue, he said, "Susannah. Do you have *any* idea why you became pregnant?"

The heat of the blush traveled up my chest to the top of my hairline. "Yes, sir, I understand about that, I know, I shouldn't have done it, I mean I know that—"

Dr. Maben tilted his head and sighed. "I don't mean *how* you got pregnant, Susannah. I think we can assume that you know the answer to that. I mean *why*." His interest was clear-eyed, abstract, and didn't seem to have anything to do with me at all. "Can you think of a reason *why* you might want to be pregnant?" He chewed on the end of his pipe.

It had never occurred to me there might be a reason. It sounded so lovely, the way he phrased it, as if you could choose to be pregnant or not, as you wished, as if you could control the paths your life would take. "Why, I don't know. I don't know if there was any *reason*."

"Think, Susannah." He puffed.

It was another area in which I was falling short. "Do the other girls have reasons?"

"Everyone has a reason, Susannah, or they wouldn't be here." His answer was kind, but frustrated, as if he were explaining something obvious.

Still, I couldn't help asking, "Why in the world would they do that? Why would *I* do that?"

"Come now." His tone was firm. "If you hadn't wanted to be pregnant, you would at the very least have tried to get an abortion. This is classic acting out. Not only did you allow the pregnancy to occur, but you allowed it to continue."

"But it was so hard to—"

"Yes, well. There's the law and then there's reality, Susannah. You and I both know that." He looked at me like he knew that I knew that we both knew a little something of the world. The statements in my head chased one another. If I hadn't wanted to be pregnant, I wouldn't have gotten myself pregnant. If I hadn't wanted to be pregnant, I'd have gotten an abortion. It *seemed* to make sense, but there was something about it I couldn't put my finger on. My thoughts wobbled, a mental teeter-totter I more and more found myself trying to balance. Dr. Maben was still talking. "We don't normally talk about theory with girls in your position, Susannah. The psychological...exigencies are too complicated." He did his head tilt. "Sometimes scientists themselves can't agree."

Inside me, Lindy rearranged herself in a little package, and without thinking I put my hand on what I guessed was her bony little bottom. "I could *try*."

During the nights I still walked the hallways, and during the daytimes the white plastered corridors narrowed just a little bit more, gently and firmly funneling me through smaller and smaller passages that became tunnels that became cracks.

Dr. Maben took his shiny pipe from his teeth and set it in the ashtray. "This isn't our usual method. But." He ran his hand over his forehead, and I wondered if he was going to produce another penny. "It's imperative that you get a grasp of your own motivations. I'd hate to see you here again in a year." He paused. "Have you heard of Sigmund Freud?"

Sort of. I knew for one thing that boys had by nature fewer emotions than girls, and that loads of us were hoping to have boys so they wouldn't miss their mothers as much.

Dr. Maben folded his hands over the mound of his own tummy and took a deep breath. "Some scientists think that out-of-wedlock pregnancy is a kind of rebellion against being a woman, a sort of secret desire to be more like a man. That it's an act of aggression and independence, possibly what Freud called a castration complex." He stopped for one moment, as if at a loss for what to say next. "In other words, let's say there are little girls who can't really accept the fact that they're not as…strong, say, as little boys. So, some of them remain sort of…*stuck* until they're grown women. They keep trying to prove they're as good as boys. As men. One way for them to do that is to join, say, a debate team." He looked at me sympathetically. "Another way is to have a baby by themselves. To show they don't need a man, you see. Otherwise they would get married first. They would behave in a more feminine way and be more…demure." He looked at me sharply. "Some of these girls become lesbians for the same reason."

At the time I had only a vague idea of what he meant by "lesbians" but could see loud and clear the inky reproach the word dragged behind it. I believed him, though. The girls in the Home *were* peculiar. Sally spent hours destroying things, mostly ripping them up, books, clothes, playing cards, sometimes fifty-two at a time, dime-sized pieces she'd throw out the window like mad confetti. And when I walked the halls at night, there was always the sound of crying leaking through those high wide transoms.

Dr. Maben was looking at me with frank curiosity. "One of the most common explanations for unwed pregnancy is based upon the Oedipus complex. That is when, say, a girl is secretly angry at her mother and wants to have her father all to herself. So she has a baby as a way to pretend, if you will, that she's in her mother's place, that she is, let's say, the mother."

I sighed. Dr. Maben had been right from the get-go. The psychiatry of pregnancy was more than I could really follow. Sure, the explanations were interesting but also distant and abstract, all those girls out there doing all those loony things. It just didn't have anything to do with me, or this ripening belly, this heavy tender body, this possibility coming to life inside me.

Still. I didn't want the doctor to think he'd overestimated my abilities.

It might be he noticed my disbelief because he stared out the window, his tone sad and distracted. "Some people think that patients see themselves as the Virgin Mary. And perhaps *that* is why they do it." He turned back to me. "Are you Catholic, Susannah?"

I nodded, but I wasn't so sure anymore and anyway, it didn't matter. In my mind I was stashed in a closet under the stairs, and sometimes I dreamed I'd taken Lindy there too but then the dream would shift and the closet was crowded with other girls, hundreds and thousands of them, all of them looking for their lost names. Just looking, searching and searching for a thing they had lost.

It will be something that has been erased.

I'd already told Dr. Maben about the dreams. Inside me, I was sure that Lindy felt them too, sure that she would feel my worry, that when she was born she too would be worried, but the doctor had assured me we were two separate entities, that there was no link between a mother's state of mind and an infant's. Dr. Maben was still talking about reasons. "Perhaps the trouble starts because a girl's parents are confused about gender. Perhaps the mother wears the pants in the family and the father is a passive sort who doesn't take charge."

I made myself look interested. On his desk were a toy train and a cast-iron spaceship, also a picture of him with a pretty red-haired lady and two teenaged girls. In the picture he was thinner and had more hair. "But sometimes a girl is desperate for attention," he said. "She reels in the first unsuspecting boy she meets."

Reels? The word yanked my attention back.

"And then charms him into a doomed romance."

And of all the things he'd said that was the thing that hit home the hardest because that's what Simon's parents must have thought too. That I was reeling in their son. For one moment I saw it too, myself, planning, no—*scheming*—to capture Simon Bloom. What was it the Joyce Jackson book said? *You may have to take the lead, but you will have to use tact!*

And maybe that was exactly what had happened.

Dr. Maben knocked his pipe against the side of the ashtray and left it there. Then he picked up the notes he'd written and glanced at them. "Now. Susannah. You are sometimes a stubborn girl. Am I right?"

I examined his face to see if I had any choice in the way I answered. I didn't. "Yes."

"That kind of behavior points toward masculine tendencies." He flipped the pages of his notes. "But my money is on anger at your mother." He looked up to check my reaction.

I folded my hands across my belly, unsurprised. I *was* angry, angrier each day, and the oddest part was that in her letters Mama didn't say a thing in the world about the baby. Mothers were supposed to ask what names you had chosen, whether you were hoping for a girl or a boy. They were supposed to shop for bassinets and layettes and lacy baptismal bonnets, for woolen booties and white cotton diapers, for salves and plastic rattles and diaper pins.

For some reason my mind landed on that sentence I'd heard weeks ago from Mrs. Bruns. *Our aim is to get them ready.*

When was that supposed to happen? And what, exactly, was I supposed to be ready for?

After the Home, there would be more days, and more years, but they existed without form, and separate, inhabited only by the Susannahs of the world, who lived in harmony with neighbors and parents and the secret workings of biology. In that place neighbors smiled approvingly, and Susannah felt right at home. But I was nowhere to be seen. Nor was my baby.

The following week Dr. Maben swiveled his chair to face me and started right in. "Susannah, can you tell me a little more about your mother?"

I was tired of talking about my mother. My body felt cramped, and my baby felt cramped, muscling around in there for room. "What about *Lindy?*"

"Who's Lindy?" Dr. Maben asked, shuffling the pages of his notes.

"The *baby.* My daughter. I want to talk about what's going to happen to her." I palmed my belly and tried to lean forward. It was more work than it used to be.

Dr. Maben set the notes on his desk and sighed. "Susannah. The time to talk about the baby is after we talk about the relationship with your mother. We have to understand the problem first."

"But that *isn't* the problem." I tried to keep my voice from sounding hysterical. "The problem is that Simon and I have to find a way to keep Lindy." Little feet kicked me from the inside.

Exasperation fluttered across Dr. Maben's brow. "Susannah. Everybody needs to be loved. Everybody. But not everybody needs it so badly they have a baby because of it. We have *got* to figure out why this happened so that you don't keep making the same mistake. Until then, you won't have the tools you need to give love. Unwed mothers can't. There's a difference between the way a normal, married woman feels for her baby and the way someone like you does. It's for *phantasy* use."

At the word, he stabbed the fountain pen on the desk.

"Phantasy use?" I couldn't tell if he was talking *to* me or *about* me, and it suddenly seemed to matter. I wrapped my arms around my waist. Lindy was quiet.

Dr. Maben closed his eyes and took a deep breath. "My dear. One is love, and the other is some manner of need-satisfaction. It's a known fact. Unweds base their decisions on their own needs, not their baby's."

I couldn't shape the question that jumped ahead of all the others in my mind.

Dr. Maben's voice grew even gentler. "Can't you see this is some manner of self-absorption?"

I tried again. "But how do you know that...that I'm not like other women? I mean how do you know that I'm not like married women?" I couldn't bring myself to say *normal*. Nor could I shape the other question. What happens to girls who aren't normal?

"Susannah. My *dear*. You yourself are Example A: a mother who wants to keep her infant over the possibility of future marriage. A mother who is hurting both herself and her child. Clearly that's not a sensible decision. And yet that's exactly what you propose to do. It's a classic inability to make rational decisions. And yet you want to be a mother. How can you possibly expect to be a good mother?"

It was only then that I began to understand. Yes, I'd gotten myself pregnant, but that was just the tip of the iceberg. Dr. Maben was telling me I had a host of other problems that had been invisible for a long time, like cancers lurking deep in my personality. The amazing thing was *I hadn't even known they were there.* How could I expect to be a mother? The past six months had been all about fulfilling my own needs. About manipulating the people around me to get what I wanted. And what I wanted was, yes, Lindy, but also Simon, and now I saw that to want both of them was nothing but self-serving. Dr. Maben was right. A woman who wanted so much for herself could not possibly be a good mother. She was simply too selfish. *Narcissistic*, that was the scientific word. Understanding finally bloomed, filling my stomach and my throat and my sinuses so full that tears began to push out from my eyes.

Dr. Maben set down his fountain pen and clasped his hands, unclasped them. "Susannah, please don't cry. Please." He started to get up from his chair but seemed at a loss as to what to do next. He sat down again. "It's something you can overcome. Really. Please." His hand found its way to the pipe again and he picked it up but did nothing with it. "We're here to *help* you, Susannah, please. You can *cure* yourself. I know it."

And in that moment I wanted to save myself, perhaps more than any one thing I'd ever wanted before. Normalcy was a club, and the first thing I needed to do, before anything else, was to find a way to be readmitted. There had to be a way. I'd prove to him I could be trusted. I'd just admit it. I *must* have wanted to be pregnant. I *must* have been lashing out at my mother. It seemed as good an explanation as anything else, and maybe I should try harder to compromise, to change, and maybe if I did change they'd look more kindly on me, and maybe they'd all of them say I was trying so hard it was perfectly fine for me to take Lindy with me. Besides, it was so much easier to agree than to disagree, so much easier to be the person they wanted you to be. To be Susannah. "I just wanted to show them," I began. The tears dried up, and the sentences flowed out of me in the psychiatrist's own words.

And Dr. Maben wrote down every word Susannah said.

11

EDIE

I did try to be nice to Trudy, I want you to know that. But now-adays I can't help wondering if there was a way to make things turn out differently. She didn't make it easy. If it was a Saturday and I wasn't visiting Simon, I invited her to the movies, but she always said no, and while I was gone she'd rifle through my things. If there'd been a sweater on the bed, it was on the bureau when I returned, and if the top drawer had been open, it was closed when I came back, the knitting I'd been working on now at the bottom of the basket under the yarn. The Saturday it happened there was a double bill, and every single one of us was late, every one of us hurrying to make it back before supper, stopping by our rooms to stash the Junior Mints or the latest *Modern Romances* we'd stuffed into our pocketbooks. I didn't want to burst in on her because I already knew how it would be, knew I'd left the drawer of the dresser open one inch, just one inch, and that I'd left my cardigan hanging down the top of it, and now it would be different. I gave a light knock so as not to catch her in the act. No one answered. I turned the glass knob.

Trudy wasn't there, and for some reason she'd stripped her bed to the rubber liner. There was something else different too, a something, a change in the atmosphere, as if Trudy's affliction had floated free of her body and lodged itself there in the cracks of the furniture and the folds of the curtains. The air had a mineral edge, and for some reason the rug was gone.

But my sweater was still in place, draped there—*positioned*—over the front of the bureau, the left sleeve hanging longer than the right, the neckline open and lifeless, just as I'd left it. And I was so bent on that one thing, you see, about how to behave when I saw Trudy, that I couldn't put the rest of it together.

Downstairs the dining room popped with so much purple excitement I got pulled right in. For once, we moviegoers and shoppers were on the outs, and it was the girls from the diet kitchen who had all the news. There'd been an ambulance, they said, and an order to stay in their rooms, to close their doors, and there'd been a swaddled figure hoisted into the back of the ambulance and whisked to the hospital.

"That's exactly what happened to my aunt," said Annette. "Her water broke and *bingo*, my cousin just popped out. Right there in the taxicab."

We counted and recounted. There were four February girls and eleven March—all there—and what, six girls due in April? All there. We counted again. And right then I knew. "Trudy." But the math wasn't right. She was in her fifth month, or maybe her fourth. If she was even pregnant.

A confused silence. Finally Therese spoke. Maybe it was the accent, but her voice came out flat. "This is the answer to the question."

What question?

"I look out the window. I see them, the doctors from the ambulance. They do not run. They are not hurrying themselves." My head felt hollow. Therese's voice echoed around in there. "They carry a person, and they do not activate the red light, the…" She twirled her index finger.

"The siren," someone said drily.

"Yes. The siren. They do not activate the siren."

Just then the kitchen door opened and Mrs. Bruns walked in, her face a shield of authority, her makeup even more inexpertly applied than usual, and something in the way she stood, the way her shoulders hugged into her body, made her smaller and older. And for some reason she was wearing a leather shoe on one foot and on the other a rubber boot.

There was quiet. The leather shoe was black. Above it, her ankle was thin and mottled. She took a breath, pulled her shoulders back. Her face didn't carry a shred of excitement. Anyone could see the color there: a charred gray despair. "You-all will have noted that there was an ambulance here this afternoon."

On the table everything was white: tablecloth, plates, napkins. I focused on my plate. Sally excused herself.

Mrs. Bruns said, "I'm afraid Trudy has had a miscarriage."

The salt and pepper shaker were white too: Chef Boyardees with holes in the tops of their white chef caps. Their eyes were dots of blue. So were the buttons on their fat little tummies.

Mrs. Bruns said, "I'll let you know as the situation develops."

I pushed back my chair. It screeched.

Upstairs I stood in the doorway of my room. I hugged myself, my belly that was thick and firm, my insides that were….what? How big was Lindy in there?

Behind me, a footfall. It was Sally. Maybe she'd had the same thought I did, that whatever happened to Trudy, it had happened right here in this room. Maybe she was counting the hours too. Five. We had been at the pictures for five hours. I'd invited Trudy, and Trudy had said…what? I couldn't remember but, yes, I'd definitely invited her.

Hadn't I?

Sally sat down on my bed. "If she had died, Mrs. Bruns would have told us."

"Would she?"

Sally colored and looked out the window. "I don't know."

"How can you die from a miscarriage?" I asked.

She hesitated. "You bleed a lot."

See miscarriage. Where had I heard those words? Luce had read them, and the corners of her mouth had turned down all funny. Emergency rooms filled up with women on Monday mornings. Women were bleeding to death on the weekends. Today was a Saturday.

That night I let myself out the back door. Behind the Home, a boarded-up orphanage blocked the noise of the traffic and the lights of the city, and ice patched the driveway where parents parked to pick up their daughters. The Dempster Dumpsters were on the other side of the lot. I carried the wicker basket away from my body as if it were a pail of garbage and opened the Dumpster's side door and tilted in the contents, and it was dark enough that I couldn't tell the skeins of colored yarn from the half-finished scarf or the paper patterns. I couldn't count how many knitting needles fell into the dark.

I leaned against the Dumpster and breathed the smell of decay. Naked vines climbed the iron fence, tangled and brittle as Sleeping Beauty vines. In the story, the princess waited for the prince to chop his way through, and at the end, he outwitted all the wicked aunts to do the right thing, and the sky and the horizon and the imaginary future all opened up with the promises of the places you could go. But where were they, those places? And how did you get there?

After Trudy left, no one mentioned her. It was like she had never existed at all.

LUCE

I'd waited all week for Mr. Watts to say yes. He was the faculty sponsor of *The Rambler*, and he kept a running list of story topics on the chalkboard, along with the dramatis personae: which students were assigned to cover which topics. On that day the list included twenty or so items: the track team's state contenders, the prom theme, the petition to wear dungarees, the new baseball coach. And there, in the middle, my idea still stood—"fathers have responsibilities too"—followed by "graduation," "Easter fashion", "spring love," and "rabbits."

Rabbits? And there, good Lord, right below the word, someone had written "Edie Carrigan."

Oh for the love of Pete. People didn't ever quit. Except that they never really started in either. It was all thrilled supposition and terrified whispers. Or maybe that was an illusion. Maybe I just imagined the unseen wave of titillation that buoyed every conversation in which her name was mentioned. I wished to God people would just say what they knew. It was the guessing that wore me out.

"Don't let it get to you." The voice was male and teacherly, but not Mr. Watts.

I set my face to neutral and turned. It was Wayne, a tall skinny bass in the glee club. I started to say, "I don't know what you mean," but instead a hot wave of anger and tears threatened to overflow my features. I glared and walked away.

His full name was Wayne Scott. Any other boy with that ridiculous name would've spent his whole life fending off jokes about carpentry and architecture, especially in a journalism class filled with word-loving eggheads. But I never once heard anyone say *wainscot*. The guy stood a little too separate and regarded you a little too carefully. Early in the year he'd been accepted to the military academy at West Point—two articles in the *Observer* and an interview on WBT. He was all history and geology and knew nothing about writing news stories. Not one thing. But that didn't keep him from doing what loads of other second semester seniors did: join the staff as an easy way to fill his last graduation requirements. He'd said it was—quote unquote—to *get a look* at the way newspapers operated. And he did do real work, I had to give him that. He'd even impressed me once or twice, though I wasn't too interested in all that military stuff per se.

I opened my history notebook, found the notes from Miss Ledbetter's hearing, set up three sheets with carbon paper, and rolled them onto the platen. But once the typewriters were clacking away, Mr. Watts pulled me aside and told me he wasn't buying the fathers idea. He had to raise his voice to be heard over the machines. "Do you realize how inflammatory an article like that is liable to be?"

"I understand that," I said. Two months until summer. So what if I was a pariah again. So what.

"I think it sounds interesting," a voice behind me said. It was him.

Both Mr. Watts and I turned to stare at Wayne Scott. His face wasn't handsome, but it wasn't funny-looking either. Heavy bones, biggish nose. Mr. Watts, who'd opened his mouth to speak, closed it.

Wayne didn't seem to realize he was out of line. Or if he did, he didn't mind. "I mean, isn't that what newspapers are supposed to do? Cover topics that are important to society?" If the question was meant to be subversive, I couldn't tell. It came out with perfect innocence.

Mr. Watts kept his composure. "It *is*..."

"I remember we had this conversation earlier in the semester." Wayne spoke to Mr. Watts like a colleague, like old pals. "Several times now she's wanted to write about integration."

I felt a wash of gratitude so sudden it seemed liquid, and not just because a boy like Wayne was defending me—if he was defending me (I was pretty sure he was). Which was certainly part of it. No, it was because he'd made the issue bigger than just Edie. As if my interest was principled, not personal. (Was that true? I didn't know, but how strange and lovely it is to be perceived as more noble than you actually are.)

Well.

Wayne carried on with wide-eyed earnestness. "I personally find these value issues to be more interesting than rabbits. I bet other people would too." This line he delivered with no sarcasm in sight. "*The Rambler* is a newspaper. That's what newspapers are in it to do. Right?"

Yes. Right indeed.

Mr. Watts stood there, blinking.

In the end, I wrote the article. It ran three columns—until Mr. Watts pulled it just as the paper went to press. That day he summoned Wayne and me to see him after school. He'd talked about it with the principal, he said, and the principal had scotched it. Mr. Watts thought it was probably best too. "It's not what we do," he mumbled. "It's not." He shook his head and said it two more times. "It's not, it's not."

I fumed.

Wayne nodded and said, "I see."

Afterwards, we stepped into the empty hallway without speaking. Then, without warning, Wayne Scott reached over and lifted my books from the cradle of my arm. "I'm sorry," he said.

"Me too." I'd never had a boy carry my books. Was that why Wayne was carrying them? Because he felt sorry for me? I didn't think it was the only reason.

Wayne swung the books up and set them on his head. It wasn't the way boys were supposed to carry girls' books, and despite what he'd said about being sorry, he seemed happy enough. He did a little imitation of Mr. Watts. "*It's not, it's not...it's not.*" He managed to get the intonation exactly right. "Isn't that the stuff that comes out of your nose when you have a cold?"

I felt my face go rigid. Surely Wayne Scott hadn't just said what I thought he'd said. Surely this boy who seemed to take everything at face value hadn't just made a second-grade joke. I studied him. "You mean phlegm?"

He spilled a grin. "No, no, not phlegm, madam, that's something else." Then, without missing a beat, he said. "That was a school of Dutch painters in the 17th century."

Aha. I scrambled for a response. "Oh, yeah, I've heard of them. They called themselves that because they invented the camera obscura...and they...they had to use flem in the cameras to capture the images."

Wayne was grinning. "No...no...They hadn't invented flem yet. Kodak did that."

Dammit. He was right.

"No, the reason they called themselves the Flemish school is because Dutchmen live in tall skinny houses that were so flemsy they swayed when the wind blew too hard."

I might have giggled, but I doubt I did. We had reached my locker. I turned around to tell him thanks.

"C'mon," he said. "I'll walk you to your bus." Wayne Scott's hair was thick and wiry, and in the afternoon sun, almost blond. I cast about for something to say. There wasn't a single thing.

"It's true about the houses in Holland, but that's not why the Dutch called themselves the Flemish school." I had to come up with something cleverer this time. "They called themselves that because they painted scenes that were really precise, and so detailed that you could see every hair on every head...down to the last flemament." It was a stretch, that one.

But Wayne smiled. "Ah...yes, the flemament...But I'm pretty sure that's something else. The flemament is the thing above us. Where the stars are. I read it in the Bible."

Amazing, how quick he'd come up with that. I didn't have but the one idea, and I couldn't help myself. Out it popped. "No, no. You mean the fundament." Good God. What on earth was wrong with me? Had I *really* just said *fundament* in front of the first boy who'd ever carried my books? Maybe he wouldn't know what it meant. But then the possibility that he wouldn't get the joke bothered me even more. "Because that's not the top, that's the bottom."

Wayne Scott threw his head back and bellowed his laughter into the schoolyard. He had the biggest laugh I'd ever heard.

> *Dear Edie*
>
> *Twice now I've gone for Co-Colas with Wayne Scott. (Yes, him.) He's only half as square as you'd think—but in a very nice way. And smart. I can tell he's trying to impress me, and I'll be honest: I'm doing the same. He doesn't really run with a crowd per se, mostly just the glee club and the chess club.*
>
> *He knows what friends you and I are. He says*  *I can't wait for you to meet him, and believe me, I have a thousand questions to ask about*
>
> *I even dragged him to one of Reverend Freeman's meetings, and he did just fine, listening and nodding his head a lot, which I think is a great start.*
>
> *In other news, the new chemistry teacher has turned out to be a perfect tyrant. We've all had a big test on Friday and everyone did poorly, even the top students. Let's hope by the time you're back he'll have settled down some.*
>
> *Don't worry.* ▆▆▆ ▆▆▆ ▆▆▆▆▆▆ *We can almost certainly save you* ▆▆ ▆▆ ▆▆ ▆▆ ▆▆ ▆▆▆▆▆▆. *I'm sure of it. More news on that soon, I hope. But don't worry, regardless.*
>
> *I have great hopes for you, Edie. We're going to have such wonderful times again. There's so much for us to do!*
>
> *Love, Luce*

12

EDIE

"We're going to need to talk about matching, Susannah." The social worker tapped his cigarette into a bean bag ashtray balanced on the arm of his chair. Mr. Henry was young and pale with black-framed glasses. He put the cigarette to his lips and watched me. It was our second appointment, and it was the second time he'd brought up the word. For weeks, he'd been inviting me to come see him, saying when I was ready to talk, his door was always open. I hadn't seen any reason to have to talk to him at all. He was the one in charge of adoptions.

"Susannah, *sweet*heart, I have high hopes for you." He offered me a Chesterfield and then held out the silver Zippo, which flared and closed with a bright snap, leaving only the sounds of our reedy inhalations, the long unthinking sigh of breath. He looked at the ceiling and exhaled. "You have to get past this stubborn streak, Susannah. It just defies reason." Then he said the same thing he'd said before, that I was almost an adult now, that I'd have to make some adult decisions. Did I realize my parents weren't going to let me bring a baby home? Adoption could be—*was*—the best solution. Didn't I want a clean slate? A chance to start again? And why did I think my parents had brought me to the Home in the first place? So I could have the baby and return to their house?

It was this last question that refused to go away. I had it too, of course, but I'd wrapped it up in a thousand layers of tissue and wasn't about to undo it now. I was here because Mama and Daddy had brought me here, that's why. I was here so that I could get ready to decide, that's why.

Mr. Henry exhaled long and slow and focused his distress on the ceiling. "Susannah, *sweet*heart. What manner of life would you be able to give your baby? Imagine, just imagine, what it'd be like to hear other children call your child, well…a bastard." He shot a glance at me, gauging my reaction.

But my mind had frozen up. I couldn't imagine a thing in the world except the sound of Mr. Henry's voice.

"Do you know, Susannah, how an unwed applies for state assistance? She has to go to court." Luce had said the same thing, had promised her father could help, her father who was supposed to be some big legal hero, and then, for no reason all that my-father-can-save-you-stuff was out the window. She'd gone completely silent about it. Now Mr. Henry pressed forward, waving his cigarette. "Think about it." I wondered if Mr. Henry had children. He wore a wedding ring. "Have you thought about where you would live?" he asked. "Do you *know* what poverty looks like?"

I didn't, of course. All I knew was the stories of victory gardens and sock-darning, or the little boys from *Oliver Twist* with their bedraggled clothes and red English cheeks. It was only fiction, obviously, but I figured there were people out there who lived in poverty, people who survived it. Look at my parents.

Mr. Henry took his glasses off and rubbed the two red spots they'd made on either side of his nose. "Sweetheart, what manner of life do you think you'd have? Sure, you have a pretty face, I'll admit it, but the kind of man who's going to be attracted to a woman with a child is not the kind of man you're going to want. Just between the two of us, Susannah, a man isn't—*can't* be expected to support another man's child. Think about it."

I'd already told Mr. Henry about Simon, but now he was pretending

I hadn't. "I will think about it, sir." The hands of the clock above his head wouldn't move, and there were still seventeen minutes left in the session, the smoke curling up and around the metal blades of the ceiling fan. Of course I knew exactly what Mr. Henry meant by matching. I could see all those thousands of wonderful couples with lovely homes who were wanting to adopt Lindy.

Mr. Henry said they weren't trying to gratify their own needs. They were people who wanted to *give* love.

But wasn't that what I was wanting too? The conversation felt slippery, like the ones with Dr. Maben, as if explanations that had once seemed firm were sliding away. Mr. Henry's words sounded sensible and noble, but I'd learned from Luce that there was sometimes a difference between the way a thing sounded and what it really and truly meant in facts, and if Luce were here she would have been able to tease out the difference, and now Mr. Henry was saying that true love was about putting someone else's needs before your own, that this was the very thing that distinguished adopting parents, because they were sacrificing their own needs for the sake of their new child. I couldn't make any sense of it, the way he made it sound like a duty. "But I thought they *wanted* the child."

Mr. Henry tapped his cigarette into the beanbag ashtray and sighed. "Susannah, need-satisfaction and love are not the same thing. Can't you see that?"

I pretended to be thinking but really and truly I found the difference too confusing. Luce would have known. But the letters from 92 Dixie Road were striped black with the laundry marker, or full of debate and current events and nothing to do with Luce herself.

Mr. Henry tamped out his cigarette and reached for another. "Can't you see how selfish it would be to keep this child when you have nothing to offer him? A mother with natural feeling would want to do what was best for her child."

I couldn't ever remember feeling so stupid, so unprepared. Dr. Maben had said rehabilitation was the first step, and I was willing to do whatever it took—except this one thing. And hadn't I told them that? But Mr. Henry kept right on pretending I hadn't, and what was worse, and what was even more mad, was that he kept insisting I had to make the choice myself, that it had to be my decision, kept saying it week after week, and then, when I told him what I wanted to do, he pretended that I hadn't.

Now Mr. Henry turned his unlit cigarette in his hand. "Look. No matter what plan you make for your baby, matching is important. That way, if you do change your mind, everything will be in place. Imagine how terrible it would be if there were no family to take him and we had to scramble around at the last minute. In your case there are special challenges because of the putative father's…background. You said he was studying for medical school?"

"Yes." I stared over Mr. Henry's shoulder at the spindly branches of the tree outside the window, and on the roofs of the low buildings behind it, and on the skinny arms of television antennae.

"And how tall, would you say, he was?"

"Over six feet."

"And what color was his hair?"

I answered the questions, every one of them, even though he made it sound as if Simon was dead.

When it came to meeting with my mother, we had to drive more than an hour out of town, just to be safe. She was afraid of running into the Methodists. Now she pinched the tip of each gloved finger and pulled the leather from her hand, then stacked the gloves on top of one another, telling the coat girl to please not store them in the pocket, that she would like a separate ticket for the gloves. They were black and matched the pillbox on her head. Father Timothy stepped around to help with the red cape, and then he helped me out of my coat. He was a baggy man with thinning hair and a chin like a "u" that had been traced right onto the flesh of his neck, and he wasn't wearing his collar. Maybe he was worried about the Methodists too.

After the waiter had taken our orders and collected the menus, Mama said, "Now, darling, I think you know this decision was already made on the night your father and I sat down with the Blooms." The sorrow that had once been in her face was gone, submerged now in something more gathered, more mustered.

Father Timothy seemed to understand Mama's resolve and was careful to step around it. He removed the cocktail pick from his martini. "Edith, you're very young." His voice was helpful. "You'll have more children." He popped the olive into his mouth and set the toothpick on the tablecloth. I rotated the fake wedding band Mrs. Bruns had handed me that morning, my finger going green from the metal. My pass was good until 4:00, three hours from now, three hours before I had to sign my name in the big brown logbook outside Mrs. Bruns' office.

Mama laid her hand over mine and struck a reasonable tone. "When you come home, darling, I'll help you redecorate your room. You've been wanting to do that for a long time. They have those marvelous embroidered bedspreads at Montaldo's and the price has come down some." Her hand felt cool and weightless. In Georgia, we hadn't owned the Buick and the air conditioner and the kidney-shaped coffee table. It was my mother who'd brought those items into being, drawn them out of thin air really, with nothing but her own effort and a few dollars. "And when you get your figure back you'll be old enough for a pencil skirt." She took a sip of her martini and gauged the effect of her words. "I think that's fair."

It was true that I'd once cared a great deal about having a pencil skirt, why, I couldn't remember, probably to look older for Simon. Surely that had been the reason.

Mama tried again. "And your father says you can look at colleges once you finish school. You know he wants your happiness more than anything in the world." I couldn't think about my father. He hadn't come today because he didn't want to see me like *that.* Instead he wrote me little notes. *Keep your chin up, kiddo! Can't wait till you come home!* Mama took a sip of her drink. "He thinks it would be a fine place to meet a boy."

I found my voice. "Mama, there aren't any boys I'm going to like better than Simon. I already know that." It was a relief to have at least one answer.

Mama unfolded her napkin, spread it smoothly in her lap. "Please don't change the subject, darling. We've discussed that part already, and it's decided." She avoided Father Timothy's gaze, but it was clear her speech was meant as much for him as for me. "For goodness' sakes, a marriage needs a year or two to stabilize. You can't just throw two people together with a baby and no job and no home and hope it all works out. You'd have your different churches and different families and no money to speak of. And an infant who was neither a Catholic nor a...Jewish."

"A Jew, Mama."

Mama tilted her head and gave me an exasperated look. "Edith."

"Neither a Catholic or a Jew. That's how you say it."

"That's just marvelous, Edith. Just marvelous." She smoothed the napkin again. "To be honest, I don't know what's come over you lately. You seem so...*disturbed*."

She looked to Father Timothy, who'd cut his pork chops into bite-sized cubes and set the knife down. He stilled his fork in midair. He glanced at the fork, set it down too. "My dear," he said. "We're all trying to help you. A child begotten in sin has to live his whole life as a reminder of that sin." He leaned toward me. "Think of this baby as ill-gotten gains, Edith, something you acquired unfairly. If you keep this child, you'll never be able to leave that sin behind. Never. You and the baby will carry it with you always." He picked up the fork again. "I'm not sure you can imagine what that will be like." Then the fork was at his lips and he was chewing.

Once, when I was a little girl, I'd confessed to taking my sister's favorite charm from her bracelet, a little sterling poodle I'd held in my fist three guilty nights because I didn't dare wear it. The priest had been Father Finney then, and he'd said the same thing Father Timothy was saying right now, that it wasn't fair to ask forgiveness without returning the thing I'd stolen.

Father Timothy impaled another piece of pork, swabbed it in apple-sauce, and pointed it in my direction. "But if you think of this child as a *gift*, if you *make* it a gift, then, well, you'll be showing God you want forgiveness."

Moments like these I couldn't understand my own muteness, like I was trapped in a block of ice. If Luce had been there, I might have known how to make my mind work again, might have been able to plan more than one step at a time. But she wasn't. "It's our *baby*," was the best I could do.

Father Timothy made a moist clicking noise with his lips that I rec-ognized as the same sound he made during confession.

My mother's voice cut in, hard now. "Don't think you are keeping this illegitimate baby, Edith. That's not what people do." The bones in her face became prominent, like metal.

I tried to keep my gaze steady. "It's what people who are married do."

A man at the next table turned to look at us. Mama lowered her voice but kept it firm and slow. "Don't make me the bad guy here, Edith. Think about your sisters. How do you think they'll feel when people stop inviting them out? It's time to start thinking about other people's needs for a change."

"What about hers?"

"Whose?" my mother asked.

"The baby's!"

Mama drew back, as if slapped, then placed a red-nailed index finger on top of my hand and waited for me to meet her eye. "You will not bring an illegitimate baby into my home, young lady. Other parents wouldn't have put up with these shenanigans for half as long as we have."

I dragged my gaze up. "Mrs. Bruns said the girls are the ones who have to decide."

Mama leaned across the table until her mouth was close enough that I could see the tiny red fissures of lipstick that bled up her skin. "You're still a minor, young lady, and your father and I have legal rights here. Your father and I forbid you to bring an illegitimate child into our home. There are certain…*actions* that can be taken."

Nowadays it occurs to me that my mother was the same age as Sally—no—younger, and Sally's words had stuck to me then and still do today. *They would let me go, you know. There'd be no bargaining with the college. There'd be no place for me to go.*

On this day I lowered my eyes. If I couldn't go home, and I couldn't go to Simon's home, what did that mean? The plate in front of me was thick white crockery: pork chops, a sprig of parsley, a pattern of apple-sauce and gravy. I tried not to think a single thing.

The next day Mr. Henry flashed me a smile and motioned me to sit. I'd never seen him so buoyant, his face awash in a happy silver light. "I found them," he grinned, elbows propped on the arms of the chair, hands steepled under his chin.

"Who?"

"The perfect family." The lenses of his glasses shone.

"What do you mean?" I knew exactly what he meant.

"Look." He tapped a manila folder. He paused. "Actually, I can't show you the file, Susannah." He blushed. "But listen. He has a secure job with a respected company. I can't tell you what it is of course, but let's just say it's a job with a grand future." His eyebrows shot up triumphantly. "And the *wife*—she's a model housewife. You should see what a beautiful home she's made, and all with her own two hands. And now she's just waiting for a baby so she can lavish her attentions on him. Or her. She already has the room done up and everything, in blue and pink because they want to have a boy and a girl. She sewed the curtains and the bassinet ruffle herself. They are both just thrilled. He's even putting a new swing set in the backyard, the kind with a miniature slide. I saw it myself." He slapped the manila folder. "And they live on a street with oodles of other young children."

Outside, it was spring. Rains had loosened the soil, the yard behind the Home a sea of mud. I'd stopped going out for fear of falling. The perfect parents, no doubt, no doubt they were, and no doubt Mr. Henry or someone like him had turned them thoroughly inside out, and maybe they did have more right to Lindy than I did. Already I hated them. "How do you know they'll want a baby that's half Jewish, Mr. Henry?"

"Because I *asked* them," he said triumphantly. "His parents are European."

European? What did that mean? English? French? *German?* "What country in Europe?"

Mr. Henry's face stilled, his mouth partway open.

"I want to know it's not Germany. Simon's father would hate that."

Mr. Henry blinked, several times, as if for once he was the one who couldn't think what to say. "Stop and think about it, Susannah. He might just be grateful."

SIMON

Simon was scared. Pre-meds were dropping like flies. The pro-
fessors didn't care. Did Not Care. If anything it was part of their crummy
mission. Separate the chaff from the wheat, the savvy from the weak. A
couple guys every month. Just gone. No goodbye, no nice knowing you,
just another empty desk in anatomy class. Simon worried that he'd be
one of them. Not because his GPA had fallen—the opposite actually.
For the first time he felt a responsibility to it, to getting into medical
school. Up to then it had stood in front of him like black dread. Edie'd
been right. He didn't want to do it. It had to do with orifices. Every
human being had nine or ten orifices, most of which he didn't want to
think about. He liked *people* fine, but what he liked was their *outsides*, the
way they looked and moved in the world, their expression, their *art*. He
didn't want to think about their insides.

But the world was changing. It was like that solarization technique
Man Ray used in his photos, for one. Every detail stood out in sharp
relief but the values of the objects, the weight and saturation, shifted.
The colors inverted, the sun black, the sky white, white, white.

Ever since the bomb at the Atlanta Temple, his Pop had been crumbling into pieces. His posture turned to shit, which was what it had
been from the get-go, but damned if he hadn't started folding himself
all the way up like a carpenter's rule. For the first time he wasn't telling
Simon what to do. He argued less and less. Forget about all the times his
father had burned him up. It broke him to see his father so shriveled, so
shattered. His mother trying to glue him back together with pots of tea.

It was a relief for all of them when Simon got the acceptance letter
from Chapel Hill. He'd finally done something right. For his parents.
For Edie. He slipped into both those roles like putting on a pair of shoes.
And, amazingly, they fit.

And Edie more gorgeous every time he saw her. She smelled the
same but different, all bread and honey and tears. Her eyes, when they
landed on him had not a shred of doubt in them. Like she could see their
path clear as a bell. Not once did she question him. Which was part of
the Man Ray photo because, yeah, he'd sure as hell questioned himself.
Oh boy did he. But the fact that she didn't meant he slid right into the

role of husband and father. Like taking care of her and Lindy was the most natural thing in the world, what he was supposed to be doing all along. And whatever he'd once thought about Edie's outsides—and he definitely still thought about them plenty—he couldn't stop thinking about her insides, and Lindy, cuddled up in there, her little knuckle in her mouth and her big old head between her knees like she was doing a bomb drill. He couldn't bear it, her huddled up in there, the thought that she'd one day have to face this smashed-up world. But he couldn't bear the opposite either: the thought of her waiting there, in bomb position, forever. Too afraid to lift her head to walk into the light.

Lindy had ten orifices too. Or would. Which was fine. Just fine. And fine for the rest of pulverized humanity. All those ears and noses and assholes. They'd been babies once too, their little toothless mouths sucking on their knobby wet knuckles, their bodies tucked up in bomb position, penitents waiting for the crash.

He'd once thought medical school was too much responsibility. Now he felt the opposite. Like it was medical school and Edie and his drowning father and hand-wringing mother and Lindy, rolled up in that same ball. Exactly the right amount. For the first time in his life he knew what to do.

The folks at Thelma's lunch counter seemed to know the deal. Like they were on their side. The owner of the place was this big Mexican guy who was always winking at him like they shared some big macho secret. It got pretty old after a while. But the waitress was all right. She didn't speak English too great, so she was always trying to act things out with big old gestures. Always making a giant hand swoop to show Edie's shape, which embarrassed them some.

Now he pushed the placemats and silverware aside and leaned across the table to grab Edie's hands. "I have good news." The words spilled from his mouth before Rufina even finished setting up his place. "My mother is changing her mind. Sort of. I think she's *relieved*, you know, that I got into Chapel Hill. That I'm actually going to go. You know how they are. They're always saying they want it to be my decision, but only if my decision is the same as theirs." Her eyes were gripping his, like she was afraid to hope. He squeezed her fingers. "Then, around two days later, she started going on about how my happiness was the most important thing to her, and then, get *this*. She said the darkroom and basement could be converted into a separate a*part*ment."

Edie froze, blinked. "How far is that from the university?"

"I mean, with the new interstate, maybe two hours." More, probably. He picked up her hands and kissed them.

"She even said she wouldn't mind doing some *baby*sitting. That you could go back to your job at Ivey's." He was leaning halfway across the table now.

"What did you say?"

"I told her I'd be home on the weekends. And she said she'd try to get my dad to come around."

"Oh." Edie's expression was wide with admiration. Like he was some kind of genius. "Do you think he will?"

His eyes landed on an empty table across the aisle.

"Maybe. I don't know. I don't want to push him. It feels...precarious. I'll know more in two weeks."

Edie nodded. "And what about your photos?" He'd dropped the job at Ivey's. Photography assistants were a dime a dozen. Less.

"I'll still have them. But as a hobby, see."

He could see the gears turning in her mind. Then she closed her eyes. Like she was trying not to cry. But she was smiling when she opened them.

Rufina brought the chicken and the French fries and a napkins dispenser for their greasy hands. He slipped off Isaac's ring and set it with his keys, picked up a drumstick. They ate, their wonderment running fast and far.

13

LUCE

The day everything turned was a Saturday in late April. Simon called me wanting to know if I'd meet him and Edie at that lunch counter. He told me that Edie was headed into her final month. He literally said that. As if I didn't know how to count to nine. As if I hadn't been looking all these months for legal ways the court could give her some independence. As if I hadn't just visited her in that horrible place.

Simon said he'd already arranged a time with Edie and did I want to surprise her with a little good luck party at a lunch counter near the mills, bring a little card, a few little gifts and such. Of course I said yes. Just—the whole thing felt odd. For one thing, it'd never occurred to me that she could leave the Home. Just pick up and *leave*.

I was also nervous about the bomb I'd delivered on my visit there. *What if your parents stop loving you? What if they don't take you back?* Worse, I'd had to confess my dad's failure, how humiliating it was going to be to win financial assistance. *My dad's not—he couldn't—what I mean is, it's going to be really hard to get any money from the state, Edie. And it's going to be public. They're going to ask you all manner of things. He'll help you, for free. It's just that—well, it doesn't always work.* Miss Ledbetter's nervous laughter still hee-hawed through my skull.

It occurred to me that Simon didn't know about my visit to the Home. Because: when would they have talked? If they had, he'd know she might not want me at their little party.

I found the lunch counter all right, an alley-shaped space with six little booths, the blue plate handwritten on a piece of cardboard in the window. Simon was at the back near the toilets, drinking a cup of coffee, a textbook as fat as a phone directory opened on the red and white oilcloth.

Turned out he'd brought a little cake in a cardboard box tied with a string, and it irritated me, you know, that I hadn't thought of that. I did bring a couple of gifts, and not baby gifts either. I didn't want to send that message. Hand lotion, warm slippers, stuff I thought she might like in the hospital. I hid the gifts on the booth bench beside me so Edie wouldn't see them right away. Simon asked me to put the cake there too, since there was plenty of room on my side, since I hadn't brought a satchel of books. And anyway, Edie wouldn't be sitting next to me.

And then the bell on the front door jingled, and there she was, big as a house. I'd been ready for the old woman version of her I'd seen in the Home. But for some reason she was better. Bigger, obviously, and more ungainly, but her skin shone and her eyes held their old laughter and her smile spread wide as the sea. She was happy. Or at least happier. Something had happened. And the effect on Simon—you can't imagine. It was like he physically changed, grew taller, more purposeful, so focused was he upon her every move. He stood to take her coat and push the table some in my direction so she'd have room.

A dark-haired waitress swooshed over, round as a wren, all smiles. "Hello there!" Her plastic name tag read Rufina, and she greeted me as if I were a long lost cousin. Then she turned that eager expression on Simon and Edie. "Hello there, my friends." As if they were old buddies. "Fried chicken?"

And they were—old buddies. Edie and Simon had been here before. *Loads* of times. Enough that Rufina knew their orders by heart. Two fried chicken plates, one with French fries, and one with green beans and okra. Sweet tea. And not once had I been invited. Not once. Not once had Simon dropped into a phone booth and said, hey Luce, we're meeting for fried chicken on Saturday and Edie would love to see you.

I remember feeling literally cold in that moment, my hands and feet like ice. Simon knew he was in the wrong because he hadn't mentioned it, hadn't said, "Hey, there's this little place that we like to go." Nope. He'd made it sound as if the idea had just occurred to him yesterday, like a thunderclap.

And yes, I noticed that he'd taken off his ring and set it atop his keys beside the salt and pepper shaker and the napkin dispenser. Of course I did. Just there, in the middle of the table between him and me. It was almost automatic, the strategizing. I couldn't help it, thinking how, if I reached for a napkin from the dispenser, and dragged the thing a certain distance from the keys and then reached for another napkin and pulled the thing under the rim of my plate I could use the plate to push it into my lap.

The problem is, once you've imagined doing a thing, once you've visualized it in your own head, you're almost always compelled to the enactment of it, the execution.

We ate our fried chicken and talked about the Home and about school. We pulled dozens of paper napkins from the metal dispenser. When Edie said she was nervous about having the baby, Simon and I made sure to talk about all the marvelous advances of modern medicine and how safe childbirth had become. I did all the right things. Ate my food and made nice talk and gave Edie her gifts and ate the little cake and told her she was going to do fine, just fine.

I felt the weight of the ring land in my lap. It would turn out to be so much heavier than that. But I didn't know that yet. At the time I figured I could do what I'd done so many times before. Wait for the discovery, for Simon to realize the thing was gone, then hold out through some of the search. After five, maybe ten minutes, insert the thing on the table somewhere, under a napkin, say. Someone would find it, and all would be well.

But that's not the way it works. You take possession of a thing, even temporarily, and you become beholden to it, for a moment or forever. *Aere perennius.* Lasting as bronze.

We finished the lunch, and the cake, and our little party, but Simon and Edie never stood up. Edie leaned toward me and said, "Oh Luce, what a treat it's been to see you again." And nobody stood to leave. Simon shook my hand like a man and said, "Thanks so much for coming," as if the place was his house, and still nobody stood to leave. Edie said, "You're the best friend a girl could have," and still nobody stood to leave. So I did. I stood to leave. And that was the last I saw of them together, sitting together on that red vinyl bench in that dumpy little restaurant, both of them watching and waving goodbye.

I felt the thing in my pocket, smug and heavy in the bottom-most seam. In that moment it still wasn't too late. It wasn't too late to draw it out and place it on the table in front of Edie and Simon and God and country. But Simon was looking at me as if he couldn't wait for me to leave and Edie too seemed to be bubbling from within, fit to burst with some exciting new possibility they couldn't bring themselves to share with me.

When I left Thelma's, I thought the ring was still in the pocket of my houndstooth.

I went back of course. Of course I did. Rufina didn't recognize me. Why would she? I wasn't Edie. Nor was I part of a beautiful young couple with an illicit problem. The waitress's face was frankly curious until I started looking under the table. Then her face creased in understanding. "El anillo. You are looking for the ring. Mr. Simon, he already search."

I knelt down on the floor then turned to Rufina's knees. "They looked under here?"

"Out there. On the floor." She swept her hand in the direction of the room. "And the mother, Miss Edie, she cry." Rufina traced her fingers down her face, like rain. My mouth felt dry as sand. I stuck my head under the table anyway, then just crawled right under. Rufina's voice congratulated me. "But you are more small!"

If you've never taken a good look under a restaurant booth, I don't recommend it. Here is what I found: several pieces of silverware, uncountable dirty napkins, many furry objects that appeared to be old food, and one dead mouse. Rufina fetched a broom and I reached it all the way back to the wall and dragged all that material into the aisle. Then the sifting: you don't want to know, Rufina's eyes wide with horror and I guess, embarrassment.

The vinyl booths weren't quite as bad. The seat rested in a plywood cradle that mostly had crumbs and change in it, a bonanza actually, more than three dollars' worth. I wrapped up the money in a paper napkin and set it on the tabletop. No ring.

I knew how it looked, what Edie would think, what in the end she would have told him. "You know she has this habit, this *problem*." Simon nodding his head in confusion, trying to understand, Edie making excuses. "It's her mom. It's her dad. She wasn't raised like you and me."

The thought of that conversation made my whole body weak.

14

EDIE

I dreamt of swimming pools, those kidney shaped ones they used to have, of floating in weightless calm, the water warm and thick against my body, the sky jagged and broken with lightning. There was no thunder, and that felt right, only the flashing of lightning like the breaking of dishes, which buzzed overhead and made the base of my spine sing electrically, and in the dream I'd forgotten I was pregnant, but now I saw that I wore a bikini two-piece bathing suit that allowed my belly to swoop forward and outward in a mango curve. In the dream I wasn't ashamed, and there was nothing in it but the expected and the mundane, my belly like a piece of fruit bobbing there along the surface of the ocean, the water warm and swirling about my legs and feet, rivulets tickling the backs of my knees.

But the sun went down, and the water chilled to a dank pool. The glare of late summer became shameful and damp. I began to sink.

A mass of sheets and blankets tangled around my legs, and the lake became my bed and then it became the narrow bed at the Home in the room I shared with a new girl, and there was water in the bed, an alarming amount of it, too much to have come from my body, and all of it pooling in the center of the concave mattress. Outside more water gurgled through the gutters, and rain patterned the windows.

And there again the buzzing, a kind of electricity pulling at the muscles of my lower back. I had two more weeks before *that*, and anyway Lee and Brenda were scheduled to go before me. My new roommate's face was pale as a moon, a filmy gossamer girl with slender hands and an accent that trailed like Spanish moss. Days she spent sitting on windowsills sucking at the filaments of her yellow hair, her chin sawing of its own accord, grinding and grinding, even as it did right now in her sleep. It would have been lovely to wake her, to ask for help with all the things that needed to be done alone in the dimness, to ask for help with the uncertainty, and the dark, and the fear of my own body, but the water in the bed mortified me and smelled so intimate I knew it had come from inside me, from my body. It was up to me to make it go away, or at the very least to hide it.

I peeled the clinging sheets from the bed, mopped up the rubber mattress too, and then piled them in a sodden mound on the floor. I spread the blankets over the naked bed and tucked them into hospital corners the way they'd instructed me on that first day, but there was no way to dry the sheets in the already damp air, so I pushed them under the bed with my foot. In the morning I'd ask Mrs. Wentzloff. I pulled my nightgown over my head and changed into the navy smock, lay down upon the made-up bed, eyes wide, and watched the moisture sliding down the windowpanes, and when the electric singing began, I held my breath and waited. Something was happening. Each time, the singing dissipated of its own accord, and many minutes passed before it came again. (How many?) I tried not to think. *Our father. Who art in heaven. Hallowed be thy name. Thy kingdom come. Thy will be done. On earth asitisinheaven.*

At some point a watery light smeared through the window, then sharpened, the objects in the room finding their outlines, and soon enough the wake-up bell rang, the clanging a message that I wasn't alone, that there were dozens of faces uncrumpling and turning wary as they roused themselves from sleep. Before my new roommate could ask me why I was dressed, I eased open the door and left.

So far everything was going just as Mrs. Wentzloff had said. Harold the janitor drove me the five blocks to Memorial, my back gripping up again during the ride. The morning drizzled blurry and grey, pairs of headlights floating up out of the fog, and Harold listening to Rosemary Clooney on the radio. *The evening breeze. Caressed the trees. Tenderly. The trembling trees. Embraced the breeze. Tenderly.* I didn't know anything. The water, yes, but the electricity in my back, not really. Or rather, I'd heard from the other girls, which was hardly the same as knowing at all. Did a girl have a right to ask about such things? Did married women? Every week the doctor who came to the Home assured me that everything was fine, just fine, that childbirth would of course be uncomfortable, but not to worry as every woman did it, and just to remember that when the contractions were ten minutes apart I was to leave for the hospital. Every woman did it.

No, it was the biology that scared me, the impossibility of it. There were English queens who'd died in childbirth.

The car slowed through the circular drive and stopped in front of Memorial's white portico, which for some reason they'd styled like cement waves in a cement ocean. Below it stood nurses in winged caps, cigarette smoke wafting into the air above them.

Harold left the engine running as he walked around the front of the car, as the radio sang to me alone. He opened the passenger door and handed me a towel to cover my head and hide my face. I got out, and he offered his arm and we walked right past the nurses to the glass doors, where the outlines of two snakes twined in perfect symmetry around a staff, each looking stunned to see his mirror image staring back. And then Harold was holding the door and patting my shoulder and saying good luck.

The foyer: giddy with fluorescent light. A nurse gave me one glance and pushed forward a sheaf of papers, and when I wrote my old name across the top of the form it felt like I was play-acting. In the labor room a fleshy lady draped a sheet across my belly while I tried not to stare at the red web of broken capillaries across her nose. Then the woman was shaving between my legs, beyond the tented dome of my belly, and inserting something there, something that made me want to go to the bathroom. She patted my shoulder. "Just a little catheter, dearie."

I'd heard the word before—in the place with the Hopalong Cassidy reruns. "Excuse me?"

"A catheter," she said. "You can ignore it." Her voice was kind enough, even apologetic. "And now I have to go. You'll be okay." She patted my hand and said gently, "Maybe it's a good time to think about how you got into all this, hmm? I wouldn't want to see you back here in a year."

I blinked. How did she know? Another nurse wheeled me into a corridor, and I shut my eyes against the brightness. Speakerless voices up and down the hall and somewhere a transistor radio playing a ballgame, or at least I thought it was a ballgame, the way the announcer's voice rushed high and thin into the air and hung there a slow moment at its peak, then sank right quick back down to the ground. Beyond that was the sound of closed-door screaming, and I tried not to think about the talk of unweds not getting anesthesia, how the doctors tried to make the labor as rough as possible so the girls would learn a lesson. Dr. Naples said the girls from the Home were treated very well at Memorial, and of course they got anesthesia, of course they did. *Our-father-who-art-in-heaven hallowedbethyname, thy-kingdom-come-thy-willbedone on-earth, asitisinheaven.*

Who was it?

And then I was in another corridor, and moans hung in the air, distantly and femalely, somewhere behind me in hidden chambers connected by snaking corridors, white and undecorated like the one I was in, corridors leading down to the labyrinthine chambers of childhood.

That one's from the Home.

How long?

Don't pay any attention.

She got herself into it, she can get herself out.

And then I was moving, wheeling along, and it didn't matter where I was going because everyone in the hospital knew about me and was making decisions for me and I wasn't but a small part of a story with an ending that had already happened. Later I had a chance to see the actual card: a five by seven index with my name across the top and the letters "O/W" written with magic marker. Out of wedlock. Below the abbreviation were the words *tractable, sometimes irrational, stubborn, secretive, high-strung, some hysteria and paranoia. Baby to be adopted. DNS.* Do not show.

A heavyset nurse covered my legs with sterile stockings and adjusted a pair of metal supports like bicycle pedals hanging in the air beyond my feet, then strapped my right foot to the right pedal. I instinctively brought my left leg closed. She fumbled with the strap, releasing her breath in annoyance. "For the love of Pete, now is a little late for modesty, don't you think?"

"Sorry, I'm not….Sorry."

There were rails on either side, like the bed I'd slept in as a little girl, and I floated above myself. I floated. They told me it was twilight sleep, and I thought again of Bluebeard and the corridors and the maze of walls that funneled and funneled until there was no place to go but through the smallest crack, the narrowness of the passages sending angry gripping waves though my body, which disappeared as quickly as they'd come, and I fell asleep and was wakened again by the next wave.

"C'mon now, girl, you're going to have to do better than that," a voice somewhere was saying. Was the woman talking to me?

Then I was back in the closet under the stairs with the sea of girls from the Home. They were all speaking at once.

I can't do it on my own.

Who would ever want to look at me again?

They've threatened to take Hank to jail if I don't do what they want.

They can put you in the loony bin, you know.

There was so much light, so many people in white uniforms and white masks moving in and out of the room, even the scared face of a candy striper wheeling a metal cart, and I thought it was silly that she should be scared when it was me who was here in this bright scientific space with the glare of exposure, strapped to the lab table like the frog Ned Babbitt and I had dissected in ninth grade biology. There had been eggs in the frog, nestled among the organs, and now my own organs were lying open to a team of nurses and doctors, here the heart, here the intestines, here the gills, here Simon's missing ring. Right here. Everyone was yelling.

Someone had set up a screen across the bed just below the level of my chin, white muslin stretched across a steel frame, and I couldn't see past, could only hear the voices and the hubbub on the other side, below my waist, in someone else's room. I gripped the side rails, and the coldness of the metal stabilized me, but my arms slipped down and away because they were so very heavy and so very long.

Sally said, "Where in the world would I go? I'd lose my job, lose my pension."

Lee said, "What I want doesn't matter."

"I can't do it."

"I don't want my child to look at me with disgust."

Someone slapped me. A nurse's voice: "For Heaven's sakes, girl! Get a grip on yourself." I didn't recognize the lady's eyes. It wasn't the one who'd called me "dearie" or the fleshy one who'd said this was no time for modesty or the scared candy striper.

And then there was the red raw sound of a baby, crying, but I couldn't see so I tried to move the screen from my face but found that my arms were strapped to the side rails, and I felt again what I'd felt in my dreams, the crush and press of close-in walls. I couldn't get to Lindy. I couldn't get there. Someone was telling me to calm down. Another voice: "Hold on, we've got a hysterical." Then someone slapped me and a brief slice of silence followed.

"It's a girl," one of the white-masked men said. "And she's got ten fingers and ten toes." He sounded so proud. Then he seemed to remember. "If it matters to you."

A nurse injected something in my arm and a man busied himself with something between my legs.

I sank.

I awoke elated. I'd given birth to a baby girl. With ten fingers and ten toes.

When I woke again, a nurse was holding up my forearm, rubbing the skin with a gauze pad that smelled of alcohol. The nurse—it was the red-faced one—reached for a syringe.

"What's that?" I asked.

The nurse held the syringe up to the light and squinted at it. "It dries up the milk."

The milk. The *milk*. I jerked my arm away.

She held the syringe in the air and looked me in the face. She shrugged. "Suit yourself. But it's not going to be pleasant."

There was policy. The nurses didn't bring babies to unweds. It would be easier on us. If we didn't see them or name them, we were less liable to miss them. Besides, what a waste to throw away a name you liked. The new parents were going to change it anyway.

And yet. It wasn't so difficult.

After two days I was going to the lavatory without help, and there were signs everywhere, and it wasn't so difficult to keep walking as if I knew where I was going, as if I'd followed the signs to the nursery a dozen times already. Behind the glass, some of the babies slept and some of them cried. I counted them. There were sixteen. I watched for a long time, until I felt a hand on my elbow and turned to see a girl in a red and white pin-striped jumper, but not the same candy striper who'd been so frightened during my delivery. This girl was my age, and fresh and blond enough to be a Myers Park student. "Can I bring you your baby?" she asked.

My answer came out in a rush. "Yes, please. It's Carrigan."

She nodded and her hair bobbed.

I had done it, exactly like Luce. That's how she got away with all her little escapades, pretending she was doing exactly what she was supposed to, pretending she didn't have a worry in her head. I took a deep breath, straightened, and stood the way my mother did. Moments later the candy striper returned with a white knobbly bundle, and the bundle was alive, and the bundle belonged to me, Edie Carrigan. I held out my hands.

Then I was lifting her, holding her, recognizing even there the ruddy face from somewhere out of sleepless nights and shapeless dreams: the bowed lips, the faintly outlined widow's peak pointing straight to the nub nose, the lashes and brows fine as spider silk, the hair on her head downy against her reddened skull, her skin so thin I could see the tender blue veins beneath, like a teacup my mother had held to the window to show how the light shone right through, and how you only got that effect with china that was fine bone.

The light shone right through. Lindy's skin was transparent—*so* transparent, the kind of pale that didn't come from my family or from Simon's. I stroked the downy scalp, the hair so blond, as fair as a Georgia peach. Viking blond.

I frowned at the candy-striper. "Are you sure, absolutely sure, that this is the Carrigan chart?"

She started. "I think so…" She glanced around. "Let me check."

Something pulsed in my throat. Lindy's hair was too-bright sunlight, that white afternoon in Atlanta, the shine of quartz and mica in the soil, Nash's gaping grave, and later, Aster's despair like a vortex that sucked me in, the vague outline of a shame too great to unveil.

The girl returned all flustered and apologetic. She hadn't known, she said, and she was *so* sorry about the mistake because the chart was stamped *OW*, and she hadn't realized the baby was OW, and she wasn't supposed to bring her at all. She held out her arms. Without thinking, I positioned my shoulder between Lindy and the girl.

She stammered. "I'm just, it's just, I'm supposed to—it's not good for you, you know. It makes it harder, I swear… Everyone says that." She didn't seem to believe her own words. Then she was pleading. "Please. You don't understand." She held out her hands, the color of fear in her face. "Think of the trouble I'll get in." She looked around for help.

I didn't think. The bargaining came straight out on its own, in one long rush. "I won't tell a soul, I'll just take her to the chapel, and you can pick her up in ten minutes." I'd already become sly.

The candy-striper took a long look down the hall, then agreed, and right away I wished I'd said twenty minutes or even thirty.

The chapel was empty, and I slipped into the last pew and scooted toward the corner, the six pews and the stained glass so plain the room might as well have been an office, all frank afternoon light and naked cross, no Jesus and no Mary. I'd assumed Lindy would be Simon's, if for no other reason than sheer odds. I didn't even count Aster. That night hadn't been intimate, but rather something too terrible to think about. The crazy part was that my mother's idea had been right. She'd wanted me to get away from Simon because there were other boys out there, other fish in the sea, but I remembered it too late and that night when Aster parked his father's station wagon in the high school lot I thought it was because he was wanting to talk, his eyes and his face full to the brim. But there was nothing coming out, no tears, no nothing, so that when he cut the ignition key from idle to off and the rumble of the big engine turned to silence, I was really and truly relieved, so that I'd been the one to open my arms to *him*, so that I hadn't been afraid when he pressed his face into my hair with a violent choking cough, and I hadn't been worried to feel the long intake of breath after each racking fit, and I hadn't been aware at what point the breaths became something else.

Even now I can't explain it, except that so much of my life had been a preparation for the advances of men and boys, from the day I'd hit puberty to that long-ago morning in the Ivey's office when I'd watched Simon watch me and had seen his desire unmask itself plain as day. So many years I'd been putting up defenses, so many years I'd spent managing other people's desires, every day girding my body and my wits, and if I'm honest I'd say that boys' desires had become a thing I'd learned to channel and to use to my advantage. But in that moment in the car I hadn't been ready because it hadn't ever crossed my mind that a boy could be overcome by grief and lechery all at the same time, that an embrace could turn into a clutch, and anguish into lust. I wasn't prepared.

I said, Aster, *don't*. Please *don't*. But it was the only thing I said. Every other thought froze before my voice could say it. And his hands were so fast, like darting birds. I pushed them away, one at a time. But they always came flocking back, and his mouth was the mouth of a baby bird's, clutching and gaping and gasping for air, for me, so that when he kissed me and then began grabbing at my clothes and pushing up my dress, I felt only a kind of astonishment because he'd never done any such thing when we were dating, and now here he was starving, and I knew I had every right to say no to him, was in fact *supposed* to say no to him, but saying the word would have required some kind of fortification, would have required finding some pocket of self-righteousness, and if I'd been able to find that anger I could have pushed him away, along with his gasping needs, and all his baby-bird hands. But I couldn't find it, that anger. He was starving for some morsel, and he'd found me, and I'd even been oddly flattered that he mistook me for something so useful. To shake him loose wouldn't have been so all-fired difficult, to shake him off and watch him flop about like a fallen nestling, but I hadn't been ready. I hadn't been fortified.

When I was dating Simon I'd lain awake worrying about whether to go to bed with him or not, as if everything had hinged upon that one decision. But the night between me and Aster hadn't even been passionate, hadn't breathed of a future, had simply been something awful that had happened. Lindy existed because I'd been unable to utter that simple syllable. No.

And when I'd returned from Atlanta, the night in the car didn't seem to matter as much, not particularly. In three weeks, Aster was in an institution, and as far as I knew that's where he was still, along with all my outrage and disbelief.

But now it mattered. I'd heard it too many times from Mr. Henry, from every one of them. No man was going to marry a woman with another man's child. A man wouldn't, couldn't be expected to care for another man's child.

Beneath my feet: empty space.

SIMON

No way around it, Simon was the only guy on the hospital ward. Girls and women stared. Followed him with their eyes. Accused him without speaking. Why are you here? Tell me where my Jim is. I know you know. He kept his eyes to himself and slogged through all that resentment. Cold mud.

Four fifteen and Edie's door hung ajar. He just stood there. Hesitating. What he feared, he couldn't say. Or wouldn't. He knocked and she answered, and there she was: bolt upright in the bed. "Hullo, gorgeous." She barely turned her head toward him. Didn't say anything. Didn't *do* anything. Like she was trapped in the middle of all that mud. He went to kiss her but stopped.

He pulled a chair to the side of the bed—so loud. She sure as hell was focused on that lunch tray, boy, moving that spaghetti from one compartment to the other like her life depended on it. He sat, reached for her hand. She closed her eyes. Like she was exhausted. Maybe she was. Of course she was. God knows how much medication they'd given her. He sat. They sat. He stroked her hand and watched her. She didn't open her eyes. Finally she said, "My mother wanted me to be around other boys, Simon."

What was that supposed to mean?

"My mother wanted me to see my old friends. Other boys. Including Aster."

She couldn't be dumping him. Not now. She pushed the tray to the side and swung her legs out of the bed, the white smock baggy against her belly. He tried not to stare, but she reached for a bathrobe anyway, closed her eyes again as she tied it around her waist. He'd never seen her like this. So changed. Jesus. Of course she was changed. She *was* dumping him. Forget about their parents: she was going to leave him this time for real. Because her parents had convinced her to find someone else. Maybe *marry* someone else. Christ. She finished tying the robe and slid her feet into a pair of slippers. Took his hand in hers but not in any kind of way he wanted and led him from the room and down the hall to a windowed room. A woman in a peaked cap moved among the infants. Edie pointed to a flax-colored girl with see-through eyes, the reddest baby there. The fairest of them all. A towhead.

It didn't mean that much. Recessive genes, that's all. Unless. What was she trying to tell him?

My mother wanted me to see other boys. Atlanta. Eriksen. Aster Eriksen. It couldn't be.

Mirror, mirror, on the wall, who's the fairest of them all?

Lindy was. Their Lindy.

Edie's Lindy.

Aster's Lindy.

Jesus.

15

EDIE

It had been four months since I'd seen Daddy, and now here he was with this big ear-wide grin. "You look as pretty as a picture." He loaded my suitcase into the trunk of the Buick, and I got into the back. It was automatic. The car smelled like French fries and cigarette smoke, and maybe it had always smelled that way and I'd just never noticed it before.

Mama seemed lighter, happier, or maybe the word was relieved. She kept turning around in her seat and saying things like, "Your color is coming back," and "You'll be wearing your old clothes in no time," but pretty quick we all ran out of things to say and she started listing my sisters' activities, that and the fact that Mosley had died. The city blocks slid past. All I could think about was Lindy behind the glass, the nurses and candy stripers feeding her from a bottle. They were all of them wholesome, professional women, not the type to let their old beaus push up their skirts on the bench seats of their fathers' station wagons, not the type who didn't know how to say no.

At some point I realized the stores and the restaurants weren't going away. There were just more and more offices, businesses, little city parks. We stopped at a light, and when the red sign of the Big Boy towered over us, I knew we weren't going home but instead past Covenant Presbyterian and the YMCA, Daddy cutting the car north toward the skyscrapers and passing the Hotel Charlotte with its whipped-cream façade. The car drew up to a white-wedding-cake of a building. He parked. Mama donned a pair of sunglasses, a scarf, handed me the same, and we all three walked toward those tiered marble stairs, where, waiting on the steps with his hands in his pockets and a briefcase beside him was you-know-who from that other place, black plastic glasses and all. Without stopping for introductions, Mr. Henry turned up the stairs and we followed him up and into the city courthouse.

Soon I was in a plain room with a lady in a navy suit, and the lady introduced me to a couple seated on a bench near the door and said they would be my witnesses. Then she told me to sit and said that Mr. Henry and my parents had to stay outside because it was the law and it was the only way for the state to guarantee that a girl's signature wasn't coerced.

The lady asked if I understood why I was there.

I nodded.

The lady gave me a stack of papers but told me not to sign anything yet, and I read the sentences and they made sounds in my head because the words contained consonants and vowels but they never did make a meaning, and after a few minutes the lady in the navy suit asked, had I read the documents?

I nodded again.

The lady said it was her job to read certain sections aloud and that I should listen and it was permanent and did I understand that the said child was a ward of the state and that there was to be no contact with the said child from this point forward. The words were rhythmic and evenly spaced, like stitches, row upon row. *Knit two together three times, bring the woolen forward. Slip one, knit one, bring the woolen forward.* There would be no parental rights, and that was without reservation, and there would be no contact. *Knit one, slip one, knit two together. Bring the woolen forward.*

Later, I'd remember the pages in front of me and the heft of the pen in my hand, its black smoothness, the relief of having something to do, and the words on the page blurring to black and white markings, a series of knitted curves and lines and shapes punctuated by blanks that sometimes made a pattern that was dense and sometimes made a pattern that was airy and light, then my own looping script swimming and flailing across the page, out of control. "I, (your name), legal mother of (child's name), a male/female born in (name of city and state) on (date), do hereby abandon and neglect my child, (child's name), without reservation, to the state. I surrender all parental rights to the said child and do permanently relinquish and transfer the same to the court of (city and state), of which said child shall be a ward...."

Knit one, slip one, knit four together. Bring the woolen forward.

"Do you affirm that you are making this decision independently, without the influence of outside forces or persons?"

Knit two together four times.

And now please sign the blank spaces.

Knit seven.

I signed.

Just there and there, if you don't mind.

Bring the woolen forward.

The lady in the navy suit pulled the pages toward her. "You did just fine, Edith. Your daughter will be placed as soon as she finishes the study home."

Those were the words that didn't fit. They sounded distorted, as if I were looking at them from below the surface of a hole where I were being buried. I looked up. "Study home?"

"She'll have to do foster care for thirty days." The lady lifted the page and studied my signature.

"Thirty days?"

"All of them do. Just to make sure there're no problems. A formality really."

"What do you mean, problems?" I heard the sound of something hit the floor. I looked at my feet and saw that it was the pen I'd been holding

The lady stopped reading and looked at me square. "You know, physical defects: blindness, deafness, retardation. It's very rare, mind you, but such things do make a child difficult to adopt out." Her eyes were large and brown and crinkly, tender blue shadows beneath them, like kindness, or bruises.

"And then what happens? If she's…difficult to adopt out?"

"Well, we don't make hasty decisions." Her voice was slow. "We might hold them up to a year perhaps, and if it's determined that there's some sort of a defect, then they would be considered unadoptable. But it's very rare. Or we might do a trial period, and then, if abnormalities develop, or if things don't work out, the new parents can return the child to the agency's care. But we would prefer to avoid that sort of thing. That's why we have the study home." She spoke very gently and didn't take her eyes from mine.

"And then what? If they return the child?"

"There are institutions for that sort of thing. I think you already know that, Edith." She covered my hand with hers. "But you wouldn't have to trouble yourself with that."

"Are you saying I might never know?"

"Well." The lady tilted her head and studied me. "Yes. It would be out of your hands."

Out of my hands. Out. And I saw them, my hands, empty, reaching for Lindy who was trapped in a cage and wearing a uniform. My fingers curled around the bars and tried to get in.

I pulled at the corner of the sheaf. I wasn't at all sure it would move, but it did.

The lady watched my face and lifted her own ringed hand. One inch.

I tugged.

She looked down at the papers and our two hands.

I tugged, and the pages came to me. I glanced again at the woman's sad and crinkled brown eyes, folded up the packet into a tiny square, and thrust it into my pocketbook.

My parents waited on a bench in the wood-paneled hallway, Daddy with his hat in his lap and Mama with her hands on the clasp of her pocketbook. "That's it, then." My father said hopefully, uncertainty undertowing his words.

"Well," my mother said, "I hope you're feeling better."

I didn't know if I was feeling better or worse, but I was pretty sure I wasn't feeling what she supposed. When Mr. Henry came down the hall I focused my eyes on the wall above Mama's head.

Mr. Henry sighed, took off his black glasses, and rubbed the two spots at the bridge of his nose. "I'm afraid we have a problem," he said.

My mother was a statue.

Mr. Henry inhaled sharply, then pushed all that air right back out in a little huff. "Look, here's what the law states. Every minor, including Susannah, has the right to make a decision about her child."

Mama rested the heel of her hand on her collarbone and the tips of her fingers on her cheek, then slowly curled the nails down her jaw and into the palm of her hand. She said, "Unless she is deemed unfit."

Mr. Henry seemed very tired. "I'm talking about right now—today. It's illegal for a minor to live on her own. Any court proceedings will take thirty days at the least.

Daddy looked hurt and surprised. "What about the Home?"

"No can do," said Mr. Henry. "There's policy. A baby poisons the atmosphere." Mr. Henry shook his head when he spoke. "It might have to be foster care. At least for the next five months, until she's eighteen."

Again. Foster care. I closed my eyes and waited for the adults to decide what to do.

In the end, the Home did take me back, for the time being. Mrs. Bruns told me they had a good deal invested in me and there'd be a lawyer to see me in a couple of days, and Mrs. Wentzloff said I needed more time for thinking. In the meantime I'd have a room on the staff wing, on the third floor above the dayroom. I wasn't to leave the hall and I wasn't to mix with the other girls as my very presence would spark wild ideas, not to mention the baby's. I'd have to take my meals in my room.

Mrs. Wentzloff gave me a kiss on the cheek and whispered, "Do not worry. You will see, Susannah." She shut the door, her last words nudging themselves into the small apartment and settling there. Then the latch clicked shut.

I held Lindy at my chest and eased into the rocking chair, Lindy melting against me, her reddened eyelids sinking to a close, body pliant and little hand slack, her mouth a hot wet spot on my blouse. For an hour she slept like that, with abandon, hair wisping up all milkweed and spider-silk on the red and blue throb of her skull, her smell like Christmas and warm baked bread.

From below the floor, a television commercial jingled, followed by the familiar sound of nervous giggling, then Mrs. Bruns's voice, and then, a few moments later, real laughter, the undertow resigned and bitter.

16

The fold-up kitchen featured a hot plate and sink, a window painted so many times it couldn't really close, and a closed door with a skeleton key hanging in the lock. Of course I tried to turn it, but the little mechanism was too old and Lindy too fragile in my arms for me to get any purchase. It was a closet maybe, like the dream closet under the stairs, and if I opened it a sea of girls with missing names would try to explain themselves, or it might be I'd find the corridors from nightmares, the ones that leaned in and closed up, channels narrowing like funnels.

Finally Lindy fell into a cranky sleep and I tried again, but the key still didn't want to turn—until it did—and then the door unstuck from the jamb with a loud crack. Dust motes, the smell of old camphor, spider webs stringing from above. A dirty light suffused the window side of the room: stacks of boxes, opaque dust, the dark shapes of prams and bassinets. Right away I knew what it was: the missing history. And here it all was, the old days, the laundry baskets stacked with nubby cotton diapers. Here they were, pale blankets transparent with age. Here they were, old-fashioned rocking cradles and wooden rattles polished smooth by many hands and baby cups in red and blue enamel and white gowns with tiny rosebud prints, rag dolls, mothy woolen booties with yarn-yellow tassels that tied to little feet, christening dresses with frail yellowed lace, chipped diaper pails with matching lids. Touching any of it raised up dust.

In the old days the men did not want them. They were ruined, bless their hearts.

But I didn't feel ruined. Or unfit. I wasn't unfit until the lawyer came to tell me so, and if I waited here at the Home, that was exactly what was going to happen.

Besides. It wasn't a prison. There were no bars on the doors. I could at least try. Look at Luce. She would've walked right out without a backward glance. She got away with nicking pens and glasses all the time.

There was considerable cleaning. I chose a carriage big enough for a two-year-old, removed the rotted mattress and lined the steel with short stacks of diapers and blankets, gowns stuffed into corners to even out the surface, and on top of that folded my two shirtwaist dresses and the suit and white gloves I'd worn to the courthouse. The shoes I swaddled in clothes and fitted into corners. I'd wear my flats.

It would have to be at lunchtime. The day after tomorrow was a Thursday, so the front gate would be unlocked for admission interviews. I figured I could walk out the door head up and bold as you please, as if it were the most natural thing in the world, the same way Luce got away with anything and everything. They wouldn't know me on the street. I could be anyone, the baby carriage my disguise. Girls from the Home didn't have such. Girls from the Home didn't have babies.

When the Thursday dinner bell sounded, I made myself count seven minutes on the clock. Then I pushed the pram along the hall to the head of the curved front stair, then carried Lindy down, laying her on a blanket in the foyer. I started the descent with the pram, which turned out to be heavy, the wheels thumping against that first step, the thump echoing through the open space, and I waited, afraid to move, my body tilted up the staircase to balance the weight. The pram pulled me toward the door, and I let it, then took the rest of the stairs one at a time, *ka-thunk, ka-thunk, ka-thunk.* Halfway down I could see the door, and through the window, a patch of green. *Ka-thunk, ka-thunk, ka-thunk.* At the bottom, I scooped up my restless girl and she wrinkled up her face as if to cry, but I held her close and jiggled, which was a thing I'd already gotten good at, and by the time I laid her in the pram she was sleeping again.

Then we wheeled straight past the hydrangeas and the rose bushes and down the walkway and into the confident May light, the walkway long and straight from the porch to the gate. I figured if I could make it to the gate, the path would drop below the horizon line and we'd be out of sight from the first floor rooms. If I made it there, to the gate, I was free. The carriage was heavy, and the rusted steel wheels wanted to catch as they rolled, but I kept pushing, and Lindy did not cry. We reached the iron gate without hearing a shout.

Except. The gate opened inward. I'd forgotten about that. I'd have to hold it open while pushing the carriage through, and then there were ten steps through the stone retaining wall and down to the sidewalk, and if I couldn't hold the carriage it would roll right down into the street. But, there, on the filigreed bench sat two colored ladies, and I could feel them watching me without watching me.

"Good afternoon, ladies," I called, cheery as I could. "Would you-all mind helping me with my carriage? I always have such a time with these steps." Lie, lie, lie.

I can tell you this. If they'd looked like my mother, I wouldn't have had the nerve to say a thing. But in those days a lot of us felt we didn't have to behave in front of colored people, as if all such women could have been Dolores who came once a week to help Mama clean, as if somehow they were all interchangeable, as if they owed us something. And I'll tell you this too: I wouldn't ever have thought about it if Luce hadn't come into my life with all her protests and marches and speeches and high-falutin ideas. But because of Luce I did. Think about it.

But I asked those ladies anyway. The two of them glanced at each other but stood. I held the gate and the handle of the pram, and one of the ladies held up the front of the pram, even though she gasped at the weight and neither one looked me in the eye. The slow warmth of deceit spread up my neck and through my face, and Dolores or no, I wondered if I should offer them money but then figured that would make it ten times worse. I thanked them instead and tried not to think what Luce would say, or if they'd tell Mrs. Bruns what they'd seen, or if they could they get in trouble for helping me out. Their bus was nowhere in sight.

The carriage had a bounce. When I pressed the Bakelite push-handle, the thing leapt right back up, and Lindy looked up from it like a tiny bonneted ghost against the stuffed white sheets, and I'm sorry to say I forgot about the ladies and their bus and even heard myself laugh. I remember feeling strangely powerful because there were loads of girls married with children who were barely older than me, and I was just another young mother and child out for a walk.

I'd double-checked the mad money in the lining of my pocketbook, plenty enough for the taxi, double-checked the address, 92 Dixie Road. Still. I figured I'd better give her a call. She'd never really wanted me to see where she lived, and I was pretty sure I knew why. Her father didn't live there anymore, and the neighborhood had turned colored, and they didn't belong to the Club, and Luce's mother wasn't anything like my mother or at least that's what I'd come to think. But none of that mattered to me one bit, not one bit, and in case you're wondering I knew Luce had not taken that ring. She would never do that, it wasn't the sort of thing she took, and even if she had she certainly wouldn't have kept it, and I never did mention her habit to Simon. I knew what I knew.

I stopped at the first pay phone. The carriage had a little brake lever and it still seemed to work, but Lindy woke right up and it wasn't until much later that I realized it was the motion, or lack of motion, that did it. Her eyes popped right open, and when I tried to step into the booth, she burst into an ear-splitting wail. I had to open the door and prop it with the handle of the carriage, Lindy's little face following my every move. The moment I broke eye contact to fit the dime into the slot she started right up again and, would you believe it, as soon as I locked eyes with her quieted right down.

I can't even tell you how that made me feel. We had only been a few days together, or at least, together out in the world.

The phone was ringing. It might sound ridiculous, but I did worry that the school secretary would recognize my voice. I even held my nose, and Lindy seemed to smile to see it. "Hello, Mrs. Braithwaite, this is Mrs. Waddell. I'm afraid we have a bit of a family emergency." A true statement, at least. "Could you bring Lucille Waddell to the telephone?"

"Are you coming to pick her up?" Mrs. Braithwaite asked.

I panicked. "No, no. Just. I need to give her an important message."

Mrs. Braithwaite sounded annoyed. "School lets out in an hour, you know."

I didn't know what to say to that.

"But I'll let her know now."

Ten minutes later she reported that Lucille Waddell was not in class, that no one, it seemed, could say exactly where she was. My mind skipped to the first thing I could think of. "Her father may have picked her up already." Good Lord was I a liar.

Maybe Luce was already at home, or at the courthouse maybe, maybe even with that boy Wayne, though I was pretty sure he was too straight-arrow to be swanning around town during school hours. But no matter. I told myself Luce's mother wouldn't be the kind to call my parents. I let myself believe it because that was what I wanted to believe. I had to.

And if she was, if she did, then she did. My parents would take me home and I'd spend the night in my own bed, and my father and mother would fall in love with Lindy's tiny trusting face, her pale peaked hair, transparent skin, the fingers that wrapped around your own.

Or, they would take me back to the Home.

An enormous white oak guarded the bungalow, the roots plowing up the lawn and the sweep of the great arms shielding the place from the street. Cats melting into the bushes when the taxi pulled up. I set Lindy in the carriage and wheeled it up the walk. The porch was covered with towers of stuff—newspapers, *National Geographics*, and hundreds and hundreds of books, many of them blossomed in green mold. Vivid mildew painted the risers of the stairs, and for some reason the front windows had been boarded up, as if in preparation for some great storm. I didn't think I could get the pram up the steps by myself so I left it in the shade of the tree and lifted Lindy out. There were two doors, one labeled "Diamond" and the other not labeled at all. I peered through the screen. The house was dark, no sound but the dribble and murmur of daytime TV.

Luce might be home by now, or her brother Martin, and even if they weren't, I wasn't some kind of prowler. I was a friend. I rubbed my thumb against the fake wedding band and conjured up my fake confident self. "Hello? Is there anyone here?" I sensed that there was. The house was live and biding, bursts of pretend laughter spattering the afternoon quiet. Lindy must have sensed something too because she stopped complaining, her face warm and waiting against my neck. I could hear the sound of Art Linkletter's tin-can voice.

"Hello? Is anyone home?"

No answer. Maybe I should wait. But that would seem peculiar.

A fan in the foyer whap-whap-whapped, and currents of air moved through the house, and with them the smell of cigarettes, and beneath that the smell of cats, and beneath that the sweetness of mildew. I passed a parlor stacked with boxes and furniture that looked to be from a boy's bedroom, Martin's I guessed. More TV laughter. The windows in the parlor were boarded up too, and a television glowed in front of them, and a La-Z-Boy reclined in front of that, and in it, a person.

It was a woman in a faded yellow duster and a single black leather slipper, her feet splayed out in front of her, one nylon stocking bunched below her knee to reveal the mottled blue of her flesh. Everything about her suggested she'd given up, straight hair wisping against her small skull, unmade face sagging like pudding, hand stretching away palm up, as if she'd been holding something when suddenly overcome by sleep. Inches away an ashtray bristled with butts and on the floor next to the chair shone a golden brown bottle. The woman was snoring, her mouth open, a silver eyetooth winking in the dim light. Two flies buzzed around her, one of them settling at the corner of her open lip.

I froze. At any moment she'd open her eyes, like Boris Karloff in *Frankenstein*, and there I'd be, a stranger, a peeping Tom, caught out.

And now Lindy was anxious too, and started to whine. I jiggled her and tried to move across the room as weightless as I could, but the floor beneath me creaked and the show on the television ended and was followed by a bright ad for Sunbeam bread. As loud as could be. Five more feet.

I opened the screen door and eased it shut behind me, the outside light brassier than before, the porch dustier, the glider more rickety. But Luce would be home soon, and she could wake her mother and talk to her in private, give her some time to put herself together.

I walked circles around the oak and the shadowed yard. The air cooled, my breasts tightened, and my bladder ached. At some point Lindy started crying again, and I sat on the glider and nursed her and rocked until she fell asleep. Only after that did a car pull up, a two-toned Plymouth I'd never seen before. A gangly boy leapt out and opened the passenger door. It was Wayne Scott. Luce hadn't told me he was driving her home from school. Or maybe she had, somewhere under all those blacked-out lines. Now she stepped out of the car with a stack of textbooks on her hip, and through the screen of the oak tree I saw the boy bend as if to kiss her, then seem to check himself and instead say something low in her ear, then get back into the car and drive away.

And then I forgot the soreness in my body and lifted Lindy out and up from the pram and set her wobbly little head against my collar, ignoring the ping of guilt I felt for disturbing her sleep. Luce was home and seeing Lindy for the very first time—and I turned my shoulder toward her, the better to show off my daughter, surprised by the flush of pride that washed me through. I had created this beautiful small person, I'd gone and done something Luce had not, something far more important than wearing pretty clothes or selling paisley blouses. Luce would love Lindy's wide flat attention and her amazement at the world, and Luce would be proud.

She stopped, stared at Lindy. Her face opened wide. "I thought you were supposed to—You changed your mind."

Changed my mind? When had I changed my mind? Or maybe she was talking about the money. That it was going to be oh-so-hard to wring money from the state and the smarter course of action was adoption. "Luce. I thought about it. I thought about it hard. I know that's what you wanted, I know it's what your dad tells girls in my position, it's just, I can't do it."

Luce wouldn't look at me, instead turning her gaze to Lindy's face. A needle of panic stabbed through me. Lindy's coloring seemed more transparent every day: the invisible hair, the red face. Nowadays of course I know I was being paranoid, that nobody ever would have known she wasn't Simon's child. But *I* knew, you see, and I was convinced that everybody else could see it plain as the noses on their faces. I actually tried to shield Lindy, but it was awkward, this business of pretending, especially with Luce. And it seemed to me that Luce knew right away about the pretending, that she could smell it, that lie, and something in her face closed, like a window sashing down. She stared and stared, as if she only now believed that Lindy was real, and the stack of books at her hip tipped over, and the textbook on the top slid over the crook of her arm and into the patchy grass. She didn't even look at it. "I am a fool," she pronounced flatly. "I didn't know."

"Luce, there's a lot—"

She shifted the textbooks from her right hip to her left. "It's not even Simon's baby, is it?"

I stood as straight as I could. "I told Simon."

"Not even Simon's." She was shaking her head almost imperceptibly. "I can't believe it. I must have been mad. Or stupid. Or both."

"Luce, it's not the—"

"I feel so stupid..." Her head swung left to right.

"Luce, listen to me—why do *you* feel stupid?"

"I thought I *knew* you. I thought we were *friends*."

"We are," I said. "That's why I—"

"You *lied* to me." Her face flushed red and tight. "After I told you everything. I thought I *knew* you."

"You *do*. I wanted to tell you. Does it matter? Why in the world does it have to matter?"

"*Because* Edie. I thought you were a person with integrity. I thought you were being your real self. That's what I tried to be with you. Throughout every bit of this, this whole time, you always struck me as the person you said you were.... I thought, I always thought you *loved* Simon, that you-all were going to get *married*. How—I thought you *loved* him. I thought it was *because* you loved him…" Her voice lowered, and accelerated, marbles rolling down a hill. "Do you know the stories I had to concoct to get information from my father? And school hasn't exactly been a cakewalk for me, you know. Everybody hints about you, where in the world you are, why you left. I've been telling the most outrageous lies. I've called people bourgeois. Unimaginative. Conformist. I wrote an editorial for the newspaper, for Pete's sake. Mr. Watts wouldn't print it."

"I know, I know. It's not the *point*."

"I wrote an editorial! And, Edie, my *dad*!" she repeated nonsensically. Then: "Doesn't Simon mean anything to you?" And finally: "Doesn't *love*?" And it was this last word, I sensed, that the conversation turned on, though whether it was love for Simon or for her I did not know.

"Look, Luce, you are more important to me than—"

But that set her off good. "Don't *lie*, Edie. Just—for God's sake—that's the one thing." She dropped the stack of textbooks, their titles splayed across the dirt. *Modern Calculus. Marriage and Family Living.* "Who was it?"

I couldn't meet those eyes. Instead I looked at Lindy, who was awake, and listening. "Aster." The words froze in my throat. "I don't know why. It was so… He was so… I just couldn't find the strength to say no to him. It just didn't seem fair."

Luce's mouth worked protestingly, punching the space in front of her like the lips of some prissy fish. "I am such a fool."

"Does it really matter? I've already talked to Simon, I've already—why in the world does it matter to *you*?" Lindy started to fuss, and moisture patched the inside of my brassiere, first warm, then cold.

"I thought you were different." Her hand slid to her front pocket to hold whatever fingle-fangle thing she'd squirreled away in there.

"Different?"

"I thought you were like me. Our beliefs. I thought you believed in doing what you said you were going to do. I thought you were a person of integrity." Her face was a wound, her voice hard. Then it receded, an undertow, smaller and further away. "Couldn't you at least have *told* me?"

Why, oh why, did we have to have this conversation right now? "No, Luce, I couldn't have *told* you. Because you would have started acting like the judge in some kind of tournament, just like you're doing now.

How can I ever tell you anything?" But that wasn't quite right either. If anything, I'd forgotten about Aster. It sounds crazy, but I'd somehow hidden the memory from my own mind. But I also knew it didn't make any kind of sense to say so. "I'm not like you, Luce. And never can be." I heard my voice rising, speeding. "I'm happy to match up to regular people, and that's hard enough. How could I ever be like *you*?"

Luce focused her eyes on mine, her face closed tight, washed orange with some other fear, some other piece of information she didn't want me to see. I hate to say it, but I thought about Simon's ring right then, and how it had simply vanished from that lunch table. "Regular people? What's that supposed to mean?"

"I—"

"I don't believe this," Luce hissed. "I can't talk about this now. I'm tired of it, Edie, tired of the whole mess. I've tried to stick by you. I've tried to defend you no matter what people said."

I put the ring out of my mind. There were more immediate things to worry about. "Please, Luce. I'm sorry. I didn't mean anything. I know you've done a good deal for me. And I need you now, to help me. Please, Luce. Just for tonight." I searched her face, hoping the words would come, whatever they were, that they'd be convincing enough. The pressure in my bladder spread, inflated, and fleshed itself out.

Luce was a hundred miles away. "We were never alike, though, were we? There is nothing alike about us. Why didn't I see that before?" She brushed past me and yanked open the screen door. It clattered against the frame.

I could feel Lindy fretting, ready to bust into a good wail, but I raised my voice to make sure Luce could hear me. "Did it ever occur to you that maybe *you're* the one who's the bourgeois square?"

Luce ignored me. She was dialing the telephone in the front hall, and I knew without asking that the number was my parents'.

LUCE

All I could do was stand on the porch. I couldn't change what I'd done, couldn't go back, couldn't leave her there, couldn't settle my mind on any one thing. I saw the house as it must look to her, the screen door ripped and the paint flaking like skin, the dead wicker loveseat sagging in the center, the magazines that smelled like cat urine and rot. Why had she come? She'd never come before. It was an unspoken agreement, and I knew she understood it because Edie understood everything. And oh God, I wondered if she'd seen her.

She hadn't mentioned the ring. She didn't need to. But the fact of it there, its absence, burned a hole between us. And now that she'd seen where I lived she'd think the worst, that I *sold* the wretched thing, for God's sake.

When the car arrived, my insides went cold. I'd expected Mr. Carrigan, or at worst the ladies from the Home. Not the flashing red light of police.

The light from the house changed too. I turned. And there she was, behind the screen door, my mother in the yellow duster. She peered out and reached for her cigarettes, put one between her paper lips, and fumbled in her pockets for the Zippo, her face red and then dark and then red and then dark. She didn't find it. And it might be that was what did it, the fact that she couldn't find that lighter. That was liable to be just as significant as the runaway girl with the illegitimate baby, or the police car in front of our house, or the men in blue uniforms getting out of the car and walking up the stairs, or Miss Diamond coming up the walkway with a shopping bag and a very wary expression on her face. At some point Mother found the lighter because for one blazing moment I saw her from Edie's point of view: the streaked hair on her naked face, the dirty housecoat, the darkened house behind her. She stepped onto the porch in a cloud of smoke. I doubt she'd been outside in many weeks, and even she seemed surprised at the clutter, there the magazines and *World Book Encyclopedias* that belonged to Dad, there the patio chairs they'd bought when he'd passed the bar, and there Edie and Lindy, the juvenile delinquent and the bastard baby, the cause of all the problems. She must have heard at least part of the conversation. I tried to remember everything we'd said. *It's not even Simon's baby, is it? Why does it have to matter? I've been telling the most outrageous lies.* Mother folded her arms around the front of her duster as the two officers paused at the step. She straightened, and I'd never disliked her quite as much as I did in that moment.

Well.

Minutes later the police officer had his hand on Edie's elbow, as if escorting her to the dance floor, but instead he guided her toward the formal black and white sedan, Edie in her black flats, the lavender scarf tied around her neck. She stepped toward the car with the baby in her arms, and how odd to see a girl get into the back of a squad car, and how odd to see her try to do it while carrying a baby. She handed the infant to the officer and lowered herself onto the back seat, lifted her hips, brushed one hand down the back of her dress, and held out her arms. The baby had started to squall, and the officer seemed happy to hand it back, then ease the door closed. The other fellow stowed the carriage in the trunk, which wouldn't close, and all the while the lights flashed red, around and around, frying the porch in irradiant light.

The police had finally come to my house, and neighbors were looking out of windows, and my mother's worst fears about me had been made real. Edie had finally seen me for who I was. The carefully separate compartments of my life had split open and spilled their contents together in one glaring lunatic mix.

Mother's face flashed again and again. All that dramatic light: I expected it to show cruelty and rage, but for the first time I saw something else in her expression: fear and illness, all of it, fright and affliction and fright again. As if it had been there all along, plain as day, but I'd never looked to see it.

EDIE

The officer at the station told me my father had called Mrs. Bruns, and that Mrs. Bruns had called the precinct to tell them the missing girl and stolen items had been found, and that I was charged with running away from a legal guardian. And theft of course. The officer had a droopy Nordic face with red-rimmed eyes and rubbery lips and seemed unexcited about both charges. He pecked the keys of a typewriter and looked up every now and then to ask a question or to return the carriage or to reach for the cigar balanced on the edge of the desk, the yellow wood already striped with blackened burn marks.

I rested my fingers on the Bakelite handle of the pram. Lindy slept, her skin more transparent than ever in the too-bright light. Yes, I told the policeman, it was true, the running away, and the theft, I said, that I hadn't had a single soul's permission to take her. I'd packed Lindy into the pram and snuck away from the Home knowing that it was wrong, I'd lied like a common criminal to the two colored ladies, all while the other girls in the Home were cleaning up the dinner dishes and doing what they were told.

The officer didn't look up from the typewriter. "Make a statement?"

"I just couldn't stand the thought of her being with strangers."

The officer stopped typing now, reached for the cigar. He held it to his tubey lips, took a long puff, and watched me through lidded eyes with what might have been curiosity. Whatever the color of his emotions, they were pale and muted.

Finally he spoke. "It's the pram, miss."

"Sir?"

"You had it in your possession when you was apprehended. The director of the Home reported it stolen"—he glanced at the page—"Uh, Mrs. Burns. Bruns."

Stolen. Of course. Mrs. Bruns had noticed the missing pram. It might be she'd noticed the missing diapers and pajamas and baby blankets too. It was only then that I understood. For the first time I understood. Taking Lindy wasn't theft. "I don't care about those items, sir. They can have them back. I don't even want them." Taking Lindy wasn't theft. You couldn't steal your own child.

The officer looked sheepish. "She wants to press charges, miss."

I felt my face collapse. It was mean, just mean.

"That's what we got, Miss…. The bad part about all this is you're going to have to stay here overnight. In the holding cell."

Why was that the bad part?

The officer continued. "But I wouldn't worry too much. In the morning you can see the judge, and then your folks can come over and pick you right up."

It was only one night. I could do it. Taking Lindy wasn't theft.

I gave the officer my pocketbook and my make-up case, and he wrote my name on two manila-colored tickets attached to brown circles of thread, and then he looped the cards around the handles of my bags and stowed them in a steel locker. Lindy opened her eyes and watched my face for a long blinking moment but she never did cry. The officer led us down a white cinder block hallway that smelled of disinfectant, the rubber pram wheels rattling along the cement floor. Inside under the awning Lindy closed her eyes. Taking Lindy wasn't theft.

The cells were made of cinder block and they really did have bars. One was empty, but in the other a woman in a green knit dress had spread herself full length on the wooden bench, her too-blond hair molded into a stiff bob, her nyloned feet crossed primly at the ankles, her left arm draped in exhaustion to the floor, and at the sound of the pram she opened her eyes, and I saw she wasn't really a woman but a girl. The officer stopped in front of the door and reached into his pocket. "A jail cell is no good place for a baby, Miss."

I nodded. It was true. A jail cell was no good place for a baby. And taking Lindy wasn't theft.

He opened the door of the cell and waited. "Don't worry. This'll all get cleared up in the morning." Waited some more. "And Officer Louden is calling your folks right now."

What was he trying to tell me?

"The baby," he added. In the carriage, under the awning, Lindy's head nestled against her chubby shoulder.

My palm wrapped the Bakelite handle. "My parents won't pick her up."

Then the officer did a peculiar thing. He touched my hand and very gently, very slowly lifted my index finger from the handlebar, then my middle finger, then my ring finger. When all my fingers had been peeled away, he nudged the pram from the door until Lindy's flushed little head was out of sight. "If that happens, Miss, I reckon we'll call your Mrs. Bruns again. She already said she'd take the baby until all of this gets cleared up." And somehow he was standing between me and the pram.

I stepped to the left, just to see better.

He stepped to the left too. "Don't worry, Miss Edith. This'll get all cleared up in the morning."

And then I was moving through the cell door, and back toward the pram—because there it was—on the other side of the bars, Lindy's little fingers curled on top of the blanket and close enough to touch, her breath even and trusting, her mouth a tiny little O.

The door clicked shut. "And a J.D. record ain't the same as an adult record."

I turned toward him. "Record?" For some reason, I thought of the records you played on a record player. "What does that mean?"

"It don't have to mean anything, miss." He was locking the door. "Unless you was ever to go to court. Then I reckon it'd mean something."

I grabbed the bars, and they were rough to the touch. "Like what? What could it mean?"

He shrank from the panic in my voice. "Just that you had a history. If you was ever to go to court, say, about something else. The court records would show that you was a J.D. At one time, that is." The officer pushed the pram toward the center of the hallway. Its black steel surface shone flatly, the white rubber wheels rolling away.

Then I understood. I would never again see that fuzzy head against my naked breast, would never again see the faint blue veins beneath her skin, would never again see the cupping fingers or the tiny fingernails. Would never again see my child. I felt again the officer lifting my fingers from the handlebar, first the one, then the middle, then the ring finger. Had he lifted my last finger? My pinkie? Or had I just let that one go? I really and truly could not remember. How was it I didn't remember? Something left me then, some physical part of my body, without which I floated on air currents with no free will of my own, and inside me sounded a wail so thin and piercing it could have been the crying of Lindy herself, wherever she was, somewhere in the building still, swaddled in the steel pram among my clothes without a single soul to hold her.

I didn't remember going back to the courthouse or meeting with the lady in the navy suit again or signing the relinquishment papers, nor could I explain it later, except to say that I'd fallen down a long doorless corridor, which in turn became a funnel that sucked me in. You were supposed to follow the rules, and when you didn't, all sorts of bad things happened. The best I could say was that in the end it was too hard to stand out there by yourself, and anyway, I'd never said I was brave. That's only what Simon said, because he needed to believe it for himself, before he'd known the truth about me. I'd certainly never said any such thing.

17

EDIE

Daddy carried the pink Samsonite from the Home's back door to the car. I carried my pocketbook, the leather strap biting against my palm, and nothing else. The trumpet vines on the iron fence bloomed obscenely orange, and the Roadmaster's chromium piping shone in the new June sun. The trunk swallowed the suitcase in its steel maw and clamped down tight.

He said he had to be back to work by 2:00 but that we'd all celebrate my homecoming that evening, that my mother was going to make lemon meringue pie, that in the meantime he'd brought me a special present. "Just from me, kiddo. It's in the back seat, if you want to take a look."

I opened the back door, where a slatted wooden milk crate leaned against the bench seat. The crate was lined with clean white towels, the way you did for a living creature, and the terrycloth moved with warmth and breath, and I could hear and feel my blood pounding through my veins, through my skull and my ears, and I couldn't believe it, you know, that my Lindy would be in that crate even as I slid it toward me.

But what I saw in the corner of the box was a copper bundle of hair, something like a wig, but then the bundle turned into a dog, a puppy staggering over the towel with its eyes closed and searching, and I couldn't make sense of it. Nor could I understand the words my father was saying. "He's a setter, a hundred percent. Setters make good dogs, kiddo." The pup blundered his way into the terrycloth wall, fell back, sniffed the air. "The breeder didn't want to let him go for another two weeks. Said he was too young." There was pride in his voice. "But I convinced him."

I wheeled. "But what about its *mother*?" My voice came out shrill.

My father looked stunned. "Edith. Jeez. Calm down. There's a farm." He held my upper arms and frowned, his face full of hurt. "It's a nice place." He patted my shoulder. "It's a real nice place." Pat, pat, pat.

My parents' house was the same as ever: there the red and white Formica on the kitchen counters, the mixer standing guard next to the refrigerator, the red-vinyl chairs with their knees bent low in ready crouch, the same bag of clothespins on the doorknob. Nothing had changed, not one thing. The house, the moment, my previous life had all been preserved in museum state, and everything I'd ever known, even the striped dishtowel threaded through the handle of the Frigidaire and that smug fat toaster, was waiting for me to come back, to reinsert myself into its daily thrum.

At dinner my sisters talked about what to name the puppy and where he might like to sleep and how big he would get. They asked how Aunt May was doing in Atlanta, but not too much really. The story was that I'd gone down there to get away from Simon and to help out my aunt, just disappear for a semester and then come back. The past had been erased and my new life was starting right away. Nobody mentioned Lindy. My own mind played a trick on me too, as if it was draping a black cloth over her memory, forcing me to look at everything else except her. In my old room the pink drapes twitched in the air-conditioning, and the stuffed lion and the blue poodle leaned against the pillow. There were the jewelry boxes and the hat boxes, there the mirror with my scarves draped over the top, there the crate with the confused setter pup, the closet full of clothes I hadn't worn in four months, there all the dresses I could fit into more or less, with their ruffles and full skirts that I never wanted to see again, the bows childish and the frills foolish, the colors out of place. And it wasn't just the dresses. I saw everything differently, like the world had become a skeleton, and the people in it naked too, and I understood the way Dotty the red-headed girl had fussed with her pocketbook when she'd come back empty-handed. I understood Sally's hollowness and Annette's brittle anger and Trudy's loneliness, how none of us had ever really believed there was such a thing as loss, or despair, at least not for ourselves, how each of us had held a secret belief that we alone would be the one to escape it, and I thought it would be a comfort to look at all those girls again, even Annette and Therese, even Trudy, to look upon their faces and search for the thing I was trying to identify, something believable and familiar, a thing I could find and touch and recognize as my own.

My breasts wept and ached and flared and wept again , and I bound them with strips of cotton so the milk would not show.

And so came the part after that when I tried to return to the merry-go-round of routine and habit that had been the structure and meaning of living, but school was over, and Ivey's had found other girls, and the summer days stretched before me like a condemnation. Still I waited for the beginning of my new life that was supposed to come blossoming up out of the nothingness, but it never did come. Or if it did, it wasn't anything I recognized.

Mama encouraged me to reduce. Skip desserts and do calisthenics, she said. She took me to her salon to have my hair done and showed me how to do liner in the natural way. I closed my eyes while my mother leaned over. "You don't want to look like a floozy, so you do it like this." She dotted the pen across the edge of my lid in a series of tiny tugs. The trick, she said, was to get the benefits of the make-up without making it seem as if you were wearing any. I could feel the light press of her hand on my shoulder and the measured breath against my forehead, a clean smell of talc and Cuticura lotion and mouthwash, and I tried to focus on the face in front of my own, her features so close, absorbed in the task, the design of this one illusion. "Stop moving," she said. "And close your eyes." At last she sighed and lowered the pencil. Without looking at me, she handed me the eye-liner and stepped back. "Your turn now, darling."

Come August I was supposed to pull myself together, enroll at Harding, and finish out my diploma, but I just couldn't imagine it. There'd be no Luce Waddell to roll her eyes and invite me to lunch, and the teachers would know something of my special circumstances, the disdain in their faces hot and obvious. The semester of school was lost, and there just did not seem a way to make it back. Instead I applied for a job as a salesgirl in Montaldo's because it was the only store in the city that had air-conditioning. The manager said I'd be fine as long as I showed a little pep.

At first the invitations came the same as ever. The problem was I couldn't make myself pick up the phone, and soon the calls tailed off. I didn't hear from Luce, and I never did connect that police car with the phone call she'd made because Luce was a lot of things, but she wasn't a tattle-tale. I knew why she couldn't stand me. I'd lied to her. I'd called her bourgeois. Most of all, she knew what a terrible person I was.

More and more the telephone sat blackly under the sunburst clock and did not ring. And then one day the Club sent my sister Deirdre home from a mixer because "All Shook Up" was at the top of the charts and Dierdre was dancing too provocatively and my father told the youth director they had no business playing that sort of music anyway, and the director came right back and said that the apples didn't fall too far from the tree, did they? Daddy just exploded. "Apples. Bullshit. What the hell does that mean?"

The days lined up one behind the other, their jackal faces hanging at the mouth, their long grooved tongues dripping thin spit.

LUCE

Every day I thought about calling her. Every day I imagined how and where the conversation might go. I practiced. Tell about the ring. Just put it out there. And then one day Mother didn't come downstairs at all and I figured it was the perfect time to dial the number.

Her father's voice boomed through the receiver. "Carrigans." The
way he said it made it sound industrial, like building supplies.

Use your best manners, that's all. "Hello, this is Luce Waddell. May
I please speak with Edie?" The question hung in the air a long moment.

A pause. Mr. Carrigan spoke without answering. "Edie's on to you,
you know."

"I beg your pardon?"

"Does it make you feel important?"

"Sir?"

"You heard me," he said.

I knew how adult conversations worked. Any answer was liable to
incriminate you.

Mr. Carrigan kept right on. "Because *you* know and *I* know that she's
out of your league. Has always been out of your league. She knows it
too."

I knew better than to answer. I could see him standing in his front
hallway, the phone clenched to his ear, that same primed football
crouch.

He said, "She wanted to *help* you. She felt *sorry* for you. And look how
you repay her."

It didn't occur to me to hang up. Instead, I just stood there in the
darkened foyer, Mr. Carrigan's large industrial voice pumping through
the earpiece and into my brain.

"You have done a lot of damage, sweetheart."

The words poured over me and then kept right on coming. I closed
my eyes and imagined them dripping, pooling on the floorboards under
my feet.

He said, "You know what happens to girls like you? I'll tell you.
Girls like you end up frigid old maids eating their dinners out of cat
food tins."

And what did I do? I stood stock still and let it all slosh over me.
All of it. And after it was over, after he'd been the one to hang up, I
replaced the receiver on the cradle. Drip, drip, drip.

She felt sorry for you. It was true, mostly. Edie and I were two different girls who never should have been friends in the first place. Edie
had been a certain kind of girl, and she'd shown me how that way didn't
work, and at the very moment I'd decided I didn't want to be like her,

Wayne had stepped in to say he liked me the way I was, that he didn't care one bit about curly hair. It made it easier to lose her, or at least for me to go in the opposite direction.

What I wanted most that day on the telephone was a chance to pass the message on, to tell her that it didn't matter, the curly hair or the Honor Society or the prom committee or even getting your byline in the paper, that those things didn't turn out to be as lovely or delicious as the two of us had supposed. They were just another set of things a person could want. There were so many bigger things to want.

But Edie's father seemed to know exactly what I had in mind.

He was wrong about the other thing. I never did tell. I was far too accomplished a guardian of secrets, especially the ones that weren't my own. Those were the secrets that mattered most, like the way my mother retreated into her bedroom for days at a time, or the sneaky way my father had packed his bags in the middle of the night, or the way my brother Martin had dropped out of school unnoticed, or the way Edie'd disappeared to have a baby in secret, and how I, Luce Waddell, had watched idly and stupidly as the young policeman guided her into the back of the squad car. These were the most embarrassing secrets of all.

I tried one more time to talk to her, on the fourth of July. I knew I'd find the Carrigans at Freedom Park, on the little hill behind the grand-stand, where the grass was thicker and they liked to set up their blanket. I arrived in the murky light of dusk, just before the fireworks, and there they were, sitting and picnicking like everybody else. They'd brought that same brown plaid blanket, and Edie was in Bermuda shorts slap-ping at mosquitoes. I sat some thirty feet away, in her direct sight. I figured eventually she'd look my way, and she would know. She always did. She would see that I'd come to find her. She would see how it was.

And at some point she did turn in my direction, several times, but it was hardly the way I expected. She looked straight through me with-out a flicker of recognition, straight down the hill toward all the other families with their blankets and portable barbecues and baskets of fried chicken, straight past, just like Connie, just like Marian Smythe and Mr. Watts and the sponsor of the Honor Society. Just like my own mother. I'd forgotten to expect the same from her. I wasn't ready to be invisible to Edie Carrigan.

Years later it occurred to me that she didn't see me that day because her attention was somewhere else, gone. And why hadn't I gone to see her later that summer? Or that Christmas? Or the summer after that? Because her father had called me *names*?

Sometimes I think it was her sightedness. It was intolerable, that vision. You knew it couldn't be good, whatever she saw inside you, those nasty petty things. Your hand pushing that ring into your lap. But at the same time you *wanted* it, wanted to be seen and loved. What I couldn't tolerate was the thought of her seeing my mother. That house, the mildewed magazines, the boxes in the dining room, Mother in the yellow duster. What if Edie had seen *that*? How much did she know? Had she seen the trace of the thing, its shadow? If she'd come into the house, she would most definitely have seen it. No matter what had happened while she was there without me, I couldn't allow her to see the thing in its entirety, that secret thing that lived in those walls and also in my gut, the ugly core of me. Edie of all people could not be allowed to see it, she who was beautiful and could not understand.

But perhaps, oh God, perhaps. Perhaps she'd seen a glimpse of it, there in that house: that Mother did not care about our home, did not care to take care of me, did not mother me. That my own mother did not could not love me.

Fourth of July was the last memory I have of Edie, sitting there on that plaid blanket in the middle of those families, her face a Greek statue, regal and blank, the months that followed so busy I scarcely had time to think about it. Instead I thought of college, and making money, and the colored girl from *Life* magazine, her expression so purposeful and decided and young. We were probably the same age, that student and I, and I kept thinking how she'd taken the bus to Washington just so she could make an impression on the president and I decided that that was what I wanted too, to be connected to change, to progress. To be connected to that girl. There were all these other things out there that mattered more than fashions and china and electric roasters and deep freezes. There was that Negro girl and all her purpose. That's what I wanted for myself.

I stopped trying to make my hair curly. As if, having learned the technique, I didn't have to do it anymore. My hair was straight, and I wore it straight in the scarves Edie had given me, and for a long time those scarves smelled like Edie. Like lavender. For a long time I thought of them not just as Edie's scarves but as Edie herself, the old Edie, the before-she-came-to-my-house Edie, as if she were always near me telling me I was splendid and that people were listening to me and don't stand on one foot and don't look at the ceiling and everyone's going to like you like you like you.

SIMON

Simon counted again. Twenty-two students, each facing a gray test pamphlet, a white answer sheet, and a cluster of yellow pencils. Five rows of male backs in gray suit jackets. Or blue. Or gray-blue. Or black. Twenty-two.

That would be his rank then. Twenty-two.

A white-haired proctor read from a script and told them to open their booklets. They had exactly three hours, he said, and time was starting now. Simon looked at the first question, then at the next. The words skimmed through his brain. He pulled at his tie and thought about taking his jacket off. Everyone else was writing. Twenty-one pencils on twenty-one pieces of paper. Friction like breathing. *Scratch, scratch, scratch.* The absurd thing was that he'd been relieved she wasn't dumping him. Nope. She wasn't. She was confessing.

At least he'd gotten to be the one to walk away.

No matter how many times she'd tried to explain it, he hadn't gotten it. But he wasn't that shocked. The shock was that she'd liked him in the first place. Some glitch in the structure of the universe. No. He wasn't shocked about Aster. It fit, damn near. That's why he'd loved her. Because she didn't belong on the road his parents had laid out for him. She wasn't *prescribed*. Not that she was a rebel—she wasn't—she just hadn't gotten the same set of instructions everyone else did. She could tell right off whether you were doing a thing because it was important to you or doing it because you'd gotten used to it. Like right now. Everyone in the room was wearing a tie. Why? Not for any good reason. Habit.

Just like the old proctor calling out their names. Mr. Adcock. Mr. Ales. Mr. Bloom. A formality, a ritual. Edie knew that if you didn't pay attention, that same ritual became what you did. Became *you*. Habit and ritual, punto, your whole life, gone, finito, and you hadn't even enjoyed it. Like these guys. Simon couldn't see their faces, but he could smell their sweat, already, in the a.m., at eight-oh-oh.

She had more life than any of them. Maybe she couldn't see where she was going, but so what. That's what made it a risk. Better than sitting here in this room. He'd wanted that unplanned thing, even a portion of it, like the faces in the portraits in the dark room. You couldn't capture everything, but you tried to capture something. That was the point. It had to be.

She could have had any man she wanted, any man in the room, but she'd wanted him. He focused on the page in front of him and saw instead the fine hairs at her temples, the way they curled around her ear, the pale column of her neck, the tilt of her eyes, her laugh, her spacious empathy. Her liveliness. Her light.

Aster was far away. In the booby hatch.

In-sti-tu-tionalized.

Some of those places had bars on the windows.

And what if the chance was now? What if it wouldn't come again?

The proctor took off his glasses and squinted at him. Simon picked up his pencil and bent his head over his exam and began to write.

18

When the doorbell chimed in the front hallway, I ignored it. It was the first week of the school year, and Mama and Daddy and my sisters were at parents' night, and I didn't want to have to make any conversations or decisions on my own. Again the chimes sounded, and I flipped through the pages of Deirdre's *Seventeen*. The models seemed younger than they used to, like children, and silly. Bangs were coming back. The doorbell stopped ringing and was replaced by a pounding, so I sighed and padded into the living room and drew the edge of the drapes, and in the driveway saw Simon's Fairlane.

He was supposed to be in Chapel Hill. It didn't make sense, except that he would know it was parents' night and he would know Mama and Daddy weren't at home. I might as well see what he wanted. He deserved that.

He wore a short-sleeved Madras and a doleful grin, and when he held up his hand I thought he was doing it to ward me off, like a witch. But then I saw the white jeweler's box, and of course I knew what came in white jeweler's boxes, just that I couldn't grasp the meaning of this particular one. He picked up my hand and closed my fingers around the box. His fingers were as long and warm and assured as ever. Then he kissed my hand. There was such melancholy in his smile. "My dad. He changed his mind. He knows you're about to turn eighteen. He's afraid we'll *elope.*"

Elope? For some reason I pictured two grass-eating animals cantering across a field.

"And you?" I asked. Simon's father wasn't the point. "What are you afraid of?"

His eyes had a new sadness, and there wasn't one thing I could do to resist it. "Life without you in it."

Simon and his father renovated the basement, hung the drop ceiling and lay wall-to-wall carpeting on the cement floors. The more temples were bombed across the South, the more Mr. Bloom changed. He stopped reading and watching the news and pounding the typewriter keys, but he seemed to do OK with the hammer and the screwdriver and the carpenter's rule. Mrs. Bloom sent the flowered couch and the Depression-era lamps down to our apartment and purchased a modern one for herself, which was something she'd been wanting for a long time. And every day she us brought cups of tea.

Simon asked me what kind of cabinets I wanted.

I said colonial.

Then he asked if I wanted a breakfast nook.

I said yes, I'd take the nook.

The new carpeting was autumn rust and smelled of glue and chemicals. The darkroom became a bedroom, which was pretty much what it had always been, except that now it was sanctified and contained an actual double bed with cubbyholes in the headboard and an eyelet dust ruffle.

Nobody mentioned the fact that I'd had a child, so I didn't either. *If you can't say anything nice*—But I wanted to talk about Lindy, about the way her nose was shaped, about the blue of her eyes, about where in the wide world she might be and what she might be doing, about the color of the clothes she might be wearing right now.—*Don't say anything at all.*

No one offered me advice, and Lindy became a person who existed for me alone, a figment that grew to fill me up, a phantom I talked to in my mind and sometimes in my kitchen. Lindy, would you like the yellow curtains?

Yes, she would.

Lindy, what would you say about the fried chicken?

She'd say it was too bland.

When I mentioned her to Simon, he said, "It's all of us. We've all had to compromise. Everyone gave up something. My parents and your parents." Which was true, I suppose. In the end the reason my parents hadn't pitched a fit was because they saw it as a last ditch way to salvage a situation that had turned out worse than they pictured. "Me, I had to give up the darkroom and the photography. And we both had to give up Lindy so that we could be together now. At least you and I have gotten to be together now."

This was all very reasonable.

In the kitchen I stacked up every kind of pot, two frying pans, a soup pot, two saucepans and a Dutch oven, Bundt molds and baking pans. It was very nice really, just what I'd wanted for cooking, back in the days I'd imagined making casseroles and Bundt cakes for Simon. But instead I slept. For astounding periods of time I slept.

Our family doctor showed me a circular rubber device that was supposed to help with spacing out births later in a marriage. He said it was against his policy to prescribe such a thing to newlyweds but that he was making an exception on account of Simon's school.

Which I thought was nice of him.

The problem was the double bed with the eyelet dust ruffle. When Simon reached for me on the weekends, his hands felt dank and amphibian. The darkroom became cellar and cell, the time we spent there drenched in windowless alluvial silence.

Afternoons I worked at Montaldo's. Mornings I spent in the basement apartment, where I hadn't gotten around to putting up pictures. I hadn't gotten around to doing very much at all. The high window in the living room leaked yellowly down the white cinder block, and the moist air locked in every impurity, every humiliation, every failure. Of course I knew you couldn't have everything, and you had to swallow the bitter with the good, including the gall that rose in your throat each month when the bloodstain on your underpants showed again that you weren't a mother, including the unused cookbooks and the emptiness of nights, the blank days that lined up one after the other. None of the decisions were really mine. Around me sounded other people's lives, the basement gurgle of water pipes, the toilet-flushings and spigot-runnings, the muffle of traffic, the permanent murmur of television. I'd given Lindy away. A man couldn't love a woman with that kind of sin on her. I knew that. A man couldn't love a woman who couldn't be a mother. The weight of nights to come washed one on top the other, their sirens and snorings and groanings and couplings, drowning me.

I took Miltown to fall asleep. During the day I napped and talked to Lindy, whom I'd given away. I'd done it, the unmother, me, Edie Carrigan. I'd gone and done it. And nothing in the whole wide world was liable to change the facts of the past or the texture of the future.

Even Luce despised me. Especially Luce. And no wonder.

19

SIMON

That first year his need to reach her turned to panic, then to desperation, then to gloom. Simon wanted to make plans, choose furniture, all that. But the truth is his parents needed his help for the first time ever and school had him in such a bind he couldn't even pay attention. And it was three hours there and three hours back. Not a minute less.

So many times he went wrong. Said the wrong thing. Didn't say anything at all. But the one he remembered most was a Friday night watching the June Allyson show. Of all things. He was bone tired that night, but he watched it with her, you know, to do it together, and it turned out to be a classic episode. *Silent Panic*, something like that, the one where Harpo Marx plays some poor slob who can't speak or hear. Can't even read for Christ's sake. Benson is his name. The only job Benson can get is working in a department store window. He's one of those mechanical men and has to dress up all spooky in white face paint with black circles for eyes and walk around all jerky and robot-like. He just keeps right on performing the same robot movements, or standing there while the people outside the window tap on the plate glass to see if he'll jump or blink. Even after the stores are closed, he stands there, stock still. But one night this bunch of gangsters comes by. They're on their way to hide the body of some guy they took out, and they're talking about it. Then they see Benson in the window, and they realize he's heard everything, and they think they better kill him too. But then they aren't sure if he's a robot or a real person. So Benson puts on the performance of his life. Convinces the gangsters he's a real live robot. Finally they leave. Of course Benson knows they're going to figure out the truth—that he's liable to rat them out. So what can he do but go to the police. The problem is, he can't make the police understand what he's trying to say, because he's mute. It's this great big deal with Benson trying to make everyone understand, and him waving his arms around and crying and imitating the gangsters. But the police never get it. They just think he's nuts.

Edie got up in the middle of the scene and locked herself in the bathroom. And what did Simon do? Just sat there in front of the set pretending everything was hunky-dory.

Jesus. What was the matter with him?

The bargain he'd made with his parents was a vise: medical school plus marriage. The only failure he'd ever imagined was school. It had never occurred to him that the failure could come from them, from him and Edie. But there she was suspended in time like one of those dolls from an exotic country, the kind with the clogs or the dirndl or some other damn thing, the whole get-up covered in a clear vinyl case. The wide blue eyes blinked but their expression never changed.

It was years before he understood why Lindy mattered so much.

In the end, there wasn't enough to bind them together and their love loosened and broke, like decomposing fruit. It was a shock, to see it prove so seasonal.

They divorced when Simon was in his third year of medical school. Later he remembered the marriage and the break-up the way he remembered other youthful transgressions against his parents' wishes. A sweet nostalgia for the thrill of the choice, then the bruised realization that his parents had been right. Again.

—

The first articles showed up later, long after he'd started in the ER. He didn't subscribe to the specialty journals, but the hospital did. The first was an account in a psych journal, then another a few years later, then a fitful stream buried in those colorless publications. The studies focused on the Homes. Girls like Edie. Turned out there were more girls from the Myers Parks of the world than there were from places like Central or Harding. There was little data on the other girls, the poor, or the immigrants, or the Blacks. And there were precious few records. They didn't have women like Martha Bruns recording every fact. But the data on the Homes. It captured you. It was consistent. Said the very things he should have known himself.

One Saturday in the 1980s, he spent damn near a whole day in the library of the medical college. In those days he was still married to his second wife, Nan. Told her he was doing research. (He was.) Because why? Because, because. Because he still thought about her, her attention, her light, the way her lilting eyes grew two sizes wider whenever you had something halfway interesting to say.

The studies reported the same thing over and over. Even the counselors had gotten it wrong. Forget it, they said. Look forward, not back.

Christ. He'd probably said the same thing, probably used those exact words. Told her not to talk about it. Keep it to herself. Good God. The two of them had never had a chance.

EDIE

After the divorce, I worked behind the cosmetics counter at Montaldo's, and it didn't matter that I was moody because the manager mostly just wanted me to look sophisticated. But something was growing inside me, a sense of outrage so strange that I didn't know what to do with it, so I stored it away, in my liver maybe, or my stomach, and I guess that's where it lived for a long while, gestating there in my organs and my bones and in every capillary of my bloodstream. No one saw it, not even the man who became my new husband.

In those days it seemed to me that the best plan was what Mrs. Wentzloff had always said it was, to begin again with a different husband who didn't remind you of your younger self, so I told myself I'd forget about the past and I'd think about my new family, that I'd do what other wives were doing, cutting out coupons and recipes from magazines and ironing my husband's handkerchiefs and hemming curtains and waxing kitchen floors and checking my husband's suits for lint. I had it easy really. It was my husband who had to worry about money, come up with the down payment on the station wagon and figure out how the mortgage worked and why the washing machine wouldn't spin and whether the bank was overcharging on the credit card interest. I had it easy. I just had to forget about the past and do my part. I could be in charge of my own home where I could make decisions about my kitchen and my parlor and my flower beds and then about my two young boys. I figured there was no reason for me to be unhappy. No reason at all. So what in the world could the matter be?

The years clicked by like railroad ties, and I found myself forever looking behind me at a point in the distance where two lines converged. Then one day the rage that had grown up inside me was full-formed enough to act on its own. It stretched its snaky limbs and flexed its live muscles, extending each toe and ugly claw with its grown-up powers, and then it began to speak, just like that. It had its own voice. One day it told my husband everything. It began with the story of Luce, and it continued with the story of Simon, and it finished with the story of Aster and Lindy. My husband listened in patient silence. Then he said he forgave me.

The word landed on me with a kind of whoosh: *forgive*, and I realized how much I'd been craving it, waiting for it to come to me, so I took it, that word, and settled it around my shoulders like a warm blanket. And for a while that made me feel different. For a while. Because that was something.

Wasn't it?

Part II

The Say-So

1984

20

MEERA

　　She found the thing in the hem of her mother's coat. It was early October, and she was parked at a strip mall between a 7-11 and a Duane Reade, trying to work up the nerve to get out of the car. The coat was one of those swing coats from the fifties, so it wasn't exactly warm: all that body heat escaping around your waist. The definition of inefficient design. And so much fabric she'd had to arrange the thing underneath her butt when she sat down in the car—and felt something—she could trace it—there, in the hem. Something hard and round and nickel shaped. But not a nickel. It was like, beveled. An extra button maybe. A ring, maybe. A bottle cap, likely. Whatever it was it had been there long before she started wearing the coat. So. Not hers.

　　This particular strip mall was one of those wacky juxtapositions in the city of Poughkeepsie. On the one hand you had this beautiful Gothic-spired campus full of three-hundred year old shade trees and glossy young people. Plopped right next to shopping centers like this one: the 7-11, the Duane Reade, the Payless Shoes, the Burger King, the Shoprite. Discarded fast food bags and empty drink cups littered the asphalt. The real America.

She couldn't bring herself to open the Chevy's door or walk into the Duane Reade or ask if they carried those do-it-yourself pee tests. Hell, she couldn't even say it to herself.

The car was heating up. She unbuttoned her mom's coat. Butt-ugly, her twin brother Alex called that coat. It was this cape-like black and cream number—*houndstooth* was the word they used back in the day. The reason she'd kept it was because it was one size fits all, the only item of clothing her mother'd ever owned that wasn't too small for her. Back in college her mom was about five foot two and a hundred pounds. Meera was tall like her dad. Even as a kid, she'd had a hand-span wide enough to spiral a football two whole months before Alex could.

She started wearing the coat after Michael dumped her. Just because. It fit fine. Loose and baggy and fine. Inside it—who's to say—she could have been five foot two and ninety-nine pounds. Could have been one of the first females to graduate from the law school at North Carolina Central, could have been one of the few women in America to actually have it all.

"On pause" was the actual phrase Michael had used. Whatever that meant. (*Press "pause" at any time. Press "play" to resume.*) It had been two weeks. She'd spent most of that time running a lot of miles on the campus track. A lot. Around and around, feet slapping the macadam, breath hammering through her head, the sound of Devo and Bruce Springsteen rocking through the stadium loudspeakers. The problem was she couldn't think. About anything really. Just the pumping of her own muscles, the pounding of her own feet, the rush of endorphins soaring through her limbs and body and brain.

Not that Michael was some sort of asshole. He wasn't. She'd met him when she was waiting tables at O'Shays, sophomore year, winter break at school. It was snowing and the place was practically empty. The Giants were in the toilet that year, but Donny the bartender had the television on, and Sandra was sitting right at the bar, which was a big crime in restaurant-land. Meera didn't give a shit about the Giants, so she stepped out onto the muffled street, and there it was, all this pin-feather snow falling under the streetlamp. Looking up into the yellow sodium glow, she could trace a single flake, so big and light they each of them emerged from the night and blotted out the lamp before floating down like stars, then like goose down, then again just like flakes. The more she watched, the more she lost herself in the illusion, the yellow-white-slow-motion blur.

Then there was some guy standing next to her saying, "I used to do this all the time when I was a kid."

She turned her gaze toward him. He wore a navy windbreaker, black crewneck peeping out of the collar, large white flakes across his hair and shoulders. He was big-boned, solid as a bungalow—more hardy than handsome, and built like a cinder block under that sweater, you could tell. She was trying to decide if he was being patronizing. But he just kept looking up at the streetlamp, so she guessed the answer was no. She tried to sound dismissive. "Yeah, well. That was a long time ago." She wasn't sure if she was talking about him or her.

He laughed. "Longer than you think."

Just then a car pulled up and parallel parked. They watched, as if they were waiting for it to finish so the conversation could proceed. But a couple got out, peered into the bistro's glass doors, and pushed them open. "That's my cue," she said.

Michael nodded but looked up at the snow again. She felt a flicker of disappointment.

She didn't expect him to follow her into the restaurant. By that time she was filling water glasses, and he was standing in the foyer and looking around the place, past the bar and into the dark corners, stamping the snow from these leather construction boots he was wearing. Like he'd just returned from some roofing job. He sat at the bar and ordered a Heineken: those sideburns, with all that russet hair, and not just on his head either—on his forearms, on his hands. He was a student for sure, boots or no, and maybe one like her. She'd grown up among kids of government employees. But once on campus, she'd felt surrounded by wealth. Michael seemed more familiar, like maybe he wasn't supposed to be at a rich school either. Like he too wasn't jetting back and forth during the break. Like he was here, working.

Whatever she guessed about him, he guessed about her. She could feel him watching when she handed her ticket to the bartender, and then a few minutes later Donny was heading downstairs to replace a keg and Michael was asking, "Why are you here?" He meant, "Why are you on campus during winter break?"

She made a sardonic face. "Making money."

He scanned the empty tables, his expression opening with humor. "I can see that." His eyes smiled before he did, these little crinkling arcs. They were dark hazel eyes, his brows darker than his hair. He had to be the only guy on campus wearing muttonchops that year. Or any year.

"You?" she asked.

"Campus security. Pick up everybody else's shifts and make bank." And that right there, that said it all. He *was* like her. Or at least kind of. Not rich and not here to fool around.

Turned out she was right. He played rugby. She played field hockey and soccer. He was an econ major on a mission to get his money's worth from school. Every lecture, every class. None of them counted until he'd added his voice, piped up, advocated, argued. He had a reputation for it, and he wore that same black crew neck and those same jeans again and again, wide and thuggish next to the artists and liberal arts majors in their tweed overcoats and red Converse sneakers. He didn't belong with the other financial types either. Too impatient to hang out and play beer games, too impatient to learn Pac-Man, too impatient for *Monty Python* or *Rambo* or *National Lampoon* or football pools or March Madness or any of that other guy stuff the guys at their school got stuck in. He called them dabblers.

Now a Duran Duran song floated from the car radio. Those pee tests were new. The Duane Reade might not have them. *Girls on film. Girls on film.* And even if they did, who was to say they were reliable? She considered turning the car and going home.

Either way she was going to be a statistic. Was *already* a statistic. The RAs gave these scare talks every fall. Half of American women had unplanned pregnancies at some point in their lives. Every ethnic group. Rich and poor. Half of those ended in abortion, most during the first trimester. One in six had abortions before graduating from college, one in four before the age of 45. Some of her friends had already made that choice, like members of some long line of women gliding toward the horizon line. It was her *turn*.

But she couldn't get her head around it. She'd won a scholarship, for God's sake. She was too close, too careful. It wasn't supposed to happen to *her*.

But the numbers said different. The numbers said she was part of some nationwide percentage. A percentage that dragged your special-ness right out of you, leaving you one among many, just another person who'd fucked it all up.

Two parking spaces over, a woman opened the door of a blue Volkswagen Beetle and stepped out with a swish of ponytail. She was about Meera's age, wearing teeter-totter heels, poodle bangs, giant hoops in her ears, and a scoop-necked full-length black unitard that looked like it was from the 70s. No coat at all. When she bent to lock the car, a little-kid wail pierced the air. The woman pressed her palm against the window. "I'll be right back. We'll get doughnuts." Then she hurried through the 7-Eleven's glass door.

The wail stopped abruptly, and the window of the Volkswagen rolled down. A hand appeared, then a face: a girl of about five, her hair swept up and tied by one of those beaded elastics, her nose red with the cold. She blinked at Meera, mainly because there was nobody else in her line of vision. Meera gave her a little wave. That held the kid's attention for about one second. Then the little girl grasped the window frame and leaned out like she was going to jump.

"No!" Meera shouted, surprising herself. The kid stopped, her attention captured. Meera didn't know what to say next. She didn't have a plan. "You have to stay in the car if you want doughnuts." It sounded terrible, and fake.

The child glanced at the 7-Eleven. Her mother stood in line talking to a young man in jeans and a black T-shirt. The silver hoops jiggled against her neck, her face prettier now, more vivacious. Then she was bumping the door open with her hip, a white paper sack and Styrofoam cup in her hand. When she saw the open window, the prettiness dis-appeared and the lips flatlined. "Victoria." The little girl—Victoria— began wailing again. "Quit it *right* now."

Meera couldn't help but picture the woman at work, sitting behind a desk somewhere, slipping those high heels off her feet and then slipping them back on when she walked around the office. Meera already knew what the woman wanted. She wanted *more*. More time with her kid, more money, a promotion, better schooling. Or maybe she wanted a man, intimacy, and love, or maybe a social life, and friends. The woman in the unitard wanted and wanted and wanted.

Meera could have told her. You couldn't have it all. It wasn't *authorized*. Meera knew that. Her mom knew that. Her mom had been one of the few women she knew with a career, but she'd been tired all the time, and she'd had a husband to help. She'd missed luncheons and cancelled dental appointments and avoided parties, even cried one time her dad suggested they host his exec officer for dinner. She was in the Officers Wives Club but never ever attended.

And then, holy shit, Meera understood something else. Her mom didn't have friends. She could count her friends on like, no hands. She didn't have them—real friends. Not one. Not now where they lived in Northern Virginia, not where they'd lived in Germany, not in the place before that or the place before that.

In the rearview she saw the blue Volkswagen pull out, Victoria's mother's ponytail swinging as she checked for oncoming traffic. The woman could be her. She could be the woman. Carrying around a grain of resentment like some unyielding seed. And sure as shit that little girl already knew that kernel was there, hard as a lacquered black pearl.

Meera smoothed the hem of her mom's coat, traced the outline of the thing hidden there, that perfect round shape. Too thick for a coin. Maybe a button or a ring. On impulse she fished out her house key and hooked the teeth into the hem. She'd fix it later. She didn't have any great sewing skills but she knew how to fix a hem for God's sake. The stitches came right out.

She pushed the object toward the opening and even before it came into view she knew she was right. It was a ring, solid and heavy and simple. A man's wedding ring. She rolled it between thumb and index finger. There, on the inside: an inscription in a language she didn't recognize—not German but something close to it. *Far mayn belibtn Itsik.* Maybe Dutch.

For my beloved Itsik. It had to be. But who was Itsik and what the hell was he doing in her mother's coat?

21

MEERA

Her parents met Michael that past Christmas at the house in Northern Virginia, where the government had put them up for a year.

Michael slowed the car and cast a long look up the street. And yes, she saw what he saw, the hundred-year-old trees, the stately brick colonials. Her hand found the bristled hair at the back of his neck, right at the edge of skin and scalp, the two cords of muscle there tight with anxiety. She pointed at the house. "That one." Red holiday lights glowed on the roofline of the porch. The house looked huge, even to her. Never mind that she and her brother had never lived there. In military families everything was always ass-backwards.

Michael edged the car up the drive. "Nice." Too nice, he meant.

"You know it's not theirs, right?" The places they'd lived in Germany were always converted barracks.

Michael cut the engine. "They're *living* in it." Meera'd seen his house. He'd spent his whole childhood in one place, a two-story in Baltimore, where kids played ball between parked cars, the sort of street that real estate developers bought up to gentrify. Something about that seemed noble to her. Made her think him capable of great feats.

Michael unbuckled his seatbelt. "The colonel drives the Sentra?"

Meera hesitated. Civilians were always so focused on rank. "Nope. The lawyer."

But it didn't take. Michael drew in his russet brows.

She slapped his leg. "My *mom*." Who was the whole reason her parents were here, in this house in Northern Virginia, because Mom was working on some high-profile case.

"Does he keep loaded guns?"

"Nah."

"Unloaded guns?"

Probably he was joking now. Probably. "It's not like he's the Great Santini."

Michael's expression softened, his eyes smiling their merry little arcs, tiny pillows of flesh crinkling below them, like a baby's. He smelled primeval, of earth and musk and forest. "All I know is my dad goes nuts whenever my sisters bring home guys."

She soaked up these comments, hungry to hear the ways other families behaved. The way nonmilitary families behaved. She pressed her hand onto his thigh. "My parents have this thing about…*infantilizing* their kids."

"Think he'll grill me?" Again, those little pillows under his eyes.

Did fathers still do that? Show their daughters' boyfriends how tough they were? Maybe. Her father'd only ever given her one piece of advice about men. Before she left for college, he'd told her and her cousin that they should never give up their professional lives for the sake of a man. He'd said, "You never know if he's going to be there to take care of you." Her cousin hadn't been too jazzed to hear that. She was older, and recently married. You could see her jaw go all tight. She was like, "I trust Jamie. And I always will." "I know you will," Dad had said. "But how do you know he won't get sick? Or lose his job? How do you know he won't die?"

It was hard for Meera to imagine her father doing some big power display now. If anything, it was the other way round. Michael was the one who had to do the proving. But she couldn't say that. It'd just make the stereotype worse. She said, "My dad's also a historian."

Sort of. For years, the cardboard box labeled "dissertation" had occupied its own shelf in their various homes. Her father never opened it, and when she'd asked him why he never finished it, he'd said that after Vietnam he just didn't have the burn, that things he'd once thought were simple had turned out to be more complicated than he thought.

Still. That box didn't go into storage for decades. Then one day it did. And by the time she really understood what he'd meant by *complicated*, that box had been gone for years.

Now her twin brother Alex bounded into the foyer, all tall and big-boned, with longish hair and a purple "All Who Wander Are Not Lost" T-shirt. He slapped his long arm across her shoulder. "Meezles! Thank God you're here." Then he leaned in theatrically and whispered, "I failed three classes."

"Holy shit. Out of how many?"

Alex raised his face up, his brows to the ceiling in mock dismay. "Everybody is *muy* PO-ed." She could see there was something under his shirt, some animal, probably the ferret. She didn't ask about the ferret or the classes. That was the way with Alex: the worse a thing was, the more they were supposed to play it like some big joke. To get serious would be like taking him out at the knees.

Now he clapped Michael on the shoulder. "Dude. Welcome to our humble abode." The ferret made an appearance on his shoulder and sniffed the air. "This is Harold." Alex always had an animal he was tending, a lizard or a rat, a hedgehog once, ant farms and terrariums. Never something normal he could cuddle but something curious and weird he could observe and study. He could spend a half an hour watching a crow pick through a bag of French fries.

"Well, hello." Her dad stood in the entryway. She saw him then as Michael must: tall and close-cropped and big-eared. Geoffrey whined and pawed at her jeans. She bent to pick him up.

"Hello, sir."

Dad extended his hand to Michael and said, "Merry Christmas. Call me Wayne." He wore the same black plastic glasses as ever, the generic style the government health insurance covered in full.

"Michael Campion. Merry Christmas, Colonel Scott."

"Nice to meet you, Michael. Call me Wayne."

"Thank you, sir."

This time Dad didn't correct him. And now her mom was clomping in and waving, the smallest person in the family but also the loudest. "Hi Michael. So glad to finally meet you." She wore slacks and some kind of flowery blouse—dressed up actually. She looked kind of cute. Normally she was all track suits. Half the time Meera was super proud of her and half the time super embarrassed. She couldn't say if her mother was pretty. When Meera was younger, it had seemed to matter a great deal, like that was the way she was supposed to measure her against other people's moms. Plus: other people's moms stayed home and baked cookies. As a kid Meera had wished for that too. Now that wish made her cringe.

Michael tipped his chin at her and extended his hand like he was honored to meet her. "Mrs. Scott!"

"Oh, please," Mom said while they shook. "Lucille." She wore her hair in a squared page-boy. That was how you recognized her in any kind of news footage. Look for the geometric hair.

"Well, thanks for including me," Michael said.

Her father looked dead serious. "That would be sacrifice number…"—he pretended to count on his fingers—"three hundred and forty-two."

Alex slid his gaze toward Meera. Half the time she could read his mind, no problem. They said it in unison. "Since breakfast." Harold the ferret nosed under Alex's collar and disappeared.

Dinner was complicated: sauces and condiments and gravy boats, Mom fussing over the pork chops. Too dry? Meera said they were great, not because they were but because her mother had gone to this big effort. And how in hell had Alex failed three classes? Mom poured more iced tea. As soon as she left the room, Meera turned to her brother. "Well?"

"Well, indeed, Sis. Very well. Thanks for asking."

"Are they axing your financial aid?"

He glanced toward the kitchen. "Don't know." Mom returned with the pitcher.

Her dad tilted his head, struck a neutral tone. "What your brother is trying to say is that all possibilities exist at this moment."

"Yes." Alex lifted an index finger toward the ceiling as if to make a pronouncement. Meera could sense the giddiness bubbling up, ready. "You see, Meezles, there's this *cat.*" He tilted his finger at her, cuing, searching out her affinity. "And he's in this box." Another finger tilt.

She leaned in, pulling up her eyebrows to keep her face from spilling. "What *kind* of cat, Varmint?" Right away it felt familiar, the same old Alex and Meera show.

"A dead one. Or a live—"

"But what *kind?*"

"A tabby, thank you very much—and—"

"But does it *shed?*"

He wrinkled his brow, then raised it in understanding. "Why, yes it *does*, Meezles."

"More than other cats?"

Deadpan now. "Yes. It's a *sheddinger* cat."

She leaned back and grinned. "Ba-dum bum." It was probably time to stop. Yeah, they had their little shorthand, but it didn't exactly include anyone else. Especially not Michael.

But Alex was just getting going. "And until you open the box—"

"Maybe he's dead—"

"Or maybe he *jumps* out. Like a rocket—" Alex leapt to his feet and threw his arms into the air. "And *lands* on his *feet!*" He stood there a beat too long, flushed in the certainty that everyone was smiling at him. Both her parents groaned, but Alex knew, and Meera knew. Even when their parents hated these displays, they loved them.

Meera gave Michael a glance, then poked her brother in the solar plexus, hard enough that he caved and landed back on the chair. "Hey. Watch out for that fall, sports fans. It's a doozy." The end.

Dad turned to Michael, tipped up his chin, and gave a sarcastic smile. "We're so *proud* of our children." Michael laughed, the sound bellying out broad as the moon. Because the thing was, they *were*. You could tell. "My wife calls them magnets. Sometimes psychically connected. And the rest of the time working against each other in perfect opposition." Meera and Alex had heard this particular metaphor about a thousand times, but Alex jolted his body straight and raised his eyebrows at her in a parody of enlightenment. Her dad shifted the conversation. "Michael, I hear you're an economics major."

"Yes sir."

But Alex wasn't ready to let go of the spotlight. He pitched a falsetto. "*Heeere*, kitty, kitty…"

Meera gave him the stink eye.

He sighed, glanced at Michael, then made an elaborate gesture with his fork. "But *please*. Enough about me. Let's hear more about *you*-all."

So. That was the end. Finally. Meera said, "Michael's family lives near Chesapeake Bay." His father had once been a policeman but had left the force for reasons she never did learn, a ghost now, pale and round, blurred by a cloud of cigarette smoke.

Dad spooned more gravy onto his pork chops. "But you spend the breaks on campus."

"Yes sir."

Mom studied Michael, like she was trying to discern what sort of character he might be. Or maybe just thinking they were only in the States for a year and she didn't feel like sharing her kids with someone she didn't know. "There's always a few people around." Meera set her hand on Michael's forearm. "Davida will be there too."

Michael's head ticked up, jerked by some kind of invisible string. Then he set his gaze on the salt shaker. Davida had been one of her housemates for two years, a psych major doing something with rats. You had to check them every day. But it wasn't just that. Meera had the impression she actually liked hanging out with the rats.

Alex chimed in. "Does that girl have an eating disorder or *what?*"

Meera felt a jab of anger. Alex really did pride himself on being an irritant. "And *why* is it any of your business?" Davida was one of those thin women who was always wanting to cook. Pasta, pesto, heavy spices.

"Just saying," Alex said. "There's such a thing as too skinny."

"But she's not it," Michael countered.

"Ah," Alex said drily. "Sounds like you would know." Meera shot her brother a look, but he was watching Michael with a sardonic expression on his face, gauging.

Meera sighed loudly in Alex's direction. He was adept at this role. The agent-of-chaos role. He could step into it like a coat. Or out of it. Meera mustered her most wilting tone, which might or might not penetrate Alex's thick skull. He had a high resistance. "And you-all get to decide what that is because…?" It bugged her, the idea of Davida feeding those rats with those little plastic droppers while they all sat around the table pouring gravy from the gravy boat and talking about her. Her mom would be jumping in any second.

But no. Her mom was studying Michael.

Alex lifted his chin piously. "Hey, I'm just a concerned citizen." But his voice carried something else, something like happiness. Or victory.

Michael's features drew themselves together. But then his face straightened and his voice came out jovial. "Citizen of where?"

"Citizen, my man. Citizen of the world."

And maybe it was that phrase, *my man*. Something in the room tightened and shifted. She could feel it, a vector swiveling in some new direction. "Ah," Michael said. He nodded at Alex's shirt. "Hence the *All Who Wander*."

Alex regarded him evenly. "Yes. *Hence*." As if the word were soiled, inane.

Michael tilted his chin at Alex's T-shirt and read aloud. "All Who Wander. Are Not Lost." Punching out each word, almost playful. "But you *are* kind of, aren't you? Kind of lost?"

Meera felt her face go stiff, the word like a slap. Alex had donned his never-give-an-inch stare, his face immobile except for his nostrils, which had somehow become bigger. He tilted his head and copied Michael's intonation exactly. "But you are kind of, aren't you? Kind of a dick?"

For a long beat the room stood still. Then Dad slapped both hands on the table, and the sound echoed like a shot. He stared Alex in the eye for a long moment, then Michael.

Meera leveled a look at Alex. The joke was off. She could tell from his face, from his eyes that flickered to hers. Next to her Michael was stone. Him she couldn't read. Her hand moved to his forearm. Under the table Geoffrey growled.

They finished their pie as fast as they could. It was a relief to clear the dishes from the table, a relief when Dad appeared with two medieval looking bottles, one in each hand.

"*You*," he lifted one bottle at Alex. "And *you*." He lifted the other at Michael. "Time for a lesson in Scotch." Without waiting for a response, he turned and marched down the hall, holding both bottles by the neck.

Alex and Michael assessed each other for a long moment, then followed. Mom tilted her head at Meera. Come.

Her father bellowed. "And di*plomacy*."

Her mom set up the guestroom for Michael. She brought up clean towels, set them on the dresser. "Thanks for the fancy dinner, Mom. Sorry
about…where everything went."

"Me too." Like they were the ones who were supposed to apologize.
She took a seat on the edge of the bed and patted the spot next to her.
"What was that about?"

"You mean Michael?"

"Well. For starters."

"I don't know."

"Maybe he doesn't appreciate Alex's brand of snark."

So. It had landed on Michael. "Alex was being a punk."

"Alex is having a tough winter."

No shit. Three courses down. Meera wasn't sure how much Mom
knew. Or whether "tough winter" meant he was suffering or that he
was failing. Her parents were pros at withholding judgment, or at least
pretending to. They didn't weigh in. They didn't tell you who to date
or which college to pick or what to major in. They were cagey—which
meant you were always trying to guess what they really thought. Your
best bet was to wait.

But Dad's so-called lesson was probably over by now, and Meera
wanted to try the Scotch too. She was pretty sure he wouldn't mind. She
and her brother had always had the same rules. Clean up your room.
This is how you pack a sack lunch. This is how you cook a grilled cheese
sandwich, a pot of rice, a roast chicken. This is how you brace your foot
against the lawnmower for a pull-start. Put some elbow grease into it.
Make yourself useful. Meera didn't think the Scotch would be any different. Instead she was stuck here waiting with her mother.

Her mom made her voice casual. "Michael is awfully charismatic. I
can see why you like him."

Meera ran her fingers along the silver chain at her neck. "But you
don't."

"I don't know him. He's certainly confident. And good looking."

Meera felt the corner of her mouth draw in. "He's way more mature than most of the guys at school." She didn't mention the fact that he was four years older. That he already had crow's feet, and hair on the back of his neck, and wrists like ankles, that she believed him capable of weathering great calamity, of looking uncertainty in the face and doing battle with it.

"Well." Her mom did this little shrug. "You're stronger than he is." Meera took a deep breath. That was her mom, all over. She didn't know thing number one about Michael, but here she was making weird pronouncements. It was all about enlarging her own kids. That was her M.O. So Meera did what she always did: listen and take everything her mom said with a giant grain of salt, including what she said next. "Are Michael and Davida friends?"

"Sure." The question annoyed her. That's not what her relationship with Michael was like.

"I'm just trying to get them straight, who knows who and such."

"All of us have friends of the opposite sex, Mom." A slow heat spread up her neck. Her parents had been out of the country for years. It was too late to be protective now. "It's not like the days when you were growing up."

Her mom drew in a slow breath. "I suppose that's true. We're all of us stuck in our own generation." She nodded, patted Meera's thigh.

"Yes." Meera tried to sound sardonic. "I'm sure he's disappointed, you know, that you're putting him in the guest room."

"Well." Her mom stared across the room, like she was sorting out all the possibilities and their various permutations. Then she returned her gaze to Meera's. "He'll get over it."

22

MEERA

Michael was waiting in front of his apartment building. Meera'd told him the bad news about the pee test. They were a recent invention, those tests, and most people didn't trust them one bit. Which was why you had to get a doctor's confirmation.

Michael wore a white cabled fisherman's sweater that was about four inches thick, and he looked good. Honest. Reliable. He opened the passenger door and settled in. There was a moment of awkwardness, as if maybe they were supposed to hug, or kiss, or something else. But they weren't. They didn't. He squinted at the coat. "Where'd that come from?"

She'd worn it on purpose. "My mom. It used to belong to her. Way back when."

"Huh."

"Nineteen fifty something."

"I didn't know you were into all that vintage stuff."

"Me neither actually."

He sank into the seat and rolled the window down. "You know it's ripped, right?"

"Yeah." She'd forgotten. That ring. None of it seemed to matter. Concrete office parks were blurring past them. Cool air lifted the hair at her temples and battered the inside of the car with noise. She could feel Michael's hope, like a buoy beneath him, and she let herself think he might be right, maybe. Maybe in a few hours they'd both be smiling at their paranoia. She let her right hand rest in her lap, but Michael didn't hold it. He was a good hand holder, or had been, the kind to interlace fingers, palm pressed against palm.

By the time they walked out of the clinic, she was thinking about hand-holding more than ever. He stopped at the car and turned to face her. The sunlight crashed onto their faces. "Well?" So much hope in his eyes, she actually thought about lying. But she didn't.

"Yeah. Positive."

He took a deep breath, and it was about the longest time in the world, the time it took him to inhale and exhale that lungful, maybe even enough time for him to take a helping of her misery and spoon it onto his own plate. That must have been why she'd asked him to come with her in the first place: for that. He stepped forward and wrapped her to his chest. She let her head rest on the scratchy white wool of his sweater and the taut muscles beneath and the hot organs inside where his heart cadenced against her ear. Maybe this was why she'd asked him, for this, this rhythm. Past his shoulder, a squirrel stuffed its mouth with acorns, sugar maples jangled in blood orange, and sweet gum leaves splayed purple across the Chevy's windshield like zodiacal stars. Autumn already. The words came out of her mouth on their own: "I don't know how I feel about an abortion."

She felt Michael's body go rigid. "That's not what I expected you to say." He was the one who was Catholic, not her. But he didn't sound happy.

She said, "I don't expect you to do anything." Which was probably a lie. She hadn't actually thought it through. Just that she felt a terrible rush to make a decision, like some giant clock over her head had started tick-tocking. Which for her was ironic. She was one of the few people she knew who'd taken almost three years to commit to a single academic major.

Michael didn't seem to hear that clock. "Let's talk about this more in a couple days." He squeezed her shoulders. "I need to think." Which for some reason annoyed her. In that moment her feelings for him loosened some, like the outer papers of an onion. For the first time she felt like they might someday fall away.

In the car she watched his profile, eyes focused straight ahead, lips pressed together in thought. He wasn't ready for this, any of it, this square beautiful man with his ready laugh and big ambitions, his construction boots and loose hanging jeans. But the future didn't have all that much to do with him, did it? And then Meera remembered her mom in that big house in Virginia, God bless her. *You're stronger than he is.* At the time, she'd done what she always did with her mom's esteem-building comments—shrug them away. But she remembered that one, on this day, as the maple trees burned orange and gold, the telephone poles *shoof...shoofed* by the open window, and a great space settled on the seat between Michael and her.

Meera and her brother had grown up during the Vietnam War, which meant a lot of time their dad was gone, as in not there. Which meant she competed with Alex for their mother's attention. Or just competed period. Like the time he pushed her off the slide and she lost a layer of skin just above the elbow. It wasn't any big horrible wound but for a few minutes it gave her her mom's uncomplicated attention. It couldn't last, she knew, but for that moment, holding her elbow under the sting of the faucet while her mother rinsed and rinsed and the water sluiced pink into the sink, for the moment she felt pretty darn good. Her mom cut the faucet off, lifted her by the armpits and set her on the closed lid of the commode. She unfolded a clean towel and patted at the red patch on her daughter's elbow. Meera felt like the queen of the world. It seemed as good a time as any to gain some points on her brother. "Mom?"

"Yes?" Her mother opened a drawer, removed a brown plastic bottle, opened the cap, smelled it.

"Who do you love the most in the world? Me or Alex?"

Her mom stopped smelling and tilted her head. She looked serious, and for some reason sad. Something beneath Meera shifted. She already knew her mother belonged to two places, with her and Alex in their house but also out there with everybody else, where people called her "ma'am" and "Counselor Scott." Now her mother upended the bottle onto a cotton ball. Finally she said, "I love your father more than anyone else in the world."

That didn't fit Meera's thinking. Her dad was a collection of photographs. He'd been gone such a long time she couldn't even remember what he sounded like. It didn't seem fair a person like that could be the winner of her mom's affection.

Her mom spread the iodine across her upper arm. "And then I love you and Alex next, whole bunches, each of you exactly the same." She cut a piece of medical tape from a roll and tacked it to the edge of the sink.

Outrage sparkled in Meera's chest. Tied for second place. "But he's not even *here*."

Her mom unwound a gauze bandage, wrapped, then taped. "He'll be back." She didn't look up but seemed instead to back into her own skin. "I miss him every day."

That was news: that there was something her mother wanted but couldn't have. That even a grown-up could wish for a thing and not get it. Meera's anger shrank some.

And her father? What was he? Mom loved him more than anyone else in the world, which meant something, she didn't know what. What troubled her was the sadness in her mother's voice, that and the idea that growing up might not be the cure for longing.

A few months later her father was home. At first it wasn't clear what his role was supposed to be. He built a swing set. He laid a patio. He bought a grill and a droop-eared pup. He took the whole family swimming at the officers club pool.

She knew how to swim, but she was afraid to go in over her head. Fine if she could ease herself into it. Fine if she could dog-paddle her way across the surface. On that day she was waiting on the diving board while her mom talked to some blonde lady with a clipboard. Meera needed her to focus on her.

But the kid behind her didn't want to wait, and the next thing she knew there were hands against her shoulder blades pushing her off the board and into the water. The bottom of the pool was a shocking, stifled world, blue-lit and wavery, slow-motioned, where sound and sight and movement did not behave as they should. Nor did her limbs. She didn't know what to do with them, or how to get up to the world of light and the blur of legs above her. She neither sank nor rose. She had no air in her lungs. Voices reached her, laughter, the tweets of a whistle, singing, but all of it far away. She understood that this was what she'd feared all along and that this was the way she would drown. The idea of death surprised her but she didn't have grasp of it enough to fear it the way she would later. Mostly she just wanted to take a breath. But a white form moved into her vision, a man all torso and arms, and so hairy that an undulant shadow wavered around him, dancing and rippling in the swimmy blue light, the furry shadow moving when he moved, and the man clasped her against the wiry hairs of his chest and swam them both up to the surface.

Sunlight and air. Air and more air. Voices. Dazzling light. The wide loud world exactly as before, the hairy man lifting her at the waist and setting her on the edge of the pool.

And it was him. Her dad.

Later that summer they loaded up the station wagon and drove to Carlsbad Caverns. The problem happened at a rest station. Her parents thought the little beagle was in the back with them, because Alex was smitten with the dog. But he wasn't. In the back, that is. The noise the tire made wasn't even a noise. More like a pause, like a flutter, a tap, this little pat of a palm.

Her dad stopped the car. "Where's the puppy?" He didn't even turn around. But her mom sure as hell did.

Alex swiveled his big old head to the left, then to the right. "Don't know, Dad." They were four years old. They weren't used to taking care of other creatures. Even Alex.

A great uncertainty edged up Meera's spine. "Dad?" That noise. It couldn't be. It hadn't been but a stutter, a breath.

"Stay in the car," he told them, and then he was gone a long time, and they could see him out there standing on the back bumper searching through the camping gear on the roof. Then he was unfolding that green entrenching spade and carrying it with him into the woods and when Meera asked Mom where he'd gone she reached over and grabbed her hand and said *Oh honey*.

The crying happened when he opened the door and started the car. Her mom put her hand on his leg and nobody said anything. But he was doing it. Her dad was crying. Alex wrapped his hands around the back of his head and rocked his whole body from side to side.

But Meera didn't really get it. It hadn't been but a flutter, a pat.

She would only hear her father cry one other time. It would sound the same as that first time, not much more than a wobble. Like he was trying to hide it. That second time she'd be twenty-one years old and pregnant and holding the phone tight in her fist and pressing her lips between her teeth. It wouldn't be so different from the time with the pup. Because there was nothing he could do to change the way things had turned out. Because something had been lost that could never be recovered. Because he hadn't been able to protect the people he loved.

But this time, she was the one who had caused it.

LUCE

There are some news items that can surprise you and at the same time confirm everything you know to be true, events that are mundane and utterly electrifying all at the same time. I felt that way about both bombshells you dropped that morning.

I was running late. I'd double checked my court briefs, slid them into my carry-on. That was the way I traveled in those years, in case the airline delayed my bags. And if the airline *lost* my bags or those court briefs: disaster.

The toaster gave a bright ping, and a piece of carbonized bread shot into the air, clearing the stainless steel and then falling back and trapping itself at an angle in the aperture. The device wasn't equipped for a single slice at a time, and neither of us had fixed it. We just didn't have time. When Wayne and I were young, we'd wanted success, even though we didn't really know what that meant. Later we learned that it meant a perennially broken toaster. There was always somebody needing something, the backlogs, the caseloads, the crushing wait, so many people's lives and careers dependent on the choices you made. The past three years had lurched past like a downhill semi, you and Alex flitting between college and the new home that had never been your home. We both felt useful, Wayne and I, necessary even, but we'd become the kind of people who scheduled our togetherness, a weekend here, four days there. Friday nights. Now I stuck a knife into the butter—I'd forgotten to take it out of the refrigerator—shaved off a hard slice, and mashed it into the crusted toast. I ate standing up, the dry crunch registering in some far away part of my mind.

I opened my Filofax and slid the passport and my plane ticket into the flap, slid the little book into my inside coat pocket. Better to keep everything on your person—there were too many kids out there as messed up as I'd been. It all came down to a system. Do everything the same way every time, and none of the pieces got lost. Keys, wallet, glasses, security badge. Important to know where everything was.

I heard the telephone, but I figured Wayne would get it. It would be the command center trying to solve some problem. That's what they did: problem-solve one international crisis after another. Wayne thrived on it, the immediate satisfactions of *doing* something. Everything was always right-now. Communist terrorist attack in Bavaria. Assassination of Middle Eastern statesman. They were all "incidents," *in cadere*, things that fell upon you. It wasn't that the command didn't see the loss of human life as a crisis or, God forbid, a *tragedy*—more that they didn't allow themselves time for verbal handwringing. It didn't get the problem solved.

My work at the VA was the opposite: long-form, bureaucratic, and slow. Most of my clients were female soldiers, most of their cases tough to prove. But we did move the wheels. Sometimes. The downside was the travel, especially now, days and days away from home, away from Wayne. I never did call myself a feminist—the word was too counter-cultural for government life. Plus we had this idea, most of us in those days, that we were more likely to get what we wanted if we weren't waving banners around. You know, smile and go after whatever it was you wanted without telling anyone you were doing it.

Now, so many years later, my qualms about the f-word seem silly. Because: what else would you have called it?

The phone had stopped ringing. I could hear Wayne's voice, at first quick and terse, then scooping up into surprise. It was 8 a.m. I knew it was you or Alex. Something dreadful stirred inside me, an ancient instinct, a great mammalian paw. My physical body strained toward your voices, my eyes and attention, yes, but also my breath, my lungs, even the hairs on my arms.

I put my head next to Wayne's, breathed his air. You didn't mince your words. "Michael and I broke up. And it turns out I'm pregnant."

Well.

Wayne answered first, slow and careful. "I'm sorry about Michael. I think you really loved him." Then he was tilting his face up to the ceiling, and swallowing.

I covered for him. First, say something comforting. Just don't give advice. That was the mistake I'd made with Edie. But what came out was different. "There are options, Meera. We can make it work." I found myself saying that I'd always been pro-choice, always been a supporter of women's rights. That we could help with the money. That it was still so early.

You listened but didn't say much for a long while. Then you said the strangest thing. "I know, Mom. It's just—remember when me and Alex were kids and we used to play smear-the-queer with all those kids on Bantam Way?"

"Every parent in the neighborhood remembers that. It was the most awful of kid games. Even without the name."

"It feels like that."

"Like what?"

"I don't know. Like, being at the bottom of the smear. Like being crushed. I can't put my finger on it."

That made no sense. "What are you thinking?"

"I mean, I guess I'm thinking about having the baby and giving it up for adoption."

"Meera, I thought you were pro-choice. You have no idea."

"I am. Pro-choice."

Wayne had gotten himself under control and seemed intent on showing so. "Ask your mother about her friend Edie from high school."

"What friend?" you asked.

I answered without thinking. "We're not friends." Even now I can't explain my reluctance. Habit maybe, the oldest one I had. Never give away information unless you have to. If I did, I'd be making Mr. Carrigan right, and he would win. By then I was old enough to know this wasn't exactly true, but I couldn't shake the conviction that it wasn't my place to tell.

But you honed right in. "You *were*."

"Your father is mistaken." That ancient shame rising up my throat. Good God. How many times was I going to have to betray her? But you were my daughter, my flesh and blood. As good a reason as any.

"Who's Edie, Mom?"

"It's just not what I would do."

"Who's Edie?"

"It doesn't matter. It was a long time ago." I couldn't tell you then, on that day. It would have required looking at the thing straight on. And I was used to being in the courtroom and used to being put on the spot. To changing the subject. "Are you prepared to go on welfare?"

"Welfare? Mom, who said anything about welfare?"

"You have to consider that. There's a good chance you wouldn't be able to do it." Silence on the other end, and a sound, maybe—a catch? I couldn't tell. "Look, Meera. You're either a mother or you're not. Both are okay, but it's impossible to do both."

"You don't think I can do it."

"I don't think you can do it while at the same time keeping yourself safe." It was time to stop. Just stop. And then there was Edie, coming down the stairs of that Home in that mushroomy smock, her face vacant, wiped clean, an old woman in a coffin. Those stupid candlesticks, all that red damask, the low light, the smell of lilies.

But I wasn't sure about the lilies. Maybe I'd made that part up.

"Mom, I can do it." You sounded so sure, so determined.

Wayne said, "Nobody can decide for you."

Meera took a deep breath. "Well. Whatever you do, we love you.

Your father and I will do whatever we can to help." There were a thousand miles between us, the Hudson River, half the Eastern seaboard, the entire state of Delaware.

Your voice was grudging now: "Thanks."

"Whatever you decide to do."

That's when you dropped the other bombshell. By the end of the conversation my head was spinning. It was many hours later at the airport that I realized I'd left that Filofax sitting open on the telephone table, my tickets tucked into the notebook's clear plastic flap.

MEERA

It wasn't exactly a picnic, talking to her mom about failure. She bottom line didn't get it. And she'd never told Meera that before. *I don't think you can do it.* Not once. But now Meera'd failed in the most basic way, and her mother couldn't face the fact that she was not like her. Not exceptional.

Soon as she could she switched to the other thing. "Mom, did you ever know someone named Itsik?" Too late she considered her mistake. Maybe he was a former love interest. Former lover.

But her mother's answer was immediate and unfazed. She was like, "Itsik? No. Not off the top of my head. Why?"

"I found this ring with that name on it. At least, I think it's a name."

Nothing.

"In the lining of your black and white coat."

Nothing.

"It has an inscription on it. It says *Far mayn belibtn Itsik.* Looks like Dutch?"

Another long pause. Then her answer, when it came, was almost a whisper, her voice stunned, impaled. "Not Dutch."

"You know it?"

Meera could hear her inhale, grabbing up more air than a person her size could reasonably fit into her lungs, then a long exhale. "Oh honey. It's been decades since I've worn that coat."

Seconds ticked away. Her mom wasn't going to answer the question.

If Meera was looking for a distraction she'd found one all right. And who was this Edie person? The friend-not-friend.

Her mother said, "I didn't know that ring was in there."

*Ob*vious, Mom.

23

It was easier to talk to Alex. He'd withdrawn from school and was taking a year off, quote unquote. He and Harold the ferret and Howie his friend had been trailing Jerry Garcia through several states. In a Vanagon no less. The last she'd heard they were headed to North Carolina.

Home of Central High School, her parents' alma mater. Which is why she had the idea.

On the phone, Alex didn't talk about getting booted from school. Instead he waxed poetic about the places they'd camped, the people he'd met in truck stops, the jobs he and Howie had taken picking apples. He was practically Jack Kerouac.

"Alex?"

"Yeah?"

"Did you ever hear Mom talk about a friend named Edie?"

"Edie? Like, from where? Virginia or Germany?" This was the way they organized their memories: according to the place they were living at the time.

"Neither. From high school probably."

"Nope."

"How about a friend who got pregnant in high school?"

"Nope."

"How about a Dutch friend, either male or female?"

"What's this about?"

"I'm not even sure. Maybe two things. I found a wedding ring in the hem of mom's coat, that checkered one, and it's inscribed in a language that looks like Dutch. When I asked Mom what it was she pretended she didn't know."

"Hunh. What does the inscription say?"

She turned the ring toward the light. "*Far mayn belibtn Itsik.*"

"That's not Dutch, you dope."

"What is it?"

"Probably Yiddish. That last word. I think it's Isaac."

Oh. *Oh.* Her mother'd known it was Yiddish too. *Not Dutch,* she'd said. Plus: she had lied. She knew exactly what that ring was.

Right away Meera started spilling everything she knew. "And Dad mentioned some high school friend who had a baby. Named Edie." For some reason she felt certain the ring was linked to the other secret: the friend. "Mom got all mad at him when he said it and made him stop talking about it." Meera didn't tell Alex why their father had mentioned the friend.

"I can't remember any of Mom's friends."

Exactly. "I mean, does she even have any?" When they were growing up, it hadn't been hard for Alex and Meera to make friends. They'd had to do it too much. If there was a summer they didn't move, their friends did. July meant goodbyes. August meant figuring out who else was looking for new friends and seeking them out. Loss and opportunity and starting brand-new. Meera had assumed it was the same for the adults. But maybe it wasn't.

Alex sounded surprised. "*That* can't be right. What about that lady she used to work with at Fort Bragg, the Black lady from the VA?"

"Julia Hayford's mom. I don't think they keep in touch."

Alex didn't want to give up. "What about at Fort Campbell? Rob and Cammie's mom?"

"Mrs. Dade?" Meera'd never been comfortable around that lady, the next-door neighbor who was always making pancakes and omelets in the mornings, even on school days. She didn't ever sit down. She'd be sliding waffles onto Cammie's and Rob's plates, then darting around the kitchen, getting…whatever, *things*.

"I don't know if Mom was actually friends with her. More like we were friends with Rob and Cammie. I think they just tolerated each other." Mrs. Dade baked killer brownies too, but there was this: Meera could eat a brownie in less than two minutes, a brownie Mrs. Dade had spent two hours making. Even if she were to eat the whole pan it'd still take a fraction of the time Mrs. Dade had spent making them. And that right there was as good a reason as any not to make brownies. Because of the arithmetic. It scared Meera, like Mrs. Dade had agreed to a life where her time meant less than everyone else's, some small bargained life filled up with make-work. Meera wondered if she'd got to the place where she wanted it that way. If maybe—good Lord—she'd trained herself selfless.

Meera didn't want to do that.

Now she took a deep breath into the phone. It was as good a time as any. "Alex?"

"What?"

"Are you guys headed for North Carolina next week?"

"Yes. Maybe. I'm not sure." Which was his way of saying he was going to do whatever Howie wanted.

"Well, can I ask you a favor?"

"Sure."

"Like, what if you actually went to Central High School and checked out the library? They must have old yearbooks there."

She could practically hear Alex pooching out his lips the way he did when he was thinking. "What would I tell them?"

"Nothing. Just act like you're a student. Just cruise in there and start looking around."

"*Meezles.*"

"What?"

"I have a mortal fear of librarians."

"Librarians or libraries?"

"Both."

"Just say your parents went to school there and you're trying to track down an old friend."

"Really, Meezles? Is this worth it?"

"C'mon. You know Howie'd like this espionage stuff. He'd eat it up with a spoon."

"So. You want me to look for an Edie in the yearbook."

"Or Edith. Possibly with a Yiddish-sounding last name."

"Remind me what the point is again?"

"Mom is hiding something from us. Some part of her past. Aren't you curious?"

"Not really."

"Plus—" Meera couldn't figure out why it mattered. That there might be something about this woman. Something that could tell her how to be. "Alex. It looks like I'm pregnant."

Hundreds of miles away and she could hear his intake of breath. "Oh...shit."

"Yeah. I know."

"*Shit.*"

"You said that."

"Jesus, Meera, weren't you guys using anything?"

This wasn't exactly the sort of thing she talked about with her brother. "Yeah, sort of. I was on the Pill. Then we broke up, so I stopped. Then we got back together, so I started again."

"So what happened?"

"You're not supposed to do that. You're not supposed to stop and start."

"Oh."

She could almost see Alex there in that phone booth, blinking at the announcement, the news of it, the unfairness. They'd both grown up believing the world was theirs to take and shape and fashion to their will. They knew about setbacks, sure, and all the unexpected things waiting to happen in a person's life. But they'd never really believed in them. Because they hadn't happened to them. Alex sounded tentative. "What are you going to do?"

"I'm having weird thoughts. Like my gut is telling me what to do."

"Get an abortion?"

"No, I don't know."

"What do you mean you don't know?"

"I can't explain it. Remember when we lived at West Point?"

"'Course." They were forever red-rovering, and hiding, and seeking, and kicking the can and relay-racing and capturing the flag and running the bases and swinging the bat. And, and, and. It was a neighborhood of clatter and competition and shouting and rallying: relentless, demoralizing, and impossible to resist. You had to be in the game because the game was everything there was. And sure, she was old enough to know about puberty and kissing and all kinds of other adolescent things that landed outlandishly on her ears, but she didn't want them yet. She knew that somewhere and someday she'd have to figure out all that stuff. But first, right then, on that street in those years, it was more important to strive. Compete. To win. To measure up. "Remember how most games began with a choose-up?"

Alex snorted. "How could I forget? That kid Randy was always the captain."

She didn't remember the captains. Just that most of the girls were picked toward the end. "You remember the other kind of game, the kind where you *weren't* picked, the kind where you were *it?*" Set apart, the person getting ambushed by the twelve-year-olds at the end of the street, or the one being tied to the hickory tree, or the one at the bottom of the smear-the-queer pile, captured by a welter of kicking sweating arms and legs, the smell of grass prickly and green against your face, each breath you gathered more difficult than the last, the panic of knowing that if one more person jumped on the pile, something inside you would collapse.

"Yeah. Kind of." He didn't sound so sure anymore. She tried to remember if he'd ever been at the bottom of that pile.

"I just feel, like, crushed. Like I'm it." A frame of ribs and bones and skin, a cage ready to fold in upon her lungs and her organs and the little muscle that was supposed to be her heart. And all of it for one reason. Because she wasn't a boy. "The idea of abortion feels like that to me. Like defeat. Like one more weight about to land."

"You mean physically or mentally?"

"I don't know. Maybe both."

A long pause. "Huh."

"I was thinking I might have the baby and give it up for adoption."

He didn't say anything. Blank, featureless silence.

"I can't explain it. It feels like I'd be doing it for myself. Like everything else right now sucks, but I can at least do this one good thing."

"I don't know, Meera."

"What are you thinking? Be honest."

"I mean…maybe that's too simplistic? Like maybe you're making an emotional decision?"

She didn't say anything.

He kept going. "I'm not saying I doubt you. I don't. I never doubt. But how's it actually going to work in the actual real world?"

"What do you mean?"

Alex was silent a long time. "I mean there's other people involved. Mainly this person who doesn't exist yet."

"You're saying I might be inflicting pain on his future life. Or hers."

"I mean, yeah, maybe. Or, like, your own. There's, like, ripple-effects. What if you're just creating more problems?"

She felt her throat go tight. Of all people, she hadn't expected push-back from Alex.

"And you don't know where this person might end up."

She nodded, even though he couldn't see her. Her throat had wadded up. She was having trouble getting out a syllable.

"You don't know whether there's other consequences. I just hate to see you—I don't know what I'm saying, Meezles. I don't know."

Noted. He couldn't come up with a single one of his so-called ripple effects. And anyway. It felt as if she'd already decided. Like the rest of her life had slipped into a bottomless hole. If nothing else, she could do this one perfect thing.

But Alex acted like he could hear her thought. "If you did it—"

"Yeah?"

"Would you stay in school?"

"Yeah." He was still talking in the conditional tense. She didn't correct him. For once, she couldn't tell him what she meant. Maybe Mom was right. Maybe you couldn't be pro-adoption and pro-choice at the same time. And maybe when you chose you were choosing that too. Who you were. Who you'd be able to be. "I have insurance. I have work. Money coming in. All I have to do is make it through this school year."

Alex was quiet for a long time. Then, "All you have to *do?*"

"Yeah."

"Jesus, Meera."

Years later she still remembered that conversation. How wise-unwise her brother had been. How she'd ignored him anyway. How she'd chosen what she'd chosen because it was the thing that required the least explaining in her head. The thing she thought she could stop thinking about once it was done.

As if.

24

LUCE

I never did like that guy, and not because you all were having sex. I was never against premarital sex per se. Better that than the mistakes my generation made: kids getting married in high school and then stuck with their choices until they figured out how to get a divorce. I just thought: why that guy, who was so clearly a tourist in your life? I found my mind drifting in your direction more than ever: things I wanted to tell you about living with a man, about being in love with one. I kept imagining you were in danger.

It was clear you weren't going to listen to me. But what was I going to do? Give you Edie's number? I didn't even have it anymore. And the idea of the two of you having a conversation without me made me cringe.

I knew you'd call back, knew you'd ask again. I felt myself caving already. And maybe there was a way. I could dig up Edie's information and write her myself. Then, if things went well, I could put you in touch with her.

But when you did call you asked about Isaac instead. Of all things. I think you thought he was some kind of ex. "Mom? Have you ever dated anyone besides Dad? Like, seriously?"

You meant had I ever had sex with anyone else besides your dad. "Meera. We met in high school. Things were different then."

"Have you been happy with him?"

I felt my body freeze. How strange for you to ask that. And for some reason I thought again of Edie. As if one or both of you were here on the sofa next to me reading everything there was to read in my face. "*Have* I been. Or *am* I?"

A long pause. "Both."

"Yes to the first. No to the second."

Another whole breath cycle. "You're not happy now."

"Oh, Meera. It's complicated."

"Oh."

"There's this woman. Sergeant Mills." Geoffrey must have heard the frustration in my voice, because he padded over and began to whine at my knee. "It's nothing. But she works in the same office as your father. She's registered a…complaint about him."

You were all silence. For a moment I wondered if we'd lost the connection. "What kind of complaint?"

"She says he wrote her a bad review because she didn't respond to his…advances."

"Advances? What kind of advances?"

"Well, that's the tricky part. It's not entirely clear."

"Like, what did she say?"

"Oh that he smiled at her and she didn't smile back. That sort of thing."

And thank God you didn't say one thing about the irony, that Mills was exactly the kind of woman I usually represented. "Do you think she's making stuff up?"

"I think there's some…misinterpretation going on." Geoffrey backed up, got a running start, and leapt onto the couch.

"No offense, but I'm having a hard time taking this woman seriously."

"I just—something is different. He doesn't want to spend time with me anymore. He hasn't wanted do make love in three—"

"Mom!"

Why was I telling you this? "I don't know what to do." Geoffrey rolled on his back with his paws in the air.

"You think it's because of this woman?"

"I don't know if it's because of her or his work or what. He seems... mad."

"At you?"

I'd already said too much. "Well. That's how I read it."

You were silent. "What're you going to do?"

"Well. The VA's sending me to Texas for the Wimberly case. But. Your father's not coming." Geoffrey nuzzled my hand.

"Oh." That syllable just sat there for a good while. "For how long?"

"You know how these things go. A month maybe. Or a couple."

"Oh."

"Maybe six."

"Six months is a long time."

"Well. It is." Something large and unwieldy filled my chest. "And then, well, we'll see."

There was a long moment of silence. "You guys always seemed like you had such a great relationship." It sat there, that comment, like judgment, and it rankled.

I took a deep breath. "Well. Nothing is ever perfect."

MEERA

Meera stopped calling her parents. Mostly she didn't want to hear any more about her mom's move, or the ring her mother didn't want to talk about, or Sergeant fucking Mills. When Alex called instead she was glad. But she couldn't bring herself to tell him about Sergeant Mills or their parents. She wanted to see if he'd say anything first. He didn't. But he did go to North Carolina and he did go to Central High School, and it turned out the place was now a community college with more librarians than ever. But the yearbooks were still there. Alex found four names, first and last: Edith Pennroy, Edith Mayman, Edith Carrigan, and one Eden Blessed Lord—which, Meera figured was a name that could only ever happen in the South.

Meera called information in Charlotte, North Carolina, and asked about all four people. But all the Ediths had either moved or changed their last names. The only one she managed to contact was Eden Blessed Lord. So that's where she started.

"I'm trying to return a misplaced ring," Meera told her over the phone. "I think it belongs to a girl from Central with the first name of Edie. I wonder if it might be you?"

Eden Lord didn't have to think about the question. "A ring? No, hon, I can't say I'm missing a ring. What does it look like?"

Meera told her. "I think it maybe belongs to an Edie who maybe got pregnant?"

Eden Lord answered right away. "Oh, honey, that wasn't me. Edie Carrigan is the person you're looking for. You have to be looking for her." Then her voice accelerated and rose. "Oh honey, are you the baby?"

"What?"

"You are, aren't you? You're the baby, and you're trying to get that ring back to your Mama."

"No, I'm—Was Edie by any chance Jewish?"

"Not that I know of. Why?"

"There's an inscrip—"

"Oh my God, they put you with a Jewish family, didn't they? And now you don't know whether you're supposed to be Jewish or not."

"What? No. I'm not Jewish. I'm not the baby. I mean I'm not Edie's daughter." Meera hadn't planned to tell her. She didn't think her mom would want her to. "I'm Lucille Waddell's daughter."

There was a beat of silence. "Oh. Her." Meera waited for more. Eden Lord seemed to sense it. "Funny. I'd forgotten all about Lucille Waddell. I literally have not thought of her…in, well since graduation."

Meera felt a needle of irritation. "She's actually a big lawyer now. For the VA. With the federal government."

"Well, isn't that interesting," Eden Lord said, without any interest at all.

Meera couldn't let it go, this weird desire to validate her mom in the eyes of this woman she didn't even know. "She married Wayne Scott. They're very happy together." Or were.

"Now I *do* remember him. What a name. Nice guy though."

"Thanks." Meera waited, but Eden Lord didn't offer any other details about her parents. "I'm trying to get this ring back to its owner. Do you have any idea where Edie Carrigan lives?"

"Oh, sugar-pop, I'll be honest, I couldn't say where she ended up. Not anywhere around here, I'd bet. And seriously, can you blame her?"

25

LUCE

Would it make a difference if I told you that the ring, once gone, changed everything? I never stole anything again, was never even tempted. Never again did the thought of having other people's possessions make me feel strong. I had lived a different reality, one in which the possession of something someone else held dear didn't make you powerful, but weak. It made you beholden, vulnerable to the whims of chance and fate. You might want a thing because you thought you could control it, but what you learned in the end was that the act controlled you. Changed your life. Launched you into the ether, cut loose, on your own, a fat-suited astronaut spinning out and out into the isolate void.

But once you'd found that ring, Meera, I had to figure out what to do. If nothing else, it was a family heirloom.

Well.

I dialed information, and the operator told me there was no Simon Bloom listed in the Charlotte area code. No Edith Carrigan either. There wasn't but the one listing, she said, and it was a Deirdre.

Deirdre Carrigan. Well. It had to be. I wrote the number in my Filofax under the heading "Edie's sister." Believe me, I thought about sending an anonymous package. A note. But on impulse I dialed Deirdre's house. Her husband picked up and gave me Edie's number without a qualm. On another day I might have talked myself out of it, jolting somebody right out of the blue like that. But on this day I didn't think. I was forty-four years old. I waited for the tone and dialed. Then there it was: Edie's voice, or rather a recording of it. I hadn't made a plan for the machine, so I just started talking. It came out as gibberish, and I was too embarrassed to tell her I actually had the ring, but it was a start. I'd done it.

EDIE

I stared at the answering machine for a long time, Luce's voice scratchier now, one generation and several states away. And it contained something new, a lovely kind of remorse I didn't remember from before. The message said the strangest thing, something about it being her fault, something about the terrible things she'd done, and I couldn't get my mind wrapped around that thought, the terrible things she'd done, or that word *forgive*, how strange it sounded. I couldn't for the life of me recollect what there was to forgive because, you see, for so many years I'd had it backwards. I had given away my child and because of that I thought that Luce was like everyone else who knew about me and couldn't bear the sight of me. She hadn't wanted me in her home and she hadn't wanted to see me ever again. For so many years I'd thought she'd only done what was normal, what everyone was expecting her to do, including me.

But the message set off something in my brain and told me that it wasn't the way it had happened, not the way it'd happened at all. There'd been a police car, for one thing, with flashing red lights, and someone had called that car, and how strange that it'd never occurred to me to ask who. I'd always assumed they just *knew*, that I'd broken the rules and everyone just *knew*. But that wasn't right. She had called them. Luce had called the police.

So instead of forgiveness what I felt on that day was a surge of anger, and it was rich, nutritious even, like some sort of milk my body had held up for years and then suddenly released. I reveled in it, that anger, because I'd just found it, you see, and I wanted to drink from it for a while, that and the thought of forgiveness, which I knew I would some-day feel but goddammit not yet. Not yet.

But still. A soft part of me liked the sound of Luce's voice, even yearned toward it, its settled sad maturity, its lacing of uncertainty, so much that I saved the message and decided I would listen to it every day until that surge of anger didn't feed me anymore, and then I would dial her number.

My second husband had stayed longer, until 1972, long enough to see the two boys into grade school in Greensboro. When he left, I was head-ing up the PTA and raising funds for charity, something I turned out to be good at. It mystified me that institutions and their representatives wanted to give me money, that the circle of everyday public opinion wasn't as important or exclusive as I'd once thought, that even after the second divorce I was able to stay inside it. Or maybe it was because of Richard Nixon and the boundaries of right and wrong blurring to include me once again. Either way it wasn't so difficult or so important as I'd once thought. Nobody cared that I was a double divorcee. They didn't know about the other thing.

And Lindy was out there somewhere, just beyond my reach, the little girl with the blond hair and the clear eyes and the ruffled dress, the little girl carrying the baby doll with the head that swiveled to the left and the right, the little girl with the two long braids. Only she wasn't a little girl. She was an adolescent, with braces maybe, and just starting to think about boys. But then she wasn't that anymore either. She was a young lady, because it was 1976, and I found myself sitting on a bench in the mall looking at teenaged girls, especially the fair ones, the pale-eyed, and I wondered about that one there in the Jordache jeans and peasant top, or that one in the sunglasses and halter top or that one wearing her school's plaid skirt.

Even my boys guessed I wanted to mother a little girl. They just didn't know it was a particular little girl I was wanting, one who was already older than they were. They didn't know I couldn't help the sharpness in my voice when I told them not to goof around on the monkey bars and then not to talk to strangers and then not to stay out late, or why in the world their rules were so much stricter than their friends'. They didn't know why their mother was so afraid.

Of course I knew I was out of step, that they laughed at me, made faces behind my back when I told them they couldn't be out past 10:00, or that they couldn't watch R-rated movies, or that they were too young to date. I knew they had elaborate ways of getting around my protection and my rules. On good days they treated me with a kind of jokey tenderness and lay their arms across my shoulders and called me "Ma," and I never did know where that came from but I liked the sound of it all the same, that single short syllable, its friendliness. Just that it sometimes felt like they were the parents and I was the child.

I hadn't told them about Lindy. *What happens when they find out they've been tricked?*

I waited.

26

MEERA

Meera was spending too much time in the library searching the periodical journals. And not for her classes either. For Central High School. Two stories in *Life* magazine, for one thing, and both had to do with the school's population of married students. Bizarre. She was also kicking herself for not asking Alex more about those four names. This Edie Carrigan, for one. It would have helped to know who her friends were. Was she on the cheerleading squad? The yearbook staff? Meera even called Eden Lord again, but Eden didn't remember any of her classmate's clubs.

The search for Edie Carrigan was the thing that brought Meera back. She stopped throwing herself into headlong sprints around the track. Started bringing in more tips at the restaurant. Started studying. Tried to figure out what kind of screenplay she was going to write for her humongous senior project. Back in the spring she'd applied to do this special screenwriting project as her senior thesis, and some committee up there in the stratosphere had thought she was a good enough candidate that they'd approved the application. But now she had to actually come up with a plan. Sure, she'd had an idea when she applied, but now she realized how bad it was.

Then for no good reason she passed out one day in the middle of a political science class. The professor sent her to the infirmary. There the doctor fitted a rubber cuff around her arm and began to inflate it. The band chuffed and plumped. Meera was still mad at the way the day'd turned out, but she also knew the sooner she spilled the beans the sooner she could go. "Actually. I just had a blood test. I mean I know why I fainted. It's because I'm pregnant." The cuff deflated with a shy hiss. "I've already had the test. Eight weeks." Almost a quarter of the way there. Already. "They said everything was normal."

"And…you're going to bring the baby to term?" The doctor was watching her. He was actually kind of nice looking, in a blonde, Baby Huey kind of way.

"I've decided to have the baby and put it up for adoption." At some point maybe it would get easier to say that.

The doctor didn't seem to know what to say, and Meera felt bad for him. She hopped off the exam table, but right as she did he sat down in the chrome chair. "Well…" Boy, he really did not know what to say. And he wasn't budging from that chair either. There weren't any other chairs in the office, so Meera sort of leaned against the exam table. The paper crackled against her butt. The doctor leaned forward and rested his elbows on his knees, touched his fingertips together. "You…have a prenatal doctor?"

At that point she figured she better just sit back down. "Yep. At West Point. My dad's in the military, so my insurance is there." Also, no paperwork.

The faster she spoke, the slower he did. He tapped his fingertips against one another, considering. "How many times have you seen him?"

"Once." She shifted on the exam table. Crinkle, crinkle, crinkle.

"And how will you find…how will you go about the adoption?" Still tapping his fingertips, just barely. His hands were big and soft, and he wore a thick gold wedding band.

Meera hadn't expected him to ask about that. But. He was a doctor. Who knew what they asked. "We haven't contacted any agencies yet."

He stopped tapping. "We?"

"My boyfriend and I—*ex*-boyfriend."

He frowned and nodded like he was doing some calculation in his head. She hopped down again. But he didn't still get up. He frowned, clasped his hand around his kneecap, leaned back and drew his knee in front of his torso, foot lifting off the floor. Then he looked at the ceiling and then down at the floor and seemed to come to some decision. "I have some friends. I mean, this isn't professional advice, but I, well I have some friends, and they're people I've known for a long time, wonderful people, hard-working, close friends, I mean they're just very good people, and they've been wanting to have a baby for a long time, five years, maybe more, and she, the wife, she only got pregnant once and it ended in a miscarriage, and I mean it was heart-breaking, and now, well, now they're looking to adopt, and perhaps, well, I don't know if you're interested in that sort of thing. I don't know all that much about it, and the truth is that I'm in no position... I just know that they'd really like to find someone."

Something in Meera froze, but she also felt bad for the guy. "Okay."

"I'm just throwing out options." He had a hard time meeting her eye. "Is that maybe, is that something you'd be interested in?"

"Maybe." She had no idea.

"Well." He flushed. "I guess I don't have their number with me."

"Oh. Oh well."

He looked at her chart. "Can I call you?"

"I guess so. Sure."

By the time he did three days had passed and she'd almost forgotten about him. This time he was practiced and professional, and he gave her a local number and said that he wouldn't call again because he couldn't get in the middle of things. He also wished her good luck.

But the number wasn't his friends'. It turned out to be the number of a lawyer. Still. It couldn't hurt to call and find out more. She sat down at the kitchen table and dialed. After two rings a woman's swift voice answered. "The law office of Larry McCann."

"Yes, I'd like to talk to Larry McCann please."

"Regarding?"

What was she supposed to say? She didn't even know the name of the couple. "Dr. Hugh Frieden gave me his name."

The secretary fired right back. "May I ask what this is in reference to?"

Meera didn't feel like explaining herself. And she didn't know the couple's name. Didn't even know this woman's name. And she sure as hell didn't feel like telling this woman the story of her life. For her to evaluate. And then what? Then maybe she'd be allowed to talk to this lawyer, this Larry McCann, who was some kind of lawyer but what kind she did not know. And then? Maybe he'd talk to her about his clients and he'd tell her certain things about them. Or not. And, if she thought about it for one second, he'd be making a fee—from *them*. Something in her balked. Whoever this couple was, they didn't trust her enough to give her their names. All she knew about them, the single fact, was that they could afford to pay a lawyer in order to avoid an agency. They could afford to buy more control and more convenience. If they found the right woman, they wouldn't have to wait in line like everybody else.

"Hello?" the receptionist prompted.

"Actually—"

"Hello?"

"No. Never mind. I changed my mind."

Her voice was bright. "Have a good day then."

That was how she decided to use an agency. There'd be social workers who cared about what happened to her child, people who believed in what they were doing, who saw their jobs as avocations. They'd be— what was the word—civic-minded. Idealistic. These were the kind of people who would keep her child safe.

Right?

Right. They'd test and probe and question. Couples would have to prove they were worthy enough and loving enough and competent enough. They'd be competing with other couples, and the best of them would get picked first. There'd be a *protocol*. And: think about it. There were thousands of couples who'd signed up for agency adoptions, thousands of people who'd undergone home studies and questions and background checks. Some of them had waited in line for years. It was one of those couples she wanted for her child.

Other people found her on their own. Weird how they always used the same phrases. *Less red tape. Adopting parents of a certain caliber. The kinds of families who send their kids to Ivy League schools. Our children have every advantage.*

Meera couldn't say why she balked. Maybe it was that phrase, *our children*. She didn't know how to tell the callers that. It was her child they were talking about. Her *child*. In her mind he was already a him. Who would be a person who walked and breathed and lived in the world, who would grow up and grow old, who would always be connected to her in some invisible, inevitable way, a person she was responsible for because she'd decided to bring him into the world. It mattered what became of him. It *mattered*, even if she didn't know him, even if she never saw him or talked to him. He'd exist because of her, through her. It was her job to make sure he was happy and loved and safe. Wealthy was a whole other thing. Not the main thing. Not the first or second or third thing.

She always told the callers the same thing. "Sorry. I think I'm going to stick with the agency."

They always answered the same way. "But *why*? We can help with the *cost*."

"It's just, that is what I'm going to do. I'm not desperate for money. I have insurance."

"But your groceries. Your *rent*, Maria." They never said *Meera*, always her legal name instead.

"I have a scholarship. And a job. Two jobs in fact."

"But you can *quit* your job. Maria. We—these parents—they *want* to pay your expenses. It's worth it to avoid the red tape. Our job is making the lives of birthmothers *easier*." That was the phrase that got her attention, the "birthmothers" part. She hadn't heard the word before. It told her there were other women out there, women who'd done this before. She wondered where they were now, what happened to them. What happened to Edie Carrigan

But the idea of taking payment for food or rent or whatever. It didn't thrill her. If she took their money she would owe them.

Besides. How would her kid feel fifteen years later when he found out how much his parents had paid for him?

27

EDIE

In January of 1985 my life changed. It started when I got a bad case of the flu and spent three brain-fogged days home from work watching one TV show after another. It was the eighties, so the programming was all talk shows and more talk shows, and my fevered little brain was having trouble keeping the guests and the hosts apart. Then Phil Donahue started up, and he was hosting some mysterious guest, a woman seated in the shadows, totally invisible except for the outline of her head and shoulders, and she started speaking in a clear schoolish voice about being coerced to give her son up for adoption, and she used all these words like "repressed" and "oppressed," and she said "we" when she talked about other women who'd lived in other maternity homes who'd surrendered other children, as if she were a part of a great and hidden group. Fever or no, I sat there bolt-straight. The woman was talking about a sisterhood who were calling themselves birthmothers and went to meetings and talked openly about their pasts and all the ways they were wanting to change their futures. She used phrases like "living our own lives" and she made it sound as if she and her friends were reformers and pioneers. They had a national newsletter, and they were mad.

Three weeks later I drove fifty-six miles on a Tuesday night to meet with the closest chapter of Concerned United Birthparents. The message from the meeting and from every other meeting after that was the same: the secret was off. A woman named Mary Jo told me that the laws about secrecy had been put in place before God was born so that kids wouldn't have to live with the stigma of being illegitimate. What a word, she said, and can you believe some rocket scientist finally figured out it might be insulting? So the hospitals decided they'd issue birth certificates with the names of the adopting parents, and the social workers decided they liked secrecy so much they wanted to keep it, and the new parents liked it even better because it meant they could pretend there was no such thing as adoption and no such thing as infertility, and everyone was supposed to behave as if. And so we did. We had. For decades. Mary Jo told me point blank that my secret was mine to own and to save and to store in an unlabelled box, or to crack open in the clean light of day. She called it "coming out of the closet."

I told myself I'd do it, one of these days, after I'd had time to prepare myself and my boys, but you have to realize that was during the time when my sons were sneaking off to parties, and kids were smoking marijuana, and the newspapers warning of cocaine and crack cocaine and something called PCP. Those were the years of my sons' breaking away, and I didn't want to give them the tools that would make it easier for them to reject me.

What happens when they find out they've been tricked?

I still had that message from Luce on my machine, and every day I returned from work and pressed the button, and every day after the messages from the telemarketers and the clients and my sons' friends all played through, there was Luce Waddell with her scratchy voice, and every day I thought: tonight. But then, after unpacking my work bag and the groceries and setting up dinner, after guessing at my sons' practice schedules, after soaping out the cat pee in the new carpet, each time I thought to do it, I found I was just too worn out, and wouldn't it be better to wait just a little longer so as to get myself more emotionally prepared?

Then one day a power outage cut the machine off and my youngest son reset the tape. A new message recorded over Luce Waddell's voice and before I could think to do a thing about it, everything changed again.

The call came at the end of a dinner party I was hosting, right at the end when my friends were clasping coffee cups in both hands, and brandy snifters sat on coffee tables next to their empty dessert plates, a tiny pitcher of cream, a tiny bowl of sugar. I was standing next to the sofa with a coffee pot in my hand when my son answered the phone and yelled down the stairs. "Ma, there's some lady on the line researching her family roots. Want me to tell her to call back later?"

The coffee pot clattered to the glass table. The pitcher of cream and the bowl of sugar jumped and rattled. Then I was at the kitchen telephone and stepping out the back door into the garage with the receiver and the cord in my hand and forgetting about the coffee and my guests, forever. I left the lights off in the garage, and the darkness was like the darkness of my own mind when I closed my eyes in my bed at night, except that the garage smelled of gasoline and grass and bicycle tires and pressure-treated lumber. Words spilled from my mouth into the receiver. "Is this my little girl? Is this Lindy?"

The other end of the line was silent. Then I heard a young woman start talking in a kind of practiced way, as if maybe she were reading. "My name is Pamela and I'm researching my family tree, and I've noticed that there are a lot of branches that are not filled in." Something like that. "For medical history reasons, it's very important for me to find out. I'm looking for the Carrigans originally out of Atlan—"

I cut her off, my voice a rush of air. "Pamela, are you my daughter?"

When she finally answered, her speech was very slow and very quiet, and I wasn't even sure I was hearing right. "I was adopted in 1959. I was born at Memorial Hospital."

Of course I wanted to ask her more, but exactly right then something swelled taut and thin-skinned in my throat, and I knew if I went too fast I would burst it open, and I managed only two croaked words. "What day?" I held my breath.

"May 17." It was a whisper.

And then that swollen thing in my throat did break open, and there were hot tears on my face and in my mouth, and a rush of snot that

choked me and prevented me speaking, and all that phlegm and snuf-
fling traveling right through to the other end of the line and God forbid
I make it any worse. Instead I wiped my nose on the sleeve of my blouse,
and the dark patch grew huge against the silk.

The young woman almost whispered. "I think I might be her."

I closed my eyes and tried to breathe, and the only thing I could
sense from the outside world was the smell of gasoline, and it seemed to
me the cleanest, most forgiving smell I'd ever breathed. Like diamonds.

Beyond that, somewhere past the kitchen there were voices very far
away, voices that stopped and started and curled themselves up like
question marks.

MEERA

The more her own plans solidified, the more the Edie Carrigan
investigation felt theoretical, maybe even fictional. Besides. Short of
driving to North Carolina, Meera didn't know what to do next. She
and Alex had made a list of all the friends their mother kept in touch
with. Which was like, four. It's not that Mom didn't like other women,
just that she seemed to do a lot of battles with them. Sometimes whole
groups. One time she'd taken on the Officers Wives Club. The whole
club. She was on some Christmas committee in Fort Benning, Georgia,
and she'd recruited this sergeant major to be Santa. Sergeant Hayford
was the husband of one of her colleagues, and about as fat as a soldier
was allowed to be, with a smile of big overlapping teeth and eyes that
crinkled like wrapping paper. He was also Black.

By Monday morning it was clear that the kids in Meera's second
grade class had noticed. A girl named Lisa was demanding answers.
"Isn't the real Santa Claus white?"

It was the first time Lisa Gaines had ever spoken to Meera, and she
didn't want to ruin it. Besides. She already had serious doubts about
the existence of Santa. A kid named Floyd answered for her. "Yeah…"
Then, for confirmation, he turned to Cheryl. Cheryl *Hayford*. Sergeant
Hayford's daughter. "The real Santa Claus is *white*, right?" Panic lifted
Floyd's voice.

Cheryl didn't move but to dart her eyes in his direction. Meera could see she had no idea. "Of course," Cheryl said.

Relief buoyed into the room. Echoes of *told ya* all around. Meera stood still as Cheryl Hayford and tried to disappear.

That evening Meera tried to tell her mother. "Floyd and Lisa said that Santa was supposed to be white." Her mother had changed out of her gray suit-suit and into the pink track-suit and was cranking open a can of Campbell's cream of mushroom. Meera watched her face.

But her mom just waved her hand as if she'd heard it all before. "A lot of grown-ups have the same idea. Your friend—*people*—like to make a big deal of these things." Meera didn't tell her Lisa wasn't her friend. "Black Santa, white Santa, what does it matter?" Her tone, her every-thing, carried the same message as ever: how silly of you to think this matters. This was an act, Meera was pretty sure. It mattered because people *made* it matter. Because they wanted it to matter. Mom tilted the can over the bowl and asked, "Do we always have to do it the same way forever?"

This was what her mother did: nudge Meera and Alex into some line of thinking they hadn't really considered. "No. I guess not." But she could still see Lisa Gaines's narrowed eyes, hear the panic in Floyd's voice. The soup landed with a *thwop*.

Her mom pressed the top of the tuna tin into the meat and drained the extra fluid into the sink, twisted off the lid, and dumped the contents into the bowl. "Think of it this way. Santa Claus is the spirit of giving. That means he can be any color." Nudge, nudge, nudge. "Right?"

"Yeah. I guess." Meera didn't tell her about Cheryl. The same way she hadn't told the kids in her class that it was her mom and the Hayfords who'd cooked up the idea of Black Santa in the first place.

28

MEERA

The agency was a glass-fronted unit in a strip mall, an H&R Block on one side and a dentist's placard on the other. The letters on the glass read "Catholic Family Services. For women, children, and families." Michael had found it. He was Catholic, so that was the direction they'd gone. Tall vertical blinds obscured the interior.

The door jangled when he opened it. A lady with feathered blond hair sat on a stool behind an enormous plastic counter, the kind that bank tellers used. The room smelled of synthetic carpet fibers and fast food. Chrome stack-chairs lined the walls, all of them empty. Michael approached the receptionist. "We have an appointment with Kimberly Boyle. The three o'clock." The blond lady eyed them. Meera figured she'd watched them in the parking lot too, trying to guess which category they were—women, children, or family. Meera was glad she'd worn her mom's coat. Like Alex said, butt ugly.

"Michael. Oh. Yes. And Maria. Oh. *Maria.*" Those three syllables released a flood of good feeling. "Sorry, you don't *look* like a Maria."

Meera was used to this reaction, but most people tried to hide it. Now the blonde woman took a frank look at Michael too. "I'm sure Kimberly will be *very* happy to meet you both."

The office was windowless and white, a crucifix and a framed copy of the Lord's Prayer on the wall. Kimberly Boyle stood to greet them. Everything about her seemed soft and edgeless, from the shape of her body to the expression on her face. She could have been thirty or fifty; Meera couldn't tell. As soon as they sat Kimberly Boyle made to reassure them. "I want you to know, Maria. You're doing the right thing." Blue plastic eyeglasses eclipsed her face, her eyes big as a Disney princess's, each lash magnified and coated in bristly mascara. The sentence caught Meera off guard. For some reason she right away felt like arguing.

"Thanks," Michael said. His hand twined with Meera's, and she was surprised to feel it there, his palm warm and strong. Bittersweet. She could feel his leg jiggling up and down.

Mrs. Boyle turned to Meera. "Think of yourself as a vessel, Maria, a vessel of Christian love. God is bringing life *through* you."

Meera's voice came out flatter than she meant. "I don't know if Michael told you, but I'm not a believer."

Mrs. Boyle blinked, absorbed this information. "That's fine then," she said. "We don't try to change people's beliefs. We're just glad you're here." She seemed to be looking for some other common ground. "So many young women want to be more like men these days."

"What do you mean?"

"Well, you know." She sounded like she was sharing a secret. "They don't want to be inconvenienced. To have to give birth."

Meera felt herself tighten, anger glittering through her. Quick and cold. "Yes. That's exactly what they want. What *we* want. Even I don't want to *have* to give birth."

Mrs. Boyle flinched, blinked at her. Michael squeezed her hand—hard. He wanted her to shut up. So she did. He was right. What mattered was her child and what happened to him. How he'd be raised. Surely that was the reason a woman like Kimberly Boyle worked in social services: because of kids. Because of *her* kid.

When Mrs. Boyle did speak, her voice assumed a careful tiptoe. "I'm obligated to tell you about our group counseling. It's required that we offer it but not that you attend."

Meera's eye fell on the picture postcards beneath the desk glass: a little girl in a white eyelet dress sitting on a bench, St. Francis of Assisi, Garfield the cat. Everything she knew about therapy she'd learned from TV. She lifted her gaze. "Do you recommend it?"

"It's up to you," Mrs. Boyle said.

Meera took a look at Michael. His expression opened, widened with expectation, and good Lord, why was she looking at him anyway? It's not like she needed his permission.

"It's just for the girls," Mrs. Boyle said. "Sorry."

And maybe it was that word *girls*, but Meera's brain jumped to some TV stereotype—teenagers with blue eye shadow and bitten-down nails and hot pink sweaters, all of them sitting in a circle of metal chairs and spilling the details of their lives. Her old claustrophobia kicked in, the weight of that pile of people, her cheek pressed against the grass, the sudden crush as each kid launched themselves onto the pile, the fear that something inside her would cave. "I don't know," she heard herself say. "Not now."

"Suit yourself," Mrs. Boyle said.

Under the desk glass, Garfield stared his half-lidded stare. She never did like that cat.

After that, she and Michael rarely saw each other. Every couple weeks he stopped by for what he called a *check in*. But such visits were wearing thin. Now, at twenty-three weeks, she'd discovered the meaning of the word gravity. The simplest activities had become chores. Like hoisting her body out of the car. Like wrangling the paper sacks of groceries out of the backseat. Like staring down three more hours of homework before she could go to bed.

She gripped the grocery sacks against her torso and made her way to the door of her townhouse. There in the fluorescent square of light behind the sliding glass door sat Michael. She stopped, tightened her hold on the bags. He was trying, she'd give him that. But it galled her to be a duty. And she didn't have time for it tonight. She thought about going back to the car, starting the ignition, and going—where? The library? Sure—if her notes weren't in the house, spread across her desk. And the groceries—the milk, the ice cream. She set one of the sacks on the stoop and slid open the glass with her free hand. Michael rose from the chair. "Let me," he said. He lifted both bags and set them on the plastic laminate counter.

"Thanks."

"No need for you to be lifting that." He picked out the desserts and fitted them into the ice-furred freezer. Milk in the fridge. They unpacked the rest of the sack together. Butter, cereal, onion bagels for Carlisle. He kept shooing her to sit down, to "take a load off."

But she just wanted to get to the bottom of the paper bag. To get to his reason for being there. To get to the point. "I actually have a lot of work to do." She'd made that bargain with herself: school plus baby. Baby plus school.

"Yeah, okay." He folded up the grocery sack. "Where does this go?"

She took it from him and slid it with the others between the refrigerator and the wall. Heard him pull out a chair and sit down. The stove clock said nine-thirty. She turned. "Michael—sorry. I have a ton of work to do."

"Fifteen minutes. I just have to tell you one thing." He put his elbow on the table and leaned forward. He wore a long-sleeved navy tee, his chest wide and solid as an armchair.

She sighed. "Okay." By this stage their path was pretty much set. And maybe that's why it seemed okay to draw the blinds, why it seemed okay to pull out a chair and ease herself into it. He could tell her whatever his thing was and she could get to work.

"I talked to my parents about it. My grandmother too."

Meera inhaled. So. They knew. That's what this was about.

He said: "We think you should give the baby to my mom and grandmother to raise."

He said: "Just because you don't want it doesn't mean we should give it to strangers. They could raise it."

He said: "It's their *blood*."

Meera felt immense, immobile, heavy as a house.

He said: "That counts for a lot, Meera."

She couldn't speak. Michael's grandmother was a short genial woman who could never remember her name. She lived in a lightless brownstone with parquet overlays on the floor, a velvet tapestry of The Last Supper in the living room, plaster crumbling on the walls.

He said: "It's their *blood*."

He said: "They could *raise* it."

She finally found something to say. "Your grandmother is in her seventies."

"My grandmother's *Irish*. My mother too."

She felt herself sinking, like water settling to the ground. To the bottom of the earth. "Your mom has a full-time job. She's already supporting like, six people." Grandmother, husband, two teenagers, Michael. Okay: five.

"They're Irish. That's what they *do*."

Maybe. Maybe it was. Maybe it was exactly what they did. But she already knew the people she wanted for her son: people who'd been waiting for years, people who were happy and smart and in love and trying to make the world a better place, people who were working on the cure for cancer but weren't too busy to play outside and tape band-aids on skinned elbows and wrestle on the floor and volunteer at school and read scary bedtime stories—not too scary of course—people who longed for family so much they'd be tempted to spoil their children but in the end were wise enough not to. People who were perfect. She said, "You don't like the idea of strangers."

"I don't like the idea of strangers." His face was inches from hers, his breathing fast and hot. She could smell it, and his body, all skin and heat, and even now she missed it. His eyes glistened, the muscles in his face and neck tight. It occurred to her that he wanted the same thing she did: the say-so. Over her body and over her child. When they were dating, he'd taken that right for granted, and she'd let him. Now he couldn't fathom what authority had shifted from his hands to hers. But that's what it was. The say-so.

Then she remembered it: the legal information from Catholic Family Services. The thought of that pamphlet shuddered through her. According to New York state law, a mother had the first claim to her infant. Once she relinquished that right, the father had the next. There was nothing to stop that father from farming out the child to other relatives and friends.

Everyone's child. No one's child. She took a long breath. "No way." It was the only thought she had in her head. "I don't want him to be someone's duty." Which was a stupid thing to say. Every child was someone's duty. "I want him to be wanted." She should have stopped there, but she didn't. "To have a sibling." Where had that come from?

His mouth hung open. "A sibling?"

She kept going, headlong, as if doing that would make her right. "And two parents." Maybe Michael had read that pamphlet from the agency, and maybe he hadn't.

"Why not? You don't want it." He didn't mention the state laws.

"It?" The pronoun made her think of a family heirloom. A silver teapot that didn't care which house it was in.

"You know what I mean."

She did. More, she knew her brother had been right. Ripple effects. This is what he'd meant. "No way," she said again. She saw Alex's metaphor differently now, like water, like waves undulating out and out. You couldn't control them all. "No fucking way."

Michael watched her for a long moment, like he didn't know who she was. Then he did a strange thing. He set his elbows on the table and the heels of his hands over his eyelids. Tears squeezed from beneath. And she knew. He didn't know about the state laws. He couldn't. And she sure as shit wasn't going to be the one to tell him.

But he could find out. Easy as pie.

She couldn't meet his eyes. Instead she sidestepped and opened the sliding glass door and stepped into the night. Because he was neither saintly enough nor evil enough. Because he'd taken too little responsibility and too much. Because he couldn't stop calling their child it.

Because he'd made her hide what she knew. And turned her into a liar.

"Correct information," the obstetrician said. He was this young soft-spoken guy. Javier Flores. Dr. Flowers. No lie. That was his name. The flowers were in the cadence of his speech, the lilt of his native Spanish. He called her "Maria" with that little tapped "r" and she never did ask him to use her other name. He leaned over the desk when he spoke, bridging the space between them. "The most important thing is correct information." The word "important" was extra pointy in his mouth. "I will give you the facts so that you can know them. In this country we have some programs. On every military base we have the Social Work Services Program." He paused for a long time, then slid a pamphlet toward her, his eyes gauging her reaction. "We have also in this country the program of WIC."

Something in her stomach dropped straight down. He was saying the same thing her mom had. *Are you prepared to go on welfare? You won't be able to do it.*

She gave Dr. Flores a long look. "You think I should keep the baby." She meant the words to come out as a question but they didn't. She'd pushed aside the opinions of so many other people, set them off separate in some other compartment where she didn't have to look at them. She didn't know if she could do it with him.

He shook his head. "How can I know these things, Maria?" He seemed to contemplate the pamphlets. "Already you know I am working in two... careers." He'd already told her he worked at the Planned Parenthood in Poughkeepsie. Because, he'd said, he had three sisters. "I see a lot of girls. A lot of girls. Some of them have lives very hard." His mouth tightened in a wry smile, his eyelashes thick and black. "I cannot tell them what to do. Or you. This is not my...privilege, I think? Like a right?"

"Yes."

"But also not my weight, I think, not my...burden. In the other clinic..." He frowned in the direction of a framed poster entitled YOUR BODY AT TWENTY-FOUR WEEKS. "Sometimes I have...opinions over the girls, the women, who have the babies." He paused, his eyes moving back to her face. "I tell you this because I do not have opinions over you." Another silence. "You will make your decision. I do not know what it will be, but it will be...correct. The best one. And I will help you with the other parts."

She closed her eyes. Not to cry in front of this gentle man. Took a deep breath. "Do you think I should be doing Lamaze?"

He was quiet again. "Yes, this is true," he said. "There are many women doing Lamaze. It is a nice thing to do, especially for the couples."

"It seems like everybody does it," she said.

"Many people." He nodded, planning his words. "I think, Maria, you are a person who wants to do the most scientific thing. This is good. But you cannot do every thing. There will always be more things."

"I want to do the most important things," she said.

He studied her. "Now you have rings." He touched his cheek below his eye. "Here."

"Circles?" she asked.

"Yes. Circles. This is from not sleeping I think. You did not have circles before."

She'd switched jobs. The restaurant had let her go because she hadn't been able to keep up with the orders. The walk-in refrigerator had reeked of rotting vegetables and the smell of the kitchen had made her throw up. Too much time spent curled over the toilet. Too many orders of pasta primavera wilting under red heat lamps. Now she was a night attendant at the college infirmary. "Are you telling me I look bad?"

He shrugged. "You look how you look. I am telling to you that which you asked. What the most important thing is. Most important is your responsibility. You are taking care of two people now. One of them is you."

Something in her lifted, some heaviness she didn't know she carried until he'd shifted it.

"Already you have enough things," he said. "Sleep is important."

She studied him, searching for the words he wasn't saying. "And you think it would be weird to be the only single woman there."

He took a deep breath, let it out. "Already you have enough."

"But what if I'm not prepared for the delivery?" she asked.

Dr. Flores crossed his hands on his desk and nodded his head gravely. "You will be prepared. I will help you."

"But what if you're not on duty?"

"I will be here." He placed his index finger on the desk. "If I have power."

She liked the way that sounded. *If I have power.* He wasn't making some promise he might not be able to keep. He was saying he'd do as much as he could. For some reason she thought of her mom. She would have liked that phrase too.

Dr. Flores shut the folder and set both palms flat on top of it, then leaned over the desk toward her. "I want to meet this baby too." He raised his index finger. "But. I have something new to show you. I think you will like it very much." He stood. "It is a machine. Come."

Minutes later she lay on the examination table while he coated the tight dome of her belly with translucent blue gel. "I know," he said. "It is very strange." He spread the gel with great care, like paint on a canvas. "The machine takes the photograph through the liquid. Because, Maria, it is the sound that makes the photograph, like, eh, el delfín."

"A dolphin?"

His face lit with interest. "Yes! The dolphin! He sees in the water with sound." He turned to the machine, adjusted a dial, checked an electronic screen. "One moment...." He held some kind of electronic reader inches from the luminescent blue soup and focused his eyes somewhere across the room, or maybe someplace even further away than that. He seemed to hold his breath. She did too.

And then she heard it: a fine tintinnabulation at the bottom of a gurgling fish tank. A heartbeat. *I'm here, I'm here, I'm here.*

Thrilling. Terrifying.

29

MEERA

She dreamt of Anna Karenina, the heroine heaving herself onto those tracks and into the path of an oncoming steam engine, slipping under the train and disappearing in a scream of brakes. Then Meera was awake, the phone ringing, the sunlight jangling through the sliding glass door, her brother Alex on the other end of the line. It was the middle of the day and she'd been sleeping—why had she been sleeping? Alex was talking, something about a winter coat, and getting it from her parents.

"Your what?" Sleep pulled at her, a miasma. "Why don't *you* ask them?"

"No way, Meezles. No can do. You know that." The sound of his voice reassured and worried her. He'd withdrawn from school, off failing somewhere on his own, just like her. The difference was that her failing had a timeline, and was finite, and his hadn't yet found a path. "Please, Meera. I can't do it right now. You have no idea. You always do everything right."

That actually woke her up. "I think you mean *almost* everything."

"Meezles. C'mon. You're like the fucking Rock of Gibraltar." He'd sent her some of his button-down shirts, size extra-large. The shirts were plaid and flannel, the sleeves flopping over her wrists past her fingertips.

"Where are you?" she asked.

"Winnipeg."

"Where's that again?"

"In Canada," he said. "One of those square states."

"There're *all* square, dumbass."

"*Please.* Just ask them. I'm freezing my nuts off." She could almost see him in a pay phone somewhere. Freezing his nuts off. Since when did the Dead tour in Canada in the winter? Whose idea was that? The last time she'd heard from him, it had been Seattle. She told him she'd been fired from her restaurant job, and he'd sent her two hundred dollars. And hadn't uttered the words *ripple effects.* "And Meera?"

"Yeah?"

"Any chance you could ask them to send my old one too? Howie doesn't have shit." Howie was Alex's old roommate, probably the inspiration for the trip. He was clever, iconoclastic, and stoned. Alex was way too invested in him. But at least Howie knew how to keep the Vanagon running.

"Yeah. I'll find out," she said.

"Thanks. That address works until next Thursday."

"Got it," she said.

Silence, the waiting kind. Alex being careful. "How's everything else?"

"You mean the baby?" El delfín. Sometimes she thought of him that way, *delfín.* Mostly she thought of him as Alexander, testing the name in her head. But she didn't know how Alex would take it. "He's fine. I think." Curled up like a comma, red and wrinkled and waiting. In the morning *el delfín,* swimming around in that soup, turning and testing the walls of his little pool, the flutter of calisthenic exercise, busy, busy, busy. He would not be a twin. And if he went to a couple that could not have kids, he'd probably be an only child. Only children had lots of toys. Only children didn't get teased before they left the house. Only children didn't get pushed off the slide by their siblings. They raced the Big Wheel by themselves, played seven-up by themselves. Team of one. Nobody knew their secrets. Nobody called them Meezles. Nobody called them from Winnipeg. Wherever the hell that was. "Alex?"

"Yeah?"

"What if you weren't a twin? What if you were an only child?"

"What? Jesus. What do you mean? Are you mad about the parka?"

"No. God, no." Parents loved each other best—that was the way it always was. "What I mean is are you glad you're a twin? Are you glad, you know, that we're brother and sister?"

There was a long silence. She could have sworn she heard wind blowing. "Jesus, Meera. Don't ask me that. I hate questions like that. But: yes. I can't even imagine it. I don't want to. I wouldn't be me. I'd be a different person."

She could feel her teeth biting against her lower lip. "Okay. Thanks for saying that. Like, really. I need it to—it helps me figure something out."

She had some power, right? Could request the kind of family she wanted, right? The problem was that Mrs. Boyle wouldn't like it one bit. But Dr. Flores had said different. *You will make the decision you will make. It will be the correct. The best.*

If only it turned out to be that simple.

"Of course they're all *qualified*." Kimberly Boyle placed the tips of her fingers on the stack between them: pages from a three-ring binder, the top one filled with typewritten paragraphs and covered with a shiny plastic sleeve. She spoke carefully, her spectacled Disney eyes watching Meera, gauging. "And our board has changed the policy." Her voice didn't cast a vote. "You girls now have the…oppor*tun*ity to see them." But her hand did not move. Meera noticed how slender that hand was, with its peach nail enamel, actually quite pretty. She tried to picture Mrs. Boyle painting her nails with one of those tiny little brushes, her lips pursed up patiently, all that time spent polishing and burnishing these ten little ellipses.

Meera's instinct was telling her to grab for the stack. Instead she held her palm against her tummy. Next to *delfín*. Alexander. Maybe his elbow, maybe his knee. He was turning into a very pointy kid. She didn't tell Mrs. Boyle about the perfect couple in her head. She knew it sounded naïve. And Mrs. Boyle kept her slender pretty hand splayed atop that stack, adjusting her glasses with her other. "In any case, I selected the couples I thought were best, just in the interest of saving time. You've limited yourself, you know, by this sibling thing."

"I know." Meera couldn't think of anything more intelligent to say. She wished Alex were with her, to help, to tell her she was right.

Mrs. Boyle removed her hand from the stack. Meera tried to slow down her heart as her hand reached for the profiles. The top one read #156. The couple was in their late thirties, married fifteen years. The husband worked in corporate business, what kind it didn't say. His wife had been a sales manager but had given up her job in order to perform her role as mother, which she felt was the most important one she'd ever have. They were active in their parish.

The only place Meera remembered seeing that word parish was in Victorian novels. Or Walker Percy ones. "What's a parish, again? Is it a county?"

Mrs. Boyle looked at her strangely. "The church. Community."

Right. She nodded. The couple had a three-year-old boy. Each child, they wrote, would have his own room. The yard was large, and the children could play. The school system was excellent. The couple said they couldn't wait to add the fourth member of their family.

Meera read the profile again. It wasn't exactly curing cancer. But okay. She tried not to think about Michael's grandmother.

The next profile was a hospital administrator and his wife. She was involved in the community "in a volunteer capacity." They too had a roomy home and an excellent school system. They too couldn't wait to have a second child.

Which seemed to Meera just fine.

The third couple was in advertising. They had everything the other couples had, and more. He was a vice president and she was a copywriter. Their application said they were satisfied with their life achievements to date. They lived in a spacious house with beautiful landscaped gardens. The profile actually mentioned landscaping. No lie.

They could have been a logical choice. Meera understood that.

They were college-educated. She was college-educated. They were in the field of communication. She was majoring in English. But there was something in the opening paragraph that hit her wrong. There'd been an ectopic pregnancy. There'd been surgeries. They'd worked and worked and suffered a great deal. They'd given it a long hard try, suffered humiliation, heartbreak. They didn't want to risk more tragedy. They felt they deserved a child and a family.

And maybe it was that, the word *deserved*.

In Meera's head, the perfect couple looked up. They were pulling their kid around in a red wagon. They said they'd be thrilled to have another baby. But they didn't say they deserved one. They didn't say their marriage depended on it.

Meera snapped open the black binder and fitted the profile back onto the metal rings. Mrs. Boyle inhaled and held her breath. There was a beat of silence before Meera heard the slow release of air. She felt obliged to talk. "It's just…I don't know. I can't put my finger on it."

Mrs. Boyle's lips thinned. "You know, I'm the only one who gets to see both sides of the equation. I see a lot of things you don't see."

Meera nodded. Well, obviously. That had to be true, right? The main thing was to be careful. Delfin couldn't do it, so she had to. There were traps and pitfalls everywhere, all around, every day, even in a single word. *Deserved.* It all came down to not stepping in them. Keeping him from falling in. That was her job, right?

Mrs. Boyle looked evenly at her. "You need to trust me." Her Disney eyes blinked behind the giant glasses.

Meera considered the statement. She *wanted* to. God, how she wanted to. "Can I ask you a question?"

"You can ask. I'll answer if I can."

"Why do you like this job?"

Mrs. Boyle straightened. "It's not always easy. There are many… challenges that you don't see. But it's…rewarding, in its way."

"Like, how? Like what's the rewarding part?"

"Just what you'd think, Maria. Seeing a couple's face light up at the chance to have a child. Their joy, their gratitude."

Meera didn't know what she'd expected Mrs. Boyle to say, but now her answer seemed obvious. And she realized: she didn't *care* about these couples, about who deserved what or who had what positions or who felt grateful. What she cared about was finding someone who knew how to love. Who wouldn't leave him or die on him. "Do you have kids of your own?"

Mrs. Boyle stiffened. "Yes. They're grown. Moved away."

"Do they visit?"

"Yes. Some."

Some of the kids? Or they visit some? "What are their names?"

Behind her glasses, Mrs. Boyle's big mascaraed eyes looked guarded and sad. "Please don't ask me that, Maria." There was loss in her voice. So. Meera didn't ask. Mrs. Boyle amended, "It's a lot of work, raising children."

Meera nodded, though she didn't understand what Mrs. Boyle was telling her. "You said you see both sides of the equation. What is it about this couple—201—that you like?"

"You know I'm not supposed to answer that."

"Is it money?"

Mrs. Boyle held herself taller, lifted her chin. "It is not. They deserve to be chosen."

There it was again, that word. Meera was starting to hate it. She nodded. They'd no doubt get a child one day. But not hers. It was too much to lay upon a kid. Besides. What about the things he deserved? "Are there any others?"

Mrs. Boyle drew herself up again, like she was trying to fortify herself. "There are." She didn't seem too thrilled about giving over the whole book, but she did it. Meera cracked it open while Mrs. Boyle watched. Among the couples who had other children, there were only thirty-one. The descriptions were written by the agency and were all less than a page. Meera took her time. She read and reread. So many men described as good providers. So many women described as homemakers. Lifelong believers. Regular churchgoers. So many deserving people. The decision felt immense. Here was one possible life, sitting right next to all these other, different lives. Each alongside the next. Other families, other cities, other sets of possibilities. But all of them similar in that one deserving way. Mrs. Boyle watched her the whole time. Meera kept returning to the same one. It wasn't the longest description, or the most florid or gushy. They weren't even both Catholic. The mother wasn't even a full-time homemaker. They were two teachers, a man who taught high school English and a woman who worked in a middle school science department. Maybe what swayed Meera was that they were service professionals. Or maybe it was because they were mixed religions and ethnic backgrounds. Maybe it was because they gave no explanation about why they couldn't have their own kids or why they were better suited than other couples. They just wanted a family. "How about them?" Meera gauged Mrs. Boyle's face.

The social worker scanned the description like she'd never seen it before. "Mmmm."

Meera had a moment of doubt. Good Lord. What was she basing this decision on? The slimmest of information. Some gut instinct. Maybe she should start all over again. Maybe she should go for one the couples Mrs. Boyle had recommended. The woman was a professional who knew what she was doing. "Is there anything wrong with them?"

Mrs. Boyle seemed offended. "Of course there's nothing wrong with them. If there were, they wouldn't be in the stack."

"Then let's pick them." Meera stacked up the other profiles and snapped them back into the notebook. Then she said it again, more definitely. "I pick them. Randall and Katrine."

Mrs. Boyle eyed her carefully, then nodded. Meera resisted the urge to grab back the stack. Mrs. Boyle opened a manila envelope and slid it atop several other documents. She slid a clipboard across the table. "We have a couple other forms," she murmured. "Both quick. This is the Thirty-Day Form. It just means you know you have thirty days to change your mind after relinquishing your child. By signing it you're acknowledging that you've been told."

Meera signed. "How many mothers change their minds?"

Mrs. Boyle looked up through her glasses. "Very few, Maria. But we do get a few girls who are...unstable."

That category—unstable—yawned before Meera like a crevasse. But she figured it was easy to sidestep. Still. The adjective bothered her. It hadn't occurred to her that Mrs. Boyle must be keeping a list of descriptors about her. But she was. Of course she was. She had to be.

Now Mrs. Boyle dipped her head to the side in a gesture that was neither a nod nor a shake of the head then pushed the clipboard across the table again. "There's one other form." *Preliminary Birth Certificate.* "Nice to have it out of the way. When the time comes, the last thing you'll want to think about is paperwork."

Meera began to print her name across the top. Mrs. Boyle watched her closely. "Caps. Use all caps. No mistakes that way." Meera wrote her name in capital letters and moved the pen to the next blank. *Name of Father.* Mrs. Boyle leaned forward. "That one's if you know for certain. Otherwise, leave it blank."

Meera felt her jaw go slack. Kimberly Boyle had already met Michael. Several times. Meera hesitated, and the pen blotted the space black. What was Mrs. Boyle trying to tell her? She lifted the nib. Holy shit. She knew. She knew. The law said that an unmarried father had first rights after the mother relinquished.

Michael's grandmother was a perfectly nice woman. She liked doing things for people, especially Michael. But she was already getting a little dotty, and Meera couldn't picture her face without seeing the velvet painting of Jesus.

Surely her two teachers would do a better job. Her two teachers of mixed religions and ethnicities who would not die. Surely. "Does my son get to see this document?" she asked.

"Not until he reaches his majority."

"And when is that exactly? Eighteen?"

Mrs. Boyle nodded. Eighteen years was a long time. Next to the word "father" were two blank lines. In capital letters Meera wrote "unknown." It would be years before she'd come to realize her mistake.

Behind the glasses, Mrs. Boyle's eyes were flat. She nodded at the form. They weren't done. "Bottom section." *Baby's Name.* Another conundrum. Meera hadn't realized she'd be able to make that choice. The name *Alexander* volunteered itself right away, and she started to write it down, then stopped. She hadn't yet asked Alex if he wanted to be the namesake of a child who was given away. Maybe he'd want his name saved for the next one, one who would stay in the family. Besides, she'd promised herself she wouldn't think of this child as her own. It felt too much like a claim, like saying hold up, it's me, here I am. I'm the one who gets to shape this new little person. Me. Mrs. Boyle was watching her. "Maybe the name is beside the point," she said. "Think about it. The parents are going to change it anyway."

So. Obviously. They'd give him their own name. Obviously. They'd probably been thinking about it for months. Or years. And now Meera remembered Edie Carrigan and wished she'd worked harder to find her. Maybe if she had, she'd know what questions to ask. Know how to imagine the future. If she had, Edie would have told her that without a name, a person wasn't real. That without a name, a person became a ghost.

Meera shut her mind off to possibilities, to doubts. She'd started seeing those undulating ripples in her sleep. Wave upon wave. Thank you, Alex. She didn't write anything on that blank line.

That was her second mistake.

30

EDIE

Lindy who was now Pamela ran her fingers over the photos in the albums, all those images of Simon and Aster, all those portraits of my parents and grandparents, the family Lindy had missed by a hair. By that time she was twenty-seven, so it would have been 1985. In some ways meeting her was exactly like television, with all that sudden joy, the repressed love leaping to the surface, the hugging, the tears, the nervous laughter, the excitement of the first meeting and the giggling comparisons. But it wasn't *only* like that. It was push-me-pull-you, really and truly. It was arguments and tests and long periods of waiting and silence.

She was a beautiful girl with straight blond hair and pancake make-up she didn't need one bit. For years my youngest son had carried around a piebald blanket just that same shade of tan, and now when I saw that color on her face it made me ache. Some days she talked to me about her wedding plans, and some days she talked about her work, and some days she asked about that long-ago day when the doctor had plucked her from my body with an instrument like a giant tweezer.

She was in public relations, which turned out to be a whole industry made up of smoothing things over and easing people's concerns and presenting the facts in the best possible light, and she'd won awards and trained other people to be good at the kinds of things she was good at. People liked her. But it always seemed to me that she had a vagueness about her, something not quite anchored, questions that hung in the air around her, and I always wondered how loud they sounded in her own head. Was her family an accident? Who might she be if she'd been raised by someone else? Where was she supposed to *be*?

Her parents were Larry and Mary Ann Devine, and she said that they'd loved her near to tears, that they'd spent years trying to conceive a child, all while everyone else's kids were learning to crawl, and then to walk, and then to pedal trikes and soon enough to get on buses and ride off to kindergarten.

I stroked Pamela's hair. "I bet. I can't imagine how that was for them, but I do know what it's like to become so focused on some desire that that's what you become. The lack of the thing. The absence."

Pamela looked uncertain. "Well, sure. They're also the kind of people who want to *help*."

The word pierced me, like always. I tucked a strand of Pamela's flaxen hair behind her perfect ear. Larry and Mary Anne had waited until she was grown before they'd divorced. "I visited them both," she said, "First my mom's new house and then my dad's. Then my mom got remarried, and she had another new house, and it was like it was their house, you know, hers and my stepfather's. Like I didn't have a stake in it. But it wasn't just that. I didn't feel like I'd *come* from anywhere either, because the people who'd raised me were no longer a couple." She ran her thumb over a photo in the album, me and Mosley on the lawn in front of the ranch house in our subdivision. "That's stupid, I know."

I didn't think so.

"That's when I started searching. They told me it was illegal. That I didn't have the right to know." And the same question hung in the air as ever. *How could you?*

Weeks went by without a word. When my phone finally rang, Pamela asked if it was a good time. Her voice was swollen with tears or beer, maybe both. "I don't want to take you away from your boys." My sons were grown then, almost out of college. But I knew what she meant. My sons who I'd born within the boundaries of marriage, my sons who I'd kept. She meant why them and not her.

"I'm sorry," was all I could say.

Pamela cried, and I cried, and it felt like a catharsis.

But three months later it happened again. *How could you?*

And then one night the telephone raised me up in the middle of some dream, and the squared red digits on my bedside clock told me it was 11:46, and Pamela was making moist noises on the other end of the line, and I heard myself pushing back, and my voice sounded fed up, even to me. "Be*cause*, Pamela, it's not so easy to stand out there by yourself and go against what everybody else says you should be doing, especially when you're young and don't even know what your options are." Maybe I didn't have a right to say what I was saying, but I couldn't talk about the law and the maternity home and my parents anymore. "So you end up going along with it, Pamela, because there's this consensus that buoys you along like a current in a river, so that you're always moving along with it, except you don't realize you're in it because everyone and everything around you is moving too. And it's only after time has passed that you can look back and see how you were borne from one place to the next, Pamela. That is how it happens." How *could* I? How could I *not*?

The other end of the line was quiet, and then my daughter said she hadn't thought of it that way before. Not exactly anyway.

I was surprised at myself, trying to figure out if I agreed with what I'd just said.

Pamela's voice floated out of the darkness. "I think I understand the idea of unseen forces. I'm trying to."

My irritation rankled. It wasn't that the Lindy in my mind and the Pamela who called in the middle of the night were so all-fired different. I'd expected that, and besides, it wouldn't have mattered what Pamela had been like, because I would have loved her anyway. It was just that the accusations Pamela made were the very same ones I'd been making to myself for so many years. Why in the world didn't you try harder? Why weren't you stronger? How could you have messed things up so badly? But when I heard them from someone else's mouth, they sounded unfair, and now, on this night in the middle of the night, something unexpected happened: I decided I did agree with what I'd told her.

How *could* I? How could I not?

When the clock read 12:16, I cut off the light and rolled away from the electric digits. There wasn't a thing in the world that had changed. Nothing had. It was just that it had been such a very long time, and somewhere I remembered what people used to say about me: that I was the brave one. Simon used to tell me that all the time, all those days sitting in Thelma's with our fingers interlaced and our legs pressed hard against each other, and even Sally, the college teacher who'd confessed to me under the hair dryers at the Home, even she had told me I was brave, and now I felt closer to her than ever before, as if I really and truly understood what Sally had known, had even *become* her in some way, and I would have liked to talk to her. But the Sally I'd known was gone, and the person she'd be now was an old woman, if she was alive at all. And anyway, there was no way to get in touch with her. I didn't even know her real name.

LUCE

In 1985, the VA had set me up in a temporary apartment at Carswell Air Force Base near Fort Worth. Which was fine. I was used to moving. Wayne was stationed in Germany again. Military life was about biding your time from one spot to the next, about living in a place and not living in that place. This particular apartment was a converted barrack, narrow hallways, shroomy spaces, the kind of unaired gloom that brought to mind my mother's boarded-up rooms.

The VA's case was motoring along. But I worried about you.

And I missed your father. I found myself imagining another home, one wholly ours, the one we'd cooked up on those vacations when we had time to dream about the future, to plan. This other home was real, already laid out, already designed: a kitchen open to a living room open to a dining room open to large windows, open to the woods. Big inside space leading to big outside space. In this future house, windows opened to the morning light, and there were flowering bushes, not roses or anything else you had to tend and manicure, but something wild, laurel or azalea, rhododendron maybe, something uninhibited and free and beautiful that stayed with you. In that other house, we had time to spend with each other. There was no Sergeant Mills, no *Christie* Mills frowning at me at the command center, arms folded flat across her chest.

The thing about loss, though, is that it's cumulative, one layer building upon the next until the weight becomes heavier and harder to carry. They added up, kids leaving home, friends moving, someone else getting divorced and falling out of touch, lapses and losses and people falling away slippery as water draining down an umbrella. You don't realize they've slid from your life until years have glided past. Too late you realize you've lost an easy or fractious relationship and finally see it for what it was: that it was love. You'd just never recognized it as such.

> ~~Dear Edie,~~
> ~~I'm sitting in these quarters in Fort Worth, Texas. Too much time to think.~~
> ~~I'm writing to determine whether you are in receipt of my phone message of December 11, 1984.~~

> ~~Dear Edie,~~
> ~~Please tell me you didn't receive my phone message from December 11, 1984.~~
> ~~It would kill me to think that you—~~

> ~~My dearest Edie,~~
> ~~It's amazing how life flies by! Wayne and I have two beautiful grown up children who amaze me with their—~~

> ~~Dear Edie,~~
> ~~I know you don't want to hear from me, but I'm trying to find Simon Bloom~~

~~Dear Edie,~~
~~I wonder if you ever think of me. The truth is that I've reached a point~~
~~in my life where I long for —~~

~~Dear Edie,~~
~~Do you remember me from high school?~~

31

MEERA

February opened into March and life became public. Meera wore baggy clothes. But she told a couple players on her soccer team. They were sitting on the grass, lacing up their cleats. It seemed as good a time as any. "So it turns out I'm not actually going to play this spring." Quitting was quitting, but she didn't feel too guilty. They weren't exactly Division I.

Robyn yanked her laces. "Don't be ridiculous. Maybe not as striker, but you'll be *in* it."

"No, I don't mean I don't want to play. I mean I can't."

Hannah was studying her.

"I have some medical stuff going on."

Robyn scoffed. "Like what?"

"Actually I'm going to have a baby."

Both of them paused mid-lace, their mouths open. Seconds passed.

Robyn glanced at Hannah. Leaned toward Meera. "Like, on purpose?"

"Yeah. On purpose. I mean it was an accident that I got pregnant. At the beginning of the semester when I got back together with Michael."

"And you decided to keep it?"

"Yeah. I mean, yes and no. I'm going to give him up for adoption."

"Shit," Robyn said.

"Radical," Hannah said.

Both Robyn and Hannah focused on suiting up for what seemed a very long time. Then Robyn: "So. Are you still going to be on the team?"

"Be on the team?" Meera hadn't expected the question.

"Come to our games. Practice with us. You know. Be the captain. Hang out."

"I guess. Yeah, I'm going to do that. Definitely going to come to the games." Even then Meera knew it was a lie. But she couldn't figure out a way to tell them she wouldn't, that she'd become selfish. It hurt too much watching them pass and chip and head the ball to each other, a team. It hurt watching their cleats pivot in the earth. It hurt just watching them pull on their shin guards. Even the smell of the grass hurt. Even the far-off distant smell of skunk.

Robyn said, "We need you." That wasn't really true. There were two other captains.

Hannah said, "I don't know if I could do what you're doing." Meera wasn't sure which part she was talking about. Hannah tried to explain. "It just seems like it would be so weird."

"Sometimes it is." The silence returned, except that now it was blank and Hannah probably wanted her to fill it.

"I think about that. What I'd do if it came to that. I mean, I guess we all do. One time I missed a period, and I was totally sure I was pregnant—I scheduled a doctor's appointment and everything—and then, boom, here came my period." Hannah paused for a long time. "I don't know, I mean I have really mixed feelings."

"Me too," Meera said.

"Wait." Robyn stopped, as if she'd just had a thought. "I thought you were pro-choice."

"Yeah." Meera let herself watch the rest of the team. Other players were starting to circle up, right legs crossed over left, doubling over in one group stretch. "I am."

Classes were less important, and more. Her screenwriting project was annihilating her GPA. Maybe her whole degree. She was supposed to be building this series of shorts, like all year and bit by bit, but she'd procrastinated from September to March. There wasn't anything she could do about it. It wasn't that she was too busy. More like the whole idea had become irrelevant. She had zero interest in writing screenplays, no matter how cool and special the opportunity was supposed to be. Zero. Nor could she think of a single thing to write about. Like her head didn't have room enough for a single act of imagination. Whenever she tried to work on the thing, the words that scrawled across the page were a series of monologs addressed to Alexander. And sure, there was a scenario where those pages turned out to be clever or poetic or postmodern or some other bogus thing. But these pages weren't. Just pages and pages of random fugitive thoughts darting around like jag-legged Jesus bugs on the surface of a puddle.

Professor Waldo held the seminars at his home, the twelve of them sitting around his colonial living room, slanted spring light slanting across the lawn through the sliding glass doors. (*Dappled*, if that word was still allowed.) They balanced their manuscripts on their knees or spread them out on the orange rag rug. Meera would have enjoyed it if she hadn't been in the process of exploding.

Today was her turn for review, her turn to sit and listen to her peers evaluate her screenplays. And it wasn't going to be pretty either. One: the plays were complete crap. Two: the plays were private, between her and Alexander. And three: nobody in the class had known she was pregnant. Ha. They'd know now. Or at least be *really* suspicious. Too bad she hadn't done a research paper in something like sociology. Too bad she hadn't buried herself in the stacks with note cards and indexes of periodical literature, facts, self-referencing endnotes. The picture of herself in the stacks was a hell of a lot more convincing than the one of her sitting here in Mr. Waldo's living room in this Puritan ladder-backed chair, this thin cloud of dread.

She steeled herself. The best she could hope for was that Mr. Waldo would give her a passing grade. In the meantime she was trying to find a comfortable position in that godforsaken chair, but the rattan was cupped just so, as if everyone who'd ever sat in the Satanic thing had

had perfect posture. And maybe they had. She figured the Waldos' friends were just like them: gray-haired and gentle and puzzled, with beautiful straight spines. From the kitchen came the sound of Mrs. Waldo and silvery little tinkle-clink sounds.

Alexander was really going at it with the calisthenics, like he was practicing karate. Like he and Meera were having this secret conversation the whole time. Good healthy kicks. Mr. Waldo tilted his head and asked the class for comments. Almost everyone was an English or theater major and almost everyone was wearing black—the color of Greenwich Village. One thing about the wealthy students that amazed Meera was that they were beautiful. Literally. Like all of them. Like they'd just stepped off the set of a Broadway play. Black jeans, black turtlenecks. The guys named Blake or Eli or Gianni or Jeremy sporting three-day-old stubble. Vintage overcoats. The girls in stirrup pants that narrowed at the ankles as graceful as vases, their tiny breasts poking against black fabric like Hershey's kisses.

Oh, and in case it wasn't clear: none of them were pregnant.

Meera wore her brown loafers. They were the only shoes that still fit her feet. She felt like an adolescent again. There'd been too much embarrassment in those days. Alex didn't suffer from it, lost in his world of terrariums and turtles, but it followed Meera everywhere, and lingered, and was sticky, that feeling, like waiting too long to be picked in the choose-up, waiting long past the time all the boys had been picked, into the time of not-mattering, the captain's what-the-heck wrist wave that meant you'd been chosen but you were a girl and he didn't much care one way or the other, and later the burn of missing a ground ball, or of saying the wrong thing, or of having a body that wasn't a male body, of training bras, of smells, of a nose too big and a chin too small.

Mr. Waldo cleared his throat. "Who would care to comment on any of these scenes?" (Or on the fact that Meera is pregnant?)

She tried to disappear. Besides, they weren't real scenes.

"Avery?" He started at the sound of his name, his eyes red behind his John Lennon glasses. He was movie-star handsome, dark-haired, black crew-necked, all the things. But he'd arrived late, which was probably why Mr. Waldo was calling on him. Avery paused now with a show of consideration, tilted his head to the side and looked at the ceiling with a squint. And right then it was obvious to Meera: he hadn't done the reading.

Ha. The joke was on him. Everybody else in the room was in on this giant secret. And he wasn't. A woman named Gretchen sighed loudly and folded her arms, caught Meera's eye and scowled in irritation. Gretchen was the only one of them who was older, in her thirties. Avery glanced at Mr. Waldo. From the kitchen came the sound of Mrs. Waldo cutting the faucet on, cutting it off. Garbage disposal on, garbage disposal off.

Avery posed theatrically, glasses in his hand. "What I appreciate about these scenes"—they weren't real scenes—"is their slice-of-life quality."

"Go on," Mr. Waldo prompted sternly. The class turned alert, not because they cared about what Avery was about to say, but because it looked for the first time like Mr. Waldo was annoyed. Like he might force a showdown.

"Oh, you know, the tactile quality of it. The smell of the air, all those physical details. These are the things that bring a piece of fiction alive."

Gretchen broke in. "You know it's a screenplay, right? Like, all dialog?"

Avery didn't miss a beat. "*Ob*viously. But I think it calls into question the nature of fiction and drama itself. I mean I really felt like I could see and *touch* these people. The inflections of their *voices*." Nobody pointed out that Gretchen meant monolog, not dialog. "Their *hands*, their *gestures*."

Meera heard a little bark of a laugh escape her mouth. The kid had some balls. She had to give him that. And *no idea* what he was talking about. She realized every face in the room was looking at her. She straightened the laugh from her face. Tried to deadpan. "I appreciate that, Avery. I do." But she was breaking the rules. They weren't supposed to say anything. The crazy thing was that she meant it. Everybody in the class knew this big thing and had opinions about it, and about her, and here came Avery, who knew nothing about any of it but didn't mind pretending like he did. Meera was no longer the biggest fool in the room.

Mr. Waldo cleared his throat again. He asked the class a question about metaphor, and they answered. A few students commented about the title. Then the rest of the discussion slid away, draining into analyses of single words and sentences, innocuous details. You could see it: they didn't know what else to say.

Mr. Waldo talked and Gretchen talked and they all made it through, and then the class was over and everyone was doing snacks and clean up and thank-yous and goodbyes and Meera stepped from the porch onto the little flagstone path and felt someone touch her on the shoulder. It was her, Gretchen. Earlier in the year the older woman had shared a series of stories about a fatal car accident and a life that had been broken into pieces and then reassembled into a more jagged shape. Her own silhouette had that same look, shredded and pasted. And she was the only student in the class who was older. It made Meera uncomfortable. Like any of them could end up her age, derailed by events lurking just beyond the edge of their plans.

Gretchen stopped walking so Meera had to too. Gretchen waited for two other students to pass, then squeezed her arm. In the center of her forehead was a scar like an asterisk. "You and I are the only ones who wrote about something real."

You and I. They had become a subset. The idea sent a bolt of panic through Meera.

"I don't just mean something that happened. I mean something that has emotional weight." Gretchen's mouth was long and wide, her lips darkened with some fuschia shade. Mouths had been appearing to Meera out of the blue, little mouths chomping everywhere, consuming, eating her up.

"Thanks, Gretchen. I really loved your stories." They couldn't be alike, the two of them. Meera couldn't be her. Couldn't be Gretchen. "They were...moving. And yes, emotional weight. I definitely felt that." But Meera was already turning her body away.

Gretchen touched her arm again. "You know the reason I took this class?"

Meera turned back, but not all the way. That shade of lipstick, almost blue. "Why?"

"Because I wanted to connect with other writers."

"Oh."

"But you're the only—"

"I'm not really a writer." The sentence leapt from her mouth and splatted on the flagstone.

"Oh, but I think—"

"No. I was just fulfilling the grade requirement. Jumping through the hoops." Why was she doing this? She waved her arm around the yard. "This is not really my thing." As if cookies and tea and Mr. Waldo's lovely writing life were some kind of torture. But she needed to get away. "Whatever I once thought about writing screenplays, I don't think it anymore. I'm sorry."

Gretchen tilted her head, trying to sort her out. Meera could see the moment she gave up.

She stepped around Gretchen. She knew she was being an ass. She just—it was something about the lipstick. Besides, it was too late. She'd made her choices and there wasn't any room for anything else. There wasn't any room to make friends. Or plans. Or think about delicious projects and careers. There wasn't even room enough to breathe.

She reached the path in the woods and pulled in the piney air. When she'd been a kid her mom had always pretended not to care about embarrassment. Pretended not to feel its stickiness. As if a person could come right in and do whatever it was she wanted, as if everything was just that easy. *Black Santa, white Santa, what's the difference?*

But maybe it was. Do what you bottom-line wanted to do. Don't think about whether people liked it or didn't. Don't think about them at all. Why Meera couldn't see that before she did not know. A March snow had melted, and the earth smelled of mud and minerals and early green grass, the creek gathering energy and silt. She'd chosen this one thing right now, this exact moment right now, in this one exact space, outside other people's opinions, outside Michael or her classes or her teammates. She'd chosen solitude. She'd chosen Alexander and this one thing right now. And there wasn't any other room for any other thing.

The path narrowed before her and the evergreens rose up on either side. She and Alexander had no secrets and no distractions. They didn't need Avery or Mr. Waldo or Gretchen. They were the strongest two people on earth.

Right?

32

LUCE

That spring it was amazement that brought your dad and me back together, at least at first. Amazement and fear. One minute we'd been a family of four, striving, and the next we were four separate people, falling. After Fort Worth, I'd relocated to Germany, back to Wayne, and the two of us had been trying to figure out our together-life ever since. The thing with Sergeant Mills had turned out to be exactly what she'd said. Eye contact, yes. Career sabotage, no. She never did get the promotion, but that turned out to be someone else's decision.

As for Wayne and me, we still had a pile of issues to work on, but we were doing it.

And now you and your baby were almost two weeks overdue. He grew and grew and made no sign of wanting to be born. His estimated weight reached nine pounds, then nine and a half. You kept going to classes, took a couple of exams, and ate what they told you to eat. The baby metabolized more calories. He grew. Still you had no contractions. Wayne and I didn't know a baby could do that: just stay. We'd been through exactly one pregnancy, and twins always came early. But here was a little boy who'd decided to take up permanent residence. In May we canceled our flights and rescheduled. In mid-May we rescheduled again. Then we called you to figure out what to do.

You sounded as if you were in some kind of a daze. "Dr. Flores said it happens sometimes. He said it's one thing to be ready in your mind and another to be ready in your organs and cells. Like the baby is holding on."

Holding on? I had an image of a child on a jungle-gym. "The baby or you?"

"Both, maybe. I don't know." So far away. As if you were on your own island, radio signals rippling into the ether between us.

Wayne's tone suggested he was supposed to know but needed a reminder. "How long can babies do that?"

"I don't know. Dr. Flores said he's on call until the baby comes." The way you talked about the man almost made me jealous. As if he could do no wrong. "He said it's not a good idea to go much longer."

I wasn't about to share the gruesome possibilities. He knew. That doctor knew. "There's such a thing as too big."

"If contractions don't start in the next three days he's going to induce labor."

Neither Wayne nor I asked about graduation. In those days a college student's health insurance ran out the day after.

"I have one more exam. I scheduled it for tomorrow. After that I check into the hospital."

This was the information Wayne was waiting for. "We'll get a flight on Friday."

I didn't say anything. It was one of the rules I'd made for myself. Don't try to influence. Don't be the heavy.

MEERA

Alexander really did not want to come out. At the hospital in West Point, it took thirty-nine hours of drugs and labor to usher him into the world. Time slipped its rails, circled around and around.

Davida was there, then she was gone, then she was there. There were intravenous drips and vomiting, Davida's voice, women's voices, Dr. Flores grim and focused, Dr. Flores peeling a pair gloves from his wrists, the sound of a trash can popping open and clamping shut. More voices, ice cubes clenched in tongs, the smell of bacterial breath, Meera's own. Deep breathing, deep sleeping, the lurch to consciousness, again.

And then he was born amid a crowd of voices, a crowd of stars. "Here we go." "Here he is." "I got him just fine." "Hold there, would you." "Got yourself an Olympian here." "Hey, big guy." "Hey, my man. You sure took your own sweet time."

There's the sound of his crying, and then he is there, this red bundle on her chest, way too big to be a newborn. Even she can see that. Tall, like her, like Alex. The nurse places her palm against Alexander's back, her other hand against his flushed skull. "Like this." She steps back and says, "Ten pounds, two ounces," then nods her head and lifts her brows like they should both be impressed. But he isn't chubby. There are no double chins, no dimpled elbows, only angles and length and new-grown leanness, like he can't wait to grow some more. "Look how beautiful," the nurse says, unwrapping the blanket. Meera thinks it's impossible, such limbs, so long, curled inside her. His knees splay like parentheses and the bottoms of his feet kiss, his little navel bandaged with tape. And his hair—fine as feathers and wet, his head untried upon his neck, swiveling and loosing in its newness.

His eyes, milk blue, look right at her, or try. They see her, and they don't. They light on her face and then her shoulder, and then beyond, upon some object behind her, and then, with another effort, back to her face. His mother. He stares open-mouthed, fascinated, trying to look at her, working hard to still the lurching of his muscles, to fix his gaze upon her.

Don't look, Alexander. Don't look, little big guy.

He tests the muscles in his hands, clenching and unclenching, the nails clear and soft and weak against the pink of his fingers. He grabs at her pinky, gripping, spasming, reaching.

And always there, her mother's voice: You won't be able to do it.

Unstable.

She sinks.

—

When she woke, a brown-skinned nurse with her hair in a poof was fiddling with something on the bedside table. "You made it." she said.

"I made it."

The nurse's voice turned metallic: "The flowers are from Michael." Like she couldn't stand the guy. Cellophane, a little bundle of flowers, something Meera didn't recognize. Freesia maybe. They were strange there, unplaced.

Meera couldn't clear the haze in her brain. Couldn't figure out why the woman was so annoyed. "Is he here?" She hoped the nurse would say no.

"He *was*. Kept wanting us to wake you up." No inflection in the woman's voice. She set a glass of water on the tray beside the bed, a little loudly, unwrapped the flowers. The flowers tilted slantwise against the lip of the glass. The cellophane she wadded and chucked somewhere past Meera's shoulder.

"What time is it?"

"Half past three." The window shades were bright. She meant half past three in the afternoon. The day had already passed. Meera had been sleeping for hours, completely absent. Three days was the time mothers and newborns stayed on the ward, three days, and Alexander would be gone. She'd already wasted one of them. How had she wasted so much time?

"The woman from Catholic Family Services called too," the nurse said, her voice just as flat. "To find out about the baby. She said she'd be by today."

Meera's parents were supposed to fly in Friday afternoon, but how many days or hours that was from now she could not say. The nurse fastened a cuff around her arm and pumped.

Then somehow the nurse was gone and time did a weird little skip, like a phonograph needle jumping ahead to the next verse. For no reason Mrs. Boyle was at the door, a clipboard in her hand. Meera was being asked to sign something.

It was happening faster than she'd expected. It never occurred to her that she might need her rights a couple days longer. It never occurred to

her to ask Mrs. Boyle to come back in a day. Or two days. Because this
was the plan, right? Why make the woman come twice? Why inconvenience her?

Still. Meera wasn't an idiot. She read what the contract said, or tried
to. Her mother had taught her two things about contracts. The first
was never to sign one without reading it. (Take as much time as you
want, Meera.) So she must have read that sheaf of papers. But she only
remembered what came afterwards, because the other thing her mother
had taught her was always to get a legible copy. There was a white copy
and a pink copy and a yellow copy. "Which one is mine?" Meera asked.
She hoped it wasn't the yellow one, the lightest. "The pink one, right?"

"Well, no," Mrs. Boyle said. "The pink goes to the central office."
She was closer to Meera than she'd ever been. She smelled girlish, like
peaches.

"Oh. The yellow one, I guess."

"Well, no. That copy goes to the court for approval. The state keeps
that copy."

"The white one?"

Mrs. Boyle's eyes grew even larger than normal. "Oh my gosh no,
child, the white one is the most important one. That one goes to the
agency. They have to have a copy."

Oh. Obviously. But. Her mom had told her more than once. "I get
a copy, right?"

Mrs. Boyle explained. "Oh, Maria, you're not going to want that
white copy, believe me. What if he comes looking for you someday and
there's no record of you in our files?"

It made sense, maybe. Or did it? Something about the logic didn't fit.
But Meera didn't know how to correct it. And good Lord was she tired.

"It's fine, Maria. We've been over this before. There's nothing new
here. Remember. We talked about the thirty days." Mrs. Boyle unclasped
the papers from the clipboard and fixed them with a paper clip.

Meera sat up, leaned on her elbows. There had to be a way to adjust
the stupid bed, but she hadn't figured it out yet. And for some reason
she couldn't let go that argument about the colored copies, couldn't
concentrate on anything but her mom's rigid rules about contracts. "I'd
like a Xerox copy please."

Mrs. Boyle slipped the papers into a manila folder. "I'll be sure to make one for you, Maria. But the truth is most girls prefer to forget."

"Can you put it in the mail tomorrow?" The problem was she felt so tired, like really inexplicably tired. She closed her eyes and gave in to the downward drag.

That was her third mistake.

In the days that followed, she didn't notice that the document never came. Later she learned that the agency had no legal obligation to provide it. She also learned that mothers forgot. They forgot conversations, the names of social workers, hospitals, doctors, dates, even the birthdates and genders of their children. It was all too much, too uncontainable. Memory constructed you some bare-boned story, and that was the one you took. The story had to be logical enough to satisfy your narrative human brain and tame enough to carry through the corridors of everyday life, hallways so narrow they held no room for the unsayable, the monstrous, or surreal.

Her housemates Davida and Carlisle showed up with cookies and oranges. They pressed all kinds of buttons on the bed until she was sitting up and looking them both in the eye. Mostly they wanted to know how she was, how she really *was*. They didn't ask what it was like, saying hello and goodbye, but that was the question Meera heard.

So. This is what it was like. There's the bare fact of him there: ten pounds of baby, his physical existence. You want to explain to him that his mother isn't there yet, that she'll be arriving in a matter of days, just a couple of days, and his new family will be perfect, because that's the bargain you've made in your mind: that you'll give them your child if they promise to be perfect.

You hold him. You worry he'll get used to your smell and your face.

You don't consider you might be too late. That he already knows you, the woman whose heartbeat has stereo-ed his existence forever and ever.

You think you might try to explain that this is for the best, that it's always been the plan, ever since the day he was a cumulus of cells against a uterine wall. You think you'll try to explain there are two other people out there waiting for news. That his family is so much better than you because they've been wanting him for years and years, that choosing a life is better than living by default. But he's doing so much work, trying to get you into focus. His muscles betray him, and waver, and jerk, and his eyes see you and they don't, lighting on your face and blinking and then on the middle distance, and then on your neck, and then, with effort, back to your face. He's trying to see you, to hold his gaze there, fixed there, on your face. On you.

As soon as her friends are gone someone knocks on the doorframe—a young man with unruly brown hair, a lab coat, a stethoscope around his neck. Somehow she knows who he is before he introduces himself. Dr. Polaski. The pediatrician. He ducks his head to the side, like he's afraid she'll yell at him. And there in his hands is a manila folder labeled *Scott, Baby Boy*.

He sees her seeing it and gives a little nod. He has a cleft in his chin like a movie star. "Your son," he says and stops. "I'm afraid his heartbeat is irregular."

She blinks.

He rushes on. "It's not uncommon. Lots of babies have it. Sometimes they call it a runner's heart."

"Oh." That didn't sound too bad. And maybe made some kind of sense. All those laps around the track.

"Probably it'll stabilize on its own—they do—but I have some concern about complications. He's a big kid. He was pretty crowded in there."

"Right…"

"I need your permission to run some tests."

"Tests?"

"Blood cultures, x-rays, maybe a lumbar puncture."

"What's a lumbar puncture?"

"Well, a spinal tap."

Fear creeping in. "For what?"

"Just to be on the safe side."

"Right…"

Forty-five minutes later he's back with Alexander in his arms. He hands him to her, the weight of her child fitting snugly against her lap. The doctor's voice nudges in. "It's not what I'd hoped."

Cold surges into her.

"I think we're going to have to send him for more imaging."

"Imaging?"

"MRI, CT scan. Like x-rays, but more sophisticated."

"Right now?" Outside it's getting dark, but this pediatrician has not gone home. It seems to her a very bad sign.

"It's a little complicated. We don't have that kind of technology here."

"Oh." The logistics seem incomprehensible to her.

"We'll have to send him to Columbia Presbyterian. In New York."

"When?"

"Tonight is best. Now, I think."

Those six words hit like cold water. Oh. "What do you think it is?"

"Probably not meningitis, but we have to check."

She's not sure what meningitis is, but she hears the words like she's under water, immersed in a pure susurrating sea. At the time she doesn't think about Alex's phrase: *ripple effects*. That doesn't occur to her until many years later.

Dr. Polaski's voice: "We're going to send him now. To be on the safe side."

"Okay..."

And then there's a flurry at the door, and, surprise, her parents are standing there with a grocery bag and this giant bouquet of flowers. She has forgotten. Today is the, today has to be—but time has lost its track and she can't get it back where it belongs and underneath the white fizz of sound her mom is saying something about flights and taxis and some kind of construction on a white stone bridge. She's wearing this crinkly paisley blouse and pink skirt, a strange outfit, a spring outfit. That's because it's May. Holy shit, it's May. Meera's dad looks bewildered. And really really scared.

In no time at all the poofy-haired nurse comes to collect Alexander. She pats Meera's shoulder and says, "Don't you worry, hon. It's probably nothing at all." On her lips, little patches of chapped white skin. "Don't you worry."

"Okay."

The nurse checks the water pitcher, fiddles with the monitors. "Just that this hospital doesn't get many newborns."

"Okay."

"Small, you know. Better to get him to the city. Just to be safe."

And then after that Meera hears nothing at all. There's the nurse's chapped lips, little white patches, her father's head bent toward the pediatrician's, her parents exchanging many looks, her mom hovering, the paisleys in her shirt like electric parameciums, and somehow Mrs. Boyle is back, or maybe she never left, and for the first time Meera is relieved to see her. Mrs. Boyle is there. She is there to catch Alexander. Meera has already signed her name at the bottom of Mrs. Boyle's pages. She's already told the world he's not hers. She's already released him, and now here he is in this freefall, the two teachers nowhere in sight, no one at all anywhere to catch him except Mrs. Boyle. And that is the next and final mistake.

Then Meera is saying goodbye, Alexander in a clear plastic box pierced by plastic tubes that run into it and into him: heart monitor, oxygen tubes, intravenous feeding. The EMTs arrive, their images pale and antiseptic, the efficiency of the staff, the fluorescent space indifferent to the outrage of the little boy without a name trapped in the box, the little boy flailing his legs loose in the empty air and thrashing his fury with open hands and feet.

And she's the one responsible, all her planning a waste, all the logic and resolve nothing but the brittle twigs of intellect. The bargain is moot. There's only the baby in the incubator, only the EMTs wheeling her child downstairs, her child who belongs to no one, who exists in freefall, alone.

Meera follows the EMTS to the garage, and no one tells her not to. And what if the teachers change their minds? What if they never come to catch him?

Dr. Polaski talks to a paramedic, his foot resting on the step at the back of the transport. The paramedic unplugs each of the wires that connect her son to the place where she is. Secures the incubator in the back of the transport and closes the double doors. First one and then the other. Walks around to the passenger side of the vehicle. Mrs. Boyle

goes with them, a clinical middle-aged woman and a tiny little boy connected to life by a series of tubes, alone in the world. He screams and
screams and screams.

Alexander, wide-mouthed in the incubator. That is the picture she
takes, the one she keeps, the one that stays in her brain forever, that tiny
face, mouth roared open in rage.

LUCE

The hospital was all astringent light and people in white, so
efficient, so styptic, so spectral. And you, split open like a watermelon,
your red insides dashed upon the ground, the EMTs glancing at each
other, the Hispanic doctor with his eyes closed, lips pressing between his
teeth, throat swallowing and swallowing.

I only heard the word meningitis once that day, but it hung all
around us, the air swollen with it.

And here myself, bloodless bystander. Spectator. Specter. Again.
My grandson-not-grandson was a beautiful blue-eyed boy, a not-so-tiny
changeling you'd chosen to bring into the world, dark hairs feathering
his skull. We weren't allowed to go with him. "Ward of the state" was
the legal phrase. I held him without holding him, held him the way you
did a neighbor's child. I wasn't going to go tumbling down that hill. I
couldn't help but think of Edie. How I'd been worrying about *her* hard-
ships. The problem with doing things over is that you're always looking
in the wrong direction.

Well. It came down to fear. You had never had the right amount,
even as a child. Especially as a child. You and Alex might find some hill
to roll down, but you were the one who found the steepest, most precip-
itous section, and not because you were testing yourself, as I might have
done, but because you didn't picture the outcome. You didn't imagine
what it was to roll down that hill and smack your head on a rock. But
Alex did. I did. You didn't *want* to picture it, and your feet took you to
the steepest pitch out of habit and out of greed. I thought of it that way
too, as greed, because the people around you were the ones who did the
worrying, who watched and imagined and held their breath.

If the baby turned out to have a disability, the adopting parents
would not want him. And if he died—well. I couldn't begin to imagine what that would do to you. As if what you were doing wasn't hard
enough.

You had risked everything, your whole life. And you'd never once
thought about it, just thrown yourself down that hill without a thought.
It made me mad. For so long I'd wanted to keep you and Alex whole
and unblemished, brand new and shiny, a promise that Wayne and I
too could be new and whole and unbroken again. I'd wanted to stow
you, wrap you up like drugstore dolls in cellophane cases, untouched,
where you wouldn't break or gather dust.

And here you were risking everything. Putting it all up for grabs. Just
because.

Now I wrapped you in my arms, even though your head towered
over mine. I was too small to shield you. And too late. I'd waited too
long, and you'd grown up. Grown way up. In a few days we might all
be caring for a disabled child. And for a long time to come.

Well. It was the self-same gamble every mother made when she
brought a child into the world. Babies got sick. You hadn't taken that
particular risk into account. It was too ordinary. I would have told you
how it was going to be, but I hadn't known how it was going to be. All
that time my attention had been directed at something else, and here
it was: plain old human illness, that ancient battering ram smashing at
the door.

Eventually you slept, your matted hair a dark wing against the pillow, and I couldn't remember the last time I'd seen you sleeping. I
couldn't remember the last time you'd been a child, the last time you'd
needed me.

You weren't like Edie. You had a choice. But you were stubborn
and once you'd decided a thing, you weren't going to re-decide it. You
were already rolling down that hill, gathering speed, your body a wild
spinning blur, your forearms drawn against your chest, big bony hands
spread to protect your face. And beneath my anger was a wild forest of
pride. Majestic. Primeval. Both you and Alex had turned out so fierce.

And then I wasn't thinking of you or Alex or Edie but of that David
Attenborough show, and elephants, and how every elephant mother

is a single mother and how the grandmothers and aunts and sisters all parent the baby, and that when a baby elephant dies the mother in her grief fondles the corpse, turning it over with her trunk and her feet, lifting the little body between her trunk and tusk. The other mothers stand so close that the great sweeping doors of their ears brush one other's shoulders. They mother the mother. On some rare occasions a bereft elephant has even been known to bend her great tree-trunk legs and kneel on the savannah grass to mourn. The other elephants don't look away, and they don't pretend not to see. But after some period of time their need for food and water rouses them, and that is when the other mothers nudge the grieving mother to rejoin her pack, her life.

Then goddamn it to hell I'm all over crying—for the elephants and for you and for Edie, but mostly for myself, for what I'd done. What I'd not done. How I'd been so afraid Edie would leave me that I couldn't see beyond my own fear. Couldn't see what my job was supposed to be. How I was supposed to mother the mother. How at the moment Edie Carrigan had needed me most I'd walked away and left her alone, kneeling in the long savannah grass on her mighty elephant knees.

I must have fallen asleep in the chair next to your bed, because your question pulled me awake. "Mom?"

"Yes?"

You still had your eyes closed. "Tell me what meningitis is."

Good Lord. You didn't even know. Or rather you did. The pediatrician must have told you something. "Inflammation in the spinal cord." I made myself say the rest. "And sometimes in the brain."

"It's serious."

"Yes. It's serious."

"People can die."

"Yes." I didn't mention the other possibilities. I couldn't. Not right now.

You were silent for a long time. I made myself hold onto hope. The baby would recover. The adopting couple would still want him. And you—I felt a dizzying fear that you would change your mind, a terrible dread that you would not. Then you said the strangest thing. "Mom?"

"Yes?"

"What's the worst thing you've ever done?"

It seemed to me the saddest question I'd ever heard. "Ah." My child, who didn't ever stop surprising. "There's a lot to choose from, Meera."

"I doubt that."

A dry little laugh came out of my mouth. Edie had been the innocent, not me. But now was not the time to think of her, or elephants, or any of it. I couldn't start crying in front of you. I felt myself smile some. "Did you know I used to steal things?"

You turned your face toward me, opened your eyes. "What? I don't believe that."

"Well. It's true."

"Like money?"

"More like trinkets. I took things from people I didn't like. Mostly little things, things they'd find missing and assume they'd lost. Things they'd look for. Pens, keys, that sort of thing. Also rings. *A* ring."

Your eyes opened wider. "But why?"

Why indeed. The tears came back then, and I tried to swallow them. You didn't look horrified, just befuddled. I pressed my lips between my teeth and looked at the ceiling, then took a big clean breath. "I don't know. It had something to do with anger, I guess. Or wanting to get somewhere I couldn't get."

You were watching me closely.

The rest of it came out too. For the first time it seemed trite, a silly thing to guard. "That ring you found belonged to a classmate's fiancé. I meant to give it back, especially after I realized it was a family heirloom. But I lost it instead. It just about killed me."

You stared at me with what could only be called fascination. "What did you do?"

"There wasn't much I could do. They knew I took it. But they never explicitly said so. They knew I was...out of control." And right then what felt like a sob turned into this snorty laugh, because it was all so absurd, and embarrassing, and how was it I'd never told you and Alex anything about that part of my life? The laugh was a relief, better than crying. But you looked so stricken I stopped and squeezed your hand instead. For a long time we both just sat there, breathing.

After a while you started to doze in and out. But then you spoke.
"Mom?"

"Yes?"

"Are you there?"

I stroked your forehead. "Yes, I'm here."

"Can you stay?"

"Yes, I can stay. I'm staying."

Part III

The Story
1985

33

MEERA

Time spreads out. It oozes like blood, and widens, and thins. Graduation comes and goes without her. She's released from the hospital. At some point her roommates load their things into U-Hauls and drive to their other homes. Her parents help her move her furniture to an off-campus apartment. Meanwhile there are low conversations about Alex, who's having some kind of meltdown in Ohio for some reason. His Grateful Dead tour is over, and there's some big mystery about it, and she can't tell if it's really a mystery or if her brain just doesn't want to put the pieces together.

Her parents rent a car to drive to Dayton. They try to convince her to come with them. She says no. It has something to do with remaining very still. Waiting to hear a piece of good news. Trying not to breathe. And the importance of remaining still. To keep from spilling.

At some point—maybe it's all the same day—she stops by the campus library by herself, which means her parents have already departed for Ohio. She pulls the building's heavy glass door and swings it toward her, the interior dim, dusty-smelling, familiar. She skips the card catalog and goes straight for the encyclopedias, a whole bank of them in six different matching sets. Grabs the first M and flips right to the entry. *Meningitis. Inflammation of the spinal cord. Inflammation of the brain. Can lead to brain damage. Learning disabilities. Seizures. Kidney disease. Death.*

She stops there. Leaves the encyclopedia open on the table and walks away. Ignores the student attendant's exasperated look.

Outside she stands on the library steps and stares out at the almost empty campus. The day is clear, hot, and hospital bright, trees and buildings outlined in the sharp acid light. A few people move around like fish in an aquarium, doing the things appropriate to their species. She has no connection to them and they have none to her. *Brain damage, seizures, kidney disease, death.*

There is nothing to do so she walks to her car and fits the keys into the ignition and backs out of the parking space. But there's no place to go. Wherever it is she's supposed to be she does not know. She turns to the right out of the campus gates, mostly out of habit. Fifteen minutes later she ends up at the grocery store. There have to be things she needs for the new apartment, right? She just can't think of what they are. In the store, more humans swim around. None of them see her or talk to her. She buys a broom. Milk and ice cream. Mint chocolate chip. She stows the bag in the footwell of the passenger seat, but the broom turns out to be too big and has to go between the bucket seats.

By the time she gets back to the library the encyclopedia is gone from the table. She checks the other sets. World. Britannica. New World. *Brain damage, seizures, kidney disease, death.* Turns the pages. Meningitis in pregnant women, meningitis in newborns. Usually bacterial, multiple causes. Pregnancy, sinus infection, pneumonia, listeria, processed meats, group living situations. Group situations. Living in groups.

When she returns to the car, the passenger footwell is covered in a livid puddle of antifreeze green. The paper grocery sack sits in the middle, a sodden island. It is not anti-freeze. The ice cream has melted. She can smell it. Mint. She has no paper towels, so she leaves the puddle where it is and the air-conditioning blows the minty sweet smell around the car until it's so cloying she has to open the window to the hot buffeting air. It occurs to her she has no paper towels in the apartment either.

She drives back to the supermarket. Buys paper towels and toilet paper. Drives back to the apartment. Cleans up the mess.

Brain damage, seizures, kidney disease, death.

She never eats mint chocolate chip ice cream again.

Alexander is four days old, the relinquishment contract three days old. Which means, what? Two days since the EMTs have taken him to Columbia Presbyterian, one day since she's left the hospital. She leaves another message for Mrs. Boyle. The assistant says she'll call the minute she knows something about the baby boy. She calls him that, "the baby boy." Meera waits. Time seeps and congeals. She needs the story. The story is everything. In twenty-six days the adoption will be final—if the two teachers still want him. His life weighs more than it did before. Hers less. She sees both of them, their lives, that had once loomed so large, full of unbounded possibilities, now receding to distant spots, tiny things, to pinpoints. The word "caregiver" hovers in her brain. Caregiver: the person who gives care. There are people whose lives consist of that. Caregivers. People who care for disabled loved ones. Caregivers.

The two teachers can't do it. That seems clear. They're professionals, with legitimate careers. Besides, why would they? All they have to do is wait for another baby. One that's healthy.

Her parents call from Ohio. Alex is shipwrecked. Sometime in the past few days he's woken up sober, straight, and bewildered in some downtown park in Dayton. His friends are gone. So is the van and his camping equipment and all his clothes. Her father sounds old when he tells her. "So much for the brotherhood of man."

"He has his wallet," Mom says, ever the optimist. "And his wits."

"That's debatable," Dad says. Meera blinks. She can't begin to process what it means. To start with, Alex will have to move in with her parents in Germany.

The words jump out of her mouth before she knows they are there. "Tell him to come here." But she likes the way they sound. She and Alex can split the rent. She thinks it is her idea. Later she realizes it's not. Her parents have seen the empty kitchen in the empty apartment, and they have told her Alex's story for a reason. They know.

And later she thinks maybe that is the job of parents, to let the children be the ones to have the ideas, to let their children save themselves. To stand afar off, even if it means they don't get the credit. Once, when they were eight, she and Alex had missed the bus so many times in a row her mother had had a conniption. Mom had made them walk to school on the shoulder of a four lane highway, their little metal lunch-boxes swinging at their sides like briefcases. It was a mile or two. Behind them chugged the family station wagon, the hazard lights blinking, the engine growling along in first gear. Years later the episode became a staple in family legend and myth, and Alex and Meera laughed about it again and again: Mom mad as a wet bird, both hands on that wheel, a cigarette pinioned between index and middle finger, watching her kids walk to school in the snow.

On the fourth day Meera calls the agency again. Someone different answers the phone—the assistant with the feathered hair. Angela. "Mrs. Boyle is out now, I'm afraid, doing a placement. You'll want to call back later."

"What can you tell me about my son, who went into Columbia Presbyterian three days ago?"

"I'm afraid I'm not allowed to give that information out."

"Oh." Meera doesn't realize she's clenching her jaw until she stops.

"Is there anything else I can help you with?"

She has only the one trump card to brandish. "Maybe. I know I have thirty days to change my mind. How do I do that?"

"Do what?"

"Rescind the surrender. Change my mind."

"Oh. *Oh.* Hold on."

A few minutes pass. Then there's a new voice. "Maria. Hi. This is Stephanie."

Meera doesn't remember a Stephanie. "Hi, Stephanie."

"You're on my list. I'm supposed to tell you that the baby boy is out of the hospital, that he's fine, that he's with his new family. As of yesterday morning."

Meera closes her eyes. The words feel like a placation. "When?" she croaks.

Stephanie pauses. Meera hears the sound of paper being shuffled, and that is what convinces her. "Nine thirty a.m."

Something in her gut unclenches. He's alive. He is living. "And the meningitis?" *Brain damage, seizures, kidney disease, death.*

"I can't say about that. But the report says healthy."

Out of the hospital. With his new family. Who still want him. Five days after the EMTs put him in the ambulance. No—four. Wait, Meera counts again. "Did you say yesterday morning?"

"Yes." Stephanie sounds pleased. "I thought you'd want to know."

"But I *called* you yesterday." Anger stabs at her, but somewhere in the distance. He is alive. He is with his new family.

"Well..." Stephanie hesitates. "You talked to Angela maybe. I was at lunch."

Another stab. "What else did they say?"

"What do you mean?"

"Well. Anything." How he'd looked when his new parents picked him up, what the doctor had said, how the diagnosis had gone. She has the outcome: He is alive. He is with his new family. The words land ebulliently but don't feel real. "Is there any way you could find out more?"

"I'll try..." Stephanie doesn't sound hopeful.

Afterward, Meera sits on the kitchen floor of her newly rented apartment with the telephone in her lap. Lunch? Had Stephanie said yesterday lunch? Twenty-four hours ago? Twenty-seven? The information feels strange, a faraway injury. But theoretical. He is alive, and he is healthy. The telephone line snakes across a field of linoleum and into the jack next to the door. She spends the rest of the afternoon there, sitting with her back against that wall and the end of the story in her lap. Say it again. He is with his new family. He is home. "Home." Home. Here, there are no rugs and no curtains and no chairs. Here there is only a futon, a metal folding chair salvaged from a campus dumpster. Outside, automobiles honk and gun their engines and the sound rips through the open windows. She hasn't left the apartment since the grocery store. The walls feel essential, like some kind of exoskeleton, a container for muscle and meat—her muscle and meat. Without that container, slick organs would ooze into the street.

She falls asleep with that picture in her mind, her organs, red and wet, slippery as silk.

⁓

She woke in the almost empty kitchen with a view of the underside of the metal folding chair. Three of the legs touched the undulate lino-leum. The fourth hung an inch in the air.

Her son Alexander was home. Home. Say it again, make it real. Or better yet, tell the story—because the story's the thing that organizes the tangle of facts and the mud of memory and the blank spaces in between. You have to have story even if you make it up yourself, the story you make about yourself, the stories you make for everyone else. So. Maybe he slept in a new crib with his belly against the mattress, his legs and knees bowed outward and his fist curled around his mouth. Maybe he cried and his new mother picked him up and walked him around and around. She was a middle school teacher, and she was up in the dead of night, but she didn't mind.

Either way there were celebrations. The teachers were telling their friends, sending out announcements. A new baby. There was this big shower, with presents wrapped in pastel colors, a yellow cake with blue icing. *It's a boy*. The three-year-old sister pressed against the crib, and a paper mobile fluttered shadows against her face and against the face of the newborn. He stared at her and she stared back.

For the first time Meera felt a little flame of relief. Something was coming to an end, or something else was beginning, she couldn't tell which. The two teachers weren't finding a cure for cancer. So. Okay. What mattered were the celebrations. People needed to know about the celebrations. For the first time she had a desire to tell someone.

Outside the sun was setting and a cotton current of air eddied across the front balcony. She carried the folding chair and set it up there, in the dusk of the long May day, forty feet above the city's arterial highway. Below her cars streamed by in currents of red and white like schools of fish, the drivers cocooned in their air-conditioned pods, moving from work to family and dinner and television and bath time and story time. Or they were high school kids, waiting to be released for the summer, cruising the city in their parents' sedans, restless with the news of freedom.

She leaned over the rail. There was no one on the balconies across the street. The wooden houses sagged and leaned, all of them white, or dirty white, Northern style—very serious. On the sidewalk below, a man carried a shopping bag with something green and leafy poking out the top. She had a crazy desire to shout hello at him, like *look, I'm here*. But he didn't even see her because he was looking straight ahead the way people did. "Hey!" She felt weirdly giddy.

He looked up. He probably thought she was crazy, but okay. She raised her hand and flung it back and forth, like some parade celebrity. Her face split open into a wide white smile. Whatever words you were supposed to say when your child came from the hospital for the first time to a home that wasn't your home—whatever those words were, she didn't know. But she needed to say something. It ended up being, "Happy Birthday." Her hand arced over her head. Let it be known. Let it be known that a little boy breathed and grieved and grew and was. That he was here, beginning, on the planet. Let his life be magnificent. Let *him* be magnificent.

The man on the street tilted his head like he thought she'd mistaken him for someone else. Or like she was drunk. But he also smiled a little. He couldn't help it, you could tell. Then he waved back in this vague tentative way—in case, you know, she was a lunatic.

34

MEERA

Time was a teeter-totter. It pivoted back and forth. One day passed. Then one more. Alex showed up with nothing but a knapsack. He and Meera ordered fast food. All that unwrapping, all that chewing, the swallowing, the long dry passage of whatever it was down your throat. Then start all over again. Another day passed. Then another.

Day twenty-two the letter came, the one the parents were required to write—agency rules. It arrived in the regular mail, between utility bills and flyers for gutter cleaning and pressure washing services. When she opened it, the picture fell right out: Alexander, flush-faced and wrapped in striped blue blankets, fists balled at the side of his head, thumbs almost touching his ears, looking at something or someone off camera. The letter was five sentences long, in this careful looped script, and focused mostly on the parents, how happy they were. How his three-year-old sister was thrilled to meet him. Meera turned the page but the back was blank. Nothing about his color, how he looked or behaved. Nothing about the paper mobile. Was he crying? Did he sleep? Were his cheeks red? What did his new house look like? What did his sister say? And seriously: what had the doctors said when they released him from the hospital?

When she and Alex were kids, her mom had made them write thank-you notes, a hyperbolic ritual enacted at the kitchen table, her and Alex squirming out of their chairs pretending they'd been shot. A five-sentence thank-you for a woolen sweater would have earned them a withering look. Yet here were two grown-up parents with five sentences to say about their new child. About *her* child. From two teachers. What did it mean?

She set the thing down, took a deep breath, then changed her clothes and laced up her running shoes and pounded down the stairs and out onto the sidewalk, the meat of her calves slapping against the backs of her nylon shorts.

The further she ran, the more she was able to breathe. Five sentences was five sentences. Still. The letter told the critical things without telling them: he actually was home from the hospital. There actually was a sister. The family actually was the family Meera had chosen.

If Alexander's mother had written it, it had to be true, right?

The adoption would be final in seven days. Meera was trying to believe her own words: that choosing a life was better than living by default, that women should take charge of their lives, that children should live in families with two loving parents.

The next day she wasn't so sure what those words were worth.

The day after that she was. And that they belonged to her.

The day after that she did not know. She repeated all the words.

The seventh day came and went.

Sometimes they'd be enough, those words, and sometimes they would not.

Then, against all odds, it was summer. She took a job doing data entry at the local newspaper because she wanted to have a schedule. She wanted to know where to go and what to do at certain times of the day. Drive the same streets she'd driven for years, shop in the same grocery store, listen to the same college radio station, all that. It felt important not to change. Important to remain very still.

Working in the professional world turned out to be a lot easier than college, and the people were mostly fine. The staffers called her "Ivy League" and teased her when she did their fact checking or Xeroxed their source material. She hadn't made a secret of her son, but the information never seemed to stick. No matter how many people she told, there didn't seem to be anyone who knew.

And after the workday finished there was only time, time when the sun was still high in the sky, seven more hours stretching out to midnight, a whole second day of time that needed filling up. She ran. She and Alex watched television—a lot—and it felt like they were both of them trying to stop thinking, or trying to think only in little bits at once, separately and together.

Something else was taking place inside her, a reconfiguring, like she'd taken all the extremes of her life and folded them into herself and taped them shut until she needed them again. The problem was she hadn't managed to save all the parts. Despite everything, she'd changed. The new parts had to be arranged to make sense with the old parts in a way she could live with. The new configuration was foreign, and distant. Sometimes she saw herself from across the pristine blue of some glacial lake, no way to get back to the other side where she'd been. Maybe she'd become the jaded friend, the Auntie Mame in the script, this sad irreverent woman who'd been everywhere and done everything and now made jokes about her figure and her ex-lovers and wore her nails too red and her hair too big. Maybe that was the role she was supposed to play. But that didn't fit right either.

In the end there was nothing for it but to go back to her regular self, the self that was waving to her from across the lake.

One night in September she returned from work and dropped onto the couch. Alex just said it. "I've had a lot of time to think." This was true. He'd been washing dishes in a steak house. The dishes came down one of those rubber conveyor belts and emptied into a great stainless steel bay. His job was to spray off the food with a giant swivel hose. Ketchup, sandwich crusts, rice and lettuce leaf, all went spiraling into the disposal at the bottom of the steel bay. "One of the things I think about is Immanuel Kant."

Meera didn't know if that was supposed to be serious or hilarious. "I mean, *ob*viously. Who doesn't?" Alex was into max-facial-hair then, and you had to look at him twice to tell if he was smiling or what. He wasn't.

"You can joke or whatever, but listen," he said. "I mean, the guy wrote a lot about what he thought ethical behavior *was*. Like how do you know what an ethical choice *is*?"

That picture seemed about right: Alex in that rubber apron, long hair curling behind his ears, hose in hand like the trunk of some elephant, chasing errant peas into the sink, him rehashing his philosophy courses while the restaurant moved around him.

Let him go back to school.

Like most of Alex's adventures, the Grateful Dead tour had started with Howie. "You know Howie," he said. "He was so crazy smart all the time. He always had a plan for this or that, and it usually worked. And somehow he had money. I mean we would work for a little while at this restaurant or that work crew, and we would have money, but then, after I'd used up all of mine, somehow Howie still had some left. So he would end up bailing me out. And weed. He always had that too. But he was always lighting it up for both of us, you know, so I never said jack. But I *noticed*. That he always had money and he always had weed. It was his way of life."

She didn't say it: Yours too.

Alex was lying on his back, staring at the ceiling, like a psych patient in a *New Yorker* cartoon. "So there we are one day, and we're in Dayton, for Christ's sake. I mean, of all places, Dayton, and it's early morning after a show, and the Dead are long gone, and we're trying to pack up our gear and all, and here come these two guys, clean-cut, you know, and one of them even has a button-down *shirt* on, and it's *yellow*. I mean, these guys have frat boy written all over them. Yuppies. *College* kids.

"So the one with the yellow shirt says, 'That's him,' and he's pointing at Howie like he's a criminal and they're in some pivotal scene on *Hill Street Blues*. And me and Maggie and Mark are just standing there, and I'm rolling up the tarp and the back of the van is open, right? With all of our stuff in there. Just hanging out.

"Well right then, here they come, back to me, so I say, 'What's the big idea?' And they say that guy there is a pick-pocket, and he supposedly took yellow-shirt's wallet and probably a poncho liner too. And I of course say, 'No way. There's no way. You've got the wrong guy.' And Mark and Maggie are yelling at these two guys already. So I say, okay, take a look in the van, if you like. This is all we have and you're not going to find your stuff.

"So they do. But the thing is, these guys are *Neanderthals*, and they start throwing stuff out on the asphalt: pots, boxes of cereal, Maggie's cassette tapes. I mean, they're being real *assholes* about it. And both of them are getting madder and madder. But the worst part is that while they're doing that I'm starting to doubt. I'm not totally totally sure I believe Howie. I mean already I'm thinking, okay, well that would explain a lot. And then they find it."

"The wallet?"

"The poncho liner, one of those camouflage things you get at the Army Navy. Big fucking deal. But Howie jumps in and says that it's *my* poncho liner and that I've been traveling around with it for the past three months. And the guys *look* at me—right?—because they're not sure. They're not totally sure whether it's *their* poncho liner or my poncho liner. And so they ask me, 'Is this your poncho liner?'

"And the thing is, I don't even think about it, I just answer automatically. I say 'no,' because, well, I don't know. Because it *isn't*. That's just what I say. It's automatic. 'No, it's not mine,' I say. And then there's this weird funny silence like everything is frozen for a moment, and then everyone looks at Howie at the same moment and then, *boom*, it's like a movie starts. Howie starts to run, and this whole crazy scene breaks out. Howie just hauls ass out across the parking lot weaving through cars like a jackrabbit and the two yuppie guys follow. Mark and I look at each other and we start following too. But it's a goddamn *parking* lot, and it's full of *cars* and people and you have to keep changing *direction* for Christ's sake, and you have to run around all those people. It's this huge parking-lot amphitheater-thing that goes on forever and ever and before Howie can get halfway across, the two frat boys catch him and all I see is Howie's head the first second and then the next second it's gone and he's down below the level of the cars, and I don't see *jack*. And by the time Mark and I catch up, we think we're in the right row, but we can't see them, and then we have to search around between rows of cars until we can actually find where they *are* and when we do, it's been maybe a couple of minutes. Not more I don't think, although I keep trying to figure if it could have been, but I think in real time it's only been maybe two or three minutes. I mean, not long, or at least, not long enough for *that*. And besides, these are *college* guys, right? *Yuppies.* But that's where we're wrong. By the time we get there, Howie is a *mess.* I mean a *mess.* There he is mushed up against the side of this Ford Escort and he looks like he's broken. I mean his face is just this bleedy *mess*, and he's just lying there on his side with his pulpy face pushed into this tire. And you know why? Beer bottles. That preppy little fucker in the yellow shirt has a beer bottle and he's going to town on Howie's face. And the other guy's *kicking* him. At a *Dead* concert. In *Dayton*, for Christ's sake. Jesus Christ.

"Anyway, long story short, they left me." Alex rolled to his side and sat up. His mouth was doing something under the beard, but his eyes looked empty.

"Wait," Meera said. She was afraid if she interrupted he'd remember he was talking to another person, to her in fact. But she might not get another chance. "Back up. What do you mean, they left you? And what happened to Howie?"

She'd dug too deep. She'd ruined it. But Alex sat back against the couch and sighed, one ankle crossed against his skinny thigh. He was wearing a black Led Zeppelin t-shirt, sneakers with no socks. "By the time we get Howie to the hospital and checked in and then come back and pack the rest of our gear up and all that, everyone is all mad, especially Maggie, and it's like I'm this big Benedict Arnold." Alex looked at his ankle, like he was watching the story unfold there. "Never mind the fact that Mark and I were the ones to chase those two away. The doctors patch Howie up and put ace bandages around his ribs and even splint his nose but he doesn't have to stay overnight or anything. They tell him he's supposed to come back in three days' time to have the wounds looked at. But here's what happens. When Howie comes out, he won't even *look* at me. I tell him I'll pay the bill, that I *want* to pay the bill, and everyone else is helping Howie back to the van while I'm charging all this to my Visa. And when I get out to the front of the hospital, where they're supposed to pick me up, there's no van. So I wait because it's only been a couple of minutes. And I wait. And then I realize. They *left* me. Took off. Dumped me. Cha-*ching*. And all my stuff is in the van. Not to mention the fact that it's *my* van."

"Shit." She didn't ask whether he'd reported it stolen. He wouldn't. It had taken him this long to tell her.

Alex looked at her. "I know what you're going to say." She didn't. Alex continued. "You're going to say you would have done the same thing." Was she? She didn't know. "But here's the thing, Meezles. Maybe you would have and maybe you wouldn't. It all depends on the way I tell it. I could tell the story in a way that makes me out to be a hero or something, like, yeah, I was standing up for justice and I got screwed. But there's another way to tell the story in which I could have saved Howie and I chose not to. I could have covered for him and maybe tried to help him later. Anyone could see that those guys were assholes. But I ratted out my best friend to them, and they turned out to be not just assholes but *thugs*. So I ratted out my friend for a goddamn poncho liner. There's that way to tell the story. That I believed a total stranger over Howie. And that story is true too." His voice was defiant, like he wanted her to contradict him. But she didn't. Mainly because both arguments had already unspooled in his head alongside each other. But also because she was thinking of a third way to tell the story. Like maybe he'd gotten fed up with Howie's bullshit and was ready to move on.

Alex looked glum. "If I were Howie, I'd certainly have liked to be given the benefit of the doubt, and I'd have liked for my friends to be loyal to me, especially if there was the threat of violence. But if I were the guy who was pickpocketed, I would have liked a little honesty in getting to the bottom of the problem. I mean in general I'd like for people to be honest with me. So which is the more important thing? Honesty? Loyalty? You want everyone to act with both of those things. So which is worse? Abetting theft or abetting violence? There's no book that tells you: okay, if you have to choose between lying and betraying your friend, here's the one you choose. That was how it was always supposed to be. There was supposed to be a clear choice, and all that mattered was that you were supposed to have the balls to make it, right? But it's not like that, Meera. Sometimes both of the choices suck. That's it. No book. That's all there is. Just do the best you can. Scares the shit out of you if you think about it."

She looked away. "I get that."

She could feel him watching her. She met his gaze. His eyes were brown and long-lashed, like a little kid's.

"Yeah. I get it," she said. "It could be noble or it could be selfish."

"Maybe it's both," he said.

She nodded. Maybe it was both.

She thought of her son whether she was awake or not. She didn't call it grief. She hadn't expected that emotion, and she didn't call it that. She didn't have a name for it, just the terrible Thing that sat at the front of her mind like a black hunkering beast. She got used to working around it.

In the spring, Alex enrolled in classes at the state university, including a course on Immanuel Kant. But after the semester was over and he'd passed the exam, he switched his major from philosophy to computer science. He said he wanted something more definite.

Within a year he'd met Kathleen, who later became his wife.

A couple years passed, and the beast moved into her cells and her bones and the blood that pumped in and out of her veins and in a few more years had become inseparable from her. She wondered if that was the reason people lit candles, to remind themselves that the beast was in there, inside them, and had once been external, a separate Thing out there in the world. As if the thing they were trying to keep alive wasn't the mourned person at all, but some earlier part of themselves.

Did the mourned person know he was being mourned? Did he care?

35

MEERA

In those years Alex and his wife conceived and gave birth to a tiny girl—born with an incurable disease, doomed before she arrived. The scientific explanation was cut-and-dried: after she'd been conceived, when she was an organism of just a few cells bursting forth with important messages coded in her DNA, another species had moved in: a cancer that attached itself to the cells that were supposed to become her central nervous system. The cancer divided and reproduced and tried to grow as fast as its young host. At first, the embryo won the growth race, and then the fetus did too, strengthening her tissues and muscles and bone at the crazy speed fetuses do, the cells of her prefrontal cortex splitting and reproducing.

The cells of the other species waited.

But now that she was a little girl, now that she had a name, the balance of power had tipped. Now it was the other species that multiplied with industry and purpose and greed, eating up Isabel's blood sugar and reproducing itself and colonizing the nerve cells of her spine.

Even after her second year, her body wasn't much bigger than Alexander's had been at birth. Even after her second year, her eyes were unfocused, reactive, her neck untried, swiveling in loose newness. She bore her suffering differently from other children, from children who had lived long enough to experience something else, healthy children who were surprised and affronted when pain moved in. For Isabel, there was no other feeling. It was what she'd known from the get-go. Her eyes lurched and her fragile limbs spasmed and kicked, but not because she was searching out escape. They did it from instinct. Crying was second nature—like breathing—the tone and pitch of her voice rising and falling to her pain, crescendoing, jerking. In easier moments she moaned, her tiny mouth working in little gulps and gasps. In difficult ones she screamed and screamed.

In those years Alex was a software designer, and Kathleen taught kindergarten. They both grew haggard, and somewhere in there they found Jesus and gripped that gospel tight. Every word of the Bible became a lifeline. Became true. For the first time, Meera and Alex's dad couldn't understand Alex. For the first time, Alex didn't understand their dad. God knows they tried, each of them sending out communiques like single-prop reconnaissance planes, little engines that stuttered bravely across the great blue abyss, the searches ever longer and more desperate, envoys that maybe did reach the other shore. Or that sputtered and spiraled and sliced straight down into the indigo void.

Imagine: Isabel died before turning two.

You can picture the funeral: there Alex and his wife swaddled in their fundamentalism, there her mother, a Unitarian who grew up with Emerson and Reinhold Niebuhr, there her dad, a dyed-in-the-wool atheist embarrassed by the South in the way only its most native sons can ever be, all of them sitting there in the first two rows of that Baptist church. The minister leverages the opportunity to gain some converts. (You have seen this before.) But there it is. It's happening. He's saying, "In real life, Isabel couldn't walk, and Isabel couldn't talk." Which is true obviously. She would never have been able to do so. But the preacher is heading someplace else, and it doesn't take him long to get there. "You should know that when Isabel got to Heaven, the first words out of her mouth, the first words she shouted, were 'Praise Jesus!'"

There are so many things wrong with this sermon that Meera shuts the preacher off, zones out. But her father, who is sitting beside her, cannot do this. It is not in his nature. If he's ever had the ability to look away from an unpleasant fact, she has not seen him exercise it. Now he turns to her and says in a voice louder than a whisper, "How does *he* know? Maybe the first words out of her mouth were, 'Why did you let me suffer so long?'"

The minister's eyes grow steely and affix themselves to some point over their heads. A woman in the front row turns around.

So. People have heard. Meera is embarrassed, obviously. Obviously there's some of that. But she also has to admit to some pride because, straight up, here is her dad who never agreed to pretend and still will not agree to pretend, his anger so clean and brisk it feels like a tonic.

The pastor talks on, now inserting the wedge just so, now slamming the mallet down with a ringing crack, now driving the metal deep into the woody pith and separating the flesh. His voice booms. "Now that she's in Heaven, Isabel walks and runs and leaps. Now that she's in Heaven, Isabel is dancing!" Mostly what Meera feels is something else, something less, weightless, groundless, a profound and permanent loss. Isabel is gone, Alex is far-off, and Meera is falling and falling, a long way with no end in sight, while Isabel, this child, this soul, this tenderness, ignites, exploding into light.

Later she stored her grief there, on Isabel, tied off like a balloon. It was easier to attach it to something that people understood. That *she* understood.

You'd think that grief would have pulled Alex and her together, but it did not. Alex and Kathleen had earned the right to grieve, but she had not. It was something they had that she wanted, and it stood between them. They were too polite to mention what she had that they must have wanted more than anything else: a healthy child somewhere out there in the world, a child she might possibly someday see.

36

MEERA

The weddings started: friends, cousins, co-workers. Which was fine for them. Just fine. But not for her. She was supposed to be doing something else, something that would justify having given Alexander away. Whatever it was, she wanted to be ready. She dated people here and there, but most of them seemed to sense she was looking past them. Like the Fordham law student in the cashmere sweater who took her to a French bistro. She liked him. She told him about herself, explaining the parts of her past she'd folded into the present, the pregnancy and the deal she'd made with herself and the months she'd lived outside the reach of public opinion. "It seemed fair to tell you now instead of later."

What was he supposed to say? You could see the facts sitting there in his mind, him trying to organize them, trying to think of a response. He looked down at his beer bottle and scraped at the label with a thumbnail. She could see that he was starting to lose his hair. It was what they were all doing, really, striding already into middle age. "That's okay with me," he said. "I mean, I'm okay with that. I guess I'd like to know what happened to the father." He looked up, pooched out his lips and puffed air through them like a musical instrument. "Whether you still see him."

This was the way conversations usually went.

A couple years later she sat with another man on another date, this time in a coffeehouse. He had receding hair too, which gave his face a long look that didn't fit the streak of silliness she already knew he had. She'd seen him do the chicken dance at weddings, seen him shop in toy stores. He was especially drawn to the gadgets that made whirring or clanging or whistling noises, the louder the better. First he bought the toys, and then he decided who to give them to. Sometimes he kept them for himself. She said the thing she always said, about having had a child, about telling him now instead of later.

He was silent for a long time. Then he said, "Huh." Then: "I have a lot of questions. Maybe for later, though." Then he touched her hand and pursed his lips, one corner dimpling with unease. He said something no one ever had. "I'm sorry that happened to you. I'm sorry you had to go through that."

Him, she thought. Perhaps she could marry *him*.

It wasn't too long before she told him everything else. About the medical stuff, the difficult delivery. How her cervix had been torn apart, that it was supposed to look like a donut but instead looked like some postapocalyptic mutant Pac-Man. So.

They were thirty when they married. Heath was way more spontaneous and youthful than she was. They lived in Knoxville and spent their weekends in the woods—what was left of them—hiking mountain gorges or climbing sandstone and quartzite rock faces with their friends. They owned two trucks, both sand-covered, both smelling like mildew. They didn't have children. Because of her damaged body. Because of all the things competing for their time.

There was more to it than that, obviously: a sense of disloyalty, like having once bartered her way out of motherhood, she wasn't allowed to change her mind. Instead she committed to theater, where she tried her hand at playwriting, then set design, then stage management, always searching out structure and meaning. Make yourself useful. That was the way you turned your life around. Turned your*self* around. She ended up in the field of puppetry arts, where she worked several angles: the shows, the children's outreach, the fundraising. By the time she was thirty-four, she was an assistant director. And that should have meant something, how she'd made a place for herself in her city's art scene.

But it wasn't enough. She'd given away a child. She didn't think it had been for this. It should have been for something else, something bigger that would prove she'd made the right decision. Something worth it.

"How many children do you have?" It's the same old question, about halfway down the page of the medical history form. She doesn't know how to answer. She writes: one. Delivery: vaginal. This doctor's visit isn't so different from others. The gyno is a white woman in her fifties, slim and bespectacled. While checking for lumps in Meera's chest, she asks her all those get-to-know-you questions that are supposed to distract you from the fact that a stranger is touching your breasts. The doc starts with what should be the safest one. "How old is your son?"

Meera pauses. It's a familiar dilemma. If she gives his age, the doc will ask the next most obvious thing. Where does he go to school? What does he like to do? Meera's learned the hard way. The best thing to do is to tell this woman the truth. And anyway. The doc's a professional, who's seen it all, right? "I had an unplanned pregnancy in college. I decided to have the baby and give him up for adoption."

The doctor's response is immediate. "Good for you! I wish more women would do that!" Her hands on Meera's chest are cool and dry. Meera shrinks from them. Does the doctor mean her other patients? That more of her patients should give their kids away? Or is she talking about abortion? That fewer women should have them? The woman senses her distrust and hurries to clarify. "You made someone extremely happy."

So. That. The doctor wishes more of her patients would give their children away. To make someone happy. Meera wonders what they're like, her other patients, and how the doctor can wish that on them. She closes her eyes and sees a young woman holding her newborn tight against her chest, left hand flat between the baby's shoulder blades, right hand cradling his little diapered butt. The person lifting the infant from her arms is the doctor. Her white lab coat hides the hurt on the young mother's face.

Meera doesn't want to have an argument, especially while she's naked under this woman's hands. Nor does she want to talk about ripple effects. Still. Some part of her wants to slow the pace of the doc's galloping conclusions. "It's not as easy as you might think," she manages. "I had good insurance. I had a lot of options. A lot of support." She was young and horse-healthy. She was—what's that word Alex used to call her?—simplistic.

"Of course it's not," the doctor says brightly. She sets a speculum on the little tray, ready for action. "That's why more people don't do it. You made a family very happy."

And *her*, Meera thinks. She's made the doctor very happy. "I didn't do it for them. I did it for myself." It sounds terrible, she knows. But it bothers her somehow, this woman imagining she had changed the course of her life for the sake of some nice deserving couple she didn't even know.

The doc sets up the stirrups and pats the exam table. Meera scoots to the edge, grateful for the silence.

37

MEERA

Her father asks her on Christmas night. She's washing the dinner pots, and he's loading plates into the dishwasher. "Do you ever think about your son?" Certain topics they discuss only while doing dishes. No eye contact required. Plus the other person has the chance to change the subject if they need an out. She scrubs the carbonized grease in the bottom of the roasting pan.

It's been twelve years since the EMTs took Alexander away. "Yeah," she says. Over the years, the topic's become heavy. If it were lighter, easier to lift, maybe she'd say she's surprised how she never stops feeling responsibility for a person she brought into the world. Or maybe she'd say it'd be better if she knew what sort of kid he's become. She could say she mourns him, but doesn't regret him. She could say she's glad to have a son out there in the world, an underground river that sprang from her body but now passes through lands she cannot see or guess, this twelve-year-old who blinks and breathes and talks on the phone and scrubs his ears, who scribbles in the margins of notebooks or stares out of windows, who has big wrists and ankles and grows like a poplar. Maybe he plays basketball or skateboards through parking lots or sits in barbers' chairs or parts his hair on the side. Maybe he carries a backpack or a clarinet. Maybe he keeps a keychain hanging from his belt loop. Maybe he has a silver dollar in his pocket. A guitar pick. A lunch card. A paperback book. Maybe he still has blue eyes.

But she doesn't say any of that.

If she did, her dad might say, "I wish we'd known how to help you more." But he doesn't say that either. Those aren't the kinds of conversations that happen in real life. Those are the kinds of conversations that happen in movies, where scriptwriters sculpt the dialogue into better, more meaningful shapes. She and her parents have shared an experience without sharing it at all. They've each of them experienced it alone, her parents in two different states busy fixing whatever happened to their marriage, and she and Alex falling, each in their own particular gravities. Then the other loss: of Isabel, a heaviness that never goes away.

They've all failed one another, all of them weaker than they wanted to be.

When her father was a young man, he'd sung the bass parts in two different glee clubs, the pauses in the bass line as important as the notes. Silence has its own speaking role, but you have to know how to listen, how to hear. Now the facts of their lives sit there between them, and daughter and father understand what the silence says: that they are small. Puny. Neither wants to think of the other this way. It shames them.

Her father dries a spatula with a dish towel. "I think about him too."

"Yeah." She turns the roaster to dump the suds, and the stainless steel clangs against the enameled sink, a welcome racket. "Thanks for saying that."

"There was a girl in our high school who went through something similar. Course, things were different then. Your mother tried to get in touch with her. But the woman never called her back." He picks up a wet serving bowl. "I always wondered what happened to her too."

LUCE

Wayne and I finally built our house in the country, high on a mountain in the woods, as much space as we wanted, which was perverse, since you and Alex were long gone. We were both scaling back some, not retiring, but looking in that direction. For the first time in years I felt as if I had time to think, which was sometimes a gift and sometimes not. Now that the world had stopped spinning at maximum speed, my mind traveled more and more to the past and to the people I'd lost, including Isabel, including my parents who didn't exist anymore, and to the question of whether they were still real. And over the years I'd decided they were real if I made them real, and kept them real, so that my father stayed as real to me as ever he'd been but my mother had long since ceased to be.

But I'd lost other people too. And some of them were still alive.

Dear Edie,
I have a daughter now, and certain events have conspired to bring you to my mind more than ever.

Dear Edie,
We've lost two grandchildren.

My dear Edie,
Yesterday I was watching that David Attenborough show — yes, it is still on — and they were doing a bit on elephants.

My dearest old friend,
Where are you?

MEERA

After eighteen years, Meera tried writing her college play again. The piece turned into a dialog with Alexander's mother. It came out terrible (again), so she wrote another. And then another. In a story there was cause and effect. The characters were free agents that caused certain outcomes. That's what made it a story instead of a list of random events. The teller arranged the parts sequentially, machine-like, where the person-as-agent set the mechanism in motion, and one gear moved another, which moved another, and so on down the line, until the causes moved the pistons toward the final event, the final effect. But some of the pieces got lost. When you told the story, those parts had to be invented. Other pieces didn't fit quite right, and they had to be left out. Pretty soon it wasn't clear who or what the agent was behind the event, and in the end the gears in the machine turned both ways.

Alexander would be almost eighteen years old. *Was* almost eighteen years old.

In a few months he could request information about his biological parents. For eighteen years she'd scripted the scene in her mind: a revelation that occurred at the agency amid lots of suspense and fanfare: there his worried father, there his protective mother, there the supportive agency personnel (they're so happy he's come to claim this gift they've held for so long). He opens the file that contains his first identity. The names and the places mean nothing to him, obviously. What resonates is their very existence, their plain typewritten letters, this genealogy that threads and reaches through history, integral and alive as his own nervous system.

His birthday loomed. She couldn't sleep for thinking about what came next. What bothered her was the word "unknown." How had she written that? Why had she written it? And what if she died before Alexander came looking? He'd never be able to find out who Michael was. What in the hell was wrong with her?

She typed "Michael Campion" into the Google search bar. Up came the website at his bank, a page of vice presidents, his solid suited self. He looked fit, but all that beautiful russet hair was gone. The muttonchops too. She clicked on the biography. The blurb said he lived in Boston with his wife and three kids. She was surprised to realize the information pleased her.

She moused back to the search bar and typed "Catholic Family Services." She'd email them, find out how to change the records. Tell them the father's name wasn't on the birth certificate, that she wanted to have the records put right. If they couldn't do that, they could add a letter to the file. It would no doubt involve filling out a form, or several forms. So what. She knew how to navigate bureaucracy, knew where to find a notary.

The search results stacked up on the screen. At the top of the list: "I am a male who was adopted through Catholic Family Services. I am in search of my birthmother."

Something in her chest turned a cartwheel.

"I was born in 1980."

The wrong year. The thing in her chest fell gymnastically.

But why had he posted this way? Mrs. Boyle had said her son would have access to his records when he was eighteen, that this was the policy of the bureau. Didn't this guy know that?

Unless.

Alexander was out there somewhere. And he was findable. That's when something inside her clicked, some forgotten switch that toggled from off to on, a low backdrop noise, a constant generative hum. Like awareness. It was also permanent.

She wrote a letter to Catholic Family Services that same day.

Once she discovered Googling she couldn't stop. She searched the word "adoption" and watched the first results tally down the screen: all those agencies asking the same series of questions: "Are you pregnant and scared? Do you need help?" None came right out and said it: that they were searching for women willing to gestate babies for nine months then give them away. Photos of smiling pregnant women beamed at her.

After Isabel had died, Alex and his wife had adopted a little girl from Korea. They'd waited in a Seoul hotel room for two blank months before they knew that Jana could be theirs. Now he was teaching her to fly fish. The first time she'd asked to go to the river with him he'd been goofy with pride. Because he hadn't pushed her into the sport. Because it was the art and craft of it that attracted her: all those feathers and hackles and hooks and leaders and God knows what else they used. How Jana's hands tied complicated little flies more easily than his giant paws. Meera listened to his happy loud complaints about the extra small waders he'd had to special-order from some company in Montana.

Jana was a healthy athletic girl. Thoughtful. With riddles in her eyes.

Meera couldn't stop wondering about her, where she'd come from, who her first mother had been. What happened to her. What happened to any of them. Why their voices were never heard.

She started researching on her days off. It didn't take her long to find the blogs, including several loud entries warning Americans about overseas adoption agencies. *It's a question of regulation. Anyone can become a baby broker. The younger the child, the more money the broker can make. Some of these babies are orphans, and some of them are purchased, and some are stolen from—*

Meera skipped to the next.

American agencies have been known to work with all kinds of places….Documents get forged all the time…. Even churches get into the action.

She turned to the author's profile, her credentials. Not a journalist, just an older woman with a cloud of silver hair, a big smile, and tilting, laughing eyes. Regal looking, even beautiful. Meera clicked on the name. A Charlotte resident…teenaged pregnancy…pulled out of Central High in 1959—Wait. Meera backtracked. Central High School. Holy shit. It was her. Edie Carrigan. *That* Edie Carrigan.

She waited five or six rings. Her mom would be scrambling around her office looking for her flip phone. Despite caller ID, she answered the way she always did, like she couldn't imagine who was on the other end. "Lucille Scott."

"It's me."

"Oh, hello!" Her surprise actually seemed genuine.

"Hey…I've been reading about a classmate of yours. Edie Carrigan."

From the other end of the line came a sound Meera couldn't place, like a squeak maybe, the kind of noise a person makes when she's on her way out the front door and realizes she's forgotten something.

"Mom?"

"Yeah..." She sounded uncertain. She didn't sound that way too often.

"You remember her?" she asked.

A pause. "I *do*..."

"She had a baby."

Another pause. "She *did*..."

Meera's throat felt fat. Which surprised her. "Mom, holy shit. Why didn't you want to tell me about her?"

A longer silence.

"Who told you about her?"

"Nobody! That's why I'm mad! I *read* it. She has a *blog*."

"A blog? Online?"

"Yes."

"Oh. I guess it's not a secret anymore."

"Mom, why didn't you tell me?"

A long pause. "I don't know, honey. I was so afraid of having an influence on you. I was in high school when—I guess I'm not proud of the way I behaved."

Her mom had been valedictorian. She couldn't have been whooping it up too much. "Is this about...that klepto problem you had?"

"Well." Her mother sounded embarrassed. "I didn't call it that."

Meera closed her eyes and waited for the thickness in her throat to go away. "So...what? This girl dropped out of school and you never saw her again?"

"Oh...honey, it was so complicated. She did drop out of school. In those days they made you. And people did make the kind of speculations you'd expect. Everybody knew, or thought they did, which amounts to the same thing. It wasn't like your situation."

This was the oblique way they talked, she and her mother. Neither of them could really name the thing that had happened, their roles, the mothers they'd been and the ones they hadn't. But always there was this tender place between them, thin as the skin of an orange segment, fragile and loaded with the promise of sweetness, but a separation all the same. Meera said, "He's coming up on eighteen."

"I know. Your father and I were talking about it last night."

Last night? Good Lord. Somehow it'd never occurred to her that her parents talked about Alexander. For the first time, she imagined them marking off the years the same way she did. "I didn't know you-all were keeping track."

Mom didn't say anything, but Meera could hear her thinking, trying to plan out the right words. "Whatever else you might say about Edie Carrigan, she had guts."

The sentence sailed toward her, this slow lob Meera couldn't possibly miss. Meera got it. Edie had guts.

38

MEERA

It seemed like Ms. Carrigan wasn't going to show. None of the women in the foyer of the Contessa Café looked like they could have graduated high school in 1959—not the graying executive with the cell phone clamped to her ear nor the ancient lady with the rubber-footed walker. Meera felt disappointment, sure, but something else too: a surprising sense of loss.

Then there was a light touch on her arm. "You *have* to be Luce Waddell's daughter."

Meera wheeled around. It was the puffy-haired woman from the blog. "Yes! Hello!" She extended her hand, and the woman pressed her fingers into it, then brought her other hand around to encircle hers in a gesture that seemed way too familiar. Then, as if the situation called for even more intimacy, Edie Carrigan cupped both hands around her shoulders and drew her in. Like they were long lost buds.

The woman's face was so close Meera smelled lavender. It was a long time before she let Meera go. She said, "You look exactly like her."

Ms. Carrigan had these very blue eyes, maps of wrinkles around them. No make-up.

Meera tried to smile. She felt a bit off-kilter. But also relieved that the woman remembered that long-ago friendship. It made sense, sort of. Her mom had been valedictorian. But Meera was more interested in Edie Carrigan, her story. All she knew was what her mom and her classmate Eden Lord had told her, that Edie Carrigan had left school to have a baby, that she'd given that child up for adoption.

Ms. Carrigan was still studying her. "Yep. Exactly like her, except more...*sporty.*"

"Ha." What a word. "Everybody's more sporty than my mom."

An adolescent girl in Cleopatra eyeliner led them to a booth, and Edie Carrigan slid onto the bench, her figure narrow at the top and full on the bottom, like a teardrop. She spread both palms on the front cover of the menu, like she had no intention of opening it. "Well. Luce is so accomplished in other ways."

The nickname stabbed at Meera. It was so effortless. Like...breezy. How was it Meera hadn't ever heard it? "She thinks very highly of you, Ms. Carrigan." It seemed safe enough.

But Ms. Carrigan looked surprised. And...hungry, somehow. "She does?"

"She said you had guts."

Ms. Carrigan studied her hands, livered with brown. Instead of a wedding ring, she wore a collection of hammered silver bands. "I've wondered about her, Meera. So many times." She looked up. "Are you here because of Luce?" The expression on her face was so hopeful Meera wanted to say yes.

"Actually I was interested in your blog."

Disappointment showed around Edie Carrigan's mouth, little lines. "Ah. The blog. It's gotten considerable chatter lately. Adoptees, parents looking, children looking. Birthmothers..." She tilted her head at Meera but didn't ask.

"That would be me, I guess. I gave up a child in 1985. I was in college."

Edie Carrigan's brows popped up, but she didn't seem particularly surprised. Instead she leaned over the table. "You know I had no choice. They made me go to one of those homes. I mean, that's just how it was in 1959." She said it the way a person would say, "You know I'm blind." As if it were the first thing Meera needed to know, like the conversation couldn't proceed until they'd established that fact. And she wasn't finished. She seemed to have a set speech. "Then, after all was said and done, I wound up in jail." Her blue eyes widened.

Meera inhaled. The woman's parents had done it, not her. Edie Carrigan was innocent.

Which meant that Meera was not.

Meera searched the other woman's face. In every state, a woman had to give written consent before she could relinquish a child. Even minors. And back in those days most states still had a revocation period of thirty days or more. In case you changed your mind. Meera braced herself for whatever the story might be. She could clamber through it, test its structure. Some stories were solid and some were not.

Then Edie Carrigan did an appealing thing. She laughed. It was a musical laugh, easy and true. "You even have the same gestures. You're wrinkling your nose. That's your mother right there. She used to do it when she didn't like something somebody said. Did you know you did that?"

Meera shook her head, caught out.

Edie Carrigan wiped at her eyes. "Because Luce didn't *either*." She delivered this pronouncement like it was straight up hilarious. "I think she imagined she was just wrinkling her nose on the *inside*, but I swear she used to scrunch up her whole face like a mouse." And then she did a perfect impression of Meera's mother.

Meera couldn't not smile. "That's pretty much dead-on."

But the next moment Edie Carrigan was waggling a long-handled iced teaspoon like an attenuated finger, pretending to scold. "You think you see how it was, you know." It took Meera a beat to realize that she actually *was* scolding. "But you don't."

"It's just that my experience was a lot different—that's all. In some ways I think of it as an accomplishment. You know, something that I made it through. Obviously it's not something I want to do again, but it's not something I regret."

"Um hmmm." Edie Carrigan's tone suggested she'd had this conversation before.

The waitress appeared. There was a flurry over forks and napkins and something to do with a customer survey. Afterwards Edie Carrigan's voice flowed like water, saturating the conversation with information about laws and advocacy. Was she for real? Meera couldn't imagine her mom being friends with her. They were too dissimilar. The woman's voice never ceased or slowed but moved to fill every low point and every lull and somehow, without being obvious, she'd turned the conversation back to Meera's mom. She picked up her fork and leaned in. "Is Luce still practicing law?"

"Part time, yes. You two don't keep in touch anymore." Meera waited for Edie Carrigan to contradict her. She could see her trying to assess what she knew.

"We were inseparable, you know."

Holy shit. Meera tried to keep her face blank. She reached for the silver chain at her neck, toyed with the pendant there. "Oh."

Ms. Carrigan sighed. "We had a bit of a falling out, I'm afraid." She looked at her hands, rubbed her thumb against the ring on her middle finger, and rotated the filigreed band. Now she seemed to be explaining something else. "It's just that I grew up with this idea that the only thing required of girls was that you look pretty and be nice to people. Everything else was sort of extra, like icing on the cake. I'm not sure you can really and truly understand that without having lived it." She paused, and her eyes traveled across the aisle, but her voice kept right on flowing on and out. "But at some point I just couldn't help myself, like once I broke the rule about being nice, I didn't know how to control anything anymore, like I didn't know how to behave after that, like everything that was true before wasn't true afterwards."

Was she talking about Meera's mom or the pregnancy? "Is that what led to the…falling out?"

Edie made a sound you could only call a snort. "That's what I mean when I say you don't get it—I mean that was it: those were the only requirements, being nice and being pretty—which sounds easy enough, but I swear it's a trap because those two things are actually really big things, and it's impossible to be nice all the time, no matter what, because it exhausts you, you know, and it's also a hell of a lot of work to look pretty all the time too, if you think about it. And you sure as shit can't always do both." Her swearing had a kind of robustness to it, or exultation, like she was working out certain muscle groups to keep them strong and fit. But beneath the swearing was a hint of self-consciousness. She twisted the wide hammered silver ring around her finger. Then she looked up and said more quietly, "But none of us knew how impossible that bargain was. I sure didn't. For half my life I was dumb enough to keep worrying away at both those things. Being nice and being pretty. So dumb. So impossible."

Meera felt herself smile. Maybe Edie Carrigan's story would show her something about her own. Show her how she was supposed to judge herself.

Go back to that first moment she knew she was pregnant, the early morning with the streetlamp casting shadows on the typewriter on her desk, that music seeping through the open window. *Girls on film. Girls on film.* That's where Meera's story began. She hadn't drifted into a decision, or waited until it was too late to make one. She'd had a choice.

If nothing else, she would do this one perfect thing. She'd once thought that. But it wasn't—perfect, that is. All the choices a single mother could make were selfish. All of them brought second guesses. Someone asked you, "Which would you rather lose? An arm or a leg or a lung?" You chose one or the other but you didn't get to keep everything. That's what made it a choice. Meera had chosen the arm, but another woman chose the lung. Another chose the leg. Every choice brought its own kind of love and its own unique cruelty. But the arithmetic was the same. The only consolation to it, the only thing dignified about it, was that each had the chance to make the choice herself.

LUCE

> ~~Dear Edie,~~
> ~~I've started this letter so many times that I~~
>
> ~~Dear Edie—~~
> ~~I have a story to tell you about Simon's grandfather's ring.~~

Oh Edie, I think of you all the time, especially now. (Bear with me, OK? This is hard for me.) I can't stop thinking about how I hurt you all those years ago, how wrong I was…

MEERA

When she wrote to Catholic Family Services she was forty. She still had that snapshot of Alexander and it was still folded in that same page of stationary. That was the deal: the agency required adopters to send a photograph and a letter. In the picture, a creamy-faced infant balled his fists at the sides of his head, blue eyes directed at someone standing to his right—his new mother maybe. The look was neither gleeful nor needy nor sad. It was curious, reserved.

So what were they like, these teachers? Obviously they made him eat his vegetables and took him to the emergency room when he had ear infections and brought his shot records when they registered him for school. Obviously they helped him with his homework and explained to him that everything that lived had to die. But had they given him a sense of responsibility to something bigger than himself? Had they taught him the names of the trees? Had they taught him to listen to the cello swells in a Beethoven symphony? Had they taught him to listen, really listen, to the way the night held its breath before the birds began to experiment with dawn?

Why should they? Maybe they taught him to pay attention to other things, like the stories of the saints, or the best quarterbacks in the NFL.

Or. There were other, darker possibilities. Not every child lived long enough to become an adult. That could have happened. Or. There'd been all those allegations about priests in the Catholic Church. Or. He could have grown up cruel or self-righteous or petty, with flaws she'd have forgiven if she'd raised him herself, just because of the person he'd been as a child, because of her memories, him drinking from a sippy cup or riding a tricycle or pasting together Christmas cards. As a parent, she could have loved him for the child he'd been rather than the person he became. But those were memories she did not have.

Then there was the other possibility: that his parents didn't love him enough. But she didn't—couldn't—believe that. Everyone would love him because how could they not? If anything his parents outmatched her. Of course they did. She loved him because he was a part of her, because she'd chosen to bring him into the world. But they had chosen to bring him into their lives. They had done the work of raising him. They loved him for that. And because they knew him. She had to believe that. She did believe that.

When the response came from Catholic Family Services she was forty-one. The envelope sat on top of a pile of junk mail on the kitchen table, the return address handwritten as "CFS."

Right off the bat she thought of Edie and her advice. *Don't expect too much, hon. Just really and truly do not expect too much.* She opened it.

It began with the worst line in the world. "Unfortunately we regret to inform you."

She blinked up at the window, realized she'd actually stopped breathing.

"There is no stipulation that adoptees with this agency have access to their records at eighteen or at any time."

He wasn't dead. They were telling her something else.

"Records are closed and can only be opened by court order."

She sank onto the kitchen banquette, relieved and sucker-punched at the same time. There is no stipulation? "I don't get it."

Just then the door opened and two dogs charged through it, her husband behind them. Both animals wagged at her feet. "Get what?" Heath said, hanging the leashes on a peg and bending to kiss her on the temple. She handed him the letter. He was a long-limbed man who carried himself with a rubbery loose-jointed ease. A flannel shirt hung over baggy cargos. The dogs vied with each other for the water bowl.

"It seems like yesterday to me. How could I remember it so wrong..."

He scanned the letter, his eyes the color of winter leaves, drooped at the edges, delicate lines at the corners. A gust of air exploded from his lips. "Makes perfect sense to me. Why *wouldn't* she lie? She was worried you'd change your mind." He tossed the page to the table in disgust. "She probably told all her clients that. Besides, it fits with all that stuff Edie told you. How birthmothers got screwed."

Her exact words: *I didn't know I had the right to know.* "Yeah, but Edie thinks *everything* the social workers say is a lie."

Heath dropped into the chair beside her, reached for her hand. "I've been thinking about this too." He turned her hand over and traced a line along the palm. "Let's find out."

"What do you mean?" she said. She knew what he meant.

"Let's find him," he said.

Something warm washed through her veins and loosened her joints all the way to the ends of her fingertips, a gush. But all she could do at first was nod and stare down at their hands. Then: "I've been looking into that. It takes a long time. You can list yourself with as many registries as you want, but then you have to wait for the other person to find those registries too. Then to contact you."

He leaned against the back of the chair and folded his arms. "Think about this. He's a nineteen-year-old kid, he's just going along in his life. He may be curious, but unless he's kind of obsessed, he probably doesn't even know about those registries."

The older dog laid his head on her thigh and looked up with longing. "I hope he's not obsessed," she said.

"Exactly," he said. "I never knew about any of those registries until you told me about them. It could take years before he hears about them. Decades."

Outside dusk was falling. The picture window reflected their faces back to them. Hers was shiny in the glass, and not young. Heath turned too, spoke to her reflection, then to her. "If you want to know where your son is, I'll bet it's not that hard. There was only one baby born in that hospital that day, right? There's public agencies that keep track of that information. The Social Security Administration, I bet. By now, some of those places must have searchable databases. I'll bet it's on public record. Somewhere." He squeezed her shoulders. "They just don't make it easy."

Meera was breathing shallowly, breaths like birds fluttering through her lungs. Did she have a right to know? Did she have a right to see the life of a person she'd given away decades ago? She thought of windows and Peeping Toms. "I'd just like to know that he's alive, and not, say… institutionalized. I'd like to know he's happy." But that wasn't exactly right. Everybody wanted to know that—if the people they loved were happy. Most of them never got to find out, even if they saw them every day. "I just want to know who and what and where he is."

Heath nodded silently, then said, "I'd like to know that too." He held her upper arms and waited for her to meet his gaze. "Let's make sure this lady didn't lie about anything else."

She pressed the heels of her hands into her eyes, nodded. Knowing was important. Without it, there were those terrible bloated images, greedy in their own power: the clear plastic box pierced with tubes, the fluorescent room, the little boy alone and unnamed, legs and arms flailing, that tiny face roaring in loose rage.

Edie waved her hand dismissively. "It's all about lying. Of course it is. Look. It's the same way every time. The birthmother is the one who needs the lawyer, right? But she's also the one who can't afford it." She was wearing a pair of those rubber gardening clogs with baggy flowered pants, the kind with an elastic waistband. On her refrigerator was a corkboard with a black and white Holstein, a pastiche of photographs and lists pinned to its flanks. The stools at the island were painted with black and white cow patterns too.

Meera rotated the pendant at her neck. "I think of all those stories as stories from the bad old days. But if this is a lie, it's just so…gratuitous." Above the kitchen table, a picture window opened onto a view of puddles and mud and the laundered bright green of a Piedmont spring. A bank of iris muscled its way up beside the back fence.

Edie ripped open a package of Wheat Thins and dumped them onto a plate next to a tumble of open cookbooks. "What they tell you doesn't necessarily have anything to do with what they put in writing."

"You think that's still true?" she asked.

Instead of answering, Edie opened the refrigerator and began rummaging around. "For me it was the word 'abandoned.' Think about it. What does that mean?" Puppies by the side of the road, a garden choked with weeds, an infant in a dumpster. Someone running from all responsibility. "Do you like Stilton or is it too smelly?"

"I like it."

Edie turned with the cheese in hand. "'Abandoned.' It's one of those words. It means a million different things to a million different people. I can tell you it was one of the things that made me angry for years and years." Her body tensed. "All those people—Mr. Henry, my parents, even that wimpy Father Timothy kept telling me, 'If you love her, you'll give her away.' Or 'This is a precious gift, a sacred gift.' But once you get into the courthouse it's a different story. You never hear the word *gift* again. That's when the *abandonment* word comes out. That's when they tell you what they really think, but then the social worker tells you the language is only for legal purposes, and that it doesn't mean any such thing, just that you have to give up your parental rights so the baby can become a ward of the state. And that's what I'm trying to *tell* you, Meera. A child had to be legally abandoned before he could be adopted." A sweep of gray hair fell over her eyebrow. She reached up and pushed it away. "I swear, that word *abandoned*, it means nothing and it means everything. Because that's what the rest of the world is told. 'Look, it says so right here in black and white. Abandoned. Bullshit. How in the hell does a kid feel when he hears that?" She was getting worked up. "Half the stuff you hear about adoption or abortion is based on that one assumption: that pregnant women are too lazy or too slutty or too selfish or too dumb, that bottom line they can't be trusted to make their own decisions. And every time some mother like that does come around, believe you me, it's all over the news, the juiciest thing ever, over and over, even if they have to import it from Australia, as if the fact that some woman lied about a dingo eating her kid just confirms everybody's suspicions about the rest of us. And don't think it's men repeating these stories either. It's *women*. And why? Because we feel *guilty*. Because we can *imagine* it. It feels true because we've each of us has had that thought at least once: Wouldn't it be nice if I didn't have to worry about these little ones? So we forget the arithmetic. We forget about the billions upon billions of human mothers who *didn't* do that and focus on the one who did. Like for some reason she's the one who really and truly represents us all. It's such bullshit." She nodded at the wine glasses. "Grab those, would you?"

Meera picked up the goblets and followed her to the back patio. Azaleas bloomed in swanky crowds of pink and fuchsia. The pin oak was beginning to leaf. Edie opened a bottle of chardonnay and poured. "Cheers."

Meera peered at the wine in her glass and started to take a sip. But right then, holy shit, Kimberly Boyle's words resurrected themselves, sat up, and blinked. *I'm the only one who gets to see both sides of the equation. I see a lot of things you don't see.* Meera's glass smashed onto the table. Edie looked scared. "What is it?"

For God's sake. "What if she lied about *everything*?" There'd been nothing to stop Kimberly Boyle from giving her child to the advertising executive with the landscaped yard. Nothing to stop her from giving him to anyone else. Worse, what if she'd lied when she'd phoned to say Alexander was healthy? What if he'd *died*?

Somehow Edie was on her side of the table, and Meera found herself gripping the other woman's forearms way too hard. "Who, honey? Who?" Edie stroked her hair, and Meera let herself be swaddled. "Oh...I know." Her face pressed into Edie's soft belly, the fibers of her sweater imprinting themselves into her cheek. "We're going to find out. This is bullshit, not knowing." Then, after a long pause, she said, "What does he know about you?"

Meera knew what Edie was getting at. He—his parents—would have built a story about her, a story constructed from whatever elements they'd been given. That could be just about anything. "That I didn't give him a name." Edie was still holding her and rubbing her back. But Meera could feel her listening. "That I listed his father as unknown."

"What else?"

"That he was taken to another hospital for tests."

Edie's hand went still. "In intensive care?"

"I don't know. They wouldn't tell me."

Edie's whole body tightened. "We have to make sure this lady didn't lie about anything else. To you or to his parents. She could have said anything." The possibilities yawned out in front of them. Edie loosened her arms. She seemed to sense it was time to change the subject. "You smell like her. Who would have thought."

Edie meant her mom. Meera pulled away from her, took a deep breath. "I have something to tell you about that."

Edie drew back, studied her. Meera took the envelope from her purse and set it on the table. The shape of the ring was visible through the paper. "This is a letter for you."

Edie looked at it, then at her.

"And I'm supposed to tell you something before you open it." That wasn't exactly verbatim. *In case she doesn't want it* was the message. But Meera couldn't say that. It sounded too rude. Edie was watching her, and now she couldn't bring herself to go forward. She was that sure she'd messed up the message. She was that lost. "Yeah...so. I don't know if this means anything to you, but I'm just repeating what she told me to say. I'm supposed to tell you—what she said was that—she said she wanted me to tell you she was wrong. That she had behaved badly and she wishes she'd done things differently and she is sorry."

Meera watched Edie's face. She'd expected bafflement, humor, some quizzical expression. But her face went still, her eyes grabbing Meera's, a blink, then two, then the muscles softening and crumpling. Knuckles in mouth, eyes closed for a long time. She swallowed twice, the skin around her eyes so thin and blue and tender looking that Meera wanted to reach out her fingers and touch it.

Edie's eyes flew open. Dutch blue and shiny with water. She reached out and grabbed the letter and squirreled it away in her apron. Then she tucked her chin, popped up her eyebrows and smiled, like the two of them shared some big secret. "You know what?"

Finally. A little information. "What?"

"Everything is going to be okay." Meera sighed but couldn't help but smile. Edie wasn't going to tell her anything. At least not right now.

Edie picked up her wine glass. "Here's to Luce." That crazy nickname.

They touched glasses. Meera waited for more. But didn't get much.

"You know what, Meera?"

"What?"

"There are people in life who give you things, lasting permanent things, but you don't really understand the gift until years later, only when it's become so much a part of you that you've come to take credit for it yourself."

"Like what?"

"Like...she showed me I could be something different."

Whatever that meant. Meera raised her glass. "Here's to my mother."

Edie took a long sip. You could tell she was settling in for some story. "You know what else?" Finally.

"What?"

"When I was young I wanted men to look at me and say, 'She looks good,' even though I knew it just meant, 'I want to jump her bones.'"

Meera tried not to frown. This couldn't be the story.

"But it was all perfectly fine as long as they didn't actually say that, and if they didn't say anything at all you could still tell when you were scoring high marks because they'd turn their heads or follow you with their eyes, and it felt good. It felt like you were worth something, like you were valuable." At this point Meera just went with it, tried to imagine what Edie had looked like as a young woman. Hair dark and shining, skin translucent. What a mismatch she and Meera's mother must have been. Seriously. Both of them so *fair*, but Edie in the Snow White sense of the word, and her mom in the social justice sense. "But then you get older and you grow out of it. You get to the place where you don't so much care how men assess you, the grade they give you, and then to the place where the very *idea* of being assessed annoys the fool out of you because who said some guy on the street has the right to glance at you and say how much you're worth? But of course the answer is *you*. *You* did. You were the one who said he had that power. That *all* of them had that power." Her eyes were wide with feeling. "And now that you're older you can't believe you ever gave that to them in the first place. And now you want it back."

Meera nodded.

"And that was the thing about your mom, Meera. She never gave them that power in the first instance. She was bent on creating a different system, some other kind of…arithmetic."

Meera nodded. The picture—it sounded about right, made her proud and sad both.

"I always wondered whether it ended up working out for her. Did it?"

"What?"

Edie was watching her. "Do you think she got most of the things she wanted?"

"I don't know. She did a lot, I guess."

Edie took a long pull of her wine. "She had you."

"And Alex," Meera said. "She's probably glad we made it through without self-destructing."

"Course she is."

"You should see her. She wears these track suits. It used to embarrass me."

Edie snorted. She was getting tipsy. "Sometimes, even now, I think about your mom, like, 'Goddamn. Luce would be able to do this. I should be able to do it too.'"

Meera barked out a laugh, relieved at last to know what they were talking about. "I've never not felt that."

Edie stared off into the twilight. She looked happy, playful. "You know what?"

"What?"

"I don't even know what a dingo *is*."

39

LUCE

The house was buttercup yellow, a low brick ranch spread across a bright and generous lawn, the garden festooned in flowers, parades of purple coneflower and pink buddleia and dots of yellow and white Shasta daisies. It looked so hopeful, so girlish.

We did live in the same state, but it was a long state, 500 miles. Besides. I was a different person. She had to be too. At the time I didn't know she'd already contacted Simon, already met him at one of those new gastro pubs in Charlotte, already folded that heirloom ring into his hand, their fingers lingering longer than either one of them had planned.

I slowed as I stepped onto the little flagstone path, the pavers interlaced with pink creeping thyme. I never did like pastels. When I was a very little girl I'd had all the things little girls were supposed to want: bows and dresses and pink angora sweaters. Mother had dressed us in chiffons and ruffles, ribbons in our hair and dolls in our arms. There was always such a fuss about this or that bow, which shoes went with what, getting the little straps just right. Those were days of picnics and birthday parties, of smiling and twirling and meeting Mother and Daddy's friends. So many desperate curtsies and pirouettes and pleading little-girl smiles.

None of it had worked. Both Dad and Martha were gone by the time I was thirteen, Martin a year later. I'd stopped curtsying. But those flowery colors, they still felt like Easter to me, like springtime and death all on the same day. Like begging.

And now here I was sixty-three years old and all kitted out in this bright summer dress, like a piece of fruit. Like an orange. Nothing fits when you're short. That's what Edie would notice. She'd take one look at me and tilt her head to the side in a way that meant *what are we going to do about this?* I remembered it perfectly, that look.

I rang the doorbell. That night long ago on that other porch the red lights flashed bright and dark and bright and dark. I really had not imagined it would be the police. But Edie's parents had called the Home and the Home had called the law, and my mother was there for the whole thing, searching for that Zippo in the red and white light.

And then the door swung in and there she was, Edie Carrigan framed in the threshold in loose linen clothes and gray hair and a big silver medallion hanging down her sternum, her face luminous, her smile enormous and white. She was wider now, and beautiful as ever, a silver bear with wide open outstretched arms.

So I did what I always did. Stepped right in.

40

It wasn't all that difficult, if you had the money and a bit of luck. It took three days for the agency to trace Alexander. That's it.

Inside her chest, an elevator dropped. There it was: an email from Family Find in her inbox. That was all. No package tied with red ribbon, no official-looking letter, no fanfare.

The email said yes, her son was alive and healthy and he had a name, and it was Christopher Robert Calloway. He had two parents and one sister. His mother was a middle school teacher. His father was the assistant principal in a high school. They'd been married thirty years.

So: yes. Kimberly Boyle had done what she'd promised. She'd placed him where she had said she would. And now Meera knew his real name: Christopher Robert Calloway. It was the name his parents had given him. It was also a history, a place to put an identity.

Later that night she reread the note his parents had written nineteen years earlier, the five-sentence one that used to make her mad. She'd long ago started picturing these people like her brother and his wife: people who loved their adopted children just as hard as Alex and Kathleen loved Jana. The letter was written in that meticulous curled script, calligraphic lines stretching straight and tense across the unlined page. She hadn't noticed it before, but now it seemed clear that the writer had used a template to guide her hand. When Meera looked at the letter now, it seemed like a piece of craftsmanship, written and rewritten many times before put to final draft. A tightrope-walk of a letter. She could almost see it: Alexander's—*Christopher's*—mother seated in her kitchen in a room with floral wallpaper, writing phrase after phrase and then crossing them out. Each line careful and balanced, painstaking, planned. "Dear Birthmother: It is impossible to convey to you the love and joy that emanates throughout our entire family since the arrival of the son we share."

Now, to Meera, that sentence seemed fine. Just fine.

A kid, the letter said to her now, is not a woolen sweater. She slid the page back into its envelope. Maybe they thanked their God instead, their prayers radioing out into the universe in concentric ripples, diffusing out and out into space and beyond.

She typed her letter. She addressed it to Alexander's—to Christopher's— parents. Because he was only nineteen. Because she wanted to know them. Because it was still their job to protect him, whether he liked it or not.

She could have used the telephone, like Edie's daughter had done. But she liked a letter better. A person could think before answering a letter. In a conversation, people didn't listen because they were too busy planning the clever thing they were going to say next, and while they were doing that the words the other person was speaking were already wafting away. Words on a page were immovable. Sure, you could look long and hard to discover what was underneath them or inside them or behind them, but the sentences themselves, the shapes of them, didn't change. You could go back and read them ten years later and they would say the same thing. And if they didn't, if the message was different, you'd know that it wasn't the words that had changed. It was you.

His parents had the right to say *no thank you*. So did he. That's how relationships worked. Even when the relationship was one with your own child. Because he wasn't a child and he certainly wasn't her *own* child, and he had the right to say no thanks.

This time around it was her turn to grope for words. She wrote that she wanted to know something of Christopher's life. There were a lot of things the letter didn't say. It didn't say that the last time she'd seen him he was screaming in mouth-wide rage. Or that she sometimes confused his rage with that of her niece's. Or that she wished she'd had the opportunity to meet his parents, to be able to carry their images and their eagerness in her mind's eye forever.

Nor was there anything in the letter that explained why the story was important, or how a name could give you a way to mourn, or how memory constructed you a story and a place to attach a wandering and nameless grief. It didn't talk about motherhood, and whether women were supposed to accept it without question. It didn't talk about choices, or how you touched them and turned them and felt their mass and texture like the weight and dimpled surface of an orange. Or how, when the decision was made, you thought it was your own. How you had to own it by yourself. The letter didn't say that women were supposed to have the say-so over their own lives. Neither did it say that she felt lucky to have a son whom she might one day meet, and lucky to have been raised at a certain period in time by a certain set of parents, and lucky to be able to make her own decisions. The letter didn't say any of that.

Still. She sealed it on a cold spring day and walked to the post office. She could have driven, but she wanted to stretch out the act of posting it to make it proportional, to give it more weight. She walked. The houses on her block lined up like colored cupcakes, done up in every shade of teal and tangerine and watermelon and pink. Some of the porches and lawns had weird modern art or mosaic-tiled sidewalks or brightly painted flowerpots, and, yeah, the line between funky and junky was thin. Chili pepper lights hung from wooden eaves. A rusted bicycle frame served as a trellis for a clematis vine. A dragon made of discarded car parts guarded a yard. It was late March, but the early hours of morning had brought a bitten clean cold and a dusting of white, and kids were home for a snow day. It felt like a holiday. Someone had scraped together a tiny snowman, but the effort had plowed up more mud than snow, and the whole endeavor was turning into a puddle of water. The streets were sunny and wet with runoff, and the pansies bloomed purple and blue in the snow, their faces mustachioed in black: little diligent uncles. Two kids on one bicycle rode up and down a side street. The smaller one sat between the front handlebars, the front wheel wobbling as the bigger kid tried to steady it, a look of furious concentration on his face.

The post office was a box made of tan bricks. Outside were two mailboxes, blue and self-important. She pulled down the steel handle and dropped the letter in. The door made a dull metallic clap.

And that was it.

Meera's mother had once been a child, and she'd decided not to be like her parents. But she'd still been reacting to them. She'd still become who she was because of them. Meera had in turn learned her mother's resolve and her belief in the persuasive power of words. She was something like her parents, and not just because of that secret information catalogued in her DNA. No, her parents' gifts came from habit and imitation, just like the flaws she'd learned from them.

Did Christopher have those same flaws?

Maybe one day she'd know. Maybe she'd learn what his parents were like, how they'd raised him, what gifts they'd given him. If not the shape of his nose then maybe the things he valued. If not the breadth of his shoulders then an ability to make people laugh. Or a love of hockey or chess. He was both mysterious and familiar to her, the two of them connected by a twisting, invisible double strand. In her mind's eye he was a young man carrying a backpack and a wallet and an unnamed longing for something he couldn't see. There were riddles in his eyes. He was analytical, like his grandmother, and he reveled in finding the thread of an argument and pulling and pulling until the whole fabric unloosed itself. He had his grandmother's logic and his grandfather's empathy, his father's ambition and his mother's stubborn arrogance. And he was alive and magnificent and alone. Like all of them.

By the time she started her walk home, the sun had melted the snow and the lawns were muddy. The intersection where the two boys had been riding was empty. Then she saw they had turned the bike into a side street, riding away from her down a hill toward an empty church parking lot. It wasn't a particularly steep hill, but it was long. Even as she watched, the bike was picking up speed. The riders seemed to have gained some skill, because the bicycle no longer wobbled. The boy in the back was wearing an electric blue coat, unzipped, lofting in the air behind them. Together they sailed toward the end of the street, a streamlined clipper ship.

At the bottom of the hill lay the new asphalt of the church lot. The bike hit the incline of the curb, lifted for a moment into unbelievable flight and then landed—*hunh!*—with a contraction and a bounce. Then, amazingly, it kept going, circling around the lot and gradually slowing. She could see the boys' faces in the sunlight, their thrown-back heads and their white teeth and their wide open laughing mouths.

Notes and Sources

The pee test came up positive. It was the 1980s, and I was a full-time college student. I'd just been dumped by a guy I thought I loved and I was trying to figure out what the rest of my life was going to look like. I was frozen with indecision. I was a kid who was attracted to every kind of career. So many could-be lives beckoned and called to me that I found it impossible to decide on just one. Even choosing a single academic major meant a dozen other fields I'd never master, a whole array of breath-taking magical lives I'd never get to live.

Single motherhood wasn't one of those lives. Besides. I knew enough to know that solo parenting required a person be *all-in*. And the idea of being all-in on any one thing scared the hell out of me. But there it was: that positive test. And all those dazzling lives? Gone.

I was pro-choice and unreligious, but for complicated reasons, many of them naïve or cocksure, I decided to bring my child to term and relinquish him for adoption. I had great health insurance. I was horse-healthy. I had support from family and friends. I figured I'd spend the next eight months carrying my child to term, continuing my waitressing job, and completing my degree. Not easy, but doable.

Right?

The decision upended my life, and not because of the difficulty of those next eight months, which was significant. Less than 24 hours after my son was born, I signed relinquishment papers—then learned the delivery had mutilated my cervix. Worse—my child was being screened for meningitis. It seemed unlikely the adopters would want an unhealthy baby, unlikely they'd feel the same sense of responsibility for him that had been growing in me for nine whole months.

I hadn't considered what now seems patently obvious: that these are the selfsame risks every mother takes when she decides to bring a child into the world: her child's quality of life—and her own. That if all other parenting options evaporate, his natural mother is the only person he has in the world.

After a few crushing days, the agency told me my son was healthy, that his diagnosis had been revised, that he'd been adopted, which was the outcome I wanted. But for years to come I felt terrified for him—and bereft.

Also alienated. I couldn't square my grief with the one-dimensional portrayals of birthmothers I saw in movies, novels, and television, women who relinquished their children, then started blissfully afresh. Was I some strange outlier, or were such portrayals simply incomplete?

As a college student trapped in my own personal dilemma, I hadn't wanted to hear other people's stories, hadn't wanted to claim the world of motherhood, hadn't wanted to spend even one extra minute in it. It felt too *gooey*. But decades later, older and less wild-eyed, here I was, still wondering if other birthmothers felt the way I did. I started reading women's stories. I fell right into the mind-boggling terrain of unplanned pregnancy in America. My research pulled me into the history all the way up to my neck. I swam around in it. It *was* gooey. There I found my mother's peers and their mother's mothers and many other mothers besides.

Enter Justices Amy Coney Barrett and Samuel Alito making the same case many other Americans have long made: that women don't need abortion rights when they can choose adoption. By the time Justice Alito drafted his opinion in the Spring of 2022, I'd been obsessing for years about the history of women who'd done exactly that. I'd found some of the answers I was looking for. I wasn't an outlier. Far from it.

The TV and movie portrayals of birthmothers—and the general public's view of the relinquishment experience—were even more over-simplified than I'd ever guessed.

These days the laws surrounding adoption are more transparent, but they vary from state to state. For example, some states stipulate that mothers cannot be under the influence of delivery room drugs when they sign relinquishment papers. Other states do not. Like women who've sought abortion rights, those who choose adoption have struggled with the very same thing: the say-so over their own decisions and bodies.

Women who choose adoption are not so different from women seeking abortion rights. All of them, all of us, are fighting for the same thing, the say-so over our own bodies and decisions.

And me? My research left me feeling lucky. The biggest difference between those mid-century "unweds" and me was that I'd made the decision myself. I'd had a choice. I'd had agency. The experience had devastated me, but it had also left me stronger and more empowered.

Over the years friends have asked my advice about their own unplanned pregnancies or their daughters'. I don't give advice. What I say is that I'm thrilled that my son walks the earth, but that the emotional cost was so much higher than I'd imagined. That there was no "clean slate" afterward, only loss. That if I were faced with the same circumstances a second time, I would probably choose an early abortion. That what saved me in the end was the ability to make the choice myself.

All other characters in this novel are imaginary. Below is a list of sources that helped me create Edie and Luce. You can find more detailed information at https://www.juliafranks.com/the-say-so-the-history.

FRONTISPIECE: "ILLEGITIMATE" PREGNANCIES

(These figures are from the US Department of Health, Education, and Welfare. See Bernstein, Rose. "Unmarried Parents," *Encyclopedia of Social Work*, issue 5, New York National Association of Social Workers, 1965, p. 797; Shlakman,

Vera. "Unmarried Parenthood: An Approach to Social Policy." *Social Casework*, vol. 42, October 1966, p. 494).

RISING NUMBER OF MIDCENTURY ADOPTIONS

Figures vary for the number of adoptions during the postwar decades, since most of them went unrecorded. Within maternity homes, some 80% of women surrendered their children between 1945 and 1970. It's likely that the same percentages were relinquished among *all* children born out of wedlock, but records are few. (See Solinger, Rickie. *Wake Up Little Susie: Single Pregnancy and Race Before Roe V. Wade*, 2nd edition. Routledge, 2000).

According to Solinger, the number of adoptions rose from an estimated 50,000 in 1945 to 91,000 in 1957, up to 175,000 in 1970. The numbers from the National Adoption Information Clearinghouse are much lower, presumably because they reflect only those adoptions documented in writing: according to written records, only 20% of white women with premarital births placed their children for adoption from 1952 to 1972. (See National Adoption Information Clearinghouse, sponsored by US Department of Health and Human Services. Accessed January 7, 2004. Online: naic.acf.hhs.gov/index.cfm).

White America considered Blacks and Hispanics unlikely candidates for maternity homes. Ergo most of the adoptions within these groups were off the record. Partly because of the informality of these adoptions, documented relinquishment rates among Latinos, Blacks, and Asian-Americans has remained below two percent throughout US history. (See Pertman, Adam. *Adoption Nation*. Basic Books, 2000, p. 30.)

Middle class Americans kept their pregnancies secret, and schools and companies expelled or fired pregnant women and girls. Thousands became invisible except as statistics in the cautionary pages of *Ladies Home Journal* and *Good Housekeeping*. But some 20,000 to 25,000 women were admitted to maternity homes each year (Bernstein "Unmarried Parents" 798; Solinger *Wake Up* 103).

PREMARITAL SEX AND ABORTION

The postwar percentages of those who engaged in premarital sex (58% of white women and 68% to 90% of white men) are from Kinsey's studies. (See May, Elaine Tyler. *American Families in the Cold War Era*. Basic Books, 1988, pp. 120-123.)

Historian Rickie Solinger reports that there were some 250,000 to 1.3 million abortions annually in the post-war decades, and Messer and May have recorded many personal accounts. (See Messer, Ellen and Kathryn E. May. *Back Rooms: An Oral History of the Illegal Abortion Era.* Touchstone, 1989; Solinger, Rickie. *Abortion Wars: A Half Century of Struggle,* 1950-2000. University of California Press, 1998, p. xi.)

PART I

BIRTHMOTHERS AND MATERNITY HOMES

Much of the information about birthmothers and maternity homes comes from Rickie Solinger's two histories. (See *Wake Up Little Susie: Single Pregnancy and Race Before Roe V. Wade.* 2nd edition, Routledge, 2000; *Beggars and Choosers: How the Politics of Choice Shapes Adoption, Abortion, and Welfare in the United States.* Hill & Wang, 2002.)

Solinger's research drew upon sources of the time period, including transcripts of congressional hearings, papers of the Child Welfare League and Family Services Association of America, papers from the Children's Bureau, papers of the Florence Crittenton Association, articles from professional journals and popular magazines. "What is extraordinary about this collection of sources…is the utter lack of contentiousness among authors within and across fields of expertise. The public and professional discussion of unwed mothers in the postwar era is a case study of the pervasive and persuasive power of consensus in this period which lasted, in the case of unwed mothers, until the early 1960s" (Solinger *Wake Up* 309).

There are many excellent histories of adoption in America. (For example: Glaser, Gabrielle. *American Baby: A Mother, A Child, and the Shadow History of Adoption.* Viking, 2021; Melosh, Barbara. *Strangers and Kin: the American Way of Adoption.* Harvard University Press, 2002; Sokoloff, B. Z. "Antecedents of American Adoption." *The Future of Children: Adoption,* vol. 3, no. 1, 1993, pp. 17-25.)

As well, dozens of birthmothers have allowed themselves to be interviewed and/or have published their own heartfelt memoirs and personal accounts. (See Arms, Suzanne. *Adoption: a Handful of Hope.* Celestial Arts, 1990; Barton, Eliza M. *Confessions of a Lost Mother.* Gateway Press, 1996; Burlingham-Brown,

Barbara. *Why Didn't She Keep Me? Answers to the Question Every Adopted Child Asks.* Langford Books, 1998; Dusky, Lorraine. *Birthright.* M. Evans & Co., 1979. Fessler, Ann. *The Girls Who Went Away: The Hidden History of Women Who Surrendered Children for Adoption in the Decades Before Roe v. Wade.* The Penguin Press, 2006; Franklin, Lynn. *May the Circle Be Unbroken: An Intimate Journey into the Heart of Adoption.* Harmony Books, 1998; Guttman, Jane. *The Gift Wrapped in Sorrow: A Mother's Quest for Healing.* Morris Publishing, 1999. Harsin, Rebecca. *Wanted: First Child.* Fithian Press, 1991; Jones, Merry Bloch. *Birthmothers: Women Who Have Relinquished Babies for Adoption Tell Their Stories.* iUniverse.com., 2000; Jurgens, Louise. *Torn From the Heart: The Amazing True Story of a Birthmother's Search for Her Lost Daughter.* Aslan Publishing, 1992; McKay, Linda Back. *Shadow Mothers: Stories of Adoption and Reunion.* North Star Press of St. Cloud, 1998; McNamara, Sally. *Beyond Happily Ever After.* Gateway Press, 2000; Messer, Ellen and Kathryn E. May. *Back Rooms: An Oral History of the Illegal Abortion Era.* Touchstone, 1989; Moorman, Margaret. *Waiting to Forget: A Mother Opens the Door to Her Secret Past.* W.W. Norton & Company, 1996; Musser, Sandra. *I Would Have Searched Forever.* Jan Publications, a Division of TM, Inc., 1979; Musser, Sandra. *What Kind of Love is This?* Jan Publications, a Division of TM, Inc., 1979; Schaefer, Carol. *The Other Mother: A Woman's Love for the Child She Gave Up for Adoption.* Soho Press, 1991; Seek, Amy. *God and Jetfire: Confessions of a Birth Mother.* Farrar, Straus, and Giroux, 2015. Taylor, Patricia E. *Shadow Train: A Journey Between Relinquishment and Reunion.* Gateway Press, 1995; Thompson, Jean (pseudonym) *House of Tomorrow.* Harper and Row, 1966; Tieman, Carol. *A Crying Shame.* Sleepy Hollow Press. 1994; Wadia-Ells, Susan, ed. *The Adoption Reader: Birth Mothers, Adoptive Mothers, and Adopted Daughters Tell Their Stories.* Seal Press Feminist Publications, 1995; Waldron, Jan. *Giving Away Simone: A Memoir.* Anchor Press, 1998; Wells, Sue. *Within Me, Without Me,* Scarlet Press. 1994.)

PSYCHOLOGY, PSYCHIATRY, AND UNWED MOTHERS

In mid-20th century America, professional psychology was coming into its own. Behavioral explanations that credited "nurture" had far more weight than those that credited "nature": people were considered to be the products of their environments, and could therefore be cured with alternative environments. Mental health professionals were thus charged not only with *identifying* what was normative behavior but also with *prescribing* it. At its worst, psychiatry became a tool for "diagnosing" and "curing" those who did not fit in, including middle-class women with "illegitimate" pregnancies. Like other misfits of the time period, they were examined, deconstructed, reformed, and ultimately reconstructed.

The mental health community believed unwed pregnancy was intentional, an almost conscious act that was a symptom of greater personality disorders. Chance pregnancy seemed too improbable. "Everything points to the purposeful nature of the act," asserted the field's most famous specialist. Leontine Young was a theorist and consultant, and for a decade her pamphlet was circulated widely among social workers and maternity home administrators. (See Young, Leontine. *Out of Wedlock.* McGraw-Hill, 1954.)

Mental health professionals agreed with her hypothesis, though they argued over the specific motivations "girls" had for getting themselves pregnant. At the time "misplaced sexuality" in women was blamed for a host of other social ills, including homosexuality in sons, henpecked husbands, and juvenile delinquency. The implication of Young's theory was that unwed mothers were mentally ill and generally unfit to raise children. By disregarding convention, they had proven they weren't responsible adults and were de facto unsuitable parents. Thus a young mother's first step along the path to mental, spiritual, and emotional health was to consciously admit her mistake by giving her baby away. Only then could she move forward to a complete recovery. (See Bernstein, Rose. "Are We Still Stereotyping the Unwed Mother?" *Social Work*, vol. 5, July 1960, pp. 22-8; Solinger *Wake Up* 102+.)

Midcentury psychiatrists held a range of hypotheses about why intentional pregnancy occurred, including adolescent maladjustment and narcissism. (See Bonan, Ferdinand A. "Psychoanalytic Implications in Treating Unmarried Mothers with Narcissistic Character Structure." *Social Casework*, vol. 44, June 1963, p. 324; Fleck, Stephen. "Pregnancy as a Symptom of Adolescent Maladjustment." *International Journal of Social Psychiatry*, vol. 2, Autumn 1956, pp. 676-681; Khlentzos, Michael T. and Mary A Pagliaro. "Observations from Psychotherapy with Unwed Mothers." *American Journal of Orthopsychiatry*, vol. 35, July 1965, pp. 779-86.)

Psychologists also enlisted Freudian theory to explain intentional pregnancy, in particular the ideas of Oedipal complex and castration complex. (See Clothier, Florence. "Psychological Implications of Unmarried Parenthood." *American Journal of Orthopsychiatry*, vol. 13, July 1943, pp. 539-548; Fleck 676-81.)

Others thought the problem was parental gender confusion, sometimes referred to as the "Mom wears the pants" theory. (See Cattell, James P. "Psychodynamic and Clinical Observations in a Group of Unmarried Mothers." *American Journal of Psychiatry*, vol. 111, November 1954, p. 338.)

Popular explanations relied on the "girl who has never been loved" theory: pregnancy as a way to boost self-esteem. (See Fowler, Dan C. "The Problem of Unwed Mothers." *Look*, July 29 1949, p. 34; White, Glenn Matthew. "Teenage Illegitimate Pregnancy. Why Does It Happen?" *Ladies Home Journal*, August 1958.)

One of the first voices to question the popular diagnosis and treatment of unmarried mothers came from the director of social services at Crittenton Hastings House in Boston, Rose Bernstein. She suspected the studies of unwed mothers were skewed because of the "acute stress" the young mothers were experiencing. Rather than interpreting the symptoms of unwed mothers as *a cause*, she said, professionals should think of those symptoms as the *result*. Bernstein suggested that even pregnant married women would look like aberrations if examined at close enough range. She also warned of the "self-fulfilling prophecy" of scientific research: "if scientists expected to see mental illness in unwed mothers, they would be especially sensitive to unusual behaviors, and these would undoubtedly be interpreted as pathologies." Rose Bernstein's voice was a lone one. Psychiatrists continued to argue the traditional view for years to come (Bernstein "Are We Still Stereotyping the Unwed Mother?" 23-25.)

Research psychology also played an outsized role in the lives of some adoptees: institutions gave scientists permission to use temporarily unparented babies as research subjects. Most notoriously, Louise Wise Services in New York City allowed psychiatrists to conduct the infamous "twins separated at birth" experiments. (For more on this kind of experimentation, see Glaser, Gabrielle. *American Baby: A Mother, A Child, and the Shadow History of Adoption.* Viking, 2021, pp. 106-110.)

COERCION

Pregnancy creates tremendous hormonal upheaval in women, and that transformation helps create the emotional bond between mothers and their fetuses. But most women planning adoption weren't prepared for this biological metamorphosis, and some changed their minds and wanted to keep their children.

But in many instances the decision had been already been made for them. No matter what station in life they came from, single mothers remember being coerced, pressured, or tricked into giving up their rights, sometimes by professionals, sometimes by freelance adoption agents, and very often by their own parents. See dozens of personal accounts listed above as well as any number of post-relinquishment studies. (See De Simone, Michael. "Birth Mother Loss: Contributing Factors to Unresolved Grief." *Clinical Social Work Journal*, vol. 24, 1996, pp. 65-76; Also Kelly, Judy. "The Trauma of Relinquishment: The Long-term Impact of Relinquishment on Birthmothers who Lost their Infants to Adoption during the Years 1965-1972." 1999. online: sites.google.com/site/birthmotherresearchproject; Also Logan, J. "Birth Mothers and Their Mental Health: Uncharted Territory." *British Journal of Social Work*, vol. 26, 1996, pp. 609-625; Also Millen, L. and S. Roll. "Solomon's Mothers: a Special Case of Pathological Bereavement." *American Journal of Orthopsychiatry*, vol. 55, 1985, pp. 411-418; Also Winkler, R.C. and van Keppel, M. *Relinquishing Mothers in Adoption: Their Long-Term Adjustment.* Monograph 3, Institute of Family Studies, Melbourne, Australia, 1984, pp. 61-68.)

During the postwar period, some professional journals suggested techniques that social workers could employ in order to persuade young women to relinquish their children. (See Coffino, Frances. "Helping a Mother Surrender Her Child for Adoption." *Child Welfare*, vol. 39, February 1960, pp. 25-8; Also Gray, Paul H. "Conscience, Guilt, and the Unwed Mother." *The Journal of Pastoral Care*, vol. 13, 1959, pp. 164-70; Also Latimer, Ruth and Florence Startsman. "The Role of the Maternity Home Social Worker in the Prevention of Illegitimacy." *Mental Hygiene*, vol. 47, July 1963, pp. 470-6.)

THE ONES WHO DIDN'T GO TO MATERNITY HOMES

Women in the poor and working classes often had more sinister experiences. Many lost jobs or couldn't ask family members for support. They didn't have the wherewithal to apply and pay for maternity homes. The perceived "value" of a woman's baby, as well as her socio-economic class (which were dictated largely by race) determined how she would be treated by the rest of the world. For some, a possible solution was to agree to surrender her child in exchange for public assistance. Another option was to work as a domestic servant in exchange for room and board, living in a kind of secret quasi-indentured servitude, or in a private "wage home," earning money for her medical care while performing services as housekeepers, laundresses, or the like. Hundreds of thousands of others turned, if they could, to their immediate or extended families, who raised the infants as part of their grandparents' households or who facilitated non-formal open adoptions with other relatives or friends. Black women faced additional bias, especially the idea that they were prone to "fecundity" and should be left to rely on their family's resources and tolerance. As a result many of these mothers ended up collecting Aid to Dependent Children (Solinger *Wake Up*).

WHAT THE CONGRESSIONAL HEARINGS UNCOVERED

In 1956 the Kefauver committee, which headed a series of congressional hearings investigating the black and gray markets in adoption, reported that some homes' "services" weren't services at all. Certain wage homes required so much housework from their residents and fed them so poorly that they actually operated at a healthy profit. Some homes told their residents that if they wanted to keep their babies they would have to pay thousands of dollars in back medical bills and boarding fees to compensate for the inconvenience they had caused by changing their plans. Young women at one highly-regarded facility in Texas placed their babies with the belief that they had a six month "grace period" in which to change their minds, but found that if they did reconsider, their children were already gone. The Tennessee Children's Home Society stole more than a thousand infants from poor and unmarried women who had been drugged or duped, then housed those same newborns without medical care and eventually sold the surviving babies to wealthy patrons. Other mothers in other facilities were told they were placing their children in "temporary care," only to find that they were gone forever. Revocation periods were not necessarily honored. Once the baby was placed with a family, such clauses were difficult or impossible for young women without legal representation to implement. A social worker could stall until the waiting period had expired. Few unwed mothers knew their rights or how to go about securing them.

Because adoption laws were inadequate, gray market adoptions were legal transactions. There were hundreds of entrepreneurs privately procuring children who could be released to adopting parents in exchange for money, sometimes very large sums of it. Some of them used legitimate means to secure custody of the children in their care; some did not. They arranged adoptions without the help of agencies, and they didn't have to answer to anyone. They presided over *more than a third of the adoptions in the country*, seeking out single mothers whose lack of financial and familial support made them most desperate. One Kansas woman housed single mothers in the basement of her home for months at a time, then delivered the babies herself and sold them to the highest bidders. Other independent brokers were driven by ideology, believing they were imposing moral order by transferring babies from irresponsible parents to more deserving ones. There were doctors and lawyers who lured single mothers to their offices and later negotiated for their babies, sometimes bringing to bear the pressure of unpaid medical bills. One Georgia court officer "made children available" by telling mothers that their babies had been born dead. Women who had had twins sometimes never knew there was a second child. Death and birth certificates were forged, records burned. If a contested case ended up in court, some judges felt morally justified in separating children from "immoral" mothers. (See Solinger *Wake Up* 32, 170-88; Weinstein, Marybeth. "Markets, Black and Gray, in Babies." *New York Times Magazine*, November 27, 1955, pp. 12+.)

PART II

THE YEARS AFTER 1963

By 1963 it was clear that there were seismic shifts in the nation's culture. The number of "illegitimate" pregnancies in America, at 300,000 plus, could no longer be attributed to individual mental illness. Popular magazines began to surmise that all these pregnancies were the result of something more obvious: an enormous number of young people engaging in premarital sex. The mental illness theories lost popularity, but the adoption practices didn't change for at least a decade.

In 1970 the number of children released for adoption reached its zenith. As many as 80% of children born to unmarried mothers were put up for adoption. In 1971 did the Supreme Court ruled that single pregnant students could no longer be expelled from school. The end of "the best solution" was nigh, and the entire edifice of belief began to collapse upon itself. Birth control was easier to come by, and in 1973, the women's rights movement succeeded in legalizing abortion. By the late 1970s, people were more willing to accept the idea of single motherhood, mostly because of the country's rising divorce rate, which was creating its own culture of single mothers. Also, the sexual revolution of the 1960s had erased the stigma of premarital sex—the term "love child" replaced the words "bastard" and "illegitimate," and the term "single parent" replaced the "unwed" label. Women were earning their own incomes, and employers couldn't fire them as easily as they could in earlier decades. Poor and working-class women became more aware of subsidized day care and other kinds of public assistance.

Adoption agencies were forced to turn to other sources, most notably to other countries, where other laws, social mores, politics, wars, or poverty levels came into play (Solinger *Wake Up*, Solinger *Beggars and Choosers*).

PART III

BIRTHMOTHERS AND GRIEF

Birthmother depression is well documented, with some studies reporting 40% of women afflicted and some reporting as many as 89%. All studies report depression among a significant percentage of birthmothers in the years following relinquishment. (See Baran, Annette, Reuben Pannor and Arthur Sorosky. "The Lingering Pain of Surrendering a Child." *Psychology Today* vol. 11, no.1, 1977, pp. 58+; Brodzinsky, Anne D. "Surrendering an Infant for Adoption: The Birthmother Experience." *The Psychology of Adoption*. edited by David M. Brodzinsky and Marshall D. Schechter. Oxford University Press, 1990, p. 305; Condon, J.T. "Psychological Disability in Women who Relinquish a Baby for Adoption." *The Medical Journal of Australia*, 1986, vol. 144, no. 3, pp. 117 – 119; Davidson, Michelene. "Healing the Birthmother's Silent Sorrow." *Progress: Family Systems Research and Therapy*, vol. 3, Phillips Graduate Institute. 1994, pp. 69-89; Davis, C.E. "Separation Loss in Relinquishing Birthmothers." *The International Journal of Psychiatric Nursing Research*, vol. 1, no. 2, 1994, pp. 63-64; De Simone 65-76; Deykin, E.Y, L. Campbell, and P. Patti "The Post-Adoption Experience of Surrendering Parents." *American Journal of Orthopsychiatry*, vol. 54, no. 2, April 1984, pp. 271-280; Logan 609-625; Millen and Roll 411-418; Sorosky, Baran, and Pannor. *The Adoption Triangle*. Anchor Books, 1984, p. 56; Weinreb, M. and V. Konstam. "Birthmothers: A Retrospective Analysis of the Surrendering Experience." *Psychotherapy in Private Practice*, vol. 15, no. 1, 1996, pp. 59-70; Winkler and van Keppel 59.)

Birthmothers also report being enraged at the common assumption that they would forget their children and enraged again to find out later that their children were treated as commodities (Solinger *Beggars* 77).

Many researchers have written about the detrimental effects of secrecy upon birthmothers' ability to heal. (See Brodzinsky 295-315; Condon 117 – 119; Davis 63-4; De Simone; Deykin, et al. 271-280; Jones; Kelly; Lauderdale, Millen and Roll 411-418; Rynearson 338-40; Sorosky et al. pp 54-58; Weinreb and Konstam 59-70; Winkler and van Keppel 61. Also Jana L. and Joyceen S. Boyle. "Infant Relinquishment Through Adoption." *IMAGE: Journal of Nursing Scholarship*, vol. 26, no. 3, Fall 1994, pp. 213-217; Wells, Susan. "What do Birth Parents Want?" *Adoption and Fostering*, vol. 17, no. 4, 1993, pp. 20-26.)

Many birthmothers report feeling as if they have lost a limb (Sorosky et al. 56; Condon 117 – 119; Lauderdale and Boyle 213-217; Rynearson 338-40.)

At least one research team has compared the experience of relinquishing a child to that of losing a child in perinatal death. They also described the unresolved nature of birthmother grief and its uniquely problematic effects, including "an increasing sense of loss" over time (Winkler and van Keppel 69-71). Another compared the birthmother state of suspended grief to grief for servicemen missing in action (Condon 117–119). Others have written extensively about the lack of closure. (See Davis 63-4; De Simone 65-76; Wells "Post-Traumatic Stress Disorder in Birthmothers" 30-32. Also Stiffler L. H. "Adoption's Impact on Birthmothers: 'Can a Mother Forget her Child?'" *Journal of Psychology and Christianity*, vol. 10, no. 3, 1991, pp. 249-259.)

Pathological guilt is sometimes a component of birthmother depression (Davidson 69-89; Jones; Logan 609-625; Wells "Post-traumatic Stress Disorder" 30-32.)

Some birthmothers suffered health problems as a result of prolonged grief, including recurrent gynecologic infections and sexual difficulties. Likewise, a high percentage of women, as many as 34%, did not have other children, in some cases due to secondary infertility (Condon 117 – 119; Millen and Roll 411-418; Rynearson 338-40; De Simone 69; Deykin et al. 271-280).

Other women became overprotective mothers when their subsequent children were born (Condon 117 – 119; Deykin et al. 271-280; Jones 2000; Rynearson 338-40).

Most studies of grieving birthmothers report that, while almost all mothers mourned, there were some women who reported being "comfortable" with their decisions, perhaps 30%. (Sorosky et al. 56; Kelly). Winkler and van

Keppel's thorough study reports a bell curve with a "normal distribution of outcomes" (Winkler and van Keppel 69-72).

POWERLESSNESS AND GRIEF

The more control birthmothers have in the adoption process, the less likely they are to regret and grieve their decisions. Many studies correlate birthmothers' lack of agency with their trauma. One researcher wrote that "depression is linked to the experience of helplessness, of the feeling that one has little, if any, control over the events (especially negative events) in one's life" (Brodzinsky 305). Other research supports these findings. (See Chippindale-Bakker, Victoria and Linda Foster. "Adoption in the 1990's: Sociodemographic Determinants of Biological Parents Choosing Adoption." *Child Welfare*, vol. 75, no. 4, July/ August 1996, pp. 337-356; Cushman, Linda F. and Debra Kalmuss and Pearla Brickner Namerow. "Openness in Adoption: Experiences and Social Psychological Outcomes Among Birth Mothers." *Marriage and Family Review*, vol. 25, no. 1-2, 1997, pp. 7-19; Davis 63-64; De Simone 65; Rynearson 338-40.)

One study proposed two portraits of birthmothers. The first portrait they called "the reluctant giver" and characterized as a woman who felt her parents or society had made her decisions for her. She felt that her baby had been stolen from her and suffered more shame and more grief because of it. Fantasies and fears about the missing child prolonged the mourning: was the child alive or dead, healthy or diseased, loved or neglected? This birthmother had no way to grieve in public, partly because she couldn't share the experience and partly because other people considered her loss insignificant. The second group researchers characterized as "grateful givers," and these women exercised more power. They felt they had choices. These women took part in the selection of the adoptive parents and had either direct or indirect communication with them. They also had some kind of control over the hospital experience and were supported by their parents and friends. They believed they were "giving a gift." They grieved for the loss of their children but were able to move on with their lives (Lauderdale and Boyle 216).

SEARCHING

Most birthmothers would like to know about the wellbeing of the children they relinquished, though many don't feel they have the right to know. Birthmothers who do contact their offspring usually wait until their children have become adults, and few have the goal of "reclaiming" their lost children or breaking up families (Deykin et al. 274). Susan Wells found that 96% of the New Zealand women she surveyed would like to be "found," and only that nine of the 262 wanted to preserve secrecy (Wells "What Do Birthparents Want?" 22-26).

Studies of adoptees show that 65-89% percent would like contact with their biological parents, and are more inclined to want contact as they age (Pertman 130). Some states allow adoptees access to their original birth certificates, with or without court orders or other restrictions. Children adopted from other countries face a host of other identity questions. If they wish to find their origins, they often face daunting searches.

BIRTHMOTHERS IN THE POST ROE V. WADE ERA

In recent decades healthcare journals have encouraged medical professionals to give birthmothers as much control over the adoption process as they can. The more agency mothers have in the decision, the easier it seems to be to accept those decisions without regret and blame. Likewise some states now stipulate that mothers cannot be under the influence of delivery room medications when they sign away their rights to their children.

Birthmother empowerment is also a feature of open adoption. In such arrangements, birthmothers may have a role in choosing a child's parents, or they may have absolute choice. They may receive a profile of the parents or meet them and visit their home. They may receive unaddressed mail or have full disclosure of address. They may be updated occasionally or have regular visits to the adopting parents' home. There have been many studies of open versus closed adoption. (Considered for this book were: Sykes, Margaret R. "Adoption with Contact: A study of Adoptive Parents and the Impact of Continuing Contact With Families of Origin." *Journal of Family Therapy*, vol. 23, 2001, pp. 296-316; Blanton, T.L. and J. Deschner. "Biological Mothers' Grief: The Postadoptive Experience in Open Versus Confidential Adoption." *Child Welfare*: 69.6, Nov/Dec 1990, pp. 525-536. There are many more updated ones.) Or you can read the many personal narratives comparing open versus closed adoption (Arms 1990; *Wells Within Me* 1994). For current state laws on adoption records, see Adoptee Rights Law Center (adopteerightslaw.com/united-states-obc/.)

CHOOSING ADOPTION IN THE POST ROE V. WADE ERA

Why did some women choose adoption in the post Roe v. Wade era? *Few studies examine why some women choose adoption over abortion.* The available research tends to focus upon why some mothers choose relinquishment and others choose to keep their children. In 1978, the most frequently cited reason birthmothers relinquished their children rather than keeping them was that they wanted them to have two parents. (See Pannor, Ruben, Annette Baran, Arthur D. Sorosky "Birth Parents Who Relinquish Babies for Adoption Revisited." *Family Process,* vol. 17, no. 3, September 1978, pp. 329-37. See also Chippindale-Bakker and Foster 337-356; Donnelly, B.W. and P. Voydanoff. "Factors Associated with Releasing for Adoption Among Adolescent Mothers," *Family Relations*, vol. 40, 1991, pp. 404-5; Leynes, Cynthia. "Factors Influencing the Decision to Keep or Relinquish One's Child." *Child Psychiatry and Human Development*, vol. 11, Winter 1980, pp. 105-112; National Adoption Information Clearinghouse, sponsored by the US Department of Health and Human Services at naic.acf. hhs.gov/index.cfm.)

Acknowledgments

When I started this book almost twenty years ago, I knew little about writing fiction and even less about writing a novel. But I read, and I imitated, and I improvised. I asked friends and family to read those efforts and give me feedback—and, oh, what a big imposition it is to ask the people you love to critique your work! It was an awkward and sometimes humiliating process. And, since most people gave me only as much constructive criticism as they thought I could handle, it was also slow. But I did figure out how the story was landing on other people's ears. And I did get better.

I owe so many thanks to Carolyn and Reid Franks, Jim Tibbetts, Richmond Eustis, Sudi Lenhart, Jill Sare, Lisa Keyes, Linda Mishkin, Jonathan Newman, Linda Shriver, Tom and Suzanne Welander, Laura Tibbetts, Andrew and Lisa Franks, Cliff Garstang, Donna Kozberg, Andrew Feiler, Karey Kramer, Kathleen Pringle, Brian Sargent, Sharon Bandy, Steven McLaughlin, Terry Roberts, Lynn Allman Roberts, Jessica Handler, Trudy Nan Boyce, Phyllis Payne, and Martina Fowler. And special thanks to Mark Beaver and Jonathan Newman for reading ten-plus versions of the opening chapter and nixing them all.

During those years I was lucky enough to work with the tremendous teachers at Sewanee Writers Conference and Tin House Writers Conference and Aspen Writers Conference, especially Tim O'Brien, Alice McDermott, Dana Spiotta, Tony Earley, Christine Schutt, Luis Urrea, Michelle Wildgen, and Robert Bausch, masters all. They taught me the craft.

Thanks too to professionals Jacqueline Hackett, Rene Zuckerbrot, Jane von Mehren, and Rebecca Gradinger, who took the time to invest in the early manuscript and educate me about the big business of publishing.

Mostly, I'm grateful to Meg Reid, Betsy Teter, and Kate McMullen for making Hub City the premier press it is today, for getting 100 perent behind every book they publish, and for believing in *The Say So* from the get-go. Meg and Betsy and Kate know just how to realign a novel in the way that best brings out its essential truths, Riley Kross has an unvarying instinct for homing in on the bits that just don't work, Julie Jarema helped get the book into the right hands, and Megan Demoss and Corinne Segal have been punctilious proofreaders. Thanks too to Charles Frazier for creating the Cold Mountain Series and including me in it.

And, as always, I am grateful to my husband Steve for his emotional support and constant everyday kindnesses.

Julia Franks is the author of *Over the Plain Houses*, which was an NPR Best Book of 2016 and was awarded five prestigious literary prizes. She has published essays in outlets like the *New York Times*, *Ms. Magazine*, and *The Bitter Southerner*. While her roots are in the Southeast, she spent years teaching literature in the US and abroad. She lives in Atlanta.

The **COLD MOUNTAIN** *Fund*
S E R I E S

NATIONAL BOOK AWARD WINNER Charles Frazier generously supports publication of a series of Hub City Press books through the Cold Mountain Fund at the Community Foundation of Western North Carolina. The Cold Mountain Series spotlights works of fiction by new and extraordinary writers from the American South. Books published in this series have been reviewed in outlets like *Wall Street Journal, San Francisco Chronicle, Garden & Gun, Entertainment Weekly,* and *O, the Oprah Magazine*; included on Best Books lists from NPR, *Kirkus Reviews,* and the American Library Association; and have won or been nominated for awards like the Southern Book Prize, the Ohioana Book Award, Crooks Corner Book Prize, and the Langum Prize for Historical Fiction.

Child in the Valley • Gordy Sauer

The Parted Earth • Anjali Enjeti

You Want More: The Selected Stories of George Singleton

The Prettiest Star • Carter Sickels

Watershed • Mark Barr

The Magnetic Girl • Jessica Handler

PUBLISHING
New & Extraordinary
VOICES FROM THE
AMERICAN SOUTH

FOUNDED IN SPARTANBURG, SOUTH CAROLINA in 1995, Hub City Press has emerged as the South's premier independent literary press. Hub City is interested in books with a strong sense of place and is committed to finding and spotlighting extraordinary new and unsung writers from the American South. Our curated list champions diverse authors and books that don't fit into the commercial or academic publishing landscape.

Baskerville
10.8 / 14.4